### LICENSE TO THRILL

"Steamy."                                         —*Cosmopolitan*

"With a sassy, in-your-face style reminiscent of Janet Evanovich, Wilde has created an unforgettable heroine."
—*Booklist*

"Hilarious as well as romantic."
—*Southern Pines Pilot* (NC)

"Hot and funny and at the same time sweet...will have you turning the pages long after the lights should be out."
—ContemporaryRomanceWriters.com

"A sexy mystery with characters that sizzle alone and even more together."

—MyShelf.com

"One of the best romps I've read in a long time. It had thrills and chills and there were a number of times I actually laughed out loud. If you like good-spirited, fun romances, then, quick, run to your local bookstore and snap this one up."

—EscapetoRomance.com

"Sexy...Wilde dishes up a delicacy that really hits the spot."

—*RT Book Reviews*

### *YOU ONLY LOVE TWICE*

"Fast-paced adventure, sexy situations, and lots of suspense will make Wilde's book appeal to a wide spectrum of readers."                    —*Booklist*

"[A] funny, fast-paced tale...Readers will be...laughing at the shenanigans."

—*Publishers Weekly*

"Super fun romantic suspense...YOU ONLY LOVE TWICE [is] a...humorous contemporary thriller worth reading."

—*Midwest Book Review*

"Wilde is a master of snappy prose...I was amazed at how much just plain fun this book was."

—TheRomanceReader.com

"Lori Wilde dishes up a perfect combination of great characterizations, action, zingy dialogue and plenty of humor...If you're up for a fun, fast-paced and thoroughly engaging read, then make sure you pick up a copy of *You Only Love Twice*."

—BookLoons.com

"Pick up this book for a great read!"

—FreshFiction.com

# MAD ABOUT
## *You*

# MAD ABOUT
## *You*

---

# LORI
# WILDE

FOREVER

NEW YORK   BOSTON

Forever
Hachette Book Group
237 Park Avenue
New York, NY 10017

www.HachetteBookGroup.com

Printed in the United States of America

First Edition: March 2014
10 9 8 7 6 5 4 3 2 1

OPM

Forever is an imprint of Grand Central Publishing.
The Forever name and logo are trademarks of Hachette Book Group, Inc.

The Hachette Speakers Bureau provides a wide range of authors for speaking events. To find out more, go to www.hachettespeakersbureau.com or call (866) 376-6591.

The publisher is not responsible for websites (or their content) that are not owned by the publisher.

# *Contents*

*License to Thrill*

*To Beth de Guzman—for giving me the opportunity to shine. Your belief in me means more than words can say.*

# *Acknowledgments*

To the people who made this book possible: Thank you to my savvy agent Karen Solem, your knowledge of the publishing industry constantly amazes me. To my editor Michele Bidelspach, your guidance and insight were invaluable in shaping this book. And most of all, to my dearest friend Hebby Roman whose expertise on all things financial brought the whole plot together. You are appreciated.

# Chapter 1

Nothing but nothing scared Charlee Champagne except black widow spiders and wealthy, long-legged, brown-eyed, handsome men with matinee-idol smiles and a day's growth of beard stubble.

In her five years as a Las Vegas private investigator, Charlee had never once lost her cool. Being alley-cornered at midnight by a stiletto-wielding transvestite produced nary a wobbly knee. Getting dragged ten feet behind a robbery suspect's Nissan Pathfinder had created not a single spike in her pulse rate.

And just last week she'd averted disaster when she'd calmly faced down a half-dozen gangbangers and convinced them the banana in her jacket pocket was actually a forty-five-caliber Grizzly Magnum.

Cucumbers had nothing on Charlee.

But something about mean mama black widows and rich, long-legged, brown-eyed, handsome, matinee-idol-smiling, beard-stubble-sporting men slid right under her skin and wreaked havoc with her bravado.

She had earned both phobias legitimately. The spider heebie-jeebies dated back to an ugly outhouse incident in rural Wisconsin when she was twelve. She had never looked at a roll of toilet paper in quite the same way since.

Her second fear, however, was a bit more convoluted. At the same time George Clooneyesque men terrified her, she was wildly, madly, impossibly attracted to them.

And the scars from those mistakes, while less noticeable than the half-dollar-sized hole in her left butt cheek, were a sight more painful than any spider bite.

As a self-defense technique, she'd developed a highly honed sense of respect for her phobias. So when the hairs at the nape of her neck spiked that Wednesday afternoon in late March, she snapped to full alert.

She sat cocked back in front of the computer in her two-woman detective agency located in a downtown strip mall, her size ten, neon blue, Tony Lama boots propped up on one corner of the desk and her keyboard nestled in her lap. She was completing the final paperwork on a missing person's case where she had successfully located a six-year-old girl snatched by her father after a custody dispute didn't go in his favor.

Immediately, her gaze flew to the corners of the room. No sign of a black widow's unmistakably messy cobweb. Slowly, she released her drawn breath, but the prickly uproar on the back of her neck persisted.

From the corner of her eye she spied movement on the window ledge. Something small and black and spindly-legged scurried.

Her boots hit the cement floor and her hand grabbed for a makeshift weapon, coming up with a well-thumbed, trade paperback copy of *Find Out Anything About Anyone*.

Pulse pounding in her throat, she advanced upon the window.

The cool cobalt taste of fear spilled into her mouth. Her legs quivered like she had a neurological disorder. Instant sweat pearled into the delicate indentation between her nose and her upper lip.

She had to force each step, but finally she hovered within killing range. She raised the book over her head, sucked in her breath for added courage, and stared down at the intimidating creature.

No telltale red hourglass.

Hmm. Charlee narrowed her eyes.

Not a black widow after all. Closer scrutiny revealed the creature wasn't even black.

Just a fuzzy wolf spider.

Oh, thank heavens.

Relieved, she sank her forehead against the windowpane and let the book fall from her relaxed grasp.

And that's when she spotted him.

Zigzagging his way through the parking lot—looking utterly out of place in the Las Vegas desert in his rumpled Armani suit, dusty Gucci loafers, and a red silk tie that appeared to cost more than Charlee's last tax refund check—meandered a fear far greater than a whole pack of poisonous arachnids.

Like a battalion of marines at roll call, her neck hairs marshaled to five-alarm status. She stumbled back to her desk, jerked open the bottom drawer, retrieved a pair of Nighthawk binoculars, fixed the scopes on him, and fiddled with the focus.

Gotcha.

Hair the color of coal. Chocolate brown eyes. A five o'clock shadow ringing his craggy jawline. Handsome as the day was long.

Her heart tommy-gunned. Ratta-tatta-tat.

Charlee gulped. Please let him go to the Quickee-Lube-Express next door. Or better yet, the massage parlor on the corner.

No such luck. He headed straight for the Sikes Detective Agency, a determined look on his face. The one thing she still had going for her—he wasn't smiling. Charlee's hand trembled so hard that she fumbled with the binoculars.

Yipes.

She had to do something. Quick.

For some unfathomable reason, guys like him were often attracted to her and she never failed to fall for their smiles and swagger. Call it a genetic deficiency. Her mother, Bubbles, God rest her soul, had been the same way.

When Charlee was seven, Tommy Ledbetter, the devastatingly cute son of the man who owned the used car dealership where her grandmother Maybelline worked as a mechanic, had lured Charlee behind the garage for a rousing game of I'll-show-you-mine-if-you-show-me-yours.

She had obliged when he threw in a pack of Twizzlers as an added bribe, only to be caught red-hineyed by Mr. Ledbetter. Tommy, the wimp, had declared the whole thing Charlee's idea. Maybelline had gotten fired over that embarrassing incident.

Then when she was fourteen and Maybelline was tending bar at an exclusive country club in Estes Park, Colorado, Vincent Keneer, whose father owned part interest in the Denver Broncos, stole a kiss from her on the ninth green. She was in seventh heaven for a few hours only to later overhear him laughing with his friends. "Getting Charlee to kiss me was easier than turning on a light switch," he had bragged.

Charlee's temper had gotten the better of her and she'd

shoved Vincent into the deep end of the pool with his cashmere vest on. Maybelline lost that job too for refusing to make Charlee apologize.

And then when she was nineteen...

She closed her eyes and swallowed hard. No, she refused to relive *that* excruciating memory. Some cuts sliced so deep they never healed.

What was it about her? She must secrete some kind of take-advantage-of-me-then-break-my-heart pheromone. Or maybe it was like how cats seemed to know when you were allergic to them and they singled you out in a crowd and insisted on crawling into your lap.

Why buck the odds? She needed all the help she could muster. Charlee snatched open the desk drawers in a desperate search for any kind of a disguise. Nabbing a pencil from the cup beside her printer, she harvested her hair off her shoulders, wound the thick mass into a twist, and anchored it to the top of her head.

Frumpy. Think frumpy.

If he so much as cracked a grin, even a little one, she was a goner.

Okay, librarian hair wasn't enough. She needed more. Charlee scuttled over to Maybelline's desk and rummaged through the contents.

Ah-ha! Her granny's spare pair of thick, black bifocals oughtta do the trick.

Charlee jammed the glasses on her face, grateful for the twofold shield. Now, not only would she look unflirtworthy in the heavy frames, but also while peering through the blurry lenses she would be unable to fully ascertain his level of cuteness. She hazarded another quick peek out the window, but had to peer over the top of Maybelline's glasses in order to see him without getting dizzy.

Who was this guy?

He stopped when he passed her cherry red 1964 Corvette convertible in the parking lot and ran a lingering hand over the fender like he was caressing a woman's inner thigh. Charlee's stomach fluttered as if he'd stroked *her* and her muscles tightened a couple of notches below her turquoise belt buckle.

Repo man?

Nah. She was ninety-nine percent sure she'd mailed her car payment, even though she did have a tendency to get so wrapped up in a case she sometimes forgot to eat or sleep or post her bills. Besides, the dude looked nothing like a repo man. Actually, he resembled a refugee from an investment banker caucus.

Or an escapee from a corporate law office.

A lawyer?

Oh, no. Was Elwood in the pokey again and looking to her for bail money? Charlee shook her head. As if her no-account daddy could afford the services of a guy who dressed like a *GQ* cover model.

A lawsuit?

Her accountant Wilkie had warned her that being sued was an eventuality in her line of work and he'd encouraged her to take out more insurance. But between keeping the business afloat and bailing out her old man when he was in between his Elvis impersonating gigs and had succumbed to the lure of another get-rich-quick scheme, she didn't have a lot of spare cash left over for frivolous things like insurance.

The guy had almost reached her door and Charlee, roosting on the verge of hyperventilation, did not know which way to jump. She stepped right, then left, ended up doing a strange little mambo, and finally jammed the binoculars under a chair cushion. She even considered ducking into the closet until he went away.

But what if he wanted to hire her? Business was business. She'd just completed her only pending case and she needed the money.

Yeah? So tell that to her stomach spinning like a whirligig in gale force winds. In the end, she leaped behind Maybelline's desk and feigned grave interest in her blank computer screen.

The silver cowbell over the door tinkled.

*Be strong. Be brave. Be badass.*

"Hello?"

Ah, damn. He possessed the deep, smoky voice of a late-night radio announcer. Charlee lifted her head and forced herself to look at the man standing in the doorway.

"Good afternoon," she replied, her tone a couple of degrees above frosty. No sense making the guy welcome. If she was rude enough, maybe he would take a hike.

The top of his head grazed the cowbell, causing it to peal again.

Dear God, he was at least six feet three, maybe even taller. And no wedding band graced the third finger of his left hand. Charlee tumbled as if she were on an Alpine ski run, a beginner who had taken a wrong turn and ended up on the black diamond expert slope with nowhere to go but down, down, down.

"Is there something you need?" she asked, making sure she sounded extra snippy and squinting disapprovingly at him through Maybelline's bifocals.

"Yes, ma'am," the paragon drawled in a smooth Texas accent.

In spite of his slightly blurry appearance, he was outrageously good-looking, right down to his straight white teeth. They had to be bonded. Nobody's natural teeth looked that perfect. His suit—while slightly wrinkled—fit like a dream, accentuating his broad shoulders and narrow hips.

He smelled like the wickedly wonderful blend of expensive cologne and the faint but manly musk of perspiration. His beautiful black hair was clipped short, making one statement while the dark stubble on his jaw made another.

Charlee wanted to rip off the borrowed glasses and feast on him like Thanksgiving turkey. The desire scared her to the very marrow of her bones.

Something sparked in his deep brown bedroom eyes and she caught a glimmer of sudden heat when their gazes met—or maybe it was just that Maybelline's glasses needed cleaning.

He sauntered toward her, oozing charisma from every pore.

Charlee forgot to breathe.

And then he committed the gravest sin of all, knocking her world helter-skelter.

The scoundrel smiled.

Mason Gentry gave the woman behind the desk his best public-relations grin. The grin—and the Gentry name—opened doors. Accustomed to getting what he wanted, Mason wanted one thing and one thing only.

To track down the floozy who'd lured his grandfather Nolan—along with a half-million dollars in family company funds—to sin city.

Mason's primary aim? Locate Gramps, drag him home to Houston (hopefully with the money still intact), and get back to the investment deal he'd been in the process of bringing in before his older brother, Hunter, had taken over and sent him after their grandfather. He was still seething about the injustice. Why did Hunter earn the plum jobs while he got scut work?

Oh, yes. One other thing. Nolan's unexpected and larcenous departure had forced Mason to postpone his engagement party.

He'd planned to ask his girlfriend of three years, Daphne Maxwell, to marry him this weekend in exactly the same fashion his father had proposed to his mother. Over veal parmigiana at Delveccio's, with fifty of their closest friends joining the festivity.

At the thought of Daphne, Mason's spirits lifted. For once in his life, he would have one up on his brother. He would be married to the perfect high-society wife.

Everyone in his family loved Daphne. She was refined, cultured, and sophisticated, with a myriad of business contacts and a pedigree she could trace back to the *Mayflower*.

Daphne was everything he'd ever looked for in a wife. They had the same values, the same friends, and they wanted the same things from life. So what if there wasn't much sexual chemistry. A good marriage consisted of so much more than fireworks.

Right?

"What do you want?" the woman demanded, squinting up at him from behind an ugly pair of glasses, her long black hair spilling haphazardly from an awkward bun secured to her head with a pencil.

Could she be the woman he was searching for?

He remembered the paper in his pocket. He'd found Maybelline Sikes's name and this address scrawled on a notepad in Gramps's bedroom. The nameplate on the desk said Maybelline Sikes, but she didn't look like a Maybelline.

She looked like nothing but trouble with her determined little chin set and her smoldering emerald eyes flashing a challenge. Unlucky for her, Mason adored a challenge.

She wore an unflattering western-style shirt, faded jeans with a rip at the knee, and the most gawd-awful neon blue cowboy boots he had ever laid eyes upon. Not a shred of makeup graced her face. Granted, with her long, dark lashes and full raspberry-colored lips she didn't need cosmetics to look good, but she did not fit the image of the busty, brash, blond femme fatale in stilettos and pearls he'd concocted in his head.

Nor had he expected her to be a private detective. Really, she was way too young for Gramps. But then again, gold diggers came in all shapes, ages, and professions.

"I'm waiting." She arched an eyebrow and he noticed she clutched a pen so tight her knuckles were actually white. The lady was not nearly as composed as she appeared.

Mason draped one leg over the corner of her desk and leaned in close until they were almost nose-to-nose, his intent to intimidate.

"I want to know where my grandfather is," he said, continuing to smile but narrowing his eyes so she would understand he meant business. "And I want to know now."

She sank her top teeth into her bottom lip and unflinchingly returned his stare, but despite her bluster he could tell from the brief flicker of uneasiness flitting across her face she wanted to back away.

"You're gonna have to be more specific. I have no idea what you're talking about."

He shouldn't have noticed the long, smooth curve of her neck, but he found his gaze lingering on the pulse point jumping at her throat. She was nervous. Oh, yeah. But very adept at cloaking her uneasiness. He couldn't help but admire her grace under pressure. He had reduced many an inefficient employee to tongue-tied stammers with his silent stares. But she wasn't buying his bluster.

"Nolan Gentry. Where is he?"

She laid the pen down, steepled her fingertips, and blinked owlishly at him from behind those hideous glasses. "Let me get this straight. Do you want to hire me to find your missing grandfather?"

"He came here to meet you. Are you telling me you haven't seen him?"

"I'm sorry, mister, I don't even know who he is. Or who you are for that matter."

"My name's Mason Gentry. I'm an investment banker from Houston and I've come to retrieve my grandfather"

"What does that have to do with me?"

She met his eyes. Their glares slammed into each other. Hot, hard, defiant.

She was a tough one all right, but he didn't miss her telltale gulp and the determined way she clenched her jaw. No matter how composed she might appear, the woman was afraid of him.

"Aren't you Maybelline Sikes?" He tapped the nameplate.

"No. I'm not. I'm her granddaughter."

Instant relief rolled over him. His grandfather had hightailed himself across the desert to see the woman's grandmother, not her. Why the knowledge lifted his spirits, he had no clue. What did it matter whether it was the granddaughter or the grandmother who was after Nolan's fortune? The results were the same.

"So what's your name?"

"Charlee Champagne."

"Beg your pardon?" he asked, not sure he'd heard correctly.

"Charlee Champagne," she repeated.

"Oh."

For no particular reason the phrase *Good Time Charlee* popped into his mind's eye along with a very provocative image of a tipsy Charlee boogeying with a lampshade on her head and wearing a very naughty black silk nightie. He could see the picture all too clearly. Perturbed, Mason shook his head to dispel the unwanted mental photograph.

Charlee sighed and then spoke as if she'd recited the details many times before. "My mother was a dancer at the Folies Bergère and had her name legally changed to Bubbles Champagne. She and my father were never married. What can I say? She was a bit frivolous. Any more questions?"

"Do you know where I can find Ms. Sikes?"

"She's incommunicado."

"Meaning?"

"She's gone on her annual fishing retreat and she can't be reached, but let me assure you she most certainly is not with your grandfather."

"How can you be so sure?"

"Maybelline hates men. Especially rich ones."

"Who said my grandfather is rich?" Mason didn't believe her for a second. No doubt she was covering for her grandmother.

Charlee waved a hand at his Rolex. "Like grandfather like grandson."

"So, you're claiming your grandmother can't be reached?"

"No claiming to it. It's the truth."

"No cell phone?"

"She can't stand 'em. Says they give you brain cancer."

"No beeper?"

"Nope. That's the whole point of the trip. Uninterrupted peace and quiet."

"I think you're lying."

Charlee shrugged. "Believe what you want."

"It's imperative I speak with Ms. Sikes," Mason said in a controlled, measured manner. He was through fooling around with Miss I'm-Going-To-Be-No-Help-Whatsoever Champagne. He wanted his grandfather found. "If Ms. Sikes can't be reached by electronic means then I will go to her fishing cabin. Give me directions."

"No."

"What?" His glare intensified. Sweat pooled around his collar. In his mad, twenty-four-hour sprint from Houston to Vegas, he hadn't even bothered to change from his business suit and he was broiling like filet mignon at a backyard barbeque.

That's what happened when you allowed single-minded focus to overcome common sense. Stubborn persistence was his biggest flaw and his greatest strength. His father often joked Mason was like an obstinate snapping turtle, never knowing when to turn loose.

"You heard me." She raised her chin, daring him to call her bluff.

He stared openmouthed. He wasn't accustomed to being refused anything. Testiness was his first instinct but something told him venting his frustration would be the wrong tactic to take. She'd most likely dig into her view. He could see she had a bit of snapping turtle in her too.

Forcing a smile, he slipped an amiable tone into his voice. "I think maybe we got off on the wrong foot. Why don't we start over?"

"Okay."

"My grandfather Nolan disappeared out of the blue with a substantial amount of money. We found a note in his room indicating he was on his way to meet your grandmother here in Vegas. We're really concerned about him. He's been behaving a bit out of character lately. I need to speak with your grandmother to find out if she has heard from him."

"Sorry," she said. "Maybelline left strict orders not to be disturbed. I can't help you."

"Can't? Or won't?"

"Take your pick."

"So that's the way it's going to be."

"Maybelline will be home in a couple of days. You can speak to her then. In the meantime, relax. Have fun. See Vegas. Enjoy a holiday." Under her breath she muttered, "With that stick-up-your-butt attitude you certainly look as if you could use one."

Like hell.

No way was he waiting a couple of days. In a couple of days Nolan and Maybelline could run through the half million at the craps table. Besides, in a couple more days Hunter would have the Birkweilder deal—*his* deal—sewn up, and would be busily collecting accolades from their father without giving Mason credit.

He gritted his teeth and fell back on his third line of offense. When authority and charm fail, there's always money. He removed his wallet from his jacket pocket, unfolded the expensive leather case, and pulled out a crisp new Benjamin Franklin.

"How much is the information going to cost me?" He slapped a second hundred on the desk.

Charlee gasped. He could practically feel the anger emanating off of her.

What? Two C notes weren't enough. Obviously, she was as greedy as her grandmother.

"Three hundred?" Mason added another bill to the stack.

"Are you trying to buy me off?"

"Let's make it an even five."

"Buddy, you can just keep peeling until your wallet is empty, because I'll never tell you where Maybelline is. There isn't enough money in the world."

# Chapter 2

Okay, he had handled the situation badly. He'd grossly misread Charlee Champagne and he'd acted like an unmitigated jackass. Mason wasn't afraid to admit when he'd made a mistake. Unfortunately, not only had she refused to listen to his apology, she had unceremoniously tossed him and his money out of her office.

He'd blown his chance with her. Charlee would never help him now.

A short nap and a hot shower later, he prowled the suite he'd taken at the Bellagio in a thick white terry-cloth bathrobe and plowed his hands through his freshly washed hair.

He was back at square one. Gramps, along with his girlfriend Maybelline and the half-million dollars, was out roaming the streets and he had no idea where to start looking.

What if they had eloped?

Mason sank onto the bed. His father would have a conniption fit. At the thought of failing and letting his family down, he groaned, lay back against the mattress, and stared up at the painted ceiling depicting fifteenth-century Italian nudes.

"Thanks a lot, Gramps. I needed this like a hole in the head."

A twinge of guilt flicked in his stomach. This wasn't about him. This was about his grandfather and what had made Gramps unhappy enough to embezzle five hundred thousand dollars and tear off in the middle of the night without a word to anyone.

He was also a little hurt. He'd believed he and Nolan were pretty close. They were both second sons in the Gentry family and understood the meaning of taking a backseat to the favored eldest. They shot a round of golf together every Sunday afternoon. They played poker with Nolan's cronies once a month. Why hadn't Gramps confided in him?

Mason's eyes traced the lines of the ceiling painting. A woman, her bare back exposed, lay on a gilded chaise lounge. He tracked the curve of her form, noticing the woman's complexion matched the exact same spiced peaches color of Charlee's skin.

What would Charlee look like naked?

Mesmerized by the concept, his imagination ran rampant as he envisioned pert firm breasts, a taut flat belly, and yards of her long coltish legs wrapped around his naked waist while still wearing her gruesome, but oddly compelling, neon blue cowgirl boots.

Startled, Mason bolted upright. Good God! He was almost an engaged man. Why in the hell was he fantasizing about another woman?

Why indeed?

A wave of embarrassment, followed by a virtual monsoon of guilt, flustered him.

"It's just because she pissed you off," Mason grumbled. "She's a challenge and you find challenges stimulating. It's nothing sexual."

*Oh, yeah?*

"Stop thinking about her," he commanded, annoyed with himself, and grabbed his cell phone.

He dialed Daphne's number. The minute she spoke, he started talking and it took a second for him to realize he'd gotten her voice mail.

"Daphne," he said after the beep. "It's Mason. I just arrived in Vegas. I'm thinking of you."

Even to his own ears the words sounded unconvincing. He left her his number at the hotel and then hung up, feeling worse than he had before he'd called. He wished Daphne were here so he could remember exactly what she looked like. He hated that he couldn't fill his mind with her instead of Charlee.

"Concentrate on locating Gramps."

All right. He could keep his mind on the task at hand. Think.

Maybelline probably lived right here in Vegas. And maybe Charlee had lied through those luscious lips of hers.

What if, instead of holing up in some fishing retreat as her granddaughter claimed, Maybelline was actually cozied up in a love nest with Gramps? Why hadn't he considered that before?

Rummaging around in the nightstand, Mason located the phone book and flipped to the S's. Ten seconds later he copied down Maybelline's home address. Ten minutes after that, dressed in chinos, a starched white shirt, and loafers, he took the elevator to the lobby.

Maybelline Sikes took a deep breath, smoothed nonexistent wrinkles from her navy blue slacks, and double-checked her lipstick in the rearview mirror. She patted her short, stylish hair she kept dyed the same flame red color it had been in childhood and climbed out of her ebony Toyota Tundra pickup truck.

Her heart gave an erratic little skip as she made her way up the sidewalk to Kelly's tavern. If she hadn't just undergone a complete physical and been pronounced as healthy as a woman half her age, Maybelline might have been worried. But turning sixty-three had nothing to do with her irregular pulse.

Outside the bar, Maybelline hesitated, her courage gone. She was nervous. Damned nervous. Not just about seeing Nolan Gentry again, but also because of the bad news she had to deliver. The past had caught up with them both.

"Go on," she urged herself. "Do it. You've got no choice."

Straightening her shoulders, she shoved open the door and stepped inside. She blinked against the contrast of bright desert sunlight and dim, smoky bar. The door creaked shut behind her. At four o'clock in the afternoon, the place was deserted.

Kelly, all muscles and tight black T-shirt, stood behind the bar buffing the counter. Barfly Bob, a perpetual regular with heavy red jowls and a bleary-eyed grin, sat on a bar stool nursing an Old Milwaukee.

But it was the man at the corner table who drew Maybelline's immediate interest.

"Hey, Maybelline," Kelly and Barfly Bob greeted her simultaneously.

Seven years ago, she'd worked for Kelly, before she and Charlee had started the detective agency. Maybelline waved a hand, but her gaze riveted on the man she hadn't seen for forty-seven years.

The man who had once saved her life.

She approached cautiously. He rose to his feet. The rolled-up sleeves of his blue dress shirt revealed still nicely muscled forearms for a man in his mid-sixties. He looked every inch the blueblood ex-actor with his perfect posture, commanding aura, and smart fashion sense.

Looking at him now, no one would suspect that over four decades ago Nolan had worked as a wildcatter on an oil derrick side by side with Maybelline's father. Only honed muscles and tanned skin gave even the faintest hint to his working-class past.

Immediately, Maybelline regretted asking him to meet her at Kelly's. From Nolan's point of view, the place was beyond seedy. But she had needed somewhere neutral for the meeting and Kelly's was safe.

Their gazes met and Maybelline's heart did the same swoony waltz it had done more than four decades ago when she'd walked out into the oil field with the brown paper bag lunch her daddy had forgotten and she'd made eye contact with the boss's handsome son.

She'd been thirteen. Nolan seventeen. He'd said "hi" to her and she'd been smitten, even though she'd known he was so far out of her league even a fairy godmother with a magic wand couldn't grant her most fervent wish.

Two years later, when he'd spotted her in town at the soda fountain and came over to buy her a Coke float, she'd just about died. Giggling, her friends had scattered, leaving them alone in the red vinyl booth.

Searching for something to say to the rich handsome man seated across from her, Maybelline told him Lana Turner had been discovered in a soda fountain. Once she got started, her passion for the movies took over and she'd gone on to tell him her greatest dream was to become a Hollywood makeup artist. Nolan had confessed he wanted to be an actor.

They'd talked for hours, until Nolan's father had come into the diner, found them sitting together, and caused an ugly scene. He'd called her trailer trash and forbade Nolan from ever speaking to her again.

"Maybelline," Nolan said, bringing her back to the present, his voice husky.

"Nolan," she murmured.

He smiled and his brown eyes crinkled with such joy, she caught her breath.

"You're prettier than ever."

In one precious minute Maybelline had the ridiculous whim everything was going to turn out all right. There she went again, dreaming of a fairy godmother.

"And you're full of horseshit."

Nolan's grin widened. "You haven't changed a bit. Still the same fiery, outspoken woman I remember."

With a flourish, he pulled out a chair for her and Maybelline sat. He hadn't ordered a drink, she noticed and wondered how long he'd been there.

He eased down across from her and she studied his face. The years had been kind to him and it occurred to her he'd probably had a few nips and tucks. Hey, if you could afford plastic surgery, more power to you.

Nolan wore glasses now, but then again so did she. He wasn't paunchy like many men his age and while he'd had some balding at the temples he still possessed a fine shock of silver hair. She remembered when his hair grew thick as underbrush and black as midnight. A strange aching tugged her stomach at the memory.

All those years gone like fallen leaves.

His gaze imprinted her face, sizing her up too. Self-consciously, she raised a hand to her cheek.

Why hadn't she worn a dress and jewelry and perfume? She hadn't worried about her looks for almost two decades. She had believed she was long past the point of wanting to appear desirable for a man.

*There's no fool like an old fool.*

"Thank you," she said. "For coming to Vegas to see me. I couldn't handle this over the phone or through the mail."

"It's my pleasure."

Kelly appeared at the table. Maybelline was so wrapped up in staring at Nolan she didn't notice the bartender approach and she jumped when he touched her shoulder. "What'll you have, Maybell?"

She looked at Nolan, and arched an eyebrow.

"Pretty early in the day for me." He raised a palm.

"You might want something to help the bad news slide down easier."

Nolan grimaced. "Is it that gruesome?"

Grimly, she nodded.

"Bourbon," Nolan said. "Two glasses."

After Kelly walked away, Nolan laid his hand, warm and rough and comforting, over hers. Something in her chest caught and hung.

"It's going to be okay, kiddo." He winked. "We've survived worse."

Maybelline took a deep breath. "Better hold your judgment until after you've seen what's in here."

She reached into her purse, took out a manila envelope, and handed her old friend a copy of the damning document that possessed the potential to destroy his entire family.

*    *    *

Dimples.

Charlee hadn't bargained on dimples. A man that long-legged, that brown-eyed, that darned handsome simply had no business possessing dimples as deep as Lake Mead and in both cheeks too! The good looks fairy had been far too generous with Mason Gentry.

Her knees were still weak. Damn him.

She couldn't stop dwelling on what had happened. How dare the arrogant, egotistic, rich, dimpled son of a bitch try to bribe her into ratting out the site of her grandmother's cabin?

The cheek. The gall. The sheer audacity!

Jerk. Pinhead. Dillhole.

She fumed around the office, working up a good head of steam.

And then she started to worry.

What if Mason was right? What if Maybelline and his grandfather had run off together? How ludicrous. Then again Maybelline *had* been acting rather odd lately herself. Plus, she'd taken off on her retreat almost a month earlier than usual.

Charlee massaged her temple, which had been throbbing ever since she'd worn Maybelline's glasses. She would love to pin all the blame on the bifocals, but Mason and his missing grandfather were as much the cause of her headache as the glasses.

Ah, crud. She couldn't calm down until she drove up to the cabin and made sure Maybelline was all right.

She locked up the office, stopped at the Swiftie Mart around the corner for a fistful of Ibuprofen and a cherry coke. With the evening sun shining in her eyes, worsening her headache, she flipped down the visor and headed over to Maybelline's place. She wanted to make sure her grandmother hadn't slipped back into town without telling her before she made the trek up to the fishing cabin at Lake Mead.

Seven years ago, when Charlee had moved into her own apartment, Maybelline sold the motor coach they'd called home ever since Charlee was five and had come to live with her. Her grandmother purchased a small lot in a retirement community, put up a nice prefabricated house on a slab, and settled down for the first time in nearly fifty years.

It was almost six o'clock when Charlee turned onto the friendly little cul-de-sac and had to swerve to avoid a white four-door Chevy Malibu intent on hogging the narrow lane.

The manufactured houses were inexpensive, but well maintained. Flowers flourished in window boxes, wind socks flew from weather vanes, white picket fences delineated property lines, pink flamingoes and kitschy plywood cutouts of ladies bending over to show their bloomers decorated freshly mowed lawns. A quiet, cozy place to enjoy one's golden years.

She knew something was very wrong the minute she spotted the door to Maybelline's trailer hanging open a couple of inches. Instantly on alert, Charlee did not pull into the driveway, but instead kept driving and parked a few houses down. She leaped from the car, tugged a small thirty-eight automatic from the leg holster inside her boot, and cautiously approached Maybelline's house.

With both hands, she raised the thirty-eight over her head and slid her back flat against the outside wall of the trailer until she came to the door. Softly, she toed it open farther.

She paused, listening.

Rummaging noises came from somewhere in the back of the house. Much louder than any four-legged rat.

Someone was definitely in there.

And she seriously doubted it was Maybelline since the Tundra wasn't in the driveway. Not knowing what she would find, Charlee extended the gun in front of her and bravely stepped over the threshold.

The damage meeting her eyes jolted her. She eased the safety off the gun. Couch cushions were slit open, knick-knacks broken, furniture overturned, pictures knocked askew on the walls.

Swiftly she navigated the mess and moved into the kitchen. Upended flour and sugar canisters dusted the floor, and dishes lay shattered in jagged shards. The refrigerator hung open and condiments had been knocked from the door. Ketchup, mustard, mayonnaise, and grape marmalade splattered out in a colorful Rorschach.

Anxiety settled like a cast-iron submarine deep inside her belly.

Whoever trashed the place was deadly serious. And from the sound of it, they were still in Maybelline's bedroom.

Tiptoeing through the silt of spilled baking products, Charlee eased down the hallway, careful not to trip over any scattered debris. The door to Maybelline's bedroom stood wide open and the rummaging noises continued. Inch by inch she crept forward until she could peer into the room.

She spotted a man delving through the closet, his back to her. He was very tall. Broad-shouldered and long-legged. For the first time since entering the house, her knees trembled.

He wore crisply ironed chinos and a pristine white shirt. How in the hell had he managed to wreak such havoc and stay so clean? He was concentrating on Maybelline's shoe boxes and he hadn't heard her creep into the room.

Striking cobra-quick, Charlee zipped across the floor and pressed the nose of her gun into his spine.

"Hands on the wall over your head. Now!" She barked out the order, trying her best not to notice how he smelled of sandalwood soap and fancy cologne.

He dropped the shoe box and a shower of old bills cascaded to the closet floor. Tentatively, he raised his arms.

"Palms splayed on the wall."

Leaning forward, he obeyed.

"Now spread your legs."

"What?"

She nudged him with the gun. "This isn't a toy pistol I've got leveled at your heart, buster. Spread your legs."

"Listen..." The intruder started to turn his head.

"Face forward."

"There's been a huge mistake."

"Yeah, like you trashing an old lady's house."

She wrapped her free arm around his chest and patted down his lean hard muscles. Her hand traveled to his waistband.

No weapon there.

She skated her shaking fingers down one long leg of his pants to his socks and back up the other leg. Her breathing rasped.

"Charlee?" he said. "Is that you?"

She should have been relieved to discover the fanny she'd just frisked belonged to Mason Gentry and not a hardened criminal. But on the contrary, her knees almost gave way.

"Gentry?" she squeaked.

"Do you mind taking your gun out of my rib cage? It's rather uncomfortable."

"Why did you ransack Maybelline's place?"

"I didn't."

"Why should I believe you?"

"Look, I'm afraid you'll just have to trust me. I did not vandalize your granny's house."

She eyed his tidy clothes again and realized he spoke the truth. Switching the safety back on, she then tucked her gun into her boot and stepped back.

Slowly, Mason turned.

He had shaved, she noticed, but instead of making him less attractive to her, she had the wildest desire to stroke his clean-shaven face, and then hold her fingers under her nose and inhale the scent of his shaving cream.

God, the man was gorgeous and he scared the living hell out of her.

Charlee bit her bottom lip to keep the terror from her expression. When she had finished her perusal and bravely lifted her gaze, she found him studying her as intently as she'd been scrutinizing him. He pinned her with deep chocolate brown eyes dangerous as quicksand.

Watch out. Watch out.

Help!

Her face heated. She couldn't be blushing. She never blushed.

*Oh, yeah? Then how come you could melt a Popsicle on your cheeks?*

Hating her weakness to the man, she hardened her jaw and bolstered her resolve not to let him know how much he turned her on.

"Why are you here?" she demanded. She knew she

sounded unnecessarily harsh, but hey, a girl had to do what a girl had to do to protect herself.

"I came to see your grandmother."

"I told you she was at her cabin."

"Then why are you here?"

"I thought she might have come home early. Your turn."

He shrugged, grinned wryly. "What can I say? You're not the only one with a suspicious nature."

Dazed, Charlee sank down on the mattress the vandal had stripped bare of its covers.

"Listen," he said. "I'm sorry if I frightened you."

"You didn't scare me," she scoffed, more to convince herself than him. Her heart rate thumped at a good two hundred beats per minute.

"Then why is your face as white as that mattress?"

"How did you break in?" she demanded, refusing to focus on her weakness.

"When I got here I found the door open and the place looking like it looks now. I simply walked in."

"Well, if you didn't trash the house, who did?"

They stared at each other.

"I have no idea. You?"

Charlee shrugged. "Could be connected with some case Maybelline was working on."

Mason waved a hand at the mess. "Stuff like this happens to you ladies often?"

"Not too often, but once in a while. Comes with the territory."

"Tough job."

"I didn't see a car in the driveway," Charlee said, changing the subject. "How did you get over here?"

"I took a taxi. The concierge at the hotel suggested

Whiskey Flats wasn't the best part of town in which to drive my vintage Bentley."

"You drove a vintage Bentley to Vegas?"

He lifted one shoulder. "What can I say? I don't care for flying."

"But a Bentley? Through the desert? From Houston?"

"Hey, I love my car. She's my refuge from the rat race."

"She?"

"Her name's Matilda and since I had to drive to Vegas, I figured I might as well travel in style."

"You named your car?"

"What's wrong with that?" he asked, his tone a tad cranky.

"Excuse me for asking."

"Sorry. I didn't mean to snap. My brother harasses me about the Bentley. Says Matilda is butt ugly, an old man's car."

"No need to explain. I've got a '64 'Vette."

His smile returned and packed the added punch of respect for her taste in vehicles. "That was your car in the parking lot at your detective agency?"

"Guilty." She couldn't help smiling back. Oh, she was sinking deep.

"Isn't a classic Corvette a rather conspicuous vehicle for a private detective?"

"Not as conspicuous as a Bentley. Besides, I borrow Maybelline's black Toyota pickup for stakeouts."

"Gramps gave me the Bentley for my eighteenth birthday. A 1955 model. He bought Matilda the same year he was up for an Oscar."

"Your grandfather was an actor?"

"Only for a year. He bought the Bentley as a reminder of the time. Sentimental value I guess. And when he found out how much I loved her, he gave the car to me."

"No kidding? Maybelline used to be an assistant makeup artist for Twilight Studios back in the midfifties."

"Gramps made movies for Twilight."

Their gazes caught again.

"That's where they must have met each other," Charlee mused. "Do you suppose they were once lovers?"

"My grandfather and your grandmother?" He snorted.

"Why did you say it like that?"

"Like what?"

"As if it were completely impossible for a rich man like your granddaddy to fall in love with my grandmother."

"Oh, so now they were in love?"

"It could happen." She crossed her arms over her chest and glared at him. "Why not?"

A soured love affair would explain why Maybelline had always warned her against getting involved with rich, long-legged, brown-eyed, handsome men. Obviously, she'd been burned. Had Mason's grandfather been the one doing the burning?

"You're carrying a chip on your shoulder about money," Mason said.

"Well, filthy lucre *is* the root of all evil," she said teasingly, but some part of her did believe money caused more problems than it solved. Her father Elwood was a case in point.

"No. Love of money is the root of all evil. Money itself is nothing but a tool."

"To use to buy off anybody you want."

He raised a palm. "Listen, I want to apologize for trying to bribe you. I was wrong."

Charlee analyzed him. He seemed genuine, but his attempt to buy her off had been instinctual. He was accustomed to using money to do his dirty work.

"What were you looking for in the closet?" she asked, diverting her thoughts. Once she clambered on her soapbox about the self-indulgent lifestyles of the rich and famous, she had trouble curbing her tongue and now was not the time or place to declare war on the upper crust.

"I was searching for correspondence between your grandmother and my grandfather."

"You came up empty-handed?"

"No yellowed love letters if that's what you're asking, but I did find a clue."

He took three long-legged steps over to Maybelline's ravaged desk sitting in front of a window and picked up a pocket date book. He tossed the calendar to Charlee.

"Check out today's date."

Inscribed in red ink with Maybelline's scratchy handwriting read the message: Meet N @ K's 4 P.M.

"I'm thinking N is for Nolan."

Charlee blew out her breath. "Maybelline isn't due home until the day after tomorrow."

"Guess she had a date she didn't share with you."

"Looks like you might be right." Poking her tongue against the inside of her cheek, she stared around Mason's shoulder and out the window. Anything to keep from peering into his mesmerizing brown eyes again.

"Any idea where K's might be?"

"I have an idea."

From the corner of her eye, she caught a glimpse of something outside the window. A shadow silhouetted against the curtain.

"So where is K's?" he asked.

Charlee frowned and came up off the bed. "Mason," she said calmly. "Move."

"What?" He blinked at her.

The shadow shifted. Someone was lurking outside the window.

"I said move," she commanded and grappled for the pistol in her boot.

"What's going on?"

She waved a hand at him. "Hit the deck."

"I don't..."

Lordy but the man was stubborn.

"Just do what I say," she hissed. "Get down now!"

"See here, Charlee, you can't just order me around," he lectured, but then all hell broke loose.

A thick-necked man in mirrored sunglasses popped up in front of the window, a gun in his hand. Instantly, Charlee sprang forward, knocking Mason off his feet at precisely the same moment the gunman fired.

# Chapter 3

She stole his breath away.

Literally.

Mason lay sprawled on the floor, struggling to suck in air. Charlee's lean, hard body flung atop his, her firm round breasts squashed flat against his shoulder blades, her warm, sweet breath fanned his cheek.

His ears rang and the silky strands of her long, jet-black hair, combined with the pungent odor of gunpowder, tickled his nose. Disoriented both by lack of oxygen and her compelling feminine scent, he simply gasped.

What in the hell had just happened?

Charlee had slammed into him like a defensive lineman sacking a quarterback at the very same instant he'd heard a car backfiring. Why in the hell had she head-butted him into next week?

The muffled sound of a car engine—was it the same one that had backfired?—revved, followed by the high-pitched squeal of tires peeling out.

"Mason? Are you all right?" Charlee sounded distant and far away, even though her head hovered just above his.

He pried open the eye that wasn't shoved into the carpet and blinked at the gentle slope of her nose.

"Are you hit?"

"Hee, hee, hee," he wheezed.

"You've just had the wind knocked out of you," she diagnosed and scrambled off his back. She stood over him, one hand on her gun, the other on her hip. "You'll be all right."

Mason finally caught his breath and looked up. Broken glass clung to her hair and clothes. He frowned, still trying to piece together what had just occurred.

She held out a hand and hauled him to his feet, power-gripping like a captain of industry. His gaze shifted from the shattered window and the glass shards spilt across Maybelline's desk, to the opposite wall where a bullet hole dug into the Sheetrock.

The truth hit him like an anvil.

That was no backfiring car.

"Someone shot at me."

"'Fraid so."

She bent at the waist and flipped her hair to shake out the glass. The slow toss shouldn't have been sensual, but the manner in which she raked her fingers through the glossy strands, tousling it first one way and then the next, captured his caveman instincts.

And the way her shirt inched up, exposing a narrow expanse of her bare back and a glimpse of purple thong panties peeking just above the waistband of her jeans sent a sharp spike of pure physical longing straight through him.

Mason blinked and shook his head. What in the hell was the matter with him?

"That's why you were hollering at me to move," he

said, turning to eye the window to keep his gaze off the provocative Charlee. "You spotted the gunman."

"Ding, ding, ding. Very good, Sherlock."

"I could have been killed."

"You weren't."

"You saved my life." Rattled and yet desperate to hide his creeping apprehension in the face of Charlee's composure, Mason shoved a hand through his hair and determinedly ignored the nervous sweat plastering his shirt to his shoulder blades.

"Don't go all Hallmark greeting card on me, Gentry. I acted out of pure reflex. Besides, I don't think he intended to kill you. If he had, we'd both be dead."

"So why shoot at all?"

"Warning."

"What for?" Mason couldn't believe they had just dodged a bullet and here was Charlee, cool as a summer salad, acting as if nothing out of the ordinary had occurred.

"I dunno. Encourage us to lay off the case?"

"What case?"

"I'm not sure."

"Do you think the shot has anything to do with our missing grandparents?"

"Maybe."

"Wow, you're a fount of information."

"Hey, I don't know, okay? I'm a detective, not a psychic."

"But why would someone shoot at me?"

"Don't take it personally."

How else was he supposed to regard a bullet aimed at his head? She expected him to simply shrug off a murder attempt?

"Probably has nothing to do with you at all." Charlee stuck the pistol in her waistband.

His eyes tracked her. He spied a tantalizing flash of flat, hard belly when she lifted her shirt. He licked his lips, dry from the arid desert air. "Who could have pulled the trigger?"

"Maybe the same creep who ransacked the place. Maybe not." She headed for the door. "You coming?"

"Where are we going?"

"To Kelly's tavern."

"K's?"

"You got it."

"Aren't we calling the police?"

"If we do, we'll be tied up with red tape for hours. You're welcome to stay here and file a report if you wish, but daylight's burning and I'm getting worried about my grandmother."

He looked from Charlee to the ruins around him and back again. She arched an eyebrow and shot him an are-you-coming-or-not look. His upbringing screamed at him to call the police. Someone had shot at them, for crying out loud, and he wanted an accounting.

But she was right. His house had been burgled before. He knew the routine. Filing a police report involved hours of paperwork and in the meantime Maybelline Sikes and his grandfather were off doing who knew what with a half-million dollars and possibly being shadowed by some two-bit thug who thought nothing of ransacking an old lady's trailer and then shooting at people through a bed-room window.

The mental picture convinced him.

"Let's roll," he said.

\*     \*     \*

Mason sat in the passenger seat. The hotels and casinos slipped past them in the gathering dusk as they drove down the Vegas Strip. The Luxor, Excalibur, MGM Grand, The Flamingo, Caesar's Palace. Tourists packed the streets, many on spring break. But Mason didn't watch the eclectic crowd or take in the bright lights. His attention was centered solely on Charlee.

She drove as she did everything. With a gritty sense of purpose. She stared straight ahead, her eyes glued to the road as she zipped around slow-moving vehicles, frequently changing lanes. Her speed continually edged over the posted limits and she often did not come to a complete halt at stop signs.

He bit down on the inside of his cheek to keep from telling her how to drive. It was her car. If she didn't mind getting it whacked, what business of his was it? He was just glad he was wearing his seat belt and paid extravagant health insurance premiums.

Ten minutes later, Charlee parked her Corvette outside a small neighborhood bar flanked on one side by a twenty-four-hour wedding chapel and a tanning salon on the other. She removed her gun from her waistband, leaned across his knees, stuffed her weapon in the glove compartment, and locked it.

Her breasts brushed lightly against his thigh in the process. Panting like a 1-900-Phone-Sex regular, Mason fumbled for the door handle and struggled to control his out-of-whack libido.

Charlee exited the car, just as she'd slid in, by hoisting her delectable fanny over the door frame Magnum, P.I., style. He tried to imagine Daphne alighting from an open-topped vehicle in such a blasé manner and he laughed out loud.

"What's so funny?" She whirled around and stabbed him with her stare.

"Nothing."

"I know what you're thinking."

"You do?"

"Typical white trash bar."

"I never said that."

"You didn't have to. I can read you like a mail-order catalogue."

"Hey." He raised his palms. "Don't assign your prejudices to me."

"What's that supposed to mean?"

"You have a problem with where you've come from."

She shrugged and turned away, but not before he caught the uncertain expression on her face. He'd nailed her insecurities. He hurried to open the door for her and she blasted him with a quelling glare.

"After you." He bowed with an exaggerated flourish.

She snorted, tossed her head sassily, and trod over the threshold into the crowded, smoky tavern. The rundown bar was a far cry from his usual watering hole, the exclusive Hidden Hills Country Club in River Oaks.

The jukebox blared a Garth Brooks classic about friends in low places. The smell of beer, menthol cigarettes, and stale popcorn filled the air. A leather-clad, tattooed crowd packed the room. They sized Mason up with suspicious glances as he and Charlee made their way toward the bar.

A few people called out greetings to her. She smiled and nodded but didn't stop to chat. She was a woman on a mission and being with her made him feel more resolute. His growing respect for her shot up a notch.

Two men on bar stools scooted over for Charlee as

she bellied up to the bar but they closed ranks around her, leaving Mason standing awkwardly to one side and fending off their glares. She spoke to the bartender, but between the loud music, laughter, and hum of voices, he couldn't hear what she said.

He tried to lean in closer, but one of the men on the bar stool jostled him with his elbow, sloshing beer over Mason's arm. He frowned and started to say something but the guy was skunk-drunk. He wrote off the shove as an accident.

"Excuse me," Mason said. "Could I please step up to the bar?"

"Can you?" the guy, who wore a black leather vest, chains, and a gold spike through his chin, challenged.

How tedious. Obviously the beer slosh hadn't been an accident. Mason sighed inwardly. He didn't have time for this crap. "Come on, mister. I don't want any trouble."

"Oh, yeah? Then how come you dragged your preppy ass in here?"

"Since you've been imbibing heavily I'm choosing to ignore that remark."

The guy looked over at his buddy. "Did he just insult me, Leroy?"

"Yup," Leroy, who had a cobra tattooed on his forearm, agreed. "I didn't go to *coll-ege,* but I do believe he just insulted you, Thurgood."

"I'm with her." Mason nodded at Charlee. "We'll be gone in a couple of minutes. No need to start something."

"Hidin' behind the skirt, are you?" Thurgood mocked Mason.

"Just move aside, please," Mason said calmly.

"Whatcha gonna do if I do this?" Thurgood plastered a hammy palm on Charlee's fanny.

"Hand off my ass, Thurgood," Charlee said over her shoulder.

Not only did Thurgood not remove his hand from Charlee's backside, but he looked at Mason and wagged his lascivious tongue.

Anger, hot and quick, shot through Mason. He slapped a hand around Thurgood's wrist and jerked him off the bar stool.

Two seconds later, Thurgood lay flat on his back on the floor, Mason's Italian leather loafer pressing against his windpipe.

"Hey, Thurgood, looks like the preppie's kicking your ass." Leroy laughed and slapped his thigh.

Charlee turned away from the bar to watch Mason with a bemused smile.

"I think you owe the lady an apology."

"Yeooow."

"Apologize," Mason said, increasing the pressure on Thurgood's Adam's apple.

"I tworry, Charlee," Thurgood rasped.

Charlee peered down at the man. "Maybe next time you'll keep your hands to yourself."

He nodded, or as much as he could manage with a shoe at his throat.

"Let's get out of here," Charlee said to Mason. "I got what we came for."

"Catch you later, Thurgood." He lifted his foot from the man's neck and followed Charlee's provocative fanny straight out the door.

"You've been holding out on me, Gentry," she said once they were on the sidewalk. "Not quite as blue-blooded as you appear. Where'd you learn those moves?"

"Fourth-degree black belt, tae kwon do."

"No shit." She shot him a pensive look and then smiled. "No shit."

"Oooh, now I'm really titillated. Cursing and everything. What would your mama say?"

"Are you making fun of me?"

"Who me?" Charlee started to slide over the door frame and into the driver's seat.

"Wait."

"What?"

Mason hurried over to the driver's side and opened the door. "A lady should allow the gentleman to open the car door for her."

Charlee shook her head. "For one thing, no one has ever accused me of being a lady, and for another, you just blew it."

"Blew what?"

"I was actually beginning to like you and then you had to go and remind me what a pompous jackass you are."

"What? What'd I do wrong?"

She slammed the car door shut and then climbed over the door frame with a glower. "Get in."

Women. Who could figure them? Try to do something nice and you ended up making them mad.

"So what did you find out about our grandparents?" he asked after she started the engine.

"Maybelline did indeed meet some guy, who sounds like he could be your grandfather, at four o'clock this afternoon."

Mason exhaled sharply. Okay. Now they were getting somewhere.

"According to the bartender, the man left with her."

"Anything else?"

Charlee swiveled her head to look him squarely in the

eyes. "I've never seen Maybelline cry. I mean not ever. Not at weddings, not at funerals. Not when I graduated high school. Never."

"So?"

"Kelly claims when they left the bar, not only was your grandfather looking pretty grim but my grandmother was bawling her eyes out."

Nolan Gentry sat beside Maybelline in the Las Vegas airport waiting for their flight to L.A. Absentmindedly he drummed the manila folder she'd given him against the metal armrest.

The contents of the file confirmed the awful news Maybelline had broken to him over the phone two days earlier. If he didn't intervene, the financial empire his father had started and he and his older brother Harry had built into a Fortune 500 dynasty would be utterly destroyed, ruining not only Nolan but his son and grandsons as well.

And the damnable thing was he couldn't say anything to anyone. Not yet. The necessity for silence was the reason he'd taken the five hundred thousand dollars from company funds. And because he hadn't known what other expenses he might incur. Such as paying off a blackmailer.

What he hoped—no, what he prayed—was that the family would send Mason to find him. It had to be Mason. Only his second-born grandson would truly understand the moral dilemma facing them.

And if they didn't send Mason?

Nolan shook his head. They would send Mason. Poor boy always shouldered the dirty work.

He peered over at Maybelline. She too had a lot invested in the outcome. If things turned out badly, her only son might end up dead.

Giving her a comforting smile, he squeezed her hand. "Everything is going to be okay."

She nodded, but he could tell from the skepticism in her eyes she wasn't buying his empty promise, not for a minute.

Her tears had damned near killed him back there in the bar. He'd only seen her cry one other time. The despair over discovering she was pregnant with a married man's baby had been so strong it sent her to the top of the HOLLYWOOD sign with the aim of ending her life.

Thank God, he'd been there to talk her down. He'd saved her life that night and now, almost fifty years later, she was saving his.

She smiled back at him and Nolan couldn't help wondering, What if?

What if he'd won the Oscar in 1955?

What if his father hadn't had a heart attack when he did?

What if he had refused his dying father's edict to come home, marry Elispeth Hunt, and mingle the nouveau riche Gentry oil-field blood with respectable old money breeding?

What if he'd stayed with Maybelline?

His old heart took an unexpected dip at the prospect. What indeed?

He gazed over at her. She was still damned beautiful in his eyes, slim and sexy despite the passing years. Headstrong and feisty. That's why her tears had frightened him so. Maybelline had never been a softie. Damn, but there were so many things he wanted to say to her. So many things he wanted to undo.

It was a useless endeavor, trying to recast the past. He'd made his choices, both good and bad. But now, the chickens had come home to roost.

She raised a hand to hide a yawn. "Long past my bedtime."

"You always were a morning lark."

"And you were the night owl. Remember when we shared the cottage in Venice Beach? You were usually coming to bed when I was leaving for work."

"I remember," he said softly. "You were three months pregnant with Elwood."

"And you'd bring me 7UP and saltines to help with the morning sickness."

Nolan patted her shoulder. "You can lean on me, May," he said. "Take a nap. I'll wake you when they start boarding the plane."

She hesitated, and then she took off her glasses, slid them into her purse, and gingerly rested her head on his shoulder.

Nolan inhaled sharply. He hadn't expected the weight of her against him to feel so good. Her hair smelled like ripe peaches and he remembered the day in his daddy's oil field when he'd seen her for the very first time.

She had worn a satiny green dress with a flared skirt that twirled when she walked and black and white saddle shoes. He recalled the dress was green because it contrasted dramatically with her fiery red hair. His fingers had itched to stroke her glossy locks.

Slowly, he reached out and traced a finger over her hair. Still soft as silk. His gut clutched.

*You're too old to be feeling this way. Much too old by far.*

She'd already fallen asleep, the gentle rise and fall of her chest luring him more surely than a siren's song. She'd always possessed the knack to fall asleep as easily as a child and nothing short of a major earthquake roused her from a sound slumber. Using his free hand, he reached for the jacket he'd draped across the seat beside him and gently spread it over her shoulders.

A tenderness so strong the feeling threatened to overrun his eyes with tears had Nolan clenching his teeth. Not once in his forty-three-year marriage to Elispeth had he felt one-tenth of the tenderness he felt right now for Maybelline. Not even when Elispeth had given birth to their son, Reed.

Maybelline was everything Elispeth was not.

She was bold and brave. When he realized Maybelline had run off to Hollywood both to escape her physically abusive father and to pursue her dream of becoming a makeup artist, her burst for freedom had given him the courage to defy his own father and go into acting. Elispeth, on the other hand, had been so timid and mousy she'd never even raised her voice. No fire. No vim. No vigor.

Maybelline did things her own way, blazed her own path. She didn't care if people gossiped about her. Elispeth followed the herd, decorating her house right down to the knickknacks exactly as they were depicted in some New York interior-decorating magazine. Elispeth had never stepped out of line. Had always done what was expected of her.

Maybelline was whip-smart and had more common sense in her pinkie than most people had in their entire bodies even though she had never finished high school. Elispeth had a masters degree from Sarah Lawrence but didn't have the good sense to call a doctor if Reed was running a fever.

And most of all, whenever he was with Maybelline, *he* was different. She made him laugh and take risks. She had once teased him into shaking off his stuffy exterior and going skinny-dipping in a pond. She'd dared him to stretch his acting talents and try for a part he never believed he could win. She had challenged him in a hundred wonderful ways. Around her, he was more alive. More of a man.

No, that wasn't fair. Elispeth had been a good woman. She'd done her best. He had no call comparing her to Maybelline. It wasn't his dead wife's fault he'd been in love with another woman when he married her.

Nolan shook his head. The scary thing was that his grandson Mason was about to stumble into the same trap he'd tripped over as a young man: marrying the wrong woman simply to appease family demands. Daphne Maxwell was a lovely girl but she was Elispeth all over again. What the boy needed was a Maybelline of his own.

To lure his mind away from thoughts he shouldn't be having, Nolan looked up at the departure board. Their flight was delayed. Sighing, he debated what to do when they arrived in L.A. Obviously, it would be too late to go to the accounting firm straightaway. They'd have to obtain a room for the night. Make that two rooms.

He closed his eyes and had just dozed off when a hand clamped down on his shoulder.

"Mr. Nolan Gentry?"

Startled, Nolan's eyes flew open. There, standing in front of him, was Elvis. Pudgy Elvis in his famous white rhinestone-studded jumpsuit.

He blinked. Was he dreaming? He half expected Elvis to launch into a rousing, hip-swinging rendition of "Viva Las Vegas."

"Mr. Gentry?" Elvis repeated.

No, not *the* Elvis, but an Elvis look-alike. The town was chock-full of Elvis impersonators.

"Yes, I'm Nolan Gentry."

"Mr. Gentry, I have a gun in my pocket. I want you to wake your companion and follow me."

"What?"

"Do you need me to repeat what I just said?"

"You've got a gun? But how did you get a gun past airport security?"

Elvis snorted. "Don't you watch nighttime news shows like *20/20* where they smuggle all kinds of weapons past the metal detectors?"

"I don't believe you have a gun. Show me."

"You think I'm gonna whip it out in public?"

Defiantly, Nolan crossed his arms over his chest. "I'm not going anywhere with you."

Elvis sighed. "Okay, let's try this another way. If you want to see the Oscar files, then you're going to have to come with me."

Nolan's gut squeezed. How did Elvis know about the stolen files? "What?"

"Yep. Believe me when I say I can make or break you, pal. Now move."

Nolan shook his head. Nothing made any sense. He had to be dreaming. Otherwise, all proof pointed to the fact that he and Maybelline were being kidnapped by the King of Rock and Roll.

# Chapter 4

Where to now?"

Charlee slid a glance over at Mason, amazed he'd asked her opinion.

He sat ramrod-straight, his seat belt snugly fastened around his trim waist, his eyes locked on the unruly Vegas Strip traffic. After his lady and gentleman crack about the way she climbed into her car, she'd pegged him as a control freak who preferred his women submissive and relegated to a pedestal.

She grinned to herself, amused at how uptight he was. She'd bet anything he rolled his toothpaste tube up from the bottom instead of squeezing it in the middle like she did. No, wait. He was probably so regimented he used a toothpaste dispenser and carefully measured out each drop. She'd wager a month's pay that he labeled his possessions, hated for the food on his plate to touch, and always counted his change to make sure he'd gotten back the correct amount.

Good thing they wouldn't be together long. She would drive him crazy with the way she stuffed underwear in the same drawer with socks, ate standing over the kitchen sink, and tossed her change in the bottom of her purse without ever looking at it.

"You're asking my opinion?"

"You are the private investigator."

"Somehow I got the impression you have a hard time letting other people take charge."

His smile was forced. "Not when the other person has more information. Vegas is your home turf. You're more than welcome to step up to the plate."

"Thank you. I will. We're going to see someone who might have an idea where our grandparents are," she said.

"Oh?" Mason leaned closer and she caught a whiff of his sandalwood soap. She wondered if he tasted as clean as he smelled. "Who?"

Charlee's mistrustful nature had her biting her bottom lip and hesitating before revealing any more information than absolutely necessary. After all, what did she know about the guy other than the fact he dazzled her like dynamite and kicked-ass at tae kwon do?

In and of itself, that fact was suspicious. How many spoiled, rich pretty boys possessed the discipline for advanced martial arts?

Once she thought about it, Charlee realized everything had been hunky-dory in her life until he'd shown up. Now Maybelline was missing, her place had been ransacked, and someone had shot at them.

What if he had lied about his identity? He could be anyone. A hit man or an undercover cop or even, heaven forbid, an IRS agent. Plenty of people would gladly line up to take pot shots at IRS agents.

"Charlee?" he prodded, more irritating than a pebble in her boot. "Who are we going to see?"

*Don't tell him a damned thing.*

She pretended to concentrate on navigating the Corvette around a slow-moving eighteen-wheeler, but he didn't buy her stall tactics.

"If the matter concerns my grandfather, I have a right to know."

As much as she wanted to, she couldn't disagree. After all, she had no real reason to believe Mason was anything other than what he claimed. Charlee reluctantly relented.

"We're going to see my father."

"From the tightness in your voice I'm guessing you two don't get along so well."

"You might say that." Charlee gripped the steering wheel far tighter than necessary. "Let's just hope my old man isn't involved in what's going on between our grandparents."

"Care to elaborate?"

Charlee took a deep breath. "No."

To her surprise, he nodded and said, "Fair enough."

Mason certainly didn't seem like the sort of guy to let things pass easily and Charlee shot him a pensive glance. Maybe something in her body language warned him off.

Whenever Elwood popped into her brain, she couldn't help tensing up. She understood even without the help of a Freudian psychologist that the roots of her prejudice against wealthy, long-legged, matinee-idol-smiling, beard-stubble-sporting men started with her father.

Mason's decision not to pressure her had a tongue-loosening effect. Charlee had no idea what possessed her but she found herself saying, "Don't get me wrong. I love my father. I mean he *is* my father after all, but a stand-up guy he ain't."

"We all have family issues."

Charlee laughed. "Yeah. Well, some of us have issues and then some of us have *issues.*"

"Rotten childhood?"

"Rotten isn't the word for it."

Why was she yammering like an Oprah guest? She wasn't a poor-me-I-never-got-over-being-mistreated-by-my-parent type. And she most certainly wasn't a whiner.

She pressed the tip of her tongue against the roof of her mouth to keep from speaking, but then Mason reached over, flicked off the radio, and casually let his fingers trail over the back of her hand. She didn't know if he'd touched her on purpose or not, but a hint of sympathy was all it took. How truly pathetic was she? Words erupted from her in a mindless purge of verbiage.

"Once upon a time, my father, Elwood Sikes, was the best Elvis impersonator in Vegas." Charlee left the Strip and downshifted as she slowed for a yield sign. "This wasn't long after the real Elvis died and Elwood's career blazed hot, hot, hot."

"Hmmm."

"Oh, he was a charming bastard. Had tons of women flocking after him, which was the main reason my mother didn't marry him even though she was pregnant with me. She might have been a naive Louisiana Cajun in over her head in sin city, but she wasn't dumb."

Charlee waved a hand. Had she ever told her story to anyone? She couldn't remember. She wanted to shut up, to keep her private life private, but spewing out her anger felt so good, she just kept blabbing.

"Anyway, my father fell for his own publicity hype. He believed the money he raked in would last forever. He bought a pink Cadillac and a fancy house with an Olympic-sized swimming pool and he wore diamond rings on every finger. The typical cliché. I'm told he bought me tons of toys but I don't remember."

"It must have been a very exciting time for him," Mason said.

"Too exciting. He started gambling. Caught the fever and lost every penny. After that he became real friendly with the whiskey bottle and they canned him from the Elvis gig for showing up drunk. Everything was repossessed. He lost it all. The money, the house, the women. He simply couldn't deal with the failure. He's spent the rest of his life trying to get it back by chasing get-rich-quick schemes and getting thrown in jail on a semiregular basis." Charlee sighed. "And I've spent a small mint bailing him out."

Mason ticked his tongue in sympathy.

"He littered my childhood with a string of broken promises. One time he swore he'd take me to McDonald's for my fifth birthday. My mother dressed me up in a pink satin dress and black patent leather Mary Janes. I can still remember the dress had a white sash with blue flowers. I waited and I waited and I waited, but Elwood never came."

"Must have been pretty difficult for you."

Charlee shook her head in denial. "Hell, I was used to him standing me up. But his reappearing acts were even worse. He'd show up, usually drunk, with some big-haired, big-chested bimbo who he expected me to call Mama on his arm and a wad of ill-gotten cash in his pocket."

"I can't even imagine."

"Worst thing, after my mother died, Elwood just dumped me on Maybelline. Not that I regret being raised by my grandmother," she added swiftly. "It's just I'd always hoped..." she trailed off.

A fire-engine siren shrieked nearby. Thank God for the interruption, otherwise she might have told him every sordid detail of her painful past.

"Better pull over," Mason advised. "I think they're coming this way."

She looked in the rearview mirror at the same time the fire truck rounded the corner. Startled, she jerked to a stop at the curb and realized her hands were shaking. Not from the unexpected arrival of the emergency vehicle but from the sheer volume of her verbal diarrhea. She could not have shocked herself more if she'd stripped off her shirt and flashed him her boobies.

The car idled softly, accentuating the quietness between them.

"Are you okay?" Mason asked, his voice heavy with concern. He touched her again and there was no mistaking the intent this time—firmer, lingering, his thumb gently rubbing her knuckles.

Charlee jerked her hand away and looked into his face. She stared at his wide, generous mouth and found herself wondering if he was a good kisser. Startled, she focused her gaze on the road.

An odd twinge twisted through her. A strange mix of anxiety, gratitude, and uncertainty.

What in the hell was going on here?

*You're just worried about Maybelline. Remember, you're highly susceptible to brown-eyed, handsome men. Nail your guard back up, pronto.*

A second fire truck zoomed by and then a third.

Struggling to appear nonchalant, Charlee tugged her hand out from under Mason's and slowly pulled the Corvette back into traffic. She smelled smoke in the air and the odor thickened the closer they came to the rundown apartment complex where her father lived.

By the time they turned onto her father's block, Charlee's heart hammered hard even before she spotted the flames licking brightly against the night sky. Dread weighed her down at the sight of firemen scurrying across the lawn with fire hoses and axes.

Apartment residents stood to one side staring owleyed as their homes flashed in a crescendo of sparks. Gawkers stopped to rubberneck.

From the corner of her eye, Charlee spied a white, four-door Chevy Malibu easing slowly down the street. She parked in the lot of a nearby dry cleaners and, without even thinking about Mason, climbed out of the car and beelined over to the small apartment complex.

*Please let Elwood be okay,* she prayed.

She tried to approach one of the firemen, but he brusquely waved her off. A ruddy-faced police officer with a Boston accent came over to escort her across the street with the other bystanders.

"This way, miss."

"My father," she said. "He lives in apartment 16c."

"Everyone's been evacuated. There've been no casualties. If your father is here, he'll be in the crowd. Now step aside."

"What happened?" Charlee fisted her hands. "I have a right to know."

"Step aside," the policeman repeated with a stern frown.

The smoke, the fire, the heat, the noise, and the chaos overwhelmed her.

Dammit, Elwood, where are you?

She wanted to argue with the cop, to demand he tell her something more, but she couldn't find her tongue. She simply stared at the dramatic flames scampering across the roof of the apartment building and she felt all the courage drain from her body.

"Excuse me, officer," Mason interrupted. He moved

closer to the man, lowered his head, and spoke so low Charlee couldn't hear what he said.

What magic he wrought, she did not know, but a few minutes later he walked over and took her elbow. "Let's go back to the car."

"Why? I want to know what's happening."

"Just do as I say."

"Listen here, Gentry…" Charlee balked, grateful to have someone to take her anxiety out on.

"Now is not the time to straddle your high horse. I've got unfortunate news."

"What?" Her contrariness vanished. She gripped Mason's forearm and imagined the worst.

"The fire originated in your father's apartment."

Charlee blinked. "Is he…hurt?"

Mason shook his head. "The apartment was empty when the firemen arrived."

"Thank God."

"They believe the fire was arson."

"Arson?"

"I hate to tell you, but the police suspect your father intentionally started the blaze."

Charlee sank into the chair in her office and forced herself not to bite her fingernails. She balled her hands into fists and dropped them into her lap. She absolutely refused to jump to conclusions about Elwood. Just because his apartment caught fire didn't mean he was up to his old tricks.

*Believe that and there's a bridge in Brooklyn someone is dying to sell you.*

Sighing, she flicked on Maybelline's computer and leaned back in the chair as she waited for the hard drive to boot up.

After leaving the scene of the fire, Mason had insisted on going back to her grandmother's trailer to help her clean up the mess and repair the broken bedroom windowpane. She'd been touched by his offer and then angry with herself for going all soft and gushy inside just because some guy did a decent thing.

Plus, she couldn't stop thinking about the way his hard, lean back—all sinewy and masculine—had felt beneath her when she'd knocked him to the floor and saved him from the gunman's bullet. Even now, hours later, the memory of his body caused the moisture to evaporate from her mouth and her pulse to speed up.

She wasn't falling for his charms. No how. No way. She understood that old song and dance. Guys were oh-so-delightful at first, at least until they landed you in their beds. After they got what they wanted, it was so long, Charlee, been nice knowing you, don't let the door hit you in the ass on your way out.

It was closing in on two A.M. but she was too wired to sleep. After dropping Mason off at the Bellagio, she schlepped down to the office to hunt through Maybelline's files in search of clues.

But instead of probing the database on the hard drive, she found herself logging onto the Internet. She never consciously decided to Google him, but the next thing she knew, there she was, typing Mason's name into the search engine.

And up popped a string of references.

Links to newspaper articles and magazine interviews and high-society pages. She discovered his family held a seat on the New York Stock Exchange.

When she stumbled across a detailed listing of the numerous companies they owned—including a silver mine in New Mexico, a flagship hotel in the Bahamas, and a top accounting firm in Hollywood—Charlee realized his family was richer than God and she was in far deeper trouble than she ever imagined.

Damn her and her illogical Prince Charming complex.

She found a photograph of Mason escorting a glossily beautiful blonde to some debutante shindig and the pinch of jealousy biting into her stomach scared her.

Good gravy. What did she have to be jealous of? She could never compete with such a woman. Nor did she want to. She'd had her fill of rich men.

Briefly, she thought of Gregory Blankensonship, the first man she'd ever loved, and winced. Would she ever recover from his betrayal?

*Oh, stop whining. You've got work to do.*

Determined, she logged off the Internet, picked up the telephone, and began calling hospitals, hotels, airlines, and bus stations. Maybelline, Nolan, and Elwood simply couldn't have disappeared into thin air.

She might not be lucky in love, but she was a damned fine private investigator. And one way or another, she would find them.

Mason had come to Vegas to find his grandfather and drag him back home in time to prevent his brother from taking sole credit for closing the biggest deal in the history of Gentry Enterprises. Retrieving Gramps should have been quick, clean, and simple.

But instead of achieving his clear-cut goal, a little more than twelve hours after arriving in town, Mason found himself embroiled in a royal mess featuring one testy lady P.I., her missing granny, a ransacked trailer house, a disgruntled gunman, and a very suspicious fire.

What he couldn't figure out was how Gramps fit into the chaos.

Mason had tumbled into bed, certain he would fall asleep within minutes, but slumber eluded him. Two-thirty and he lay wide awake listening to the bedside clock tick off the seconds. Dammit. Charlee had promised to come around for him at six A.M. so they could start searching for their grandparents again.

Charlee.

Now there was one hell of a woman. Tough and unflinching, she didn't coddle her fears or back away from the truth.

It was a thrill watching her mind work. He could actually see her mental cogs whirling. It was in the tilt of her jaw, the furrow of her brow, the tightening of her facial muscles. The way she focused on whatever task lay at hand was a thing of beauty.

And being with her was strangely exhilarating. As if by proxy her fervor would rub off on him. He wondered if she realized how the intensity came over her. The way her green eyes changed colors and took on a lively ferocity when she was on the hunt.

She was a woman warrior, proud and strong. He thought of the way she'd looked at Maybelline's house, gun in hand, a determined set to her chin. Suddenly his senses were as full of her as they had been at the moment the gunman fired.

The womanly aroma of her hung in his nose, the imprint of her firm body lingered against his back, the sound of her rich, smoldering voice haunted his ears. She stirred his imagination and aroused a dormant passion he never realized he possessed.

He liked her long, lean limbs and the bronzy glow of her skin. He liked the straightforward scent of her—

honeysuckle soap and crisp spray starch. Not frilly or overdone. Just clean and honest and free.

And her luscious tresses. Masses of straight black hair hanging down her back in a curtain of sheer delight or bouncing provocatively when pulled back in a sleek pony-tail. Too bad...

*Too bad what, Gentry?*

Too damned bad he was stewing in his hormones. Charlee Champagne was strictly off-limits for so many reasons he couldn't begin to count. Groaning, Mason stuffed a pillow over his head and willed his mind empty.

He must have finally dozed off, because he woke with a jerk when the telephone rang. Blindly, he fumbled for the receiver in the dark and brought it to his ear.

"Lo," he mumbled.

"Gentry, it's Charlee."

As if he didn't recognize her sexy, smoky voice. "What time is it?"

"Four o'clock."

"What are you doing up?"

"Couldn't sleep."

"Go away for a couple of hours, will you?"

"Can't. Got some hot news." He could tell from the thrill in her tone she was jazzed up. A cougar on the prowl.

Shaking his head to clear away the cobwebs of aborted sleep, Mason propped himself against the headboard. "I'm listening."

"I did some digging and I found out Nolan and Maybel-line booked a red-eye flight to L.A. last night."

"They're in L.A.?"

"No, they never got on the plane."

"So they're still in Vegas?"

"That's what I aim to find out. I'm headed over to the

airport to interview the gate agent and figured you might wanna come along."

"Sure. Sure." Mason yawned and ran a hand through his hair.

"See you there in twenty minutes," she said and hung up the phone.

Twenty minutes later, Mason parked his Bentley in the infield parking garage, then walked over to wait on the curb outside the terminal.

Charlee screeched her Corvette to a stop in a passenger loading zone and leaped from the car. She wore a straw white Stetson cocked back on her head and twin braids streamed down her back. She looked absolutely adorable; although he had the impression she was shooting for badass. Daphne would proclaim her a fashion disaster, but Mason appreciated that she dressed the way she pleased, in-vogue styles be damned.

He pointed at the NO LONG-TERM PARKING sign. "You're not going to leave your car here."

"Nobody's gonna tow me away at this time of the morning." Her fast-talking disregard for the posted sign told him she was wired on adrenaline and so eager to leap into the investigation she couldn't be bothered looking for a parking space.

"Don't count on it."

"I'm on the hunt. I need my vehicle at the ready in case I need to make a quick exit."

"Parking in a passenger loading zone and risking being towed is not the way to achieve your goal."

"Oh, hush. How are they going to know I'm not loading passengers? We won't be long. Come on."

Mason didn't budge. "Charlee, move your car," he insisted.

"Relax, Gentry. Boy, you are uptight. Love the sheet creases by the way." On her way past him, she reached up and lightly fingered his cheek.

Her touch burned electric. Mason growled, desperate to deny the tingle of awareness warming his face.

Blithely, she stalked into the concourse and he had no choice but to follow or get left behind. Fine, let her car get towed.

In spite of himself, Mason found his eyes locked on the sassy sway of her blue-jeaned behind. Good thing she wasn't his girlfriend. They would clash like cymbals over every little thing. He couldn't imagine living with someone so stubborn.

Girlfriend? What in the hell prompted that outlandish concept?

*Because she's the girl of the dreams you never even dared to dream. She's wild and free and full of spirit. And she would scare the living hell out of your family.*

He shook his head. Blame his crazy meandering thoughts on his poor sleep-deprived brain. He was officially losing his marbles.

*Gramps, you owe me big time.*

Charlee pranced through the security checkpoint, but Mason set off the buzzer. The attendant motioned him aside for a wanding. They required him to empty his pockets and remove his shoes before they were satisfied he wasn't planning on blowing the place to kingdom come.

He hurried through the terminal. His impatience escalating when two thick-necked guys in black sunshades bumped into him. If he hadn't been so intent on locating Charlee, Mason might have paid more heed to the duo, but because he was in a hurry, he blew off their rudeness. By the time he caught up with her, she was deep in conversation with a gate agent.

He walked over and touched her shoulder. When she turned away from the gate agent, he was startled to see her normally golden skin had gone pale. The look on her face sliced a chill straight through his bones. He felt confused, angry with whomever or whatever had created her obvious distress. He fisted his hands, ready to beat someone to a pulp on her behalf.

"Charlee? What's wrong?"

She quickly gained control over her emotions, smoothing out her forehead and pressing her lips firmly together.

"We're in luck. The same gate agent is still on duty. He remembers Maybelline and Nolan. They left with some guy just before the plane arrived."

"What guy?"

Charlee didn't meet his gaze and he realized instantly she was keeping something from him.

"Charlee?" he prodded.

"I dunno, but the gate agent said he watched all three of them head over to the rental car area."

He narrowed his eyes. "Is that everything?"

She hesitated.

"What aren't you telling me?"

She studied the scuffed toe of her boots, jammed her fingertips into her front pockets. "Our grandparents were arguing with the guy. Like they were upset and didn't want to leave with him. Actually the gate agent even offered to call security, but your grandfather told him everything was all right."

"Does he remember what the guy looked like?"

Charlee took a deep breath. "Yeah. He was wearing a white, rhinestone-encrusted jumpsuit."

"That's certainly memorable. Sounds like Elvis Presley."

"Or an Elvis impersonator."

Their eyes met and he knew what she was going to say before the word left her mouth.

"Elwood."

# Chapter 5

Foreboding slithered through Charlee's insides like a snake shedding its skin. Why would Maybelline and Nolan run off with Elwood? She had a bad feeling about the whole deal. Mason's grandfather had arrived in Vegas with a large sum of money in his pocket and large sums of money attracted Elwood like flies to cow patties.

Her father had been jailed for many penny-ante schemes from peddling weed to hoodwinking tourists with three-card monte to blackmailing a high-profile exlover. However, none of his crimes had merited a felony charge. Maybelline had washed her hands of him years ago, but Charlee couldn't admit defeat when it came to her father no matter how many times he disappointed her.

Maybelline rarely spoke to her only child. Why would she leave the airport with him when she'd planned on catching a flight to L.A.?

Unless...

Charlee started to gnaw on her thumbnail and realized Mason was studying her. Shamefaced, she quickly tucked her hand behind her back.

"Let's go talk to the rental car people," she said in a decisive tone and stalked toward the counter.

The woman behind the desk didn't glance up from her tabloid magazine. Charlee splayed her palms against the black Formica countertop and cleared her throat.

"Excuse me."

Unhappy at being dragged from her celebrity gossip, the woman glared at her. "Yeah?"

"A middle-aged Elvis impersonator along with an older couple rented a car from you earlier this morning. I'd like to know where they were headed, please."

The woman frowned. "I can't release that kind of information."

"I'm a private detective," Charlee said in her most professional tone and flashed the woman her ID. "And I'm investigating a possible crime. If you could do a little finger-tapping on your computer keyboard I'd really appreciate it."

"Sorry, no can do."

"It's a matter of life and death. I must know where they're headed."

"You're not the police. I don't have to tell you anything." She continued reading her gossip rag.

Charlee gritted her teeth and contemplated shoving Ms. Congeniality out of the way and commandeering her keyboard, but before she had time to discard the idea as a not particularly viable one, Mason placed one finger on the woman's magazine and slowly pushed it downward so she was forced to look him in the eyes.

"Hi there." He shot the woman a grin so dazzling even an ardent man hater could not have resisted him: and clearly she was no man hater.

"Oh, my!" the woman gasped breathlessly as if one of

the movie stars from her magazine had sprung to life right in front of her. "Where did you come from?"

Mason leaned nonchalantly closer and studied the name tag situated just above the woman's breast. "Lila," he crooned. "What a lovely name."

"Why thank you," the woman simpered and batted her eyelashes. "I was named after my great-grandmother."

"How do you do." He offered his hand.

"I'm doing very well now that you're here." She angled a sultry glance at him and pumped his hand as vigorously as if she were pulling the handle on a slot machine.

Charlee snorted. Enough with the friggin' foreplay, Gentry, get to the point.

"Listen, Lila, I'm hoping you can do me and my"— Mason glanced over his shoulder at Charlee—"sister here a favor."

Sister? Charlee burned a hole through him with her stare. What was the big idea telling Ms. Congeniality she was his sister?

"She's your sister?" Lila asked.

Mason lowered his voice. "I know. Her manners are so atrocious you'd never suspect we were raised by the same parents."

"No indeed," Lila whispered back as if Charlee weren't standing right in front of her.

Mason murmured something else that Charlee couldn't quite hear. Lila giggled girlishly and then typed into the computer. Let some rich handsome guy smile at her and ole Lila folded like a house of cards.

"The party you're interested in rented a red and white Chevrolet camper. License number LYG-123. It's supposed to be returned to the Tucson office on Monday."

Monday? Why so much time? It didn't take but maybe

eight or nine hours to drive to Tucson. Why keep the rental until Monday? Charlee nibbled on her bottom lip and tried to figure out what stunt her father was pulling.

"Thank you so much, Lila." Mason gazed deeply into the clerk's eyes and flashed her his dimples, looking like some swoonily gorgeous soap opera star. "You've been an immeasurable help."

"Hang on a minute." Lila was practically panting. She tore off a scrap of paper from the yellow legal pad on her desk, jotted something on it, and slipped the note into Mason's hand. "Call me." She winked.

Charlee rolled her eyes, wagged her head, and mocked the awestruck clerk by silently mouthing, "Call me."

See. Precisely why she didn't trust wealthy, long-legged, brown-eyed, handsome men any farther than she could toss 'em. They would do anything to get their way. Completely shameless, the lot of them.

"Bye." He wriggled his fingers at Lila, and took Charlee by the elbow. "Let's go, sis."

"What's up, Slick?" Charlee untangled herself from him the minute they were out of earshot. "The gossip rag queen gave you her phone number?"

"Not that it's any of your business, but yes."

"You gonna call her?"

Mason frowned and tossed the woman's number in a nearby trash can. "Of course not."

Charlee shook her head. "Cruel bastard. You trifled with that woman's affections."

"All for a good cause."

"And by the way, what was that remark about my being your sister?"

"Hey, it got us what we needed." He guided her through the concourse, which had grown more crowded since they'd first arrived. "Do you think she would have opened up to me if she thought you were my girlfriend?"

"I'm not your girlfriend."

"I know that and you know that, but Lila didn't know that."

"You're such a liar."

"Sounds like sour grapes to me."

"What are you talking about? Sour grapes over what? That Lila was drooling on you? *Puh-leeze,* I could care less."

"You're just testy because my method worked and yours didn't. You can catch more flies with honey, sweetheart. Remember that."

"Hmmph," Charlee mumbled under her breath while at the same time her pulse revved to realize he'd inadvertently called her sweetheart. Oh, this was completely disgusting. How could she let herself get all flustered and fluttery over some pretty boy?

Perturbed at her reaction, she searched for something rude to say. "Honey my ass. You snagged her with the matinee-idol smile and your sultry brown-eyed stare."

"Pardon?" He lowered his head to hers, those very eyes in question twinkling with a mischievous light. "I didn't quite catch that. Did you just compliment me?"

"Ahem. I said, the red and white camper is only a few hours ahead of us. If we pick up the pace, maybe we can overtake them before they reach Tucson."

"That's what I thought you said."

"Yeah. Right."

"Really, Charlee, you've got to learn to express your opinion more often," he teased.

"Leave the sarcasm to me, Slick. It doesn't suit you. Stick with your forte."

"And what is that?"

"Conniving women."

"Ah, so that's my forte. I always wondered what it was." He ran a hand over his beard stubble. The soft, rasping sound knotted her stomach.

"Smart aleck."

"So tell me, Charlee, if tempting women is my forte, how come my charms don't work on you?"

What in the hell was wrong with him? Mason berated himself. He didn't flirt. He wasn't a hound dog. He respected women. Considered them his equal in every way. He was about to become engaged. Daphne trusted him and Mason honored that trust. He would not allow something as insignificant as sexual magnetism orchestrate his downfall. Not when he was so close to achieving everything he'd ever wanted.

Maybe the impending engagement was the problem. Maybe, somewhere deep down in his subconscious, since he was out of town, away from his normal surroundings, he was simply letting himself go one last time before settling down.

*You're just flirting with Charlee, not seducing her. What's the harm? You flirted with the rental-car woman and that doesn't bother you.*

Charming the rental-car clerk was business. He had needed information. He turned on the charisma. He'd gotten what he wanted from Lila.

And what about Charlee?

What did he want from her?

Stunned, Mason paused. Nothing. He wanted nothing from her. He only wanted to find his grandfather, bring him back home, and get on with his life. If things went according to plan, bright and early Monday morning, he'd walk into his father's office to close the Birkweilder account, successfully wresting his deal back from Hunter.

At the thought of the look on his brother's face when he showed up to overturn his competitive coup, Mason smiled.

And the sooner he and Charlee got on the road after that camper, the better. Even if it meant throwing himself into the nerve-wracking crucible of Charlee's hot rod Corvette and enduring her gawd-awful driving for the next several hours. Whatever it took to achieve his goal, he would do it.

What about the Bentley?

What indeed? The idea of leaving his baby in the airport parking garage gave him hives. He would insist Charlee follow him to the Bellagio to drop off the Bentley before they headed for Tucson.

He turned to her, but she'd already sprinted ahead of him, running through the automatic doors to the passenger loading zone where she'd parked.

"It's gone!" she trilled and threw her arms in the air. "They towed my Corvette. Dammit!"

Mason opened his mouth to murmur a smug, "I told you so," but before he could get the sentence out, she whirled around and shook a finger under his nose.

"Not a word. Don't you dare say a word."

He clamped his lips together.

"And stop smirking. I know a smirk when I see one."

Mason shrugged and tried hard to stop smirking.

"Crap." She paced and smacked a palm repeatedly against her forehead. "Crap, crap, crap. I don't have the money to get it out of the police impound and both my thirty-eight and my cell phone were locked inside the glove box."

She looked so distraught that his temptation to gloat disappeared. He had the strangest desire to haul her into his arms, hold her close, and promise her that everything would be all right. He had no explanation for the urge. She wasn't the damsel in distress type and he knew she'd sooner poke him in the ribs with her elbow as thank him for his attempt to comfort her, so he sensibly kept his hands to himself.

"Calm down," he said. "I'll pay to get your car out of the impound."

"No. I can't let you do that."

"Why not?"

"I've had bad luck when it comes to borrowing money from men. It never works out. When you owe men money, they have certain expectations."

"Expectations?" He arched an eyebrow.

"Oh, come on, don't force me to spell it out for you."

Startled, he met her gaze. "Do you mean sexual favors?"

"Well, duh."

"There have been men in your life who have given you money and then expected sexual favors in return?"

The idea of someone treating her like a disposable sex object caused a ball of anger to clog his throat.

"I said men expected it from me, not that I did it. Jeez, what do you think I am?"

"I didn't mean . . . er . . . that's not what I meant to suggest."

*Oh, great. Way to stick your foot in your mouth, Gentry. You basically called her a prostitute.*

"So you can understand my reluctance to accept your offer of financial assistance."

"Charlee, I am not other men. Besides, this is an emergency. We need to get on the road as quickly as possible if we have any hope of overtaking the camper before it reaches Tucson. They've got several hours on us."

Hesitating, she pursed her lips and looked as if taking his money would literally kill her. "Okay. But the minute we find Maybelline, I'll get the money from her and pay you back."

"That'll be fine."

He reached in his jacket pocket for his wallet. Hmm. He almost always placed his wallet in his front left pocket. Maybe in the haze of hurrying to the airport he'd put it in the right pocket instead.

He patted the other side.

Nothing.

A sickening feeling sank to the bottom of his belly. He checked the back pockets of his trousers.

Not there.

No wallet. No credentials. No money. No credit cards.

Grinding his teeth, he recalled the two thick-necked men in black sunshades who'd bumped him as he'd come out of the security checkpoint.

Panic surged through him. It was an overblown corollary that didn't match the circumstances. He could cancel the credit cards and wire home for money. He could call the police and report the theft. No need for alarm.

Except time was critical if he wanted to catch up with his grandfather.

And there was the niggling little voice in the back of his mind. The same voice that had been whispering negative messages to him ever since he was a kid trying to compete with Hunter for their parents' attention.

*If you're not a Gentry, who are you?*

Without his ID, he wasn't a Gentry. Without his driver's license he couldn't even drive his Bentley.

How was it Charlee had so eloquently expressed herself? Crap, crap, crap.

Somehow crap just didn't seem strong enough.

"Something the matter?" Charlee asked.

"My wallet," he said. "It's been stolen."

"Give me your car keys." Charlee held out her palm.

"What?" Mason stared at her as if she'd suggested sacrificing his firstborn child to Pele the volcano goddess. What in the devil was she yapping about?

"Give me your keys," she repeated and curled her fingers in a "gimme" gesture he would have found cute if he hadn't been so upset. "We'll have to take the Bentley."

"No."

"Look, we don't have a choice. My 'Vette's been towed."

"It was towed because you recklessly disregarded the passenger loading zone sign and, I might add, my advice not to park there."

"Oh, here we go." Charlee sank her hands on her hips. "Mr. Uptight-by-the-Rules is giving me a lecture. Go ahead, let me have it, get it out of your system."

She was looking to pick a fight, but he refused to give her one. This wasn't the time or the place. "Chastising you isn't part of my agenda. I'm more concerned about the loss of my wallet. If you'll excuse me, I'm going to make a phone call to the authorities."

"Well, while you're calling the cops, I'm going after our grandparents before Elwood does something truly stupid. Hand over your car keys and I'll be on my way."

"You're out of your ever-loving mind if you think I'm letting you take off across the desert alone in my Bentley."

"You really have a problem relinquishing control, you know that?"

"Me? You're saying *I'm* a control freak?" Incensed, Mason splayed a palm over his chest.

*Easy, you know she's just gigging you because she's mad at herself.*

"Do they drink tea in China?" She jerked her chin up, the look in her eyes challenging him.

"I'm the control freak? You're the one who refused to move your car simply because you didn't want to take my advice." Okay, so he couldn't keep his mouth shut about the damned car.

"That's sooo not the reason I didn't move the 'Vette. And just look at you." She waved a hand at him. "Your clothes are perfectly pressed. Not a hair out of place. Your friggin' shoes are even shined. Only a control freak is that put together at six o'clock in the morning."

"Or someone who happens to take pride in the impression he creates."

"Yeah, the impression of a control freak."

A plane took off overhead, drowning out his reply, which was probably a good thing. The woman could try the pope's patience.

"You can't even let the wallet go, can you?" he heard her say after the plane had cleared the airport. "Gotta run to the police."

"My driver's license is in there. And my credit cards. My triple A card. Not to mention eight hundred dollars in cash."

"It's gone, Mason. The cops won't be able to get it back for you. Be realistic. But you can't let anything go, can you?"

He gritted his teeth hard. Calm down. Breathe deep. "You don't understand."

"Control freak."

"Woman," he ground out and sent her a don't-mess-with-me warning, "you have a talent for pushing a man to the limits of his patience."

"I'm trying to get you to quit your yammering and get on the road before something serious happens to our grandparents. We're wasting precious time." Charlee tapped the face of her wristwatch.

"I'm not so convinced a crazed trip through the desert is the most prudent move. How do we know for sure that's where they're going?"

"We don't, but do you have a better idea?" She cocked her head and spread her arms wide. "I'm open to input."

He paused, then admitted, "I don't have any better ideas."

"Okay then, Slick. Let's hit the highway."

Thirty minutes and twenty-five desert miles later, Charlee was seriously regretting goading Mason into the road trip. He'd been on his cell phone to his secretary, instructing her to report his credit cards stolen and wire money to him in Tucson.

He had also talked briefly with his father but Charlee noticed he didn't give many details about what had happened. He just told him that he had discovered Nolan was on his way to Tucson and he was following him. He never mentioned either Maybelline or herself.

It was strange listening to the one-sided conversation. She had the feeling Mason tiptoed around a lot of hot button topics with his father. Like stolen wallets and Elvis impersonator kidnappers and sassy lady private investigators who didn't drive to suit him.

He had hated giving her the keys to his Bentley, but when she suggested he go ahead and take the wheel even though he didn't have his license, he had actually lectured her from the highway safety manual.

She could tell by the way he had painstakingly pulled the keys from his pocket he would much rather have a tooth extracted without Novocain than let her behind the wheel of his vintage vehicle. But apparently his sense of right and wrong was so deeply engrained he couldn't conceive of driving without a license.

Too bad for him. Nice for her. She got to pilot a Bentley.

Ah, but at what cost.

"Slow down," Mason demanded, his face the color of a yucca in full bloom as Charlee took a bump in the road at seventy-five miles per hour. The Bentley glided through the dip on marshmallow shock absorbers—smooth and sweet. "What's the speed limit through here?"

"Control freak."

"If you say that one more time . . ."

"You'll what?" she dared, surprised by the quick thrill of pleasure pulsing through her at his threat. "Take me over your knee and spank me?"

"Not that you couldn't use a good spanking." He glowered. "But I don't strike women."

"Not even if I like it?" She winked, both terrified and turned on by her naughty boldness. He was so damned stuffy, she couldn't help but try and shock him. Shocking this uptight blue blood, however, was a bit like dynamiting carp in a horse trough.

She was so busy teasing him, the right front tire left the road and strummed irritatingly across those wake-up-you-desert-hypnotized-ninny strips.

"Keep your eyes on the road," he yelled.

Startled, she jerked the steering wheel, ended up overcompensating and weaved slightly into the northbound lane. Luckily, there was no oncoming traffic.

"Shit!" Mason exclaimed and lunged for the wheel.

She jabbed him in the rib cage with her elbow before he could slap his hands on the steering wheel. "Back off, I'm driving."

"Oww." He rubbed his ribs. "You're a lunatic. You know that?"

"Don't grab the wheel when someone else is driving."

"Where the hell did you get your driver's license? Britain?"

"That's a pretty good one actually. Maybe you do have a sense of humor."

"I wasn't trying to be funny. Stop the car."

"Don't get your knickers in a knot. Nobody was coming. And besides, I wouldn't have wandered into the other lane if you hadn't hollered at me."

"Stop the car."

"So what, now you're going to drive? I thought you couldn't drive without your license." Charlee peered over at him. She started to make another smart remark, but she saw the muscle in his jaw tick and realized just how angry he was.

"I do want to see my grandfather one last time before I die. I'll take my chances. Stop the car."

"Wooo. Now you're breaking the law."

"Hush, woman," he commanded.

His tone told her to back off if she didn't want to see a Texas aristocrat lose his temper. Trying hard not to grin, Charlee slowed the Bentley and pulled onto the shoulder. She cut the engine and scooted over to the passenger side when Mason got out.

She darted a look over her shoulder. He stalked purposefully around the car. A delicious little shiver, like a cat running up stair steps, scampered through her. What was it about the proud set of his shoulders, his determined ground eating stride, the way his hair tapered down the back of his neck that so tickled her fancy?

Mercy.

*Knock it off, Charlee, unless you're looking to get hurt. Stop thinking about him. He's nothing but trouble with capital letters.*

Fat lot of good that lecture accomplished.

Something about him—exactly what she couldn't say—touched her in a way she'd never known. Her emotions were confused, muddled. She was sexually attracted to him, oh, yeah, but her feelings for him were more than just that. It was passion taken to a whole new level. The sensation burned inside her chest sharp and clean and bright. But she couldn't name the feeling, even if someone had offered a million tax-free bucks to do so.

The pulse at the hollow of her throat jumped and sweat popped out on her brow as a myriad of naughty fantasies flashed through her mind. She could almost feel his strong masculine hands on her body, his fingers tickling her tender flesh.

He slid behind the wheel and slammed the car door after him, breaking her from her illicit reverie. Charlee's hands shook so hard she had to sit on them.

She'd been too long without sex. That's all there was to it. She had to stop her flights of fantasy.

"You okay?" he asked gruffly. "You're looking a little weird."

"I do?"

"You're all red in the face." He arched an eyebrow. "Like someone caught watching a nudie peep show."

"Excuse me?"

Immediately, she went on the offensive. Maybelline had drilled into her head the best defense was a good offense and boy, was she ripe for defending herself before Handsome Dimples here discovered just how much power he wielded over her.

"Are you embarrassed about something?"

"This is the desert, in case you haven't noticed it's over a hundred degrees outside. That's why my face is red. No other reason. Now get the engine started and crank up the AC."

"Anything you want as long as I'm driving," he said, pulling back onto the road. He turned the air conditioner on high and then stuck a Charlotte Church CD into the CD player.

Eww. Ick.

She should have known he would have highbrow taste in music when what she wanted to hear was something loud with a strong, throbbing beat. On second thought, perhaps Charlotte was the better choice. Nobody could have sexual daydreams with that glass-shattering noise.

Sighing, Charlee forced herself not to notice what an exceptionally fine profile Mason presented and instead directed her gaze out the window at the arid roll of landscape stretching out before them.

It was going to be a very long trip.

Just then Charlee caught the reflection of a white Chevy Malibu in the side-view mirror. They were the only two cars on the road for as far as the eye could see.

Something in the back of her brain niggled.

For the third time in the last twenty-four hours she'd spotted a four-door white Chevy Malibu. The car was a common enough make and maybe she was jumping to conclusions, but the first time she'd noticed a white sedan had been outside Maybelline's trailer after it had been ransacked. The second time had been at the apartment fire. Coincidence?

She didn't think so.

While Miss Church trilled her earsplitting soprano, Charlee kept an eye on the sedan. It stayed a good ten car lengths behind them.

"Speed up," she told Mason.

"I'm already doing seventy."

"Just speed up."

"Why?"

"Do you have to be a privileged pain in the ass about everything?"

"I don't want to get pulled over. Lest you forget I have no driver's license."

Charlee sighed. "Remember when we were in Maybelline's trailer and I told you to duck and you wouldn't listen to me?"

"Yes."

"Well then, speed up."

"Are you saying there's a mad gunman after us?"

"Maybe."

Mason sped up.

Charlee squinted into the side-view mirror.

The Malibu sped up too.

"Slow down."

"What?"

"Please don't make me repeat myself."

Thankfully, he didn't argue, but slowed the Bentley.

The Malibu decelerated.

Charlee sucked in her breath. No doubt about it.

They were being followed.

# Chapter 6

I still can't believe your son kidnapped us." Nolan shook his head and for the hundredth time tested the ropes binding his hands behind his back.

He and Maybelline were locked in the back of a rented camper together and without the benefit of air-conditioning. A swelter of sweat dampened the back of his shirt and his arthritis nagged at him to shift positions.

The camper's side windows were wide open but the blast of desert air was anything but cooling. Maybelline's kid was a jerk, but considering who his daddy was Nolan wasn't too surprised.

"I should have left him on his father's doorstep when I had the chance," Maybelline grumbled.

"You were too good of a mama, you couldn't have abandoned him."

"Good mama. Ha! That's awfully sweet of you to try and make me feel better, but if I were a good mama would my son be such an asshole?"

"You raised your granddaughter and from what you tell me she's turned out great," Nolan soothed.

"I raised her because my no-account son wouldn't do

his duty." Maybelline paused. "Charlee is the best thing in my life, but I worry I did her a huge disservice. Moving around like I did. We never stayed in one place longer than a year or two."

"Why's that?"

"After growing up in Red Bay, Texas, you've got to ask me that question? I didn't want any small-minded, small-town attitude painting Charlee with the same brush I got painted with. Every place was a new start, a grand new adventure. And she never complained."

"But?"

Maybelline shrugged. "She has trouble making friends. I mean she has a lot of acquaintances, people she can hang out with, but nobody she tells her secrets to. She never learned how to get close to people. I figure that's all my doing. I wanted her to be free to choose her own life, not be defined by what others thought of her. I taught her to be tough, to stand on her own two feet and not depend on anyone. Well, she's free and independent all right, but I worry she'll never be able to trust a man enough to let him love her."

"Hmm, strong, brave, independent, and knows her own mind. Charlee sounds a lot like someone else I know," Nolan said.

"I don't want her to end up like me."

"What's wrong with the way you ended up?"

Maybelline didn't meet his eyes. "It's a lonely way to live."

Her pain cut him to the quick. For the last forty-seven years, while he'd been surrounded by his loving family, Maybelline had been out in the world struggling to raise first her son and then her granddaughter alone.

"I'm sorry about Elwood," he said, not even beginning

to know how to apologize to her for the loneliness she'd suffered. He felt guilty somehow that she'd never found anyone to love. "We can't be held responsible for what our grown kids do, Maybelline."

"Try telling Elwood that. He blames me for everything gone wrong in his life."

Nolan thought of his own son and winced. Reed was bound to blame him for the mess he'd gotten the family business into and with good reason. He was to blame.

"What's with the Elvis costume?" Nolan asked, changing the subject. "You'd think Elwood would want to be as inconspicuous as possible. Seeing as how he's committing a felony."

Maybelline snorted. "Obviously you don't know my son. He craves attention. Got a big dose of his daddy's theatrical blood in him. Wears that damned white jumpsuit everywhere he goes. Sometimes I think he imagines he really *is* Elvis."

"What do you think he's planning on doing with us?"

"I don't know. I never could decipher what went on in that boy's head." Maybelline sighed.

"Don't worry, I'll get us out of this mess and without hurting your son."

She eyed him skeptically. "Nolan, you can stop being so protective. I'm not that pregnant sixteen-year-old you took under your wing."

"Even back then it took an act of Congress to get you to let me help you."

"I've been fighting my own battles for a long time and the last thing this old bird needs is for some man to start blowing smoke up her dress. I'm a realist. Elwood is not the brightest bulb in the package and the odds of something getting screwed up in his little kidnapping scheme are pretty high. In fact, I've been sitting here composing my obituary."

"Still bracing yourself for the worst." Nolan looked her squarely in the eyes.

Maybelline notched her chin up in that stubbornly defiant way of hers. Lord, she was a fighter, in spite of her silly speech about writing her obit. "I didn't get life handed to me on a silver platter. The school of hard knocks kinda takes the rosy shine off positive thinking."

"No need to snap at me because you're feeling guilty," Nolan said, reading her like a road map. "What Elwood is doing is not your fault. Everything is going to work out fine. You'll see."

"Your cockeyed optimism is treading on my last nerve," she groused.

"I know." He grinned. "And you love me for it."

"You've gotten kinda egotistical in your old age, Nolan Gentry."

"You think so?"

"Maybe not. Maybe you were always egotistical and I just forgot."

The camper hit a bump and bounced Maybelline against his shoulder. The contact was comforting. He wished his hands were free so he could wrap an arm around her.

"The boy drives like a maniac," she said, but didn't try to inch away.

Nolan liked having her next to him, even if their combined body heat raised the already miserable temperature in the camper. He wondered if she liked the closeness too.

"Where do you think he's taking us?"

"I've been racking my brain over that question for the last hundred miles trying to second-guess him and can't come up with an answer. I just hope it's not Mexico. He's got a fascination with Mexico."

"What I don't understand is why he won't give us the files, take his blackmail money, and go on his merry way."

"I think that's the rub. I think he's lying. I don't think he has all of the files. Just a few papers like the copies I gave to you. Not enough to prove anything in court."

"Sooner or later he's got to stop to let us out. We'll try to talk some sense into him then," Nolan said.

"Either that or we'll bash him over the head and take the camper," Maybelline said grimly.

"Woman, you are bloodthirsty." Nolan chuckled.

"If I'd whopped his britches when he was little maybe he wouldn't have turned out like he did."

"It's going to be all right. Have faith."

"Easy for you to say, old man. You've had lots of experience with things turning out the way you want them to turn out."

"Well, you're with me now, Maybelline, so you better get used to things turning out right for you too."

She made a derisive noise but he saw a flicker of hope in her eyes. "I'll believe it when I see it."


Mason felt edgy in a way he couldn't define. Tension knotted the muscles across his back so tight they ached. Every time he glanced in the rearview mirror and saw the Malibu, an angry testiness soured his gut.

Who were the people following them and what in the hell did they want? Out here on this lone stretch of highway he and Charlee were incredibly vulnerable. What if the white Chevy tried to run them off the road? Then what? His knowledge of tae kwon do was no match for two men with a gun. Too bad Charlee had left her weapon in the Corvette.

Whatever happened, he would fight to the death to keep her safe.

"We're going to have to ditch the Bentley in Phoenix," Charlee said.

"What?"

"We'll never be able to elude our *compadres* back there while we're driving this white elephant." She jerked a thumb over her shoulder and her braids bobbed provocatively from beneath her battered straw cowboy hat.

"Hey, no insulting Matilda."

"Hell, Gentry, we might as well be piloting a Goodyear blimp. There's no such thing as incognito in a vintage Bentley."

"We're not leaving the car."

He stubbornly clenched his jaw. His attitude might not be practical but Matilda was his prize possession and he wasn't about to abandon her. The car had been his ticket to freedom when he was sixteen, allowing him—if only briefly—to escape the high demands of his family. He would sneak off in Matilda during his parents' business parties when he was supposed to be currying political favors. But even more than that, Matilda represented the lurking wildness inside him that had all but disappeared after his best friend Kip was killed.

Matilda was the one solid thing that kept Kip alive for him. They'd shared their first beer together, sitting on Matilda's hood in his parents' garage, listening to Nirvana and talking about girls. They'd cruised the local strip, listening to Boyz II Men and trying to pick up girls. They'd parked by the lake, listening to UB40 and trying to get to second base with the girls they'd picked up.

He wondered what Kip would think of Charlee and he knew immediately they would have been rivals for her affections. Kip had always gone for the sassy ones.

At the memory of his buddy, a lump tightened his throat. It had been almost ten years since the accident but the loss still gnawed at him with a painful sting.

He would never stop feeling responsible. He had never stopped trying to make amends by staying on the straight and narrow and doing exactly what his family expected of him. It was the least he could do to pay for his gravest mistake.

*Yeah, but Kip wouldn't hold you responsible and you know it. He would be mad because you've stopped doing what you loved.*

Unable to handle the thoughts of how he'd failed his friend, Mason stiffened his upper lip and stared straight ahead.

"I know a woman in Phoenix. We can leave the Bentley with her and borrow her Neon," she persisted.

"Over my dead body," Mason growled. He knew it was prideful of him to be so mulish. Vain even. But he didn't care. Charlee would just have to deal with it.

"Don't tempt me." She looked completely serious with her dark eyebrows drawn into a V and her lush full lips pursed.

"I'm getting the distinct impression you're frustrated with me," he said.

"You pick up on that all by yourself?" She glared.

"I don't understand why you're so upset."

"For one thing, I'm worried about my grandmother and you're putt-putting along at sixty miles an hour. We'll never catch up to the camper at this rate."

"How serious can it be? They *are* with your father."

"Which is precisely what I'm worried about. You don't understand. My father is both unpredictable and easily influenced by others."

"All right," Mason conceded. "I'll drive faster." He sped up to sixty-five.

Charlee groaned and rolled her eyes.

"What now?"

"You drive like a little old lady on Zoloft. Hands at ten and two o'clock, eyes straight ahead. I swear, Gentry, you're old before your time."

"I drive by the rules of the road."

"You live your entire life by someone else's rules, is what you do," she mumbled.

"What?" He cocked his head. "I didn't quite catch what you said."

"Nothing."

"You muttered something. Let's hear it."

Charlee folded her arms over her chest. "I said, lest you forget, we're being followed."

"That's not what you said."

"Pretend it is."

He knew exactly what she'd said and she was right. He was a law-abiding man. Where would society be if everyone threw the rules of civilized behavior out the window? Charlee probably went for those swaggering bad boy types who broke the law and broke her heart with equal ease.

"So let them follow us."

"Need I remind you my grandmother's trailer was ransacked, we were shot at, and someone torched my father's apartment complex?"

"Your father did that."

"No he didn't."

"Whatever you say."

"What does that mean?"

"I'm tired of arguing with you." The woman could wear a professional filibuster into the ground.

"Oh, no, no, no." She shook a finger. "You don't believe me and simply saying you do doesn't change your mind. You can't just give in because you don't want to argue."

"Yes I can. See, I'm shutting up. No more arguing with you."

Gleefully, Charlee found the chink in his logic. "Good, then let's ditch the Bentley."

"No."

"Thought you weren't going to argue."

"Sit back and hush."

He wondered if he was going to have to kiss her in order to shut her up. Why was kissing her such an appealing idea?

This had to stop. He was almost engaged.

Think of Daphne.

Determined, he tried to call up Daphne's image and his mind went blank. He struggled to summon her scent but instead of the floral aroma of Daphne's expensive perfume, he could only smell Charlee's fresh soap scent. Instead of mentally seeing Daphne's sleekly coiffed blond hair, he saw long, jet-black tresses twisted in beguiling braids. Instead of hearing Daphne's dulcet acquiescence, his ears vibrated with the sound of Charlee's deep, throaty-voiced firmly held opinions.

Something about Charlee called to that wildness inside of him he'd buried along with Kip. The wildness that scared him because he knew what trouble it could cause. The wildness he missed and feared with equal intensity.

Why did she stir him so? Not just physically. That was easy. The woman was a looker with a body that wouldn't quit. No, there was an energy about her, a power that compelled him on a level he could not explain.

She moved him in ways far beyond his experience. Her courage sparked a corresponding bravery inside him. Her audacity dared him to rise to the challenge. Her toughness engendered his strength.

Charlee was a force of nature that had blown into his life and altered everything.

His stomach lurched but he convinced himself it was because he hadn't eaten breakfast. They drove for several miles in dead silence. Eventually they approached the outskirts of Phoenix. Mason struggled not to glance over at Charlee again, but no matter how hard he tried he could not seem to deny the unsettling awareness radiating between them.

Was this what people meant by chemistry?

In spite of his best intentions to the contrary, he found his gaze veering from the highway stripes to the woman at his side. She was gnawing on a thumbnail and when she realized he was watching her, she jerked her hand from her mouth and dropped it into her lap.

"Nervous?"

"Who me? What have I got to be nervous about?"

"The Chevy Malibu."

"Oh, yeah. That." Charlee checked the rearview mirror. "Are they still behind us?"

"I don't see them, but I know they're back there."

"Maybe we can lose them in the Phoenix traffic."

She nodded. His gaze traveled from her face, down the curve of her neck to the skin exposed beneath the opening of her collar. He moistened his lips, mesmerized by the swell of her breasts and the way they moved when she breathed.

Heaven help him, he was ogling her. Mason jerked his gaze back to the road.

"Get an eyeful?" she asked tartly.

The woman didn't miss a trick. When was he going to realize Charlee was sharp as a suture needle and twice as prickly?

"I apologize. I shouldn't have stared at you."

"Damn skippee. I'm not some amusement park ride for the slumming rich boy."

"I don't think of you in that way," he protested, flustered because he'd been caught visually undressing her like some horny fifteen-year-old.

Charlee pushed the brim of her hat up with one slender finger and peered down at her breasts as if trying to fathom the appeal. Surely the woman was aware of just how sexy she looked.

"You know," she said a few moments later. "After my mother died and Maybelline took me in, she bought us a travel trailer. She showed me the kind of life skills they don't teach you in school."

"Odd view on child rearing."

"She said she didn't want me to get in trouble the way she had when she was young. She worked odd jobs to support us. Mechanic, bartender, hotel maid, even drove a school bus. She took me with her everywhere she went." Charlee paused.

Mason contrasted her past with his childhood. His entire life spent in one place, raised by nannies and housekeepers, seeing his parents only on occasion as they flitted from party to party, from one business deal to the next, from Paris to Japan to Timbuktu.

"I remember one time, when I was, oh, about fourteen, Maybelline got hired as a housekeeper for a state senator in Utah. I developed early figure-wise and the old letch couldn't keep his paws to himself. One afternoon he cornered me in the kitchen pantry and stuck his hands up my blouse. He told me if I'd do him a few favors he'd pay me handsomely.

"I told him if he didn't get his grubby mitts off me I was going to send his balls up to visit his throat. I always wondered what made a man think he could manhandle his servants."

"Charlee," Mason said, feeling awful to the core, "I hope you don't think I'm that sort of man."

"Of course not." She grinned. "I was just pondering the power of boobs."

Disconcerted, he too pondered the power of boobs. Why did Charlee excite him in a way Daphne never had? And not just Daphne. None of his elegant, refined female counterparts had ever made him yearn to do something totally rash and reckless the way this pert private detective did.

A sense of longing swept over him, for something he'd never had. The freedom to follow his heart.

And if he married Daphne, he never would.

There was the rub.

He felt as if Charlee held the key to his freedom if only he was brave enough to reach out and take it.

Was he?

For one crazy, foolish second, he envisioned Charlee as his fiancée.

Mother would faint. Father would have a coronary. Hunter would gloat and say something like, "Way to make me look good."

If he was married to Charlee he'd be whispered about behind his back. His social contacts would dwindle, his

business accounts would suffer. He had seen the phe-
nomenon before when anyone in his circle married someone from the outside. Never mind that this was the
new millennium. High society still operated on a class
system.

Besides, why would he want to do something so cruel
as to cage a bright, vibrant woman like Charlee in his
claustrophobic, walk-on-eggshells-or-get-ostracized world?
He would never be that selfish.

"So whatever happened with the senator?" he asked,
changing lanes and passing a slow-moving tractor-trailer rig.

She studied him for a long while before replying. "The
guy ended up paying me not to squeal on him to his wife
and I gave the money to a women's shelter."

"Pretty resourceful for a fourteen-year-old."

"Told you, Maybelline was determined to give me a
real life education and that she did."

"Maybe too much of an education. You grew up way
too soon."

"Not soon enough. If I'd really been resourceful, I
would have gone to the newspapers, created a scandal, got
the sucker thrown out of office before he used his power to
disgrace some other poor maid."

Mason looked at her. He thought of his own housekeepers and of the servants who had worked for his parents. He
realized with a disturbing jolt he never considered them as
anything more than his employees.

Sure, he paid well, did his best to treat them with compassion, but he'd never imagined what their lives were like
when they weren't cleaning his house or taking care of his
needs. Guilt needled him and he swore to himself when
he got home he would take more of a personal interest in
the people he employed.

"The Malibu's right behind us," Charlee said.

Mason swore under his breath. He'd forgotten about being followed.

"Slow down. Let them get closer."

"What for?"

"Just do it and don't give me any grief for once, okay?"

She'd been right on the previous occasions. Resisting the urge to ask for more details before embarking on her plan, Mason slowed the car.

"Get in the middle lane."

He turned on the blinker and moved over.

"Thank you," she replied tartly and stuck out her tongue at him.

"You're welcome." He fought the strange thrill darting through him at the sight of her glorious pink tongue.

Holy guacamole but her sauciness inflamed him.

"Slower." Her eyes were trained on the mirror, her body tensed, her muscles on alert.

"I'm practically crawling as it is."

"I want them right on our tails so when you radically veer off at the next exit ramp they won't have time to follow us."

"Oh." He checked the rearview mirror too and saw the Malibu was on his bumper.

"Here we go." Charlee inhaled audibly.

Up ahead Mason spotted the Los Angeles exit sign.

"Keep driving, keep driving."

"But I thought you said . . ."

"Wait, wait."

If he waited any longer it was going to be too late to make the exit ramp.

"Floor it, floor it, change lanes, go, go, go." She barked orders like a prison warden.

Dear Lord, there were a string of cars in the inside lane. "Now!"

He couldn't do it. He couldn't drive erratically on purpose and risk their lives. What if they had a wreck? What if they hurt someone?

*For one damn time in your life, don't overthink things. Just friggin' let go and do it.*

Mason stomped the foot feed. Matilda leaped to the challenge. She shot forward like a torpedo. He swerved across the white line, barreling straight for the exit ramp.

*Holy crap, we're going to die.*

He braced himself for an impact and prayed Matilda could handle whatever came her way.

Car brakes squealed. Horns blared. The smell of burning rubber spewed into the air. The brash flavor of raw adrenaline flooded his mouth as they sped pell-mell up the overpass, leaving the Malibu stuck below them on the other freeway.

They were free.

"Yippee!" Charlee hollered and raised a palm. "We lost them. High-five me."

Mason had never high-fived anyone in his privileged life, but he didn't hesitate for a second to slap his palm against Charlee's. His heart pounded, his gut turned upside down, but damn, he was having fun.

Their skin contacted with a solid splat.

And ripples of awareness blasted through his hand and up his arm.

He met her gaze. Her eyes rounded with surprise and he knew she felt it too. This surge, this splurge, this pure spill of thrill.

Ah, hell, this wasn't good.

Not good at all.

# Chapter 7

*I'm not falling for him,* Charlee argued with herself as she propelled the Bentley toward Tucson. *I'm not.*

Liar, liar, panties on fire.

She'd only known the guy twenty-four hours. She couldn't be falling for him.

Maybe not, but every single time he leveled his brown eyes and cocked his dimples at her, she broke out in a cold sweat.

Ah, jeez. She was screwed.

*I won't fall for him. I won't, I won't, I won't. I don't care how cute and brown-eyed and long-legged the man is.*

She had to keep her guard up and her tongue sharp if she hoped to survive this jaunt through the desert with her dignity intact. So what if he thought she was a bitch. It was better than getting her heart broken. Again.

Moistening her lips, Charlee inched her Ray Bans down on her nose with an index finger and sneaked a quick peek over at him.

Mason was leaning back in the plush leather seat, his long legs folded at an uncomfortable-looking angle. She found herself tracing a path from his expensive leather shoes up the length of his body to his broad chest. She caught her breath and flicked a look at his face.

Thank God his eyes were closed and he hadn't caught her giving him the once-over. His hands lay folded across his stomach and his chest rose and fell in a smooth, steady rhythm.

She studied his profile. Regal nose, solid jaw, high cheekbones. She felt kind of soupy inside, like she'd drunk too much water too quickly. She recalled when they'd high-fived each other and a fresh shiver of something nice mixed with something very scary tangoed through her.

After the great escape back there on the freeway, Mason had pulled over, taken the keys from the ignition, dropped them into her hand, and said, "Take over, Champagne. I'm not cut out for high-speed chase stuff."

Amazed, she simply accepted the keys and switched places with him again, but she couldn't help pondering his change of heart. After he'd successfully eluded the Malibu, he was downright triumphant. He'd grinned like a kid, his eyes feverish with the thrill.

He'd *enjoyed* it.

Perhaps, Charlee postulated, that's what bugged him. He didn't know how to cut loose and have a good time. Mr. Buttoned-down pops a button and doesn't know how to handle himself.

*And don't be getting any wise ideas about becoming his teacher.*

Oh, but wouldn't he make a glorious teacher's pet.

Stop it!

Her palms grew sweaty on the wheel and her heart reeled drunkenly against the wall of her chest. She was headed for deep trouble, entertaining such thoughts. She was not going to fall again. No way, no how. No, no, no.

Who was she kidding? It was all she could do not to pull the car over and jump his bones right here and now.

Damn her hide but she'd always been attracted to sophisticated men who were so far out of her league she couldn't reach them with a high bounce on a trampoline. She knew better than to tumble for another rich brown-eyed handsome man.

They were opposites in every way. He was the kind of guy who'd dip a toe in the water, testing the temperature before going for a swim. She dove right in and took what she got. He was a linen napkin kind of guy. She was paper towels. His life was planned, well ordered. Hers was chaos and she liked it that way.

Unfortunately, something about him whispered to the soft feminine side of her she'd stuffed down deep a long time ago. He made her feel smart and savvy and admirable. He respected her. That was a first from guys like him.

And he made her want things she had no business wanting.

Rather than think about the potent male beside her, Charlee jammed her sunglasses back into place and returned her focus to the road. White-hot heat poured from the cloudless blue sky and bounced a shimmer of radiant waves up from the asphalt. She studied the desert, the wide expanse of dry barren land most people eschewed but which an intrepid few embraced.

While some might find the desert a lonely, desolate place, she felt differently. The desert was alive with nature. You just had to know where to look for it. To Charlee the desert was home. What made her feel lonely and desolate was not water-starved land but the emptiness gnawing at her when she was in a roomful of people.

She imagined Mason's busy life was jam-packed with

people. His parents, his brother, his grandfather, his friends. His business partners, his colleagues, and high-society debs. He hailed from a foreign place where she did not belong and could never fit.

Shaking her head, she forced herself to think about something else and speculated on the men in the Malibu. Who were they and why had they been following them? She tried to tie everything together—their grandparents, the half mil Mason's grandfather embezzled, her father, the men in the Malibu, Maybelline's ransacked trailer, the bullet through the trailer, Elwood's apartment fire, but no matter how hard she tried, Charlee couldn't paste together the link. Too many pieces of the puzzle were missing.

What concerned her right now was their destination. Were they on a wild-goose chase? Since Mason had turned the keys over to her, she'd driven a steady eighty-five miles an hour hoping against hope to spot the red and white camper.

Maybe Elwood and their grandparents weren't on this road, she fretted. What then? They might not even be in Arizona.

Charlee nibbled her bottom lip. Up ahead she spied a small crossroads with a gas station and a convenience store. Noticing the gas gauge had slipped to almost a quarter of a tank, she pulled over.

Mason didn't wake up when she stopped. Poor guy must be exhausted. She filled up the tank, and then saun-tered into the convenience store. She grabbed a couple of packages of Twinkies and snagged a six-pack of iced Pep-sis from a barrel next to the checkout counter.

"Hey," Charlee asked the pimply-faced clerk as he rang up her purchases. It was a long shot, but what the hell?

"By any chance has a red and white camper stopped by here in the last few hours?"

"Some guy in an Elvis suit at the wheel?"

"Yeah." Charlee arched her eyebrows in surprise. "You saw him?"

"Who could miss him?" The clerk shrugged. "He paid for his gas with quarter rolls."

"About how long?"

The clerk scratched his goateed chin. "Maybe three, four hours ago."

"Hey, thanks. Keep the change." Charlee gathered up her drinks and Twinkies and started for the door.

"He didn't get back on the road to Tucson though," the clerk said, stopping her in mid-exit.

"No?"

He shook his head. "Nope. Took the back road up to the old movie studio lot."

"What movie studio lot?" Charlee frowned.

"They used to make westerns there in the forties and fifties. My grandmother claims John Wayne was once a regular around these parts. He even autographed the back of a movie ticket for her. *Rio Lobo* I think it was."

"No kidding?"

"Studio lot is closed down now. Abandoned. Boarded up. Except local kids go up there sometimes to drink, smoke weed, and get laid. Don't know why the Elvis guy went up that way. Road dead-ends in the studio lot. Nothing else up there but rattlesnakes and tumbleweeds."

When Charlee got back to the car, Mason was awake. She climbed in and tossed him a Twinkie.

"What's this?" He held the cellophane wrapper gingerly between his index finger and thumb as if it would jump up and bite him.

"Thought you might be hungry." She ripped into her own Twinkie and sank her teeth into the sponge cake. "Yummm."

"These things are filled with preservatives and bleached white flour."

"So?"

"They are not part of a healthy diet."

"Oh, my, call the food police."

"Go ahead, make fun."

"Jeez, Gentry, lighten up. One Twinkie isn't going to kill you."

"I think I'll pass." He sat the snack cake on the console between them.

"Okay fine. I'll eat it."

He narrowed his eyes. "How in the hell do you stay so slender eating junk?"

Charlee brushed cream filling off her chin with the back of her hand and grinned. "Lucky I guess. I'm blessed with a high metabolism."

"I need real food," he grumbled.

"Well, Joe's Stop and Snack isn't the place for five star cuisine, sorry. It's Twinkies or nothing until we hit Tucson. Unless you want me to go back in and get you a bag of pork skins."

"No thanks. I can wait."

"Suit yourself." She spun the Bentley out of the parking lot and took off down the narrow dirt road a few yards to the right of the store, a rooster tail of red dust kicking up beneath the tires.

"Hey." Mason sat up straighter. "Where are we going?"

She told him what she had found out from the clerk.

"Why would your father whisk our grandparents away to an abandoned movie set?" He scowled.

"I've been thinking about that."

"Come up with anything?"

"Well . . ." Her suspicions weren't pretty and she didn't want to alarm Mason but he had a right to know. "I'm thinking he might be holding them for ransom."

"You're kidding?"

"It crossed my mind. He's kidnapped before."

"What!"

"Settle down. It's not as bad as it sounds. He snatched a Vegas headliner's Yorkie. The little dog was vicious, chewed his fingers up. He had to go to the emergency room and of course that's when he got caught. The Yorkie's owner dropped the charges for old times' sake because she and Elwood used to be lovers way back when, so he never did any time or anything."

"Why didn't you tell me before?"

"I didn't want you to bust a gut. Like you are now. Besides, it was just a dog. Not a person."

"Well, it looks like he's made the jump from kidnapping canines to holding humans hostage."

"Don't worry. Elwood's not violent or anything. He won't hurt them."

"How can you say that? My grandfather's life is at stake!" Mason hollered.

"So is my grandmother's and you didn't hear me raising my voice or the veins on my forehead getting purply and popping out."

"For all I know"—Mason glowered—"you and your grandmother are in on the scheme. Nothing but bad things have happened to me ever since I met you."

"I resent that. You're the one who turned my life topsy-turvy. I was perfectly happy sitting in *my* office minding my own business until *you* strutted into my life."

He paused. "All right. I was out of line with that last comment. I really don't believe you and your grandmother are in on it."

"Thank you."

She really did like the way he could admit when he was wrong. Most of the men of her acquaintance were busy trying to find someone else—usually her—to blame for their unhappy circumstances.

Mason reached over and lightly touched her arm. "I can get rather aggressive if I think my family is in danger."

Yeow! His touch sent a brush fire of emotions sweeping through her body. Desire, excitement, restlessness, and fear. Yep. Mostly fear.

"Mmmm," she mumbled, unable to speak past the lump of terror in her throat. He was touching her again and she was feeling way too susceptible.

*Whatever you do, Charlee Desiree Champagne, do not make eye contact with those dreamy brown peepers of his. Don't you dare.*

She wished he would take his hand away but he kept touching her. She felt that sudden, wild, almost irrepressible urge again to pull the car over, fling herself into his arms, and kiss him like there was no tomorrow.

It had been a very long time since she'd been with a man. His touch made her desperate to feel something hot and wild and womanly. She'd been hiding her femininity under her boots and jeans and cowboy hat for quite some time and her hormones were rebelling.

She batted his hand away roughly.

"You're mad at me."

"I'm not."

"You are. I can tell by the way you shoved me away."

"I'm not mad. Your hand was just hot. This car is hot."

She fiddled with the air-conditioner vents. "Are you sure this heap has freon?"

"Charlee," he said, his voice sounding extra deep and throaty. "Would you look at me, please?"

No! No!

"I apologize if I offended you in any way."

"I accept your apology," she whispered. "Okay?"

"I can't believe you until I can see your eyes."

"Look, Gentry," she snapped as panic surged through her. "I'm driving here. I'm not in any mood to gaze into your eyes."

"All right."

Thank God. Charlee sighed in relief as he let the issue go.

She gripped the steering wheel so hard her fingers cramped. Flexing first one hand and then the other, she realized they had driven almost thirteen miles with nothing in sight but cactus and rocks and a Gila monster or two.

"Are you sure the clerk wasn't pulling your leg?" Mason asked.

"Maybe it's on the other side of the mesa."

"How far are you going to drive before you admit defeat?"

Charlee hardened her jaw. "I never admit defeat."

"Never?"

"Ever."

"Determination is an admirable quality, Charlee, but sometimes you gotta cut your..." Mason's voice trailed off as they rounded the mesa and the road dead-ended at a padlocked iron gate.

They spotted a weathered, barely readable sign proclaiming: TWILIGHT STUDIOS. Then below it, a smaller, newer sign printed in thick block letters. PRIVATE PROPERTY, KEEP OUT. TRESPASSERS WILL BE PROSECUTED.

They looked at each other.

Twilight Studios. The same movie studio Nolan and Maybelline had once worked for.

Happenstance?

Charlee didn't think so. But what was the bond? Why had Elwood brought them here?

A high wooden fence divided the studio lot, but time and the desert had eroded the once stately planks into slumping, thin gray posts staggering across the red dirt like teeth sliding forward in an aging mouth. Several boards were missing from one area and a narrow trail told the story. Someone or something entered frequently through the opening.

Charlee parked the Bentley beside the fence.

"If your father brought our grandparents here, then where is the camper?"

"Inside the studio lot?"

"How did they get in? The padlock is rusted shut."

"Maybe Elwood knew another way in."

"What now?" Mason asked.

"We go in."

"The sign says no trespassing."

She stared at him. "What planet are you from?"

"Are we going in on foot?"

"Unless you've been holding out on me and you've got a magic carpet in your back pocket, yes, we're going to trespass on foot." Charlee opened the car door.

"But I'm wearing loafers and I left my sunscreen back at the hotel."

"That's why I have on cowboy boots and a hat," she replied tartly.

"Oh, yeah?" he retorted. "I thought it was because you wanted to look tough."

"That too," she confessed. "Come on." She was halfway to the hole in the fence before he even got out of the car.

He shut the door, shaded his brow with his hand, and looked around. "Do you think the Bentley will be safe parked here?"

"I don't think any gangbangers will be stealing your mag wheels if that's what you're asking."

"No, it's just if anything were to happen we'd be stranded."

"What about your cell phone?"

"That's assuming I can pick up a tower."

"You're unnaturally attached to your car, you know that, don't you?"

"Yes," he grumbled. "I'm aware I place too much value on a car. Can we get on with this, please?"

"Oooh, hit a touchy spot."

"Do you want me to bring up your towed Corvette?"

She raised her palms. "I surrender. No more cracks about the car."

"Thank you. I appreciate that."

Charlee led the way through the fence and into the lot. They walked side by side into the false facade of an Old West town. The first building they came to was an aged saloon with the obligatory hitching post, as dusty and weather-beaten as a real saloon might have been a hundred and twenty years before. The sheriff's office came complete with tumbleweeds and had the windowpanes knocked out while the nearby livery stable hosted a rusted anvil and bent horseshoes. The town ended at the dry goods store with barrels of fake food sitting out front.

"I think I've seen this set in an old western or two," Charlee mused. "Ever see *Shane?*"

"Twilight didn't produce *Shane*."

"They could have used the set."

"Don't think so. According to Gramps, back in those days the studios were pretty territorial. They practically owned the actors."

"Yeah, Maybelline mentioned something like that."

The sun lasered down. Sweat collected along Charlee's collar and a vague uneasiness settled in her belly. The place was dead quiet. Not even the scratch of a scurrying lizard. The eerie theme song from *The Good, the Bad and the Ugly* drifted through her head.

"No one's here," Mason said.

A dread of dizziness washed over Charlee. Something wasn't right. If Elwood brought their grandparents here, then where were they? What if her father had crossed the line from small-time-get-rich-quick schemer to big-time felon?

She simply couldn't believe that. Regardless of his numerous faults, her father, no matter how much trouble he was in, would never hurt his own mother.

But what if there were other people involved? Don't forget the goons in the white Chevy. She didn't know if they had anything to do with Elwood kidnapping Nolan and Maybelline or if they had been following the Bentley for some other reason.

What if the Malibu goons were debt collectors and they'd been tracking her in order to get to Elwood? The possibility was a very real one. It wouldn't be the first time her father had owed money to the wrong people. Once, he'd even ended up in the hospital following a debt-related beating. Her uneasiness grew.

Elwood was here. He had to be. They needed to keep looking. She took off down movie-land street.

"Where are you going?" Mason asked.

"Every good western has a farmer's barn. It's gotta be around here somewhere."

They found the barn squatting at the end of the lot next to the facade of a farmhouse. The barn was for real, however, and the donkey's bray that broke the silence was just as authentic.

Charlee jerked her head around in time to see someone disappearing around the corner of the barn.

Without dithering, she went in hot pursuit.

She could hear Mason's footsteps pounding close behind her. She rounded the barn in time to see a man desperately trying to scale the mesa. She tackled him at a dead run and knocked him to the ground. That's when Charlee realized the guy was at least sixty and wearing ratty gold prospector clothes.

"Please don't hurt me, sister," the old man panted. "I swear I don't know nothing about these weird goings-on."

Mason, Charlee, and the old prospector, whose name turned out to be, oddly enough, Waylon Jennings, sat on moldy hay in the barn out of the direct heat of the relentless sun, sharing the Pepsis Charlee had bought at the convenience store.

"Yep," Waylon said, "I thought I was seeing things when Elvis Presley got out of the camper. Seein' mirages are pretty common when you spend a lot of time alone in the desert but I couldn't figure out why in the hell I'd be having a vision about the King. I never cared much for his music and as for his movies, well they flat stank. 'Cept I kinda liked *King Creole.*"

"Forget the movie criticisms," Mason interjected. "What happened?"

Waylon shot him the evil eye, then spit a stream of chewing tobacco juice at his shoes. Mason jumped aside and the old prospector turned his attention back to Charlee. "When Elvis pulls an older couple out of the back of his camper and I see he's got them tied up I start thinking maybe it's for real and I'm not imagining things, so me and Jackass—that's my donkey—come down off the mesa for a closer look."

Mason watched Charlee's face as she studied the old man. The woman was intensely focused. He could actually see her listening. He realized she was probably a very good private investigator.

Somewhere along the way, however, his attention shifted from respecting Charlee's interrogation skills to admiring the way her faded jeans curved tight over her perfect butt.

Maybe it was the desert heat, maybe it was lack of sleep and food, maybe it was sheer desire, but without warning, Mason was lost in a very sexy vision of his own and it startled him. He wasn't driven by sexual impulse. At least not usually. But something about tough, irreverent Charlee Champagne tapped into his baser instincts and made him want to throw back his head and howl with lust like a lonesome desert wolf.

What in the hell was the matter with him? Why, after twenty-seven years, had his libido chosen this particular moment to go haywire?

But even more disturbing than his physical desire for her were the other, more subtle feelings she roused in him. Affection. Tenderness. Happiness.

Dear God, he realized with a jolt. He was happier when he was around her. Happier than he'd been in years. Even when they argued, even when things went haywire, even when she was so stubborn he wanted to wring her sweet neck, he was happy.

Stunned, he could only gaze at her in wonderment. Surely he was mistaken. It had to be something else.

"Pepsi tastes real good," Waylon said. "Ain't had a soda pop in close to five years. The stuff costs too much."

"The older couple," Charlee gently nudged him back on topic. "And Elvis?"

"Oh, yeah. Where was I?"

"Elvis took them out of the camper."

"Yeah and the lady was saying he better untie them or he'd be sorry and you could tell Elvis wasn't about to untie her 'cause she looked like she was going to put her foot to his backside real hard. Feisty she was."

Mason wanted to yell at the old man to "get on with it" even though he wasn't in the mood to dodge more tobacco juice. In his normal life, he was a take-charge guy, accustomed to maintaining a tight rein over both his job and his body, but out here, tempted by Charlee's unexpected appeal, away from the defining manners and mores of his world, he was clearly a guppy on parched soil gasping for oxygen and he hated feeling out of control.

But Charlee was running the show and she merely nodded patiently at Waylon. "Go on."

"The lady and Elvis got into a shouting match and when Elvis wasn't looking, the older man got loose from his ropes, sneaked up on him, and cracked Elvis on the head with one of those big Igloo thermoses from the back of the camper. Elvis went down like a sack of sand."

*Way to go, Gramps!* Mason mentally cheered.

Charlee winced. "That must have hurt. What then?"

"Well, sir, I mean, ma'am...the older man untied the woman and then they hopped into the camper. They spotted me as they were driving off and they stopped and asked me if I needed a ride. Said they was on their way to L.A. Hell, I ain't got any use for that city. Left there in nineteen and eight-one when my ex-wife kicked me out and I ain't regretted it for a second. I told that nice couple thanks, but no thanks."

"What happened with Elvis?" she asked.

"Well, not long after the couple left, Elvis came to, got on his cell phone, and called somebody. I guess it was about an hour later, though it might have been longer, this black limousine pulls up and guess who gets out?"

"Who?"

"Go on, guess."

Charlee shrugged. "I don't know."

"Take a guess."

"Marilyn Monroe," Mason spouted and got to his feet.

Waylon frowned at him. "Don't be dense. Marilyn Monroe is dead."

"So is Elvis."

Waylon needed a minute to process that before resuming his dialogue. "Anyway, one of them old-time western movie stars gets out of the limo. I can't remember his name but I know his face."

"John Wayne?"

Charlee glared at Mason. What was she getting testy about? She was the one who had sacked the old guy and now she was acting like they were best buds. "Don't pay him any mind. He's from a big city and doesn't know any better."

"No, not John Wayne," Waylon said, a waspish note in his voice. "You think I don't know the Duke?"

"Okay, if it wasn't John Wayne, who was it then?" Mason asked.

The old coot had spent way too many years baking his brains in the Arizona sun searching for some nonexistent gold mine. He didn't know if they could trust a single word the guy said.

Waylon snapped his grizzled fingers three times, trying to jog his memory. "He was in that movie with Walter Brennan. He played a gunslinger."

"Oh, that narrows it down," Mason said.

Charlee speared him with a do-you-mind expression. Actually, he did mind. He was hungry and hot and horny beyond all common sense. He needed a meal, a bath, and a bed. But mostly, he needed to find his grandfather and get the hell back home where he belonged before he did something irrevocably stupid like have crazed monkey sex with Charlee and ruin his family's best-laid plans for his future.

"It's okay, Waylon," she said. "You don't have to remember the guy's name. It's not important."

"Give me a minute, I know I can think of it."

"Let's just say some famous movie star showed up in a limousine to pick up Elvis and then they drove away together. Is that how it happened?"

Waylon nodded his shaggy, unwashed head. "Yep. That's it exactly."

"You know." Mason glanced at his watch and tapped his foot impatiently. "Now we know our grandparents have eluded Elwood and are on their way to L.A., we should get back on the road. Let's roll."

Forward motion. He had to regain control. Move things along. He'd allowed Charlee free rein but now it was time he took charge. If he didn't... Helplessly, Mason found his gaze drawn back to Charlee's curvy rump.

Forget distractions. He had a goal. Find Gramps. Nothing else mattered.

Determined, Mason started for the car without even waiting to see if Charlee was going to follow.

# Chapter 8

*Nowhere Junction Next Exit. Last Chance for Food and Gas Next One Hundred Miles.*

Nowhere Junction. Now that was truth in advertising. Mason figured the only place more isolated than here was the dead center of Antarctica.

"We gotta stop," Charlee said as she blew past the sign at a good ninety miles an hour. "My stomach is about to eat a hole through the bottom of my feet and my bladder's threatening to explode."

Mason gripped the armrest with both hands and clenched his teeth. He shouldn't have let her behind the wheel again after they left the abandoned movie studio lot, but she'd had the keys in her pocket and she'd simply slid into the driver's seat without asking if he wanted to drive. He was conflicted about that on so many levels.

On the one hand he did hate driving without a license. Breaking laws, even small ones, went against everything he stood for. On the other hand, she drove like a banshee with a firecracker clenched between her teeth. But when he'd outrun the Malibu, the capricious thrill blasting through him unnerved Mason so deeply he had insisted she drive.

He didn't like unplanned emotions. He was a cool, calculating guy, known in business for his unruffled aplomb. Faced with the evidence he could get just as embroiled in a car chase as some joyriding teenager had been a startling revelation to say the least. He thought he'd outgrown that irresponsible wildness after Kip's death.

But now, because of Charlee, he found himself longing for freedom. She made him want to break with tradition. She made him want to stand up to his folks and tell them he was tired of living the life they'd chiseled for him. Dammit, but she made him want to have fun.

"Ah hell," Mason muttered when he spotted the giant fiberglass hamburger perched atop a square little diner located next to a truck stop.

He was irritated with himself for his lack of self-control and annoyed with her for making him want to embrace that recklessness. His fickleness put him in a bad mood.

The pungent aroma of diesel fumes mixed with the smell of lard long past its prime filled the air. And all the vehicles in the parking lot were either pickup trucks or eighteen-wheelers.

"What?"

"This is the last food for one hundred miles? Deep-fried grease?"

"You were expecting maybe the Russian Tea Room?"

"I was hopeful to find something with fresh vegetables."

"This *is* the desert, Gentry." Charlee pulled into the parking lot.

"You can't park here."

"Why not?" She blinked at him.

"It's in the direct sun."

"Everything in Arizona is in the direct sun."

"Park under the shade cast by that giant hamburger." He pointed.

"Sheesh, Gentry, sometimes you can be a real pain in the butt. Anybody ever tell you that?" Charlee complained but backed up the Bentley and moved it under the shade of the hamburger.

Actually no one had ever spoken to him so frankly and he appreciated her for it. She deflated his ego with one prick of her sharp observations and unstuffed his stuffiness with her down-to-earth common sense. Mason unclenched his jaw. Maybe he was acting too persnickety. Lighten up.

"Thank you for moving the car," he said contritely.

Charlee seemed surprised by his apology. "You're welcome."

The wind gusted, sandblasting them with red Arizona topsoil as they got out of the car and entered the diner. Men in dusty jeans, boots, and cowboy hats sat on stainless-steel stools at the front counter. A fry cook in a dirty white apron doubling as a waiter leaned against the counter, a spatula gripped in one hammy hand. A country and western song twanged from the jukebox in the corner.

Every eye in the room turned to give them the once-over as the door closed behind them. The locals sent Charlee an appreciative stare, sizing her up as one of their own.

"I gotta go to the bathroom," she whispered, leaning in so close he caught a whiff of her unique scent. "Be right back."

Charlee took off for the ladies' room. The men's gazes narrowed on Mason and classified him for what he was—rich, well heeled, and as out of place as Shaquille O'Neal at a midget wrestling match.

Ignoring them, he picked out a red plastic booth in

front of the big picture window. He wanted to sit where he could keep an eye on Matilda. He noticed the men had spun around on their stools and were gawking at the Bentley.

A few minutes later Charlee returned and slid across from him, the chipped Formica tabletop sandwiched between them. She'd taken her braids down and her dark hair spread across her shoulders in a cascade of curls. She plunked her hat on the seat beside her.

He stared, dumbfounded. She was bewitchingly beautiful and he couldn't stop eyeballing her.

She flicked a long dark corkscrew of hair off her shoulder in a gesture so feminine he wondered if she was subconsciously flirting with him. He'd read somewhere when women were interested in a man they fiddled with their hair. Some kind of primal mating call.

"What?" She rubbed at her cheeks. "Have I got something on my face?"

"No, no." Mason forced himself to look away.

The fry cook wandered over and thrust two grease-stained menus at them. "What'll ya have to drink?"

"Coffee," Charlee said.

"Water. Lots of ice." Mason opened the menu.

The fry cook/waiter grunted and went after their beverages.

"Gotta have some Java," Charlee confessed and suppressed a yawn. "I'm having trouble staying awake after not getting any sleep last night."

"Now you tell me. I should have driven."

She shrugged. "I like driving the Bentley." She consulted the menu. "I think I'm going to have the cheeseburger basket. What about you?"

Mason searched the list of options looking for anything

remotely healthy, finally admitted defeat, followed suit and ordered the cheeseburger basket when the fry cook arrived to deliver their drinks.

Charlee stretched out her feet and her boots collided with his shin. "I'm sorry," she mumbled and jerked her legs away.

But the damage was done. The contact, even through the dual barrier of her boots and his pants leg, launched a rocket of desire straight through him.

Restlessly, she shook a package of Sweet'N Low into her coffee. "So," she said after taking a long sip of what looked as if it could have passed for forty-weight motor oil. "Do you have any idea why our grandparents are going to L.A.?"

Mason shook his head. "No. Only thing I can think of is our family owns controlling interest in an accounting firm in Hollywood. But why Gramps would go there I have no idea. He's been retired for two years."

"That's the same accounting firm that's responsible for counting the Oscar votes."

"Yes. How did you know?"

Charlee gave him a smug smile. "I'm a private investigator, remember."

"You ran a profile on me."

She shrugged. "I had to make sure you were who you said you were. A girl's gotta protect herself."

Mason smiled. Smart and pretty. A deadly recipe. He was going to have to watch out for this one or end up regretting their trip through the desert.

And he never wanted to regret having known her.

"Okay," she said, resting her elbows on the table and propping her chin in her hands. "Let's suppose your grandfather *is* going to check on the accounting firm, although it's highly possible something completely unrelated is going on."

"Agreed."

"What does that have to do with my grandmother? I mean, why is she involved?"

"I don't know."

"We've assumed that they met each other years ago when they both worked at Twilight Studios. Then my father kidnaps them and takes them to an abandoned Twilight Studios movie lot. Doesn't that seem awfully coincidental to you?"

"You're saying there's a connection."

"Seems odd is all I'm saying."

He tended to agree, but for the life of him he couldn't figure out what Twilight Studios had to do with his grandfather embezzling half a million dollars from Gentry Enterprises and taking off to Vegas to meet Charlee's grandmother without a word to anyone. It was totally out of character for Nolan. Maybe his father and Hunter were right. Maybe Gramps was simply going senile.

Yeah? Then explain the men in the Malibu.

Maybe they hadn't been following him, but Charlee. Maybe the gunshot through the window had been meant for her. It made perfect sense. She was a private detective and over the years she had probably collected more than her fair share of enemies. Maybe chaos theory did indeed rule and nothing was connected.

Too bad he was so tired and hungry. He was missing something here and in his dulled haze of sleep-deprived starvation he couldn't think straight. Food. He needed food. Even a greasy hamburger would help.

Mason rubbed his eyes and stared out the window, checking on Matilda. The wind tossed dust eddies across the desert. He cringed as a small whirlwind passed over the Bentley. First chance he got, they were pulling into a carwash.

"When did your grandfather disappear?"

"What's today? I've lost track of time."

"Thursday."

He looked at his watch. Five-thirty in the evening. The trip to the movie studio had cost them a good three-hour detour. "My brother Hunter discovered the missing funds on Monday evening. When we went to confront Gramps on Tuesday, we discovered he was gone. I left for Vegas right away."

"Driving instead of flying so obviously you didn't feel as if the matter was that urgent." She peered at him over the rim of her cup.

"I told you I don't like to fly. And we did figure Gramps was probably just letting off some steam. Retirement doesn't suit him."

"So why not just leave him be?"

"He did steal half a million dollars from the family business."

"And then you arrived in my office yesterday afternoon," she said.

Had it only been a little more than twenty-four hours since he'd first laid eyes on Charlee Champagne? It seemed he had known her for years. Of course they had been together pretty well nonstop for the last twenty-four hours. If you averaged that up in dating time, saying a typical date lasted four hours, they would be on their sixth date.

*Date? What the hell are you talking about, Gentry?*

He had to stop this. His hormones were messing with his emotions. He was letting the circumstances wreak havoc on his brain. He needed to stop reacting from his gut and his heart and start thinking with his brain.

Pronto.

"Okay, so your grandfather takes off and in his room you find my grandmother's name and address."

"Well, actually, it was the address to the detective agency."

"Come to think of it, Tuesday morning was when Maybelline said she was leaving for her fishing retreat. Usually, she spends weeks preparing and talking about it and then, just out of the blue, she tells me to hold down the fort and takes off."

"I'm thinking that Gramps had hired her to work on a case for him."

"But what case?"

Mason shook his head. "I have no idea."

"Of course now there's a bigger question."

"Which is?"

"How do we find them once we get to L.A.?"

He paused a moment, pondering the question. "Gramps has a few old friends there. He doesn't see them much anymore, but we could give them a call and find out if they've heard from him. In fact, when we get back to the car I'll give them a ring. I can also phone home to see if Gramps has touched base with the family. Plus I'll check my voice mail to see if he's tried to contact me."

"It's a start," Charlee said. "I can check my answering machine too. And once we get into LA. I can start calling hotels, see if our grandparents checked in anywhere. I'm assuming they'll stay somewhere upscale if your grandfather is anything like you."

"He's got five hundred thousand dollars in cash, he can pretty much stay at the most expensive hotel in town if he chooses." Mason's eyes met Charlee's and he could tell she was thinking the same thing he was. Their plan was lame but it was all they had.

"Maybe they're on some kind of trip through memory lane," she mused. "Recalling their misspent youth."

"Maybe. But that doesn't explain why Gramps stole the money or why your father kidnapped them or why the guys in the Malibu were following us or why some old western actor showed up in the desert in a limousine to give Elwood a lift."

"Touché."

"Something big is at stake."

"Yeah, like half a million dollars."

"It feels bigger than that. The whole thing makes me uneasy."

"How come your family sent you to Vegas?" Charlee asked. "Especially since you're not keen on flying."

"Pardon?"

"Why didn't your brother come after your grandfather or even your father?"

Mason shifted against the hard plastic bench and toyed with the paper wrapper from his white plastic dinnerware. "Because it's my job."

"It's your job to baby-sit your grandfather?"

"No. It's my job to play cleanup. Hunter is the front man. The mover, the shaker, the deal maker. I tie up the loose ends. It's up to me to maintain customer service. Make sure everyone is happy."

He tried hard to keep the bitterness from his voice. He was resigned to his position in the family hierarchy, but sometimes he couldn't help but begrudge the fact that he'd been relegated to second place simply by birth order. No matter how hard he tried, Mason always seemed to fall short in comparison to his older brother.

"So essentially you're the family janitor. Mop up the messes and whatnot."

"It's not like that," he protested.

She raised an eyebrow.

"It's not." He could hear the defensive tone in his voice. Who was he trying to convince? Charlee or himself?

"And what about you?" she prodded.

"What about me?"

"Are you happy, Mason?" She peered deeply into his eyes in a maneuver that made his gut hitch. "Do you like being the janitor?"

*When I'm with you, I am.*

Her perceptive question took him off guard. He had no idea how to answer. "Sure I'm happy. Why do you think I'm not happy?"

"Well, for one thing you're glowering."

"I'm not glowering," he denied and smiled purposefully.

"Now that's just plain wrong."

"What is?"

"Denying how you feel. Pretending to be happy when you're not. What happens in your family when you express your displeasure?"

"What is this? Twenty questions? We're talking about our grandparents here, not me."

"What happens?" she persisted.

"I don't know."

"You don't know? What does that mean?"

Good Lord, the woman could worry a wart off a frog. "I've never openly expressed my displeasure."

"For real?"

"My parents aren't emotional people. We Gentrys prefer to stay reserved. It facilitates peace."

"Peace at all cost, huh. Explains a lot."

"Explains what?"

"Why you're so screwed up."

"I'm not screwed up." Annoyance surged inside him at her half-baked psychobabble. "You think I'm screwed up?"

"How old are you?"

"What's that got to do with anything?"

"Thirty-two, thirty-three?"

"I'm twenty-seven."

"Oh. Sorry." She looked chagrined. "You seem much older."

Before she could elaborate on her theory concerning his supposed screwed-up-ness, their cheeseburger baskets arrived, sidetracking them from further talk.

In spite of himself, the aroma of grilled onions made his mouth water and when he bit into the cheeseburger he sighed involuntarily at the delicious flavor.

"Good, isn't it?" Charlee grinned and dunked a french fry in ketchup.

Good? The fatty cheeseburger was sheer heaven but he wasn't about to admit that to her. Not after all the bitching he'd done. Feeling contrite, he dabbed his chin with a paper napkin.

"Mmmm." Charlee's soft little moan of pleasure just about stopped his heart.

He looked up and the expression of delight on her face caused his breath to come in short, ragged gulps. Charlee's lips glistened in the cheap fluorescent lighting and her eyes glowed luminescent.

And when she slowly licked a morsel of melted cheese from her finger his entire body tightened and the swell of heat swamping his groin was almost more than he could bear.

Jesus. What in the hell was the matter with him? Talk about your mental turmoil.

He was not the kind of guy who vacillated. He didn't have conflicted feelings. Mostly, he ignored his feelings. So why couldn't he do that now? Why the constant struggle? He wanted her so badly and yet he didn't want to want her. He was screwing up his life. Ruining everything he'd built. Letting himself be tempted by a litany of "what ifs?"

This was wrong.

And yet the notion of kissing those provocative lips felt so damned right.

He was going to have to break up with Daphne and that's all there was to it. He'd barely thought about his girlfriend in the last twenty-four hours. And how could he commit to Daphne when he couldn't stop fantasizing about bedding a certain very sexy private eye?

The wind howled around the corner of the diner, escalating as sharply and rapidly as his desires. Dust bathed Matilda's windshield. Overhead the ceiling creaked and groaned.

"Let's get out of here." He wiped his hands on a napkin and then reached for his wallet. "I'll get the check."

Belatedly, he realized he had no wallet and no money.

Instead of heading on into Tucson where he'd had his secretary wire him money, they had immediately headed for L.A. after Waylon Jennings told them Maybelline and Nolan were headed there. He was still without cash flow and he hated being broke.

"You're broke, Gentry," Charlee pointed out, a little too gleefully for his tastes. She had an uncanny ability for pushing his buttons and shooting down his pretensions. "My treat." She pulled a wad of ones from her jeans and approached the cashier.

Damn if he could stop himself from eyeing the incendiary swish of her back pockets.

She paid for their meal and came back to retrieve her hat from the seat. She plunked the straw Stetson down on her head and turned to gaze at the windstorm.

"Maybe we ought to lie low until the dust devil passes," she said.

"No, no. It'll be all right." Mason wanted to get on the road. The sooner they got out of here, the sooner they'd get to L.A., and the sooner they were in L.A., the sooner he and Charlee could go their separate ways. "Give me the keys." He held out a palm. "I'll drive from here on out."

"Whatever." Charlee dropped the keys into his hand.

The metal roof groaned again, louder and more insistently. He took Charlee's elbow and guided her toward the door.

Was it his imagination or did she tense beneath his touch? Too bad. He'd been raised a gentleman. She was stuck with his deeply ingrained manners, like it or not. Besides, he liked touching her.

He leaned forward and reached to push open the front door of the diner, but the wind snatched it from his hand. At the same moment the roof stopped its low-level groaning and instead let loose with a sharp, metallic, bone-chilling shriek.

The whole building shook as the shriek gave way to a deep, heavy rumbling.

And then came a crash loud enough to rival a wrecking ball smashing into a dilapidated building.

Bam. Boom. Splat.

In unison, the truckers and cowboys seated at the tables and counters jumped up and ran to the window.

"Holy shit," someone exclaimed.

Charlee gasped and clutched Mason's shoulders, her fingernails digging into his flesh.

Mason froze, his mind refusing to accept what his ears had witnessed.

"I'm so sorry," Charlee murmured.

Slowly, in millimeter increments, he turned his head.

The giant fiberglass hamburger that forty minutes earlier had been perched jauntily up on the roof of the diner now lay squarely on top of Matilda, squashing her flatter than aluminum foil.

# Chapter 9

The thermostat is busted." Maybelline wiped her oil-stained fingers on a white paper napkin and slammed down the hood of the camper.

"So we're stuck here." Nolan splayed a palm to his forehead. He regretted leaving his cell phone at home. He hadn't brought it with him because he was afraid his family would call and he wouldn't be able to resist answering the damned thing.

"Until I can jury-rig something and we can make it to the next gas station, yes."

Nolan sank his hands on his hips and let his breath out slowly. "May, it's imperative we get to L.A. before the Oscars on Sunday night."

"I'm aware of that, but it is only Thursday evening. Relax. We'll get there."

"I'm worried about Elwood finding us again."

"Yeah, me too."

"The sooner we get to Hollywood the better. I need time to plan an offensive counterattack."

"I'm doing my best," she said calmly, took a map from the glove compartment, then leaned against the hood and opened it up. "Our current location isn't even on the map."

They had decided to stay off the main roads after ditching Elwood at the abandoned Twilight Studios lot. Unfortunately, staying off the beaten path had been a calculated risk that wasn't paying out.

"As the crow flies, we're only a few miles from the interstate and a place called Nowhere Junction. Maybe we could hitch a ride there."

"Except when was the last time we saw another car on this road?"

Maybelline sighed and folded up the map. "Not for hours."

"Face it, we're stranded."

The sun squatted on the horizon. Nothing could be done tonight.

No point taking his prickliness out on Maybelline. At least she knew enough about engines to try to repair the broken thermostat. His manhood took a ding on that one but it couldn't be helped. The gizmos underneath the hood of a car were a complete mystery to him. Might as well make the best of a bad mess.

Fifteen minutes later they were ensconced in the back of the camper. They sat side by side on the bare mattress, their backs pressed against the cab. Nolan took an orange from the sack of supplies Elwood had left stashed in the front seat of the camper, peeled the skin away, and broke off segments for Maybelline. The tangy sweet smell of citrus fruit filled the small confines.

"Not exactly the way I imagined spending the night with you," he murmured.

"You imagined spending the night with me?"

"Hell, yes," he growled. "About a thousand times on the plane trip to Vegas and about ten thousand since then."

She leaned against his shoulder. "I never knew you thought of me like that."

"Like what?" he asked out of pure devilment. He wanted to hear her say it.

"You know. Sexually."

"I married you, didn't I?"

"That was in name only. You were just trying to protect me. I never thought you actually wanted to *sleep with me,* sleep with me."

"Christ, woman, what is the matter with you? The whole time we were married and living in that bungalow on the Twilight Studios lot and you were six months pregnant, I wanted you."

"I never knew."

"Come on. You never had an inkling?" He put his arm around her shoulder, drew her closer, and fed her an orange wedge. When her lips brushed against his fingertips, his old heart sang.

"I thought you were just a really sweet guy from back home who married me to save my reputation."

"Well, you were wrong."

"The whole three months we were married you never once even tried to kiss me." Maybelline leaned up and traced his chin with her finger.

"You were pregnant with another man's baby and I thought you were in love with him."

"I might have been. Once. Or I was in love with the image of who I thought he was. Until I discovered the cheating bastard was married."

"You were going to fling yourself off the HOLLYWOOD sign over him. What was I supposed to think?"

"That I was pregnant and unwed back in the fifties when girls were judged rather harshly for that sin."

"What about you? Not once did you let on that you thought of me as anything more than a friend. And when you filed for the annulment..."

"Oh, come on, Nolan."

"What?"

"I knew I wasn't good enough for the likes of Nolan Gentry. Your daddy made that fact clear enough the time he threw a hissy fit when he caught us together at the soda fountain."

"My daddy was an ass."

"No. He was right. He knew you were Dom Perignon and I was Ripple."

"Dammit, don't put yourself down like that."

"I know who I am, Nolan. I've never labored under the illusion that I belonged in your world. The only reason I agreed to the marriage in the first place was because I would have lost my job at the studio if they'd discovered I was unwed and pregnant."

"It hurt me, May, when you got that annulment behind my back and took off without a word."

"I couldn't stay married to you when your family was planning on you walking down the aisle with Elispeth Hunt. I wasn't about to ruin your life just because I'd ruined mine. And when that gossip columnist started snooping around the set and asking questions, I knew I had to do something to protect you. I could just imagine what would happen if your father found out you'd married me out of pity."

"I didn't marry you out of pity, dammit. I married you because I loved you."

"If that was true, Nolan, why did you make everyone on the set swear to keep our marriage a secret? Thinking back on things it was a miracle no one gave us up to the gossip rags."

He swallowed hard. "I was a coward."

"No you weren't."

"I let the love of my life walk away because of my family."

"I hid from you."

"I should have searched harder."

"Your father had a heart attack. What else could you do but go home? And let's call a spade a spade. You married me because you wanted to feel like a hero."

"That's not true, but I am sorry," Nolan said vehemently, "if I ever made you feel like you were anything less than special to me."

"You never made me feel bad. I just knew we weren't right for each other."

"You were wrong about that."

Maybelline said nothing. He peered down at her in the gathering gloom. It was almost too dark to see her face but when he put out a hand, he felt the dampness of her cheek and knew she was crying.

"Ah," he said. "Ah, sweetheart, don't."

And then he was squeezing her tight, pulling her close to his chest, and kissing her like he should have kissed her forty-seven years ago.

Charlee stared at the car in horror.

"Matilda." Mason's voice cracked as he stood beside the massacred Bentley. The plaintive sound sliced a hole through her heart.

"Mason, I'm so, so sorry."

He dropped to his knees and ran a hand over the piece of bright red metal that used to be a fender, poking from beneath the giant murderous hamburger.

"It's my fault," she said. "If I hadn't insisted we pull over for a meal...."

"She's the only car I ever had," he murmured in the hushed reverential tones reserved for funerals.

The diner patrons stood in a circle around them, mumbling their sympathies.

"I lost my virginity in the backseat," Mason continued. "To Blair Sydney. She was home on spring break from Vassar the summer I turned seventeen."

Charlee squatted beside him, laid a hand on his shoulder. She felt lousy as hell. She was the one who had parked the car directly underneath the burger, even if it was at his demand. She should have ignored him and parked where she wanted.

"You shouldn't torture yourself."

"You don't understand. Matilda represented something important to me. Freedom from my family. A piece of my own identity."

"A shit load of money is what she represented," one of the cowboys muttered. "I'd hate to have his insurance premiums."

Charlee shot the loud mouth a quelling frown and the cowboy had the good grace to look embarrassed. "Come on, Mason, let's go back inside. Nothing can be accomplished out here."

He appeared to be in a trance, staring at the violated car as if he were peering into a crystal ball and seeing an unpleasant future. He sat for the longest time not saying a word. Just when Charlee thought she was going to have to pinch him to remind him he was alive, Mason spoke. "I should have listened to you. I should have left Matilda in Phoenix with your friend."

God, she hated being right. Hated seeing him so disheartened. She imagined her cherry red Corvette compacted beneath the oversized sesame seed bun and empathy pains knotted her stomach.

This wasn't good at all.

She had to snap him out of his funk.

Twilight deepened and the lights from the gas station next door came on. The other diner patrons meandered off, but Mason just kept sitting on the ground, shaking his head and reciting a litany of memories associated with the car—his college graduation, summer vacations, and cross-country trips. He was holding a wake for Matilda. The only thing missing was whiskey and Irish lament songs.

He worried her. Big time.

Allowing him to descend into self-pity—however understandable under the circumstances—was a luxury they couldn't afford. They had to get their heads straight and come up with a way out of here, ASAP. They had no car, very little money and now even his cell phone was D.O.A in the wreckage of Matilda.

Tough love. That was the answer. She made the conscious choice to aggravate him.

"You gonna sit there and feel sorry for yourself all night, Gentry?" She cocked her head and leveled him a stern stare.

He didn't even look up at her, which scared her even more.

"What? You want me to go find a preacher to eulogize the car?" She was desperate. If she couldn't break through to him she had no idea what to do.

He didn't move.

She snorted, exaggerating the sound for his benefit. "Great. Just what I might have expected from a spoiled, pampered, rich blue blood." She laid it on thick, gesturing with her arms and raising her voice in a desperate attempt to attract his interest.

"Having a frickin' pity party over a car. Boo-hoo, poor baby." She paced behind him, hands on her hips. "I got news for you, pretty boy, while you're indulging yourself, our grandparents are God knows where, maybe even being chased by nasty, menacing people while you sit on your duff and..."

"That's enough!" Mason snarled, leaped to his feet, and whirled around to face her in a movement so sudden and fluid Charlee choked on her words.

*Ulp.*

"Not another peep out of you."

For a long moment, she just stood there in disbelief, like the time when she was a kid and she'd been petting her hamster and it bit her so hard her thumb bled.

Mason's chocolate eyes smoldered with a perilous fire. His jaw was set, every muscle in his body tensed. His dimples, which were beguiling when he smiled, dug into his face like ominous burrows when he glowered. He stalked toward her with a loose hip stride that promised more trouble.

He looked very, very dangerous.

Charlee gulped and took a step backward, stunned by the changes in him. Was this the same man she'd just driven four hundred miles beside? Where was the self-controlled, self-contained guy she'd met in her office yesterday afternoon? Gone was all semblance of civility. In Mason's place stood a total stranger.

"I've had it up to here." He sliced his hand across his neck. "You push and you push and you push. A man has limits, Charlee Champagne, and I want you to know I've reached the edge of mine."

Okay, she'd snapped him out of his near catatonia but this certainly wasn't what she'd bargained for. He kept coming, his features a mask of unadulterated ferocity. Her stomach careened up to her throat.

And Charlee kept backing up, her eyes growing wider with surprise. She raised her palms in a defensive gesture.

"Now, Mason..." She started to explain why she had been so hard on him but he wasn't in the mood to listen. "Take a deep breath."

"I don't want to hear it." Gravel crunched beneath his feet. *Crunch, crunch, crunch.*

Her heart slammed against her rib cage like an un-seat-belted crash-test dummy bashing repeatedly into the windshield of a Yugo.

His teeth were clenched. A vein at his forehead throbbed.

Charlee slowly edged one foot behind her hoping that if she moved without haste she would defuse his anger. "Settle down."

"I don't want to settle down." He was utterly pissed. He looked as if he wanted to tear her to shreds with his bare hands, bit by tiny bit. "I'm tired of settling down. I've been settled down for twenty-seven years and where has it gotten me? Stuck in the middle of the Arizona desert with an infuriatingly aggravating woman, that's where."

Another sliding step back. Another and another.

And then her boot heel hit smack-dab up against the outside wall of the diner.

Nowhere to run.

Charlee held her breath.

He slapped his palms against the wall on either side of her head, effectively pinning her in.

Uh-oh.

A tiny burst of panic exploded inside her. She'd created a monster. She could feel his pain, see it in his eyes, but there was something more than hurt and anger lurking in those blazing brown depths.

Passion, desire, and hungry sexual need smoldered there too.

Oh, God, oh, God, oh, God, she was in trouble.

Her blood ran hot and her insides were all jittery and jammed up. She couldn't let him know how she felt. Vulnerable and willing and turned on like a faucet. She sank her top teeth into her bottom lip and curled her fingertips into her palms to stay the rush of her surging emotions.

She had to lighten the mood. She had to think unsexy thoughts. She had to get her mind off the fantasy of making love to this brown-eyed handsome man. Going on the offensive had only provoked his ire. It was time to try something else. Humor maybe?

"Ever since I met you nothing but bad things have happened," he continued to rant. "I've been shot at, made fun of by creeps in a bar, had my wallet stolen, been in a crazed car chase, and now the vehicle that's dear to my heart has been smashed by a giant hamburger."

Charlee's upper lip twitched and an almost irrepressible urge to laugh pushed through her. When you thought about it, their circumstances were really sort of funny. Laughter might offer a wonderful release valve for her, but she had the distinct impression Mason would not appreciate a hysterical giggling fit.

"But none of those things were my fault," she squeaked as her mind frantically raced to think of something sarcastic and witty and fitting but she came up empty-handed. The drastic change in him was just too intimidating.

"Maybe not, but you attract trouble like a television screen attracts dust. I can deal with all that chaos. I can even deal with my car getting crushed. What I can't deal with is being insulted by a smart-mouthed private detective who thinks she knows it all because she grew up the hard way."

"I don't think 1 know it all," she denied.

He ignored her refutation. "Yes, I was raised in the lap of luxury. So sue me. It doesn't make me a bad person. I don't have to put up with your derision and your sarcasm and your holier-than-thou attitude."

"I . . . I didn't . . . I don't . . . That's not . . ." she stammered, hardly able to form a coherent thought.

He narrowed his eyes to slits and he leaned in closer. His lips were almost touching hers. His masculine scent invaded her nose.

Her breath came in hot, rapid gasps. The pulse in the hollow of her throat throbbed erratically. Heat swamped her body. The flavor of raw sexual desire filled her mouth.

God, but she was so aroused.

Charlee had never wanted anyone more than she wanted him right now. Her fingers itched to rip the shirt from his body. Her lips ached to ravish his. Her legs quivered with the urge to wrap themselves around his muscled waist.

And then, over his shoulder, she caught a glimpse of something that instantly dampened her raging libido.

A white Chevy Malibu pulling into the gas station behind him.

Oh, no. Not now. Not when her brain was swamped in hormones and not functioning properly.

What to do? What to do?

Think.

She had to create a diversion. Had to do something to make sure they weren't immediately spotted by the Malibu goons. She had to buy them some time.

But how?

Only one idea occurred to her. One single, awful idea that promised to plunge her even deeper into emotional danger, but it was all she had.

The men were getting out of the Malibu. The one from the passenger side was glancing around.

If he spotted them...

Not knowing what else to do, Charlee grabbed Mason by the collar and pulled his face close to hers. "Kiss me," she demanded.

"What?" He looked as if she'd asked him to jump into the Grand Canyon buck naked.

"Kiss me now. Kiss me hard. Kiss me like you mean it."

"Huh?"

"Just do it, dammit."

Mason stared at her, his mind a chaotic jumble. Charlee's chest rose and fell in rapid succession, her breasts rubbing lightly against his inner forearms. Her lips glistened moistly. Her gaze was desperate.

Was she as turned on as he?

Her sense of sexual urgency surprised him, igniting a fire in him like a blowtorch to ten-year-old kindling. When had his sorrow over losing Matilda turned into all-out desire for the dark-haired, green-eyed woman captured between his arms?

He pillaged her lips. He was a plunderous pirate claiming his booty. He was a ruthless bounty hunter bringing his prisoner to justice. He was a cold-blooded cutthroat taking what didn't belong to him.

From the very moment he had clamped eyes on her in that small dusty detective office, he had yearned to kiss her.

Years of pent-up feelings surged through Mason. A

river of underground sensation. Too long he'd suppressed his basic emotions and now they were tumbling out of him in a pure, explosive purge. Anger mixed with raw sexual desire mixed with sheer shameless need. Burning euphoria mixed with voracious carnal hunger.

She wrapped her arms around his neck and pulled him closer. Her hair brushed against his face and he just about came unraveled.

Mason thrust his tongue past her parted teeth and damn if she didn't moan and wriggle against him. She tasted like hamburger heaven.

He stroked the inside of her mouth with his tongue, surprising himself with his bold technique. He ran his hands down her feminine hips to cup her butt in his palms. As he enjoyed what was happening between them, he forgot about everything else.

The rest of the world was a blur. He forgot about Daphne, his job, his parents. He didn't think about Matilda or Gramps or the fact that a dozen truckers and cowboys were staring at them through the diner's plate-glass window.

He ignored the chugging, wheezing sounds and the choky diesel odors of the eighteen-wheeler engines idling at the gas station behind them. He didn't care that they were stranded in Nowhere Junction with no way out of here or that he had no money, no ID, not even a change of clothes.

Time hung suspended and nothing mattered but the silky slide of Charlee's lips against his. He felt liberated and feral and authentic, as if he had at last unearthed the real Mason. He felt consumed by a shadow self who had been prowling in his subconscious for years, just waiting for the chance to pounce free.

Charlee moaned into his mouth and her tongue took off on an adventure of its own. His body reacted vehemently, pulling him deeper into treacherous territory.

He allowed his hands to glide down her spine to her waist and then lower still. Her smallness surprised him. Because she acted so tough, toting that gun and spouting strong talk, she seemed larger-than-life. But right here, right now, in his arms, she felt soft and willing and womanly and surprisingly delicate.

His fingertips reached the waistband of her jeans and his groin ached with the desire to yank down her zipper and shuck those denim britches right over her hips.

Just when he was at the point of suggesting something so completely out of character that anyone who knew him would have sworn pod people had taken over his body, Charlee wrenched her mouth from his.

"Okay. You can quit now," she said. "They went inside the gas station."

"Who did?" Lust-addled, Mason could only stare at her.

"The men in the Chevy Malibu."

"What?"

She nodded toward the gas station behind them. Slowly, Mason turned his head and spotted the Malibu. Understanding dawned. Charlee hadn't asked him to kiss her because she was overcome by passion. She'd just been trying to avoid being spotted by the guys in the white Chevy.

He felt stupid and foolish and thick-witted. To think he'd actually believed Charlee had wanted to kiss him. But it had been nothing but a ruse, a ploy, a plot to keep them from being identified by their pursuers. His pulse kicked hard against his neck vein, embarrassed, ashamed.

Chagrined, he stepped back from her, lightly fingering his lips.

"The hamburger is hiding the Bentley from their view but I don't think it'll take them long to figure out we're here." Charlee gripped his arm.

"They're coming after us," Mason said flatly and stuffed down his mortification. He felt the way you did when someone waved at you from across the room and you waved wildly back, happy to be recognized, only to realize the person was waving at someone behind you.

"I'm afraid so."

"What do we do now?"

"I don't know. I gotta think." Charlee bit down on her thumbnail.

At that moment a chartered tour bus—with the destination sign mounted over the cab spelling out Los Angeles—rumbled into the parking lot. The bus pulled to a stop between the diner and gas station, blocking their sight of the Malibu.

"Maybe we could talk one of those truckers into giving us a ride," Charlee said.

The door to the tour bus whooshed open and the driver got off but Mason didn't really pay much attention.

"We could pay someone to give us a ride." Instinctively, his hand went to his pocket before he remembered again that his wallet had been stolen. He swore under his breath.

"Oops, looks like your money isn't going to help us get out of this one."

What was the matter with her? What did she have against money? Or against him for that matter?

"Don't worry, big spender. I've got it covered." Charlee unbuttoned two more buttons on her shirt, revealing an eye-popping amount of skin.

She handed him her straw cowboy hat, then bent over from the waist to brush her fingers through her hair. When she straightened, her curls had a wild, tousled just-rolled-out-of-bed look. She licked her lips to moisten them.

"What in the hell do you think you're doing?" he growled and grabbed her elbow as she started to stroll away.

"Just like you told me. Trying to catch flies with honey."

With breasts like that on display and that madcap hair corkscrewing everywhere she could snag every fly on every pair of blue jeans in the diner. Jealousy, mean and hungry, chomped into him at the thought of those men ogling his Charlee.

"Over my dead body. I'm not going to let you expose yourself in exchange for a ride."

"Got any other bright ideas? If so I'd like to hear 'em. I'm open. Oh, and hurry. I did happen to notice when those goons got out of the Malibu that they were wearing shoulder holsters under their jackets."

"You're saying they're dangerous."

"I'm saying they've got guns and we don't."

"Excuse me, folks."

Charlee and Mason glanced over to see the beefy, ruddy-faced tour bus driver standing next to them, a clipboard clutched in his hand and a harried frown pulling at his brow.

"Yes?" she asked.

"Are you Skeet and Violet Hammersmitz?"

Mason opened his mouth to deny it and Charlee promptly trod on his toe.

"Ow." He glared at her. If he wasn't so jealous and upset and embarrassed and confused, he might have been quicker on the uptake.

"Excuse us." She fluttered her eyelashes at the driver who was busily checking out the cleavage she'd forgotten to button back up. Mason had an irresistible urge to plant his fist in the guy's face and the intensity of his response shocked him. "My husband and I are having a little tiff. What did you say?"

Husband? What was the little minx up to?

"Are you the couple who missed the bus in Tucson and called in to say you'd meet up with us here in Nowhere Junction?" the driver asked.

"See any other couples around here?" Charlee waved a hand.

"Well come on then, get on the bus. We're running late as it is and we got a schedule to keep. We're supposed to be in L.A. before midnight and it looks like we're not going to make it before two." The driver turned and headed back to the tour bus.

"What in the hell do you think you're doing?" Mason hissed once the man was out of earshot. "Telling that guy I'm your husband? I don't like lying."

"I'm getting us a ride to L.A., doofus."

"Oh." He paused a minute. "But, Charlee, that's not right. What about the other couple? What happens when they get here and the bus has left without them?"

"Let's forgo the ethics for once, Eagle Scout."

"There's nothing wrong with having standards."

"Yeah, yeah, it's admirable and all that but let's be sensible for once. The other couple doesn't have armed thugs following them. Plus obviously they've got another ride, or how else would they get out here? Don't worry about Skeet and Violet. They'll be just fine."

"Good point." He conceded.

The driver tooted the horn and motioned for them to get a move on.

"Well?" Charlee angled her head toward the bus.

"Which is it? A free ride out of here or a showdown with those two *Soprano* wannabes?"

Just as she asked the question, the two men from the Malibu stalked into view, heading straight for the diner. With a jolt, Mason recognized them.

"Hey," he said. "They are the same guys from the airport. The ones who stole my wallet." Angrily, he started forward, his intent to challenge them.

Charlee grabbed him by the belt loop. "Whoa there, where do you think you're going?"

"They've got my wallet."

"And if you confront them you're gonna end up in the trunk of their car. Trust me on this. I know unsavory characters, and those two are as sleazy as they come. They've already stolen your wallet, you wanna add your life to their list of accomplishments?"

"No." He hated to let this go. Every male instinct urged him to fight for what he knew was right.

Charlee inclined her head. "The bus?"

When she put it like that, the choice was easy. Pretend to be Charlee's husband on a bus trip to L.A. or end up in some shallow grave in the desert.

He shot a backward glance at Matilda and his heart tugged. Nothing more he could do for her anyway. Squaring his shoulders, he followed Charlee to the bus.

# Chapter 10

Charlee climbed the bus steps, Mason right behind her. His warm breath tickled the back of her head and the hand he placed at her waist, well wowza. Her head still swam from the power of his kiss. Her lips and cheeks and chin still burned from the abrasion of his beard stubble.

She wanted to snap at him to move his hand away, but she was pretending he was her husband so she had no recourse. She was stuck with his proprietary gesture.

"Violet! Skeet! Welcome, welcome, we were so worried you would miss the bus again." A short, plump, middle-aged woman with a perpetual smile locked into place enveloped Charlee in a lilac-scented hug and then stepped back to pump Mason's hand after they'd climbed aboard the bus. "I'm Edith Beth McCreath, your tour director."

"Nice to meet you, Edith Beth," Mason enunciated carefully, obviously trying hard not to lisp on the woman's unfortunate name.

"Gosh," Edith Beth said, craning her neck upward.

"You're a tall one. Must come in handy when you're reaching for shoe boxes on those high stockroom shelves."

"Excuse me?" Mason frowned.

Edith Beth looked stricken for a moment, plucked a day planner from her pocket, and started ruffling through the pages. "You are a shoe salesman, right, Skeet?"

"Yes, right. Sure. A shoe salesman."

Charlee rolled her eyes. She'd never seen a lousier liar.

Edith Beth jabbed at an entry in her journal with a stubby index finger. "Yes you are. It says so right here in my trusty notes. A shoe salesman from Des Moines. And, Violet, you sculpture fingernails for a living. Let me see those hands."

Before Charlee could stop her, Edith Beth grabbed her hands and stared down at her ragged fingernails.

"Oh."

She jerked her hands away and hid them behind her back.

Edith Beth laughed. "Must be a case of the cobbler's children going without shoes, eh?"

The tour director glanced from Mason's dirty Gucci loafers to Charlee's scuffed cowboy boots. She tried to gauge what the woman was thinking but Edith Beth was well schooled in the art of displaying a perky grin in lieu of real emotions.

"Put 'em in a seat, Edith Beth," the bus driver growled. "I'm pulling out."

"Yes, yes," Edith Beth twittered and escorted them to the last empty seat on the bus. "Don't mind Gus. He's a bit grumpy, but he's a very good driver."

Once they were seated, Edith Beth stepped to the front and picked up a microphone. "Everyone, let's have a hearty 'welcome aboard' for Skeet and Violet."

"Welcome aboard, Skeet and Violet," the other passengers recited.

"A shoe salesman?" Mason whispered to Charlee. "I'm a shoe salesman from Des Moines?"

"Could be worse, could be an undertaker from Chattanooga."

"But a shoe salesman? I don't know anything about shoes."

"Yeah, well, try being a nail technician who bites her fingernails." Charlee sat on her hands.

"I bet you make a horrible living, Violet dear. Good thing you married me so I can support you selling Hush Puppies and Reeboks."

Charlee peeked over at Mason. He seemed to have gotten over Matilda and was actually trying to crack a joke. Thank God.

"I can't tell a lie. You are my Prince Charming, Skeet."

She felt a tug on her shoulder and looked across the aisle at the petite blonde seated across from her.

"Hiya." The woman grinned. "I'm Francie Pulluski and this is my husband, Jerry." She wrapped an arm around the big bear of a man sitting next to her, who grinned and shook first Charlee's hand and then Mason's. "We just got married Sunday before last. How long have you guys been hitched?"

"A month," Charlee said at the same time Mason said, "Three weeks."

Francie chuckled. "Well, which is it? A month or three weeks?"

"Um, well, we eloped a month ago, but then his family insisted we have a regular ceremony," Charlee lied smoothly. "So Skeet considers that date our real anniversary, don't you, honey?"

"That's right, sweet 'ems." Mason gave her a tight-lipped what-in-the-hell-did-you-get-us-into grin.

Charlee almost laughed. She'd bet her last dollar the man had never before said "sweet 'ems" in his entire life.

"Did you see my ring?" Francie flashed her a modest diamond and Charlee made the obligatory oohing and aahing noises. "Now let me see yours."

"Um, it's at the jeweler's. Skeet bought it too big. You know how men tend to overestimate size."

Francie tittered. "I hear ya."

"So how did you two meet?" Jerry asked Mason.

Mason arched an eyebrow and she could tell by the look on his face it was payback time for that crack about men overestimating size.

"Why, the minute I saw the bartenders at Quintero's pub hose down Violet at the Wednesday night wet T-shirt contest I knew she was the gal for me."

"You were in a wet T-shirt contest?" Francie's eyes widened. "You brave girl! I could never do anything like that."

"She wasn't wearing a bra either." Mason winked. "It was true love at first sight."

"Drunk," Charlee said, giving Mason the evil eye. "I was totally drunk. I don't even remember meeting Skeet that night."

Mason's gaze locked with hers. "Oh, but you sure remembered me when you woke up in my bed the next morning licking my ... er ... toes."

To her utter shock, Charlee felt her cheeks heat as if she actually had been in a drunken, bra-less, wet T-shirt contest and gone home with him for a night of debauchery.

"Got yourself a wild one there," Jerry said, a touch of envy in his voice.

Francie frowned, apparently not wanting her new husband to dwell on the mental picture of Charlee in a wet T-shirt, and she changed the subject. "Aren't you guys just excited to death to be going on the twenty-first-century version of the *Newlywed Game*?"

Um, the *Newlywed Game?* What was Francie talking about?

"You betcha," Mason said, really getting into his Skeet role. "We can't wait."

"You're gonna have to work really hard to beat us, though." Francie patted Jerry's thigh. "We know everything there is to know about each other, don't we, baby."

Jerry looked a little uneasy. "Uh, everything," he echoed, giving Charlee the distinct impression the guy had kept a secret or two from his new bride.

"No way are you winning," the husband of the couple seated behind Jerry and Francie exclaimed. "We're gonna take the grand prize. We couldn't afford a honeymoon and this is our chance."

Charlee looked around at the other passengers and realized everyone on board were young couples. She counted sixteen pairs, including her and Mason. Were they all *Newlywed Game* contestants? She asked Francie covert questions and discovered the bus was on a public relations jaunt. It had started in New York and was making media stops at various central locations around the country and picking up contestants as they went. The last stop before L.A. was Tucson. She was unable to ascertain, without making Francie suspicious, why Skeet and Violet from Des Moines were picking up the tour in Tucson.

She felt guilty then at the thought of robbing Skeet and Violet of their chance to out-couple the other couples on national television. She tucked her remorse to the back of her mind. It couldn't be helped. They'd done what they had to do to get out of Nowhere Junction.

"Don't worry"—Mason leaned over to whisper in her ear—"when all this is over I'm going to hunt up Skeet and Violet and surprise them with a second honeymoon."

It was as if he'd read her thoughts. Charlee smiled at him and something in her heart gave a strange tug. He might be a rich, spoiled, stubborn control freak, but he was also a nice guy.

Warning, warning! Danger, danger!

*Stop having warm fuzzy thoughts about him. You know how much trouble you get into when you let yourself think pleasant things about wealthy, long-legged, brown-eyed, handsome men with matinee-idol smiles. Wise up!*

"Everyone!" Edith Beth boomed over the microphone. "Time for travel games."

"Travel games?" Mason asked. "What are we? On the bus to summer camp?"

"Oh, it's fun," Francie said. "Just wait and see. We've been playing on and off since we left Tucson."

Edith Beth explained the rules. It was a memory game where one person started with a word and the next person had to come up with a word that used the last letter of the first word. The following person had to recite those two words, then come up with a third and so on. The upshot being whenever anyone missed a word, the entire bus had to kiss their mate.

Oh, crap. No way. Charlee caught her breath at the thought of having to kiss Mason again. The last kiss had short-circuited her brain and got her feeling all soft and mushy toward him. No more. No can do. Nuh-uh.

She had to find a way out of this or face some pretty dire consequences.

Like the loss of all common sense when it came to drop-dead-gorgeous George Clooneyesque men.

Amid much giggling, the game started. When the sixth person forgot a word, Edith Beth tinkled a cowbell. "Everyone kiss!"

How the hell had she gotten herself into this situation? Mason looked at Charlee and gave a little shrug. He leaned over to kiss her.

She doubled her fist. "You do and you die."

"It's all for the good of the cause. We wouldn't want to get found out as impostors and risk getting thrown off the bus."

"You're just trying to take advantage of the situation." She narrowed her eyes at him.

He smirked and flashed her those sinful dimples.

"You can pretend to kiss me," she said. "For the good of the cause. But that's it."

"Whatever you say." Mason leaned perilously close to her lips and almost, nearly, barely, touched her mouth with his. His gaze was locked on hers, his eyes burning a daring challenge.

The air in that tight space between them vibrated with tension and anticipation.

Gak! This was worse than kissing him. She felt keyed up, on edge, hypersensitive.

The game went on and they got away with feigning their kisses. Until it was Charlee's turn.

She tried to remember the cycle of words but Mason's body heat distracted her and she flubbed.

Edith Beth rang the cowbell.

Once again Mason almost, nearly, barely brushed her lips with his.

Charlee shivered.

"Oh, no, no, no," Edith Beth said, walking down the aisle to their seat and shaking her head. "That will never do. You're kissing her like she's your sister, Skeet. This woman is your wife. Lay a big wet one on her."

"Don't even think about it," Charlee whispered fiercely through clenched teeth.

Mason shifted away from her and confessed to Edith Beth, "I'm sorry, but I've never been comfortable with public displays of affection."

Thank heavens he'd heeded her words. He was trying to get them out of this. Heck, he probably didn't want to kiss her any more than she wanted to kiss him.

Yeah? So how come she felt a little disappointed?

"We're not the public," Edith Beth said. "These are your fellow *Newlywed Game* contestants. Come on, Skeet, plant a kiss on Violet she'll never forget."

"Kiss, kiss, kiss," everyone chanted.

"You guys," Charlee pleaded with the group. "Skeet had onions on his hamburger back at the diner and his breath is really pungent."

"I've got a mint," Francie offered and dug in her purse for a peppermint.

"Aren't you helpful," Charlee said and it was all she could do to keep the sarcasm from her voice.

Mason popped the mint and grinned at her. *All for the good of the cause,* his expression declared.

Charlee squirmed. She felt trapped and panicky and freaked out. She feared if he kissed her, really kissed her, the way he had back there in the truck stop parking lot, that every bit of rational self-control she possessed would fly right out the window and she'd turn into a quivering pile of estrogen Jell-O.

"I'm not moving until you give her a real kiss, Skeet Hammersmitz." Edith Beth folded her arms over her chest and tapped her foot against the floor.

"You do and so help me God, you'll pay for it," Charlee murmured in his ear.

"Tit for tat, sweetheart," he murmured back. "You started this back there at the diner."

He had a point. She had no one to blame but herself. Oh, and the goons in the Malibu.

His eyes met Charlee's and her stomach took the express elevator straight to her boots. Her heart pitter-pattered.

The last time she'd kissed a wealthy, brown-eyed, handsome man she'd gotten her heart shattered into a gazillion little pieces.

*Buck up. You're older now. Less gullible. You can handle this. It's just a friggin' kiss, Charlee.*

He hesitated.

Edith Beth clapped her hands and got a rousing round of "Skeet, Skeet, Skeet, Skeet" going.

Charlee didn't want him to kiss her against his will. She raised her voice to be heard over the chanting. "It's okay, folks. Skeet doesn't have to kiss me in front of everyone. I know he loves me."

"Prove it," someone from the back of the bus shouted.

"Kiss her, Skeet, kiss her, Skeet, kiss her, Skeet!"

"Oh, just go on and get it over with," she snapped.

And then Mason was kissing her even more passionately than he'd kissed her in the diner parking lot and that kiss had been pretty darned passionate. He curled her into the crook of his arms, bringing her close to his warm, firm chest. She felt the heady lub-dubbing of his heart through the soft material of his shirt.

*Don't give in. Fight the feeling. It's just lips.*

Correction. Not just lips. Hot, moist, demanding lips. Lips that tasted of peppermint. Lips that glided like silk over hers. Lips that took her breath and refused to give it back.

Lips that belonged to a wealthy, long-legged, brown-eyed, handsome man with matinee-idol smiles and a day's growth of beard stubble.

She was screwed and she knew it.

His kiss, his touch, his smell, all felt too good, too irresistible.

What the hell. She threw in the towel and succumbed to the moment.

Her eyes shuttered closed and she allowed herself to drift into uncharted waters, to fully experience the promise of his mouth. This was different than the rough, demanding way he'd kissed her before. This kiss was both hungry and tender. At once lazily languid and intensely urgent.

A hot, overwhelming rush of desire thundered through her. His tongue thrust past her lips and delved deeply into the warm recesses of her mouth.

Sensation stormed through her body. Waves of it, crashing one on top of each other in a blind, mad rush. Sweetness and heat and pressure. Moistness and pleasure and pure, honeyed desire.

"Wooooooooo," the whole bus chimed in unison.

Happy now, everyone?

"Okay," Edith Beth interrupted. "You get a gold star, Skeet. Let's move on. Your turn to recite the memory string."

But Mason completely ignored Edith Beth, his focus—and his mouth—centered on Charlee.

"Ahem," Edith Beth cleared her throat.

Charlee pried open one eye and saw him waving the tour director away. His own eyes were closed as he too savored the moment. Charlee's belly tightened.

"Somebody hand me a water hose," Edith Beth joked.

"A water hose was what got them into this," Francie said with a giggle.

"How come you never kiss me like that," Charlee heard one newly wed wife whisper to her husband.

Mason grinned against her mouth and she found herself grinning right back.

"All rightee then," Edith Beth said, admitting defeat. "We'll leave Skeet and Violet to it and get on with the game. Next!"

"What are you doing?" Charlee whispered into his mouth after Edith Beth had moved on but Mason continued to kiss her. "You can stop now."

"I'm enjoying the benefits of being your husband. Believe me, there's enough negatives in this relationship, I'm taking the good where I can."

"You're not really my husband and we don't have a relationship."

"You want to call Edith Beth back over here and explain that to her?"

"No. I guess you'll just have to go on kissing me."

"Guess so."

She knew they were using Edith Beth's game as an excuse to capitalize on the sexual allure that had been simmering between them from the very moment they had met. She knew she was susceptible to the charms of rich, brown-eyed, handsome, long-legged men. She knew she was careening straight for Heartbreak Hotel. But no matter how hard she tried to pull away, once started, she simply could not stop kissing him.

He was like a horrible, horrible addiction and she couldn't get enough, so she convinced herself there was nothing wrong with satisfying her physical craving as long as she didn't get her mind or heart or soul involved. She could kiss and simply walk away. This didn't have to mean anything more than sumptuous bodily pleasures.

Denial. The junkie's tool in trade.

The bus traveled on into the night and long after Edith Beth's game had ended, Mason and Charlee continued to kiss. They were like fourteen-year-olds sitting in the back row at the movies experimenting with their first flush of sexual desire. They slid down low and rested their heads against the back of the seat. Charlee was practically in his lap, her legs dangling over his knees.

Kissing was a heady, invigorating, and totally stupid thing to do.

They did it anyway.

Even when their lips started to chap they kept kissing.

Nothing was inside her head except the moment. She forgot about Maybelline and Elwood and Nolan. She forgot about the men in the Malibu. She forgot about the fact she had a terrible track record with men. She operated on pure animal instinct and indulged herself in the sensual pleasures of Mason's mouth.

Soon enough, reality would intrude. For now, they were on a honeymoon bus bound for Hollywood and the *Newlywed Game*. It was a world removed from where they'd come and where they were headed.

When they finally opened their eyes and came up for air, they noticed everyone around them was kissing. Mason grinned. "Look what we started."

"Forget the Love Boat. We've got the Love Bus."

"Wonder if this was what it was like back in the free love era of the sixties."

"Seems very decadent."

"And very arousing."

His brown eyes crinkled at the corners and he gave her a come-hither look that had her knees liquefying and her pulse leaping over tall buildings in a single hop.

*You're digging yourself a deep one, Charlee. Remember*

*Gregory. Everything was all fun and games with him too, in the beginning.*

"We shouldn't be doing this," she said.

"No," he agreed. "We shouldn't."

And then he reached for her again.

Sometime around midnight, Mason woke with a start to find Charlee curled snugly against him, her head resting on his shoulder. His arm had gone to sleep and tingled with an achy numbness but he hated to disturb her slumber by moving.

The bus was silent except for the steady strumming of the tires rolling against the asphalt. Everyone around them was sacked out, cuddled together under sweaters or blankets. The sight was touching and darned romantic. For one brief moment he actually wished they were Skeet and Violet Hammersmitz on their way to compete in the *Newlywed Game.*

He studied Charlee's face in the light of moon glow slipping through the bus windows. She looked so relaxed, so peaceful. Her lips were parted slightly and her dark hair spilled over her shoulders in an inky cascade. He shifted, turning to relieve the numbness in his arm without waking her. Snuggling with her had its advantages and disadvantages.

It felt so right to have her tucked into him, to feel her soft, warm breath fanning the hairs on his forearm, to experience the comfort of her body heat.

"Mason," she mumbled dreamily in her sleep and wrapped her arms around his waist.

Something tightened in his heart. An emotion he was afraid to name. Closing his eyes, he bit down on the inside of his cheek.

What was happening to him? He was a disciplined guy. He didn't allow unwanted emotions to rule his life. That was one of the things he liked about his relationship with Daphne. She never made him feel wild or crazy or out of control.

Daphne.

Guilt as tall as Hoover Dam stacked his conscience. He had never done anything remotely dishonest and now he was sneaking around behind his girlfriend's back kissing Charlee. He was being unfair to both women.

He had no excuse. He'd gotten caught up in the moment. All the old rules of order had been turned topsyturvy. Add to that the powerful pull of sexual attraction between him and Charlee and well...he'd been weak.

But his greatest fear was that his attraction to Charlee went far beyond the physical. He was scared to explore the thoughts, nervous about prodding the emotions growing inside him. Most of all, he was afraid to trust his feelings. Afraid to let go.

The last thing he wanted was to hurt either her or Daphne. But the fact that he could feel something so intense for a woman he'd known less than two days told him what he'd already begun to suspect. He simply could not ask Daphne to marry him as he had planned.

And as for Charlee?

He owed her an apology. A big one.

Plus, he needed to keep his hands and his mouth to himself for the remainder of their trip. Easier said than done when her body was entangled with his.

"Charlee," he whispered and gently shook her shoulder.

"Hmmph."

"Could you let me out? I need to visit the facilities."

She sat up blinking and he felt weirdly sad once the

weight of her was gone from his body. She stretched her hands over her head, giving him a delightful view of the soft curve of her upper arms. In spite of himself, he stared.

God, but she was compelling. Her hair was tousled and her eyes narrowed into a cute little squint. She splayed a palm over her mouth to suppress a yawn.

He climbed over her knees, his shins brushing against her jeans in the process. Sudden heat hit him like an explosion.

What was it about her that commanded such a spontaneous response in his unruly body? Perplexed, Mason rotated his numb shoulder, trying to shake out the pins and needles.

He stumbled toward the back of the jostling bus in the darkness and scrambled for a handhold when they smacked into a pothole. He missed the back of a seat he grabbed for and found himself propelled forward onto his knees.

His face made contact with the back window glass. The bus leveled out and he pulled himself to his feet but what he saw out the back window shoved his stomach right into his throat.

There. In the darkness. On a long, lonely stretch of arid desert highway, the bus was being followed.

By a white Chevy Malibu.

They arrived in Los Angeles a couple of hours later. Even at two-thirty in the morning, the indomitable Edith Beth was perky. If he'd had a gun, Mason would cheerfully have shot her.

"Good morning, everyone," she chirped over her microphone as Gus turned on the interior lights. "Welcome to the City of Angels."

Everyone squinted and grumbled.

"Wakey, wakey!" She clapped her hands like a seal on uppers. "We'll be at the studio lot soon. And I know it's the middle of the night, but we've got to get you sorted out into your bungalows where you can finish up your naps, shower, and change clothes before the welcome breakfast at seven-thirty."

"Will there be lots of coffee?" Jerry asked.

"Oh, six or seven different flavors." Edith Beth beamed. "You're our stars. Twilight Studios has done an all-out media blitz promoting the contest and our *New Millennium Newlywed Game* contestants. We're expecting a huge media turnout because reporters from all around the country are already in Hollywood for the Academy Awards on Sunday night."

"Ah," Charlee whispered to Mason. "So we're the warm-up act for the Oscars."

"Looks like it."

Mason craned his neck toward the back of the bus to see if he could spot the Malibu, but their seats were too far away from the back window and if he made another trip to the bathroom Charlee was going to start thinking he had a bladder problem. Sooner or later, he would have to tell her they'd been tailed from Nowhere Junction.

"What's the matter?" she asked. "You look jittery. Nervous about being on the *Newlywed Game*?"

"We're not actually going on the game show, Charlee. Soon as we hit the studio lot we're getting a taxi out of there. ASAP."

"At two-thirty in the morning? Why can't we sleep at the bungalow for a little while first?"

"Because we don't have time."

"What aren't you telling me?" She narrowed her eyes at him.

He sighed. No pulling one over on her. She didn't miss a single thing. How was a guy supposed to protect a woman like that? So much for his vain attempt at handling the matter on his own.

"The Malibu is behind us." He jerked a finger at the back of the bus.

"They figured out we got on the bus."

"Well, I can't imagine it was that hard to put two and two together. Smashed Bentley, only couple at the truck stop, and then we disappear at the same time the tour bus does."

"I've got half a mind to walk right up to them and ask them who the hell they are and what they want."

"Don't you dare," he growled, but kept his voice low so the other passengers wouldn't overhear them. "They're armed and dangerous."

"You were all for tackling them when you realized they were the ones who stole your wallet."

"That was me, not you."

"Oooh, Gentry, you're getting all protective on me." She lightly traced a finger over his bicep. "That is sooo sexy."

"Knock off the teasing, Charlee. I'm serious."

"Me too." She gave him an impish grin.

Fresh guilt assaulted him. Obviously she'd read more into last night's kisses than he intended. He had to set things straight with her.

"About last night..." he started to say but then Francie leaned across the aisle and interrupted him.

"Aren't you just over the moon excited?" she enthused. "This is the most thrilling thing that's ever happened in my entire life. I bet I won't be able to sleep a wink after we get to the bungalow."

"What about our wedding night, babe, that was pretty thrilling," her husband Jerry interjected.

Francie waved a hand. "That was fine, sweetie, but this is live television. Imagine. Common ordinary everyday people like us on TV."

Charlee and Francie chatted up a storm and Mason never got the chance to apologize for kissing her. A few minutes later, the bus pulled up to the studio lot and checked in with the guard at the security gate.

A spotlight shone on a large banner spanning the entrance. It read: TWILIGHT STUDIOS CONGRATULATES BLADE BRADFORD ON HIS SECOND OSCAR NOMINATION.

Blade Bradford.

Hmm. Mason had completely forgotten that Blade Bradford, the actor who had beaten out Gramps for best actor, had recently made a silver screen comeback with a small budget film the previous year that had earned him a best supporting actor nomination.

Charlee nudged him. "Twilight Studios? Is this just happenstance or could this have something to do with Maybelline and Nolan?"

"It is weird but I don't see how this *Newlywed Game* thing and our grandparents are connected."

"I don't trust coincidences," Charlee said. "Keep your eyes open for a link."

Edith Beth got on the microphone and started in on her spiel. "Blade Bradford's Oscar nomination has resurrected not only his own flagging career but has been the saving grace of Twilight Studios that until the unexpected hit of *The Righteous* was on the verge of bankruptcy. Between Blade's coup and developing television shows like *The New Millennium Newlywed Game,* Twilight is poised to return to its glory days of the 1950s. So see, you guys are part of a history-making event. So give yourselves a big hand."

On cue, the bus broke out into applause.

Gus pulled the bus to a stop under bright security lights outside a collection of bungalows.

"Back in the early days, actors actually lived in these bungalows while they were making movies," said Edith Beth. "You'll be rooming two couples to a bungalow. I'll call out your names and your bungalow numbers and give you the door key as you get off the bus."

Mason reached over and squeezed Charlee's hand. "Here's where we make a break for it."

Charlee giggled. "You sound like an escapee from some cheap prison flick."

"I *feel* like an actor with a third-rate script," he said. "Keep an eye out for the Malibu. I'm hoping they weren't allowed on the lot."

They stood in the aisle and waited their turn to disembark. Edith Beth herded everyone outside while Gus unloaded luggage from the right side of the bus.

"When you get off," Mason instructed, "head around the front of the bus and go left."

"Wow. Gentry, taking control. I like your macho side."

"Charlee, this is no joke."

"Sorry. Just trying to lighten the tension."

She was right. He was tense. If he clenched his jaw any tighter, he'd snap off a tooth. Charlee climbed off the bus in front of him and immediately darted to the left. Mason followed right behind.

"Skeet, Violet!" Edith Beth snapped her fingers. "This way. You're in bungalow five with Jerry and Francie."

"Hurry," Mason said. "Before Edith Beth gets hold of us."

Charlee sprinted ahead and rounded the corner of the

closest bungalow before he did, but he hadn't taken more than two long strides when she did an abrupt U-turn and almost plowed smack-dab into him.

"What?" Startled, he put out an arm to stop her forward momentum and grabbed her wrists between his fingers.

"Go back, go back." Charlee moved her hands in a shooing motion. "They're here."

"Who are here?"

"Our Malibu buddies and they're coming toward us and they don't look happy. Move it."

That's all it took. He grabbed her arm and hustled her back round the front of the bus to face the frowning Edith Beth.

"You two enjoy being mavericks, don't you?" the tour director asked in a snippy tone. "Now pick up your suitcases and go to your bungalow."

Two suitcases remained on the curb. Everyone else was shuffling off in the dark toward the row of cottages. Charlee looked at Mason. "Do you suppose that's Violet and Skeet's luggage?"

"Who else would it belong to?"

"But how come their luggage got on and they didn't?"

Mason shrugged. "Who knows? People and their luggage get separated all the time."

"Maybe they were making out in the bathroom of the bus terminal."

"Maybe."

Mason hurried over to pick up the suitcases. When he bent down, he darted a quick glance under the bus and spied two pairs of legs on the other side.

"Skeet, Violet, hurry up," Jerry called. "We're waiting for you guys."

# Chapter 11

Make the best of a bad situation, Charlee told herself. As long as the Malibu goons were lurking outside, they might as well get some shut-eye. They could worry about escaping after daylight. Sensible advice until she saw the size of the bed she and Mason were expected to share.

"Oooh," Francie called out from the bungalow's other bedroom. "Aren't these beds nice and cozy. Just perfect for snuggling."

Cozy, hell, in that twin bed wannabe, they'd be stacked on top of each other like Pringles in a can.

Mason dropped the suitcases on the floor and turned to look at Charlee who hung back in the doorway.

"We sleep in our clothes," she decreed.

"I'm not arguing."

"And no touching."

He cocked his head at the tiny bed. "Be reasonable."

"Okay then, we sleep back-to-back."

"Why? Afraid you'll be tempted?"

"Of what, kicking you out of bed?"

"You can relax, sweetheart. I'm much too tired to even think about molesting you, much less work up the energy to do it." He peeled off his shoes and flopped down on the bed.

The truth of the matter was, she was *very* tempted and a little disappointed he wasn't even going to try to molest her.

*What in the hell is the matter with you?*

It was the idea of lying next to him on that itty-bitty bed that had her thinking crazy thoughts. All she had to do was look at his long form stretched out on the mattress and her stomach performed a three-hundred-and-sixty-degree loop-de-loop.

She was *not* getting emotionally involved with him. She just thought he was kinda sexy and a very good kisser.

Well, stop thinking like that, she chided herself and edged cautiously toward the bed. She left the bedroom door open just in case Mason changed his mind in the night and decided to get frisky. She could make a quick getaway if necessary.

*And speaking of getting away, concentrate on how you're going to get away from the Malibu goons. That's what's important.*

She kicked off her cowboy boots, turned off the bed-side lamp, and gingerly lay down next to Mason.

He didn't move. Propping herself up on her elbows, she peeked over at him. He appeared to be sound asleep already. Good. She would close her eyes for just a few minutes while she thought about how they were going to get out of this mess. She would plan for tomorrow. She'd plot a way to find Maybelline with or without Mason's help.

She was not going to think about how solid Mason's body felt pressed against hers or how the steady sound of his breathing reassured her. Not for one single minute was she going to notice how his long legs hung off the end of the bed or how his beard stubble gave him a roguish appearance in the muted glow of the night-light. She was not going to remember how vulnerable he'd been back in the diner parking lot when that hamburger had smashed Matilda to smithereens or how angry he had gotten just before he'd kissed her for the very first time.

No siree. He was completely out of her head. She was giving herself a mental Mason vaccination. From now on, she was one hundred percent immune to his charms.

Charlee paced the closet-sized dressing room where she and Mason had been told to cool their heels before the live broadcast began at nine.

Before leaving the bungalow that morning, Mason had tried to make a phone call to his brother only to discover the cottages weren't equipped with telephones. Charlee had peeked outside to see the Malibu still parked in the studio parking lot, although there were no signs of the two gun-toting men.

Not knowing what else to do and faced with Edith Beth shooing them along, they had followed Francie and Jerry and the other couples to the breakfast buffet. The media had interviewed them and then the couples had been ushered over to the studio.

And so, they waited.

Charlee was dressed in the least offensive outfit she could find in Violet Hammersmitz's suitcase. That meant she was stalking back and forth in a red flouncy-skirted micro-mini, a black faux leather shirt with shoulder pads and four-inch, scarlet, ankle-strap stilettos. She looked like a streetwalker version of Joan Crawford.

She was within inches of putting her sweaty, two-day-old

jeans and T-shirt back on and saying to hell with it. Especially since the stilettos were a size too big and she kept falling off them.

Poor Mason hadn't fared much better. He had gotten stuck wearing Skeet's gaudy purple, hula girl print Hawaiian shirt, beige Bermuda walking shorts, and bright yellow canvas deck shoes.

Must be hard, she thought with a touch of sympathy, for a pampered blue-blood accustomed to the finest designer haute couture to find himself outfitted in Cheapo-Mart red-light-special duds.

"I don't want to go on the show," he repeated for about the twentieth time in the last five minutes.

"It'll be fine."

"We'll be on national television. Representing ourselves as Skeet and Violet Hammersmitz."

"Don't sweat it. You'll live. I'll live. Skeet and Violet will live."

"You just don't understand. What if my family sees the show?"

"Something tells me the Gentrys from Houston Texas are not big fans of daytime television."

"Somebody my parents know might see us."

"And that would be the end of the world?"

"Three days ago, I would have thought so. But now, after all we've been through, what's a little parental disapproval in the grand scheme of things?"

"That's the spirit," she encouraged. "Rebel. Buck the system. I'd say you're about ten years overdue."

"You don't understand," he said darkly. "Gentry Enterprises is a high-profile company. We live in a fish-bowl. People watch what we say and do. My family is very conscious of their public image."

"No kidding."

"You're awfully young to be so sarcastic."

"And you're awfully old to let your family pull you around by the nose."

They glared at each other.

"It's going to be a disaster," he muttered.

"Look, Mason, going on television beats the alternative. We either go on the show, which gives us time to come up with a plan for eluding Rocko and Bruiser out there, or we might as well just get fitted for cement shoes, go climb into the trunk of their Chevy right now, and be done with it. Come to think of it," she mused, "cement shoes have got to be more comfortable than these medieval torture devices." She bent to tug at the straps biting into her ankle.

"You don't wear high heels much." His gaze, tracking the length of her bare legs, sent heat waves shimmering through her.

"What was your first clue? The fact that I keep twisting my ankle?"

"There you go with that smart mouth again."

If he only knew what was going on inside her body. Her sharp tongue was her singular defense against the hot and bothered way he made her feel. The lone barrier that kept her heart safe.

"I'm also guessing you don't wear short dresses either considering the fact you're swishing that skirt around so hard you keep flashing me your panties."

"What!" Aghast, she plastered her hand to the back of her skirt. "Oh, crap, how am I ever going to be able to sit down without giving the audience squirrel shots?"

Mason laughed so hard he almost fell off his chair. "I can't believe you said that."

"What?" Charlee narrowed her eyes at him. "What's so funny?"

"I don't think I've ever heard a woman say 'squirrel shots' and not be discussing wildlife photography."

"That's because the only women you're ever around are those hoity-toity stuck-up society women. Squirrel shot is a perfectly legitimate term."

He was still laughing; his dimples tap dancing their way into her heart. So much for the mental Mason vaccination she'd given herself last night. Apparently his strain of charm was so virulent no adequate inoculation existed.

A heavy sense of inevitability weighted her. She felt like one of those shooting gallery ducks going around and around on the mechanical track, listening to the *ping-ping* of ricocheting bullets, never knowing when she was going to get hit but certain the blast was coming.

"Just keep your legs crossed very tightly and don't squirm. You'll be okay."

"I swear this was the longest skirt in Violet's suitcase. The woman is a floozy, I'm telling you." Charlee kept yanking at the hem, trying to make it stretch lower.

Mason eyed her legs again. "If Violet looks anything like you do in that outfit then Skeet is a lucky, lucky man."

"That does it. I'm going back to the bungalow and putting my blue jeans back on. I can't have you ogling me like a hunk of bologna."

"Sweetheart," Mason said and arched an eyebrow. That simple word sent an arrow of longing straight through her very soul. "Forget bologna. You're filet mignon all the way."

She thrust a thumbnail into her mouth and started to gnaw.

"Stop that."

"Stop what?"

Mason got up from the stool parked next to the lighted vanity table that hosted makeup, nail polish, cold cream, and other beauty supplies. He walked over to extract her thumb from her mouth.

"Sorry," she apologized. "It's a bad habit I can't seem to break."

"Sit down," he said and nodded at a chair on the other side of the tiny room.

"What for?"

"I'm going to paint your fingernails bright red and every time you start to bite them you'll see that flash of crimson and stop."

"Get out of here."

"I'm serious. Noshing your fingernails completely negates your tough girl image."

"I know."

"So sit." He pulled the chair next to the vanity and patted the seat while he plunked down on the stool.

Charlee eased down across from him. Mason rummaged through the bottles of nail polish and selected a screaming vermilion color.

"Give me your hand."

Reluctantly, she stuck out her hand. He shook the polish, and then uncapped it. Taking her hand in his, he stroked the brush over the nail of her pinkie.

She forced herself not to shiver at his touch and read the label on the polish bottle to distract herself. "Be Still My Heart."

"What?"

Her gaze leaped to his. He cocked a grin with his dimples on full-out assault.

"The polish," she said in a rush, not wanting him to

think she was saying he caused her heart to stop. "That's the name of the color. Be Still My Heart."

"Oh." He lowered his head again, moved on to the next finger.

"Where did you learn to paint fingernails, Gentry? Don't tell me you have a secret life dressing up in women's clothing."

"No, nothing like that. I'm afraid the truth is much more mundane. I built model cars when I was a kid. Hundreds of them. I spent hours holed up in my room, gluing and painting."

"Really? Rich as your family is I would have supposed they'd have hired someone to build the models for you."

He flashed her another look. This time he was clearly irked. "Money isn't everything, Charlee."

"That sounds like someone who's never been broke."

"I don't want your sympathy, so don't think that's why I'm telling you this, but I was really a lonely kid. My folks weren't hands-on parents." He didn't sound bitter, just matter-of-fact. "That's what money will buy you. Nannies so that you don't have to fuss with the mess of daily child rearing. No kissing those skinned knees and risk mussing your makeup. No rushing home from parties to put your kids to bed. No tedious bedtime stories. Hired help will do it all for you." He laughed but Charlee realized that chuckle held a note of hurt. "But, hey, at least I had both my parents. You got cheated out of both of yours."

"Maybelline was enough." She stared in fascination as he finished painting her left hand and motioned for her to give him her right.

"What happened to your mother?"

Charlee shifted on the seat, uncomfortable with the conversation. She didn't like talking about herself. Exchanging personal information resulted in closeness and she'd already told Mason way too much about Elwood. That's as close as she wanted to get.

She said nothing.

"Come on, Champagne, it's your turn to share." He gazed at her. She saw intelligence, understanding, but worst of all an overriding compassion. She didn't want him feeling sorry for her.

*Just tell him and get it over with.*

"She was onstage one night and her headdress slipped. Didja know those things can weigh up to fifty pounds? She tripped on the stairs and broke her leg. She died in the hospital after a blood clot went to her heart." Charlee paused as the memory washed over her. "I was at Maybelline's watching cartoons and eating a peanut butter and jelly sandwich when she got the call."

"It must have been hard on you."

Charlee shrugged, pretending the pain didn't run river deep. "I don't remember her much."

He didn't say anything else and Charlee recognized his technique. He was waiting for her to fill the silence. She refused.

The ticking of the wall clock sounded like a gong in her ears. The air in the room seemed stale. Dust motes cavorted on the shaft of sunlight slanting in the window blinds.

"There you go. All done," Mason said at last and capped the fingernail polish. He blew on her hand to dry her nails. His warm breath sent chills of anticipation skittering up her arm.

Charlee jerked her hand away, disconcerted by the emotions pumping through her. She stared at her vermilion fingernails. *Be Still My Heart.* Her hands looked as if they belonged to someone else. Someone soft and giggly and feminine, and she was none of those things.

"Your nails look nice. I'd love to do your toenails next. There's something incredibly sexy about painting a woman's toenails."

"Lord, don't tell me you have a foot fetish."

"I think I have a Charlee fetish." And then he did the unthinkable. He leaned over and ran a hand up the edge of her skirt, his fingertips brushing lightly over her upper thigh.

She slapped his hand away. "Knock it off," she growled. He ignored her.

"Mason," she jabbed a stern note of warning in her voice.

"Yes?" He arched a devastating eyebrow and she couldn't find her tongue. Dammit, where had she put the stupid thing?

He pulled her off her chair and onto his lap and peered down into her eyes with that knee-melting brown-eyed stare of his.

"Don't you dare," she threatened.

"Dare what?"

"Do what you're thinking."

"What am I thinking?" His eyes challenged her with a lusty gleam.

Her heart pounded and her palms grew wet. Ah hell, she grew wet in another place not too far away from where his hand lay.

"No more of that kissing nonsense we were doing last night."

He dipped his head lower and pursed his lips. "Why not? You really seemed to like it on the bus last night."

"That's exactly why not," she squeaked. "I did like it. Too much."

"I liked it too." His voice was deep and masculine and packed with sexual tension. "What's wrong with that?"

"We're wrong. You and me."

"If wanting you is wrong, I don't wanna be right."

Why did he have to say that?

*Charlee, you're in deep trouble. Get up. Get out of his lap. Run away.*

"We can't do this," she whispered. "My fingernails are wet."

"I don't intend on kissing your fingernails."

"Smart-ass."

She thought she could forget about last night and that heady, Edith-Beth-word-game-induced make-out session they'd indulged in. She thought how his kisses had made her feel special and cherished and appreciated.

She thought she could treat it lightly. She'd told herself repeatedly those kisses meant nothing.

Ha! She was falling faster than a barrel tumbling over Niagara Falls.

"I know why you're so cranky."

"I'm not cranky," she denied and tried to squirm out of his lap but he held her flush against him and the more she squirmed the more aroused he became, leaving no doubts as to where his perverted thoughts lay.

"You are definitely cranky."

"Am not."

"You've been hiding your femininity for so long behind that tough-talking attitude and your gun and those cowboy boots and faded blue jeans that you've completely forgotten what it feels like to be admired for the sexy, desirable woman you are."

"Oh, you're so full of it," she said, even though his

words hit the bull's-eye with such unerring accuracy her throat clogged.

"You can't fool me, Charlee Champagne. I see right through your streetwise persona." He lowered his voice. "Deny it all you want but I know that deep down inside you're soft and vulnerable and tenderhearted."

"Stop grinning at me like that," she snapped, terrified he was going to spy the hungry longing reflected in her eyes for something she could never have.

How many times had she hoped that a man would gaze at her exactly the way he was gazing at her? How many times had she dreamed of strong loving arms around her? How many times had she longed to be swept off her feet and carried away into happily-ever-after?

She'd dreamed, yes, but she knew it was all a fantasy. Real life simply didn't work that way. Hadn't Maybelline drilled it into her head and hadn't Charlee's life experiences supported her own disappointment in love?

"I don't want this."

"Liar."

"You're becoming really pushy, Gentry. I'm not sure I like this new side of you. I'm not..."

Before she could finish castigating him for having the audacity to ogle her with such frank desire, he took her mouth hostage.

She wanted to tell him that she wasn't his for the taking. That she wasn't some scullery maid eager to lift up her petticoats for the lord of the manor anytime his appetites led him to the kitchen. But she did not say a word. She breathed in the dark scent of him and savored the rich aroma. Damn her and her shortsighted weakness for brown-eyed handsome men.

Charlee succumbed, all fight and denial and fear

vanishing in the heated taste of his lips. She relaxed her neck against his forearm, the top of her head resting against the wall.

The pressure of his mouth was ticklishly light at first. Soft, warm, teasing.

Dizziness assailed her and she reached up to thread her trembling fingers through his hair and pulled his head down closer to hers. So what if she got fingernail polish in his hair, it would serve him right for starting this.

Last night's kisses had been no fluke of nature. The man could kiss with a mastery that took her breath.

Step by step he increased the pressure, cajoling her lips apart. The mild brush of his tongue was measured and indolent, seducing her in steadily escalating notches. Her head spun recklessly as he took the kiss deeper and deeper still.

His palm cupped the curve of her hip. An instant chemical reaction exploded inside her. The material of her borrowed black blouse grew damp from the anxious perspiration pooling between her breasts.

She tightened her fingers in his hair, pulling lightly, and heard him growl low in his throat as his breathing quickened.

She should put a stop to this. Right now. Get up. Move. Poke him in the eye. Anything to snap herself out of the languid dream state he'd woven over her.

But he smelled like orange juice and tasted like the sinfully delicious eggs Benedict they'd been served for breakfast.

She knew she was going to pay for her recklessness. It wouldn't be the first time she had paid a high price for her imprudent desires. She'd learned the hard way that nothing this sweet came without expensive strings attached.

Kiss in haste, repent for the rest of your days, Maybelline had drilled into her. And so far her grandmother had been right to warn her.

But Mason's mouth was moist and hot against hers, blurring the edges of reality and sucking her down into momentary bliss. Ah, what a foolish slave she was to her hormones.

He stroked her with firm, tender circles and she trembled beneath his touch, her body's response as unstoppable as an earthquake. From outside the dressing room came the sound of the *Newlywed Game* theme song played to an updated hip-hop beat. The steady pounding bass vibrated up through the floor and into the steamy air beneath them.

Her blood skipped through her veins with the strumming rhythm and gathered heavily in her groin. She ached to be filled with him.

Because of their circumstances she was safe from her own headlong recklessness. No matter how tempted she might be to take this lurking passion to its natural crescendo, she knew they couldn't get too carried away. Not when any moment they were expected onstage.

That remembered knowledge eased her earlier misgivings. She was free to explore this sweet interlude without fear of going further than she wished.

Or so she thought until Mason's hand slipped up her thigh and his fingers hooked inside her panties.

*Charlee no,* her mind warned but her body, oh-her-wicked wicked body was on fire for him and she writhed against his lap while his inquisitive fingers gently explored.

Too late for regrets.

Pure animal instinct took over when his lips left hers to trail a path of blazing heat over her chin and down her throat to the ticklish juncture where her collarbone intersected with her neck. She groaned at the tactile pleasure of his mouth against her skin.

He gave a low, throaty chuckle of pleasure and laved her with his tongue while his fingers continued to stroke the delicate tissue hidden by her panties. He sounded triumphant and a tad egotistical that he had dragged her down to such depths, but she was too lost in physical bliss to care.

One hand was undoing the buttons of her blouse, exposing her aching breasts to the hot air of his breath. While her pulse leaped and revved in answer, his naughty hand slid under her back and she felt the hooks of her bra spring open. The guy knew what he was doing.

Charlee arched her back, practically beseeching him to take her nipples into his mouth. She rocked her pelvis against his hand begging for more. She shouldn't do this, but she was the helpless product of biology. Her body quivered and pulsated and yearned for more.

Forget common sense. Ignore prudence. Deny rational thought, whispered the pleasure centers of her brain. Stop thinking and simply enjoy.

When he sank a finger into her, she gasped and tightened her muscles around his warm, wet digit and almost came right then and there with his hand in her panties.

Moisture filled her mouth. She hadn't been this hungry for a man since, well, Gregory.

*And look where that got you,* whimpered the rational side of her brain, which had been all but bushwhacked by her wildfire libido.

Mason raised his head and peered down into her face, sensing her mood change. His dark eyes gleamed with not only lust, but with something deeper, something more. It wasn't the lust that scared her, but the something more. Was that tenderness skulking in his gaze?

Mesmerized, Charlee stared back, unable to look away, unable to stop herself from slipping pell-mell into the abyss of those dark brown eyes. They hung suspended like that for one long breathless moment. Their gaze locked, her blouse unbuttoned, her bra flapping loose, Mason's hand in her panties, his finger inside her, his erection impossibly huge and hard against her buttocks.

And she felt an inexplicable sadness as she imagined things that she could never have with him. A wedding night. A home. A baby.

A knock sounded at the door at the same time a fresh-faced young woman with exotic almond eyes and honey-colored skin poked her head around the door.

"Mr. and Mrs. Hammersmitz...oh, my...oh, no...I'm so sorry." Flustered and flushing to the roots of her glossy dark hair, the girl spun on her heels and turned her back to them.

Charlee jumped from Mason's lap, buttoning her blouse as she went.

"Stupid, stupid, stupid," the assistant muttered to herself. "You've got to learn to stop walking in on newlyweds."

"It's all right," Mason assured the woman. His voice seemed loud in the confines of the small room. "We're the ones who should apologize for not locking the door."

She peeked over at him and saw that his hair was sexily disheveled and his mouth was plastered with the vixen red lipstick the makeup artist had caked on her lips. And she saw that his eyes reflected an unexpected happiness. A happiness bordering on pure joy. She had caused that look.

Charlee caught her breath at the glorious realization of her power over him.

The young woman still did not look at them. "They're

ready for you on the set now," she squeaked, then scurried away.

"I think we traumatized her for life," Mason joked.

"I think you traumatized me for life," Charlee confessed before she realized what she was going to say. The last thing on earth she wanted was for Mason Gentry to know exactly how vulnerable his happiness made her feel.

Lust was one thing. Love was something else entirely.

# Chapter 12

Maybelline woke to find her bare legs entwined with Nolan's. When she turned her head, she was treated to a spectacular view of his broad, muscled back. Sometime before dawn he'd put his boxers back on, making him both modest and adorable.

Her cranky old heart careened into her chest as unbalanced as a drunk staggering out of a bar at two A.M. Last night had been incredible and she couldn't thank Nolan enough for making her feel like a desirable woman again. He'd given her a whole new lease on life and the fortitude to face what lay ahead of them.

*What you're feeling is way more than gratitude, Maybelline, and you know it.*

She was in love.

The dreamy teen who had hidden her love from him forty-seven years ago because his father had told her a white trash Sikes would never be good enough for a Gentry had sent her fleeing to Hollywood. And she'd ended up sleeping with a married man simply because he'd looked like Nolan.

That same young girl who'd had the stars smacked

from her eyes by an unplanned pregnancy and a man unwilling to assume responsibility for his own son.

That spunky kid had carried a large burden on her small shoulders and she'd done the best she could. But Elwood's father had turned Maybelline hard and cynical inside when it came to love and romance.

She grieved now for her lost innocence. She felt guilty too, for coloring Charlee's view about men and life in general. She felt guilty about a lot of things. About the way Elwood had turned out. About the way he'd blackmailed Nolan.

Her lover had been wonderful, however, never blaming her for what Elwood had done.

Her lover.

Maybelline smiled up at the ceiling. She was sixty-three years old and Nolan Gentry was her lover at long last. The lover who made her feel like a giggly, girlish sixteen-year-old all over again.

Something good had come of Elwood's criminal behavior. Unfortunately, there was still a whole lot of bad they had to clean up before they could take their budding relationship one step farther. Too many things hung in the balance. Like the Gentry family fortune.

Maybe Nolan's father had been right. Maybe she did spell nothing but trouble for his son.

"Morning, sunshine. What's got you concentrating so hard?" Nolan reached over and rubbed the frown line between her eyebrows with the flat of his thumb.

She looked into his dark brown eyes and smiled. "You."

He tugged her into his arms and held her against his chest for the longest time. They lay not speaking, listening to the sound of their synchronized breathing and reveling in the rekindled love they'd found.

Finally, Nolan kissed her and said, "We have a long day ahead. We should get up, get started."

Maybelline nodded but neither of them moved. She feared that if they got out of bed she would realize it was all a dream.

He nuzzled her neck and planted small kisses along the underside of her jaw.

"Best not start something you don't plan on finishing," Maybelline whispered. "Because I can't be held responsible for what I do next."

"You issuing a threat, honey? Or a promise?"

"Why don't you take a chance and find out."

An hour and a half later, sexually sated and voraciously hungry, Maybelline and Nolan sat on the tailgate of the camper eating a bag of popcorn for breakfast. Maybelline kicked her legs back and forth, munching contentedly.

"You deserve brunch at the Four Seasons," Nolan said.

She waved a hand. "That sort of thing means nothing to me."

"Oh, just wait until you come to Texas. I'm going to spoil you something rotten."

"Well, old man, don't count your chickens before they hatch. We've got a lot of damage control to do before we can start making plans for the future."

Nolan frowned. "I was trying not to think about all that for a few minutes."

"That's because you're the idealist and I'm the realist."

"How did I manage for so long without you?" he asked.

She grinned. "You did pretty well by yourself. A high-society wife, a son, a huge investment firm. I wouldn't have been an asset in your world, Nolan, and you know it. Your daddy certainly knew it."

"Well, my daddy's gone and my world has changed. I'm not the easily influenced young kid I once was."

"Let's not talk about this right now," Maybelline said. "You keep an eye out for passing cars while I take another look at that thermostat."

She had been tinkering under the hood of the camper for about twenty minutes, alternating cussing out the thermostat and sweetly cajoling it to work, when Nolan called out, "Car's coming."

Maybelline straightened and tucked the one tool she had—a toothbrush-sized wrench she kept in her purse for emergencies—into her back pocket. Nolan was standing at the edge of the road, windmilling his hands in an attempt to get the car to stop.

She wiped her hands on a napkin and narrowed her eyes at the vehicle. Damn if it wasn't a big black stretch limousine, right out here smack-dab in the middle of the Arizona desert. It looked as incongruous as a gold prospector at a high school prom.

As the limo drew closer she could see the windows were tinted. It pulled to a stop at Nolan's feet. Maybelline sauntered over to stand beside Nolan, a queer anxiety shooting through her veins.

Slowly the electric windows rolled down and she found herself staring not only into the face of the man who'd impregnated her forty-seven years ago, but down the barrel of a bull-nosed thirty-eight as well.

Mason's blood raced through his veins. He felt like a caged beast. Restless, pacing, hungry to be free.

Calm down. It's just stress.

Stress. Yes.

That was the only excuse. Ever since losing Matilda

he'd been acting crazy, out of character and out of control. Once the trip was over, once he'd found Gramps and ironed out this obvious misunderstanding, he would go back to being his old self.

Except oddly enough, some not-so-small part of him did not want to go back to his life the way it had been before he'd met Charlee Champagne.

Before Charlee everything had been nice and safe and predictable. *He'd* been nice and safe and predictable. The good son, doing what he was told, scheduled to marry a woman his parents approved of, doing the job they'd picked for him.

He'd been living someone else's life.

And now?

Well now, things were in utter chaos. But in a weird, wonderful way, the chaos felt great.

Charlee made him itch for all the childish, carefree things he'd missed in life. Things he'd never even known he'd missed until he met her. Undisciplined, unruly, impetuous things like making out in the balcony of the movie theater or skinny-dipping in the lake at midnight under a full moon or feeding each other a banana split at Baskin-Robbins.

He glanced over at her. God, but she was extraordinary. Impulsive, yes, but cautious too. She made decisions quickly—like getting them on the bus—but she was vigilant with her emotions, never letting him know exactly what she was feeling. She was smart and witty and determined. She was confident and generous and brave.

And in that sexy little outfit that had once belonged to Violet Hammersmitz she absolutely took his breath away. He was halfway in love with her already.

They were on a sound stage seated in a cheap plywood

box, decorated with wedding bells and doves, that probably looked very nice on television, but in reality Mason feared getting splinters from the unfinished boards.

Francie and Jerry sat in the box next to them. All four of them had just won the first game and had advanced to the play-off round. This, in spite of the fact that he and Charlee had done everything within their power to answer the questions incorrectly.

It seemed some weird cosmic synchronicity compelled them both to choose the same wrong answers. Call it fate, call it destiny, call it kismet. New Agey as it sounded, Mason feared the universe was hell-bent on shoving them into each other's arms, no matter how they struggled against it.

He was surprised to discover the notion didn't scare him. Not in the least. In fact, he craved the heady excitement of falling in love and he knew this was what had been missing from his relationship with Daphne.

Francie wriggled her fingers and mouthed, "Good luck," at the same time the music swelled and a spotlight came on to showcase the Bob Eubanks look-alike who came popping out from behind the curtain.

The live audience broke into immediate applause.

"Good morning, folks! And we're back for the grand prize round. I'm Manny Mann, your host for Twilight Studios' *New Millennium Newlywed Game*. Let's give a big hand to couple number one Skeet and Violet Hammersmitz from the heart of America, Des Moines, Iowa!"

The spotlight shone on him and Charlee. Obediently the crowd clapped and Manny Mann went on to introduce the remaining couples.

Mason peered over at Charlee again. She looked more nervous now than she had in the first round, poor kid.

Winning had kicked the stakes up a notch. They simply had to lose this time.

She was so tough and self-reliant he kept forgetting she was covering a soft, vulnerable core and that she hadn't had the advantages in life that he'd enjoyed. Advantages like private tutors, Harvard Business School, a life coach, a media coach, and a mentor. Smiling his encouragement, he reached over and squeezed her hand as the production crew cut to a commercial and the emcee joked with the audience.

"You're doing just fine," he whispered. "I know we'll lose this time."

She nodded but instead of his touch reassuring her, he was surprised to find she trembled even harder.

"Charlee? Are you okay?"

Before she could answer, the same young assistant who had interrupted them in the dressing room came over to escort the ladies offstage to a soundproof room.

Thirty seconds later, they were back from commercial and the Bob Eubanks clone, Manny Mann, jumped right into the program.

"Husbands, here's your first question." He paused while dramatic music played. "Would you say your wife's chest is more like a watermelon, a grapefruit, a peach, or a strawberry?"

The audience twittered.

"Skeet?" Manny prompted him with a smug smirk. "What fruit are Violet's breasts most like?"

The spotlight shone on Mason. What a stupid question. He forced a smile. He was stuck here, he might as well play along.

"Are we talking size here, Manny, or flavor?"

The crowd hooted and guffawed enthusiastically at his response.

"Either or, Skeet. Just answer the question."

"A peach." He'd just discovered firsthand that Charlee's breasts were round, soft, and perfect. Just the right size for cupping into a man's palm.

And on went the stupid questions. Mason was never so relieved in his entire life when at the next commercial break they brought the wives back in.

Charlee seemed to have recovered from her stage fright. She was laughing and joking with the other women. That is until she sat next to him again. The smile left her face and she nervously started to chew on her thumbnail but stopped herself before she could nibble off the flashy Be Still My Heart crimson polish.

Then a curious thought occurred to Mason. Maybe Charlee wasn't afraid of being on television or of winning the game. Maybe she was afraid of *him*.

Charlee afraid? Impossible. He thought of how she'd used her body to block his from the bullet shot into her grandmother's trailer. How she'd tackled the old gold prospector at the abandoned studio lot. How she'd boldly bluffed her way onto the tour bus. Charlee was the most courageous woman he'd ever known.

"Okay, ladies, now we'll see how well your answers matched your husbands'. Remember in this round each correct answer earns you five points. Violet, how do you suppose your husband answered?" Manny Mann asked and then repeated the ridiculous fruit question.

Charlee glanced at her chest, and put an exaggerated comic expression on her face. "Well, Manny, most people would probably say a strawberry, but my Skeet is really generous so I'm gonna say a peach."

A bell sounded. "That's absolutely correct. Skeet, hold up your card."

Mason raised the placard the assistant had placed in his lap at the break.

Charlee grinned.

"Aren't you going to kiss him for being so generous about your dimensions?" Manny asked a little too lewdly for Mason's taste. He noticed the emcee kept glancing at Charlee's chest and he frowned pointedly at the man.

"Oh, sure," Charlee said, then hastily leaned over and kissed Mason's cheek. The sweet smell of her lingered on his skin.

"Remember"—Mason leaned over to whisper to her once Manny had gone on to quiz Francie and Jerry—"we don't want to win this thing. Try to give wrong answers."

"I was," she protested. "I figured for sure you'd say strawberry."

"Oh, come on, Charlee, your breasts are perfect. Not too big, not too small. Firm and pert and..."

"Mason!"

Had he shocked her? It wasn't easy shocking Miss Streetwise P.I., but yes, he did believe she was blushing. He grinned.

Manny was back with another question and damned if she didn't get that one right too. Even though it was a question about the nonexistent apartment they shared. By the time the five-point round was over, she'd answered all three of the questions correctly and they had more points than any of the other contestants.

Just before the assistant came over to escort the husbands offstage, Mason murmured in her ear, "Remember, answer the opposite of how you think I would answer."

"Okay, all right." She nodded. "I've got it under control."

"Violet," Manny said after the commercial break. "Can

you tell us how old was your husband the very first time he made whoopee?"

Charlee hadn't meant to answer with the truth. Honestly, she hadn't. But her pride over the fact that she knew that Mason had lost his virginity in the backseat of the Bentley when he was seventeen with Blair Sydney took over and she blurted out exactly that and then belatedly slapped her hand over her mouth.

"No, Manny, that's not correct. I'm wrong. He wasn't seventeen."

"Too late, Violet." Manny winked. "You've already spilled Skeet's dirty secret. He's a late bloomer."

Charlee cringed. Mason was going to skin her alive. She imagined how embarrassed he would be if his most private sexual history got back to his parents.

God, she was an idiot. What possessed her to tell the truth?

Perhaps she'd subconsciously wanted to pay him back for embarrassing her about her peachy breasts? Was she that petty?

"Violet," Manny returned to her after all the other women had answered the virginity question. "What was his parents' reaction the first time Skeet introduced you to them?"

Charlee tried to imagine meeting Mason's parents and almost snorted out loud. No doubt the Gentrys would hate her and everything about her just as Gregory's parents had hated her.

Think opposite of reality.

"Manny, Skeet's parents welcomed me with open arms and even asked me when we were planning on giving them grandchildren."

There. No way on earth would Mason get that question right.

"Ladies," Manny said after they had answered the remaining ten-point questions. "This is it. For twenty-five points, what is your husband's favorite food?"

Oh, getting this one wrong would be like falling off a log. "Violet?"

"Cheeseburgers, Manny. And french fries. Skeet loves greasy fried foods."

Feeling self-satisfied that she'd done well, Charlee leaned back in her seat and gave Mason a thumbs up as the husbands filed onto the stage.

They were a team, she realized suddenly. Charlee admitted to herself she *liked* the feeling. She'd never felt this close to anyone, save her grandmother. It had always been her and Maybelline against the world.

Until her grandmother had run off with Mason's grandfather.

The shift in her thinking was disconcerting. All her life she had believed that she had no one on her side except for Maybelline. Certainly not her irresponsible father. And losing her mother at such a young age had only strengthened that belief.

*Fool. You're setting yourself up for disaster. You know better than to fall for this guy.*

She knew better and yet she could do nothing to temper the sweet, mushy feelings sprouting inside her the minute Mason took his place as her pretend husband.

*It's just lust,* she assured herself. *He's one helluva hottie and a crackerjack kisser. Nothing wrong with physical attraction as long as you don't let it become something more.*

When Manny asked Mason the virginity question and he got it right, Mason shot Charlee a look of alarm.

*What in the hell ?* his expression said.

Charlee shrugged and looked apologetic. How could she explain her need to let the world know she was privy to Mason's secret when she didn't understand the motivation herself?

"Skeet, what was your parents' reaction the first time they met Violet?"

Mason looked uneasy. "Well, Manny, they welcomed her with open arms and even asked when we were going to start a family."

*Ding, ding, ding,* went the bell.

"That's correct, Skeet, earning you another ten points." Charlee offered him an I'm-so-sorry-I-screwed-up smile. Her stomach churned. Was he mad? Her anxiety level skyrocketed.

"And now, gentlemen. For that all-important twenty-five-point question. The question that can make or break you. What is your favorite meal, Jerry?"

"This is a cinch," said Jerry, rocking back in his seat and puffing out his chest with absolute self-assurance. "My favorite food is lasagna."

The buzzer sounded, signaling a wrong answer. Jerry blinked and shook his head. "What? What?" He glared at Francie.

"No, Jerry, your wife Francie says your favorite meal is pizza."

"Pizza, lasagna, they're both Italian food. Come on, Manny, cut us some slack," Jerry begged. "Francie gets pizza and lasagna mixed up. Come on over to our house the next time she makes pizza and see for yourself."

The buzzer blasted another raspberry.

"Sorry, Jerry, you're out of the running."

The next two couples managed to get the answer right, tying them up with Charlee and Mason.

"Skeet and Violet Hammersmitz, if you answer this question correctly, you'll not only be our grand prize winner but you will have proven you know each other more intimately than any of the other fifteen couples in the contest."

*Please get it wrong,* Charlee prayed and clenched her fist. *I know you hate hamburgers.*

"For a total score of sixty points, Skeet, and a two-night stay at the famous Beverly Hills Grand Piazza Hotel along with special VIP tickets to this year's Academy Awards ceremony on Sunday night courtesy of Twilight Studios, what is your favorite meal?"

The crowd and Charlee held their collective breaths. She crossed her fingers and her toes and closed her eyes tight.

*Say sushi, say Chateaubriand, say anything besides hamburger.*

Because her heart hung in the balance. For the life of her she couldn't imagine anything worse than spending the night with Mason in a luxury hotel.

Just the two of them.

All alone.

In a fancy hotel.

With champagne and room service.

Given those circumstances Charlee knew she was not strong enough to resist him or if she even wanted to. Not when all it would take to get her stripped naked was one flash from those darling dimples.

"Well," Mason drawled in that sexy Texas way of his that never failed to set her pulse flailing erratically, "Manny, I just love cheeseburgers and french fries."

# Chapter 13

Directly following the broadcast, Charlee and Mason found themselves surrounded by news media. In a blur of activity, they were interviewed and then whisked away in a limousine.

As their driver pulled out of the Twilight Studios parking lot, Charlee spied the thugs leaning against the white Chevy Malibu glaring at them.

She nudged Mason in the ribs and nodded out the window at the men. "Winning the contest was one way of getting away from those goons."

"They'll just follow us," Mason predicted gloomily and sure enough, not two minutes later, the Malibu pulled up behind them in the traffic on Sunset Strip. "We're stuck for now, but once we get to the hotel, I'll call my family and have them wire money."

A confident gleam sparked in his eyes as if he had everything figured out. He seemed different, more sure of himself. He sat up straighter and assumed a regal air in spite of Skeet's hideous tourist clothes. Mason was back in his milieu.

By the time they arrived at the Beverly Hills Grand

Piazza he was back to being a Gentry again, the same controlled, calculating executive who'd marched into her office on Thursday afternoon.

Gone were all traces of the open, adventuresome man who had cut loose back there in the desert. The man who had kissed her all night long on the honeymoon bus. The man who said her breasts were perfect as ripe peaches.

That was a good thing. Right?

This way, she didn't have to worry so much about falling for him. Still she felt sorta sad that Skeet was gone for good and Mr. Straight-and-Narrow was back at the helm.

The minute the hotel valet opened the limo door, a second contingent of reporters and another perky representative from Twilight Studios were there to greet them.

The representative introduced herself as Pam Harrington and bustled them into a reception area.

"Are all these people for us?" Charlee stared in disbelief at the milling throng gathered in the hotel ballroom and lining up for a lavish buffet.

Pam smiled. "Well, we are waiting for Oscar nominee Blade Bradford. He was supposed to be here to congratulate you on winning the game but I guess he's running a little late."

Blade Bradford, huh? Blade was her grandmother's least favorite actor. She'd done makeup on him back when she worked for Twilight. Even though Maybelline wasn't one for trashing people, she'd only had bad things to say about the Oscar-winning actor.

And because of Maybelline's unhappy experiences in Hollywood, Charlee herself had never been starstruck. As her granny was fond of telling her, movie stars put on their pants one leg at a time, just like everybody else.

Pam cast a nervous glance at her watch. "If you'll

excuse me, I'll just go make a couple of phone calls. Help yourself to the buffet."

"Ah," Mason said after Pam had bustled away, his tone suggesting he'd just died and gone to heaven. "Caviar."

He went straight for the black fish eggs.

Fish eggs. She should have known that would be his favorite food.

Blech! She looked at the salmon pâté, the foie gras, the oysters on the half shell, and the sushi rolls spread out across the elaborate buffet.

She was hungry but not *that* hungry. She settled for a dry wheat cracker and ended up having to guzzle half a glass of champagne to wash it down.

Charlee snagged one of the tuxedo-clad waiters by the arm. "By any chance you wouldn't happen to have a jar of Skippy chunky peanut butter hidden away somewhere in the kitchen, would you?"

The waiter rolled a haughty expression down the end of his nose. "Madam, this is the Beverly Hills Grand Piazza."

"And?" Charlee one-upped his hoity-toity look with her own particular brand of a hard-edged stare she'd perfected in the dark alleys of Vegas.

He squirmed under the intensity of her glare but maintained his snooty countenance and added a flippant head toss. "I'm afraid we do not stock Skippy chunky peanut butter."

Charlee was about to tell the guy to pluck the stick out of his ass when Mason glided over and smoothly intervened.

"But I'm sure you carry some brand of peanut butter. So run off to the kitchen and get some for the lady," he said pointedly in his most superior tone.

Apparently his commanding voice and the way Mason

set his facial features overrode Skeet's garish outfit. Even when it was disguised in Cheapo-Mart duds the waiter recognized aristocracy when he saw it.

"Yes, sir"—the waiter bowed contritely—"I will bring the lady her peanut butter."

"Thank you." Mason smiled like a shark on chum patrol.

"You didn't have to stick your nose in." Charlie sank her hands on her hips, irritated that he had gotten results from the wormy waiter where she'd failed.

"You looked like you needed the help."

"It must be nice," she said sarcastically, "having people fall all over themselves to do your bidding."

"Why are you mad at me? I got the peanut butter you wanted."

"I should have been able to get my own peanut butter off that lippy waiter."

"You're being unreasonable."

"Am I?"

"This is Beverly Hills."

"Meaning?"

"Different things work in different worlds."

"What are you talking about?"

"If I'd waltzed into Kelly's bar and ordered caviar what do you think would have happened?"

"Good point," she conceded.

The waiter reappeared, rushing over with a fat dollop of peanut butter centered on a leaf of butter lettuce and riding atop a fine bone china plate.

"Is Madam pleased?" he asked her, but his eyes were on Mason.

"Madam is very pleased," Mason assured him. "You will be be commended to your supervisor."

The waiter nodded and hurried off.

"You're really great at this greasing-the-palm stuff, aren't you?"

"Makes the world go round, babe."

"Babe? Oh, horrors. Better watch out, you're slipping back into Skeet vernacular," she said.

"Thanks. I appreciate the warning." He flashed her an intriguing expression she couldn't interpret, but it made him look kinda sexy. Charlee downed the rest of her champagne in a desperate hope it would make him look less attractive.

Bad move.

He only looked cuter through the sweet sheen of high-dollar bubbly. When a waiter offered her another glass of champagne, she took it, even though her head was already helium-balloon floaty.

She could quaff a quart of rotgut whiskey just fine but champagne shot straight to her head. The more expensive the brand, the faster she succumbed.

According to Maybelline, Charlee's mother had been the same way and Bubbles adored bubbly so much she had even named herself after it. Judging from the way her head was reeling, the effervescent stuff must have set Twilight Studios back a pretty penny.

By the time the food was gone and Blade Bradford still hadn't appeared and the grumbling reporters began to clear out, Charlee was seriously regretting that second glass of champagne.

Pam walked over. "I'm so sorry. It seems Blade can't make the reception."

"Probably three sheets to the wind in some hooker's bed," mumbled the photographer trailing after Pam.

"But we're going to take a publicity photo anyway. I'll

just stand in for Mr. Bradford." Forcing a smile, Pam sandwiched herself between Charlee and Mason and draped
an arm over their shoulders for the photographer. Charlee
smiled dopily for the camera and held up two fingers for
bunny ears over Pam's head.

"What's going to happen," Charlee whispered to
Mason after Pam had moved away to ply her public relations skills with the reporters, "when they figure out we're
not Skeet and Violet?"

"We'll deal with that problem when it arises."

"Come, come, come." Pam was back, grinning and
snapping her fingers. "Now for the moment you've been
waiting for. Let's go see your honeymoon suite."

She escorted them through the lobby and toward the
elevators. Charlee wobbled precariously on Violet's four-
inch stilettos and at first she was grateful when Mason put
a steadying hand to her elbow.

But his touch, combined with the dizzying effects of the
champagne, made her feel all warm and fuzzy and receptive. And she hated soft, squooshy emotions like those.

Soft, squooshy, girlie emotions only got you into trouble.
*Take a note. Remember that.*

"Here we are." Pam slid a card key through the electronic eye sensor and pushed open the door.

Charlee had been in luxury suites many times when
she'd worked as a hotel maid, but that was in Vegas where
everything was ornate, flashy, and gaudily overdone. This
room was pure elegance.

From the cherrywood canopied bed to the eggshell
satin duvet to the silver champagne bucket with a bottle of
iced Dom Perignon nestled on an antique teacart the place
whispered money, money, money.

On the classy bureau sat a gigantic fruit basket. Beside

the basket rested an artfully arranged bouquet of colorful spring flowers and a half-dozen flickering candles giving off the scent of honeysuckle.

"Wooo, fancy-schmancy," Charlee said.

"I'll just leave you two alone to enjoy your prize. If you need anything, here's my beeper number and your Oscar tickets." Pam handed Mason an envelope.

"Thank you." He stuffed the envelope in the back pocket of his shorts.

"The reporters will be back on Sunday afternoon to interview you before the Academy Awards. And tomorrow I'll take you shopping on Rodeo Drive for your Oscar ceremony clothes. All courtesy of Twilight Studios."

"No kidding," Charlee murmured. "New clothes too. What a kick."

Guilt needled her. This should be Violet Hammersmitz's big adventure, not hers, but in spite of herself she was enjoying this Cinderella gig.

"Have fun," Pam said, looking distracted, and left the room.

Once the door snapped closed behind her, Mason and Charlee turned to stare at each other.

"Wow, Gentry"—Charlee spun around the room, her head swirling—"do you live like this all the time?"

"What do you think of me? I don't live in a hotel. I have a house, I go to work, I volunteer my time to charities. I have a normal life."

"Yeah, but do you eat caviar and sleep on four-hundred-thread-count sheets and have people waiting on you hand and foot every day?"

"It's not that big of a deal."

"Oh, maybe not to you, but to me this whole thing seems surreal."

"It is surreal. The fact that you and I are stuck here pretending to be husband and wife has little basis in reality."

"Hmm, I don't know about that. I'm real and you're real and if I pinched you hard on the fanny I bet you would holler."

"I think it's time I made a few phone calls," he said, ignoring her "pinching him on the fanny" remark and heading straight for the white and gold phone centered on the Queen Anne writing desk.

Giggling, Charlee fell backward onto the satin duvet and immediately slid whiz-bang onto the floor. She sprawled on her spine, her neck resting awkwardly against the footboard.

"There's a trick to lying down on satin," Mason said without even looking up from punching his calling card number into the phone.

"So I gather." Charlee stared up at the ceiling and willed her head to stop whirling.

From this angle, she had a tantalizing view of the length of Mason's leg.

Man-o-man-o-man.

Her eyes tracked a path from his thigh to his knee and down to his muscled calf. An irresistible urge took hold of her. She wanted to scoot across the carpet and sink her teeth into the fleshy part of that calf to see if it tasted as juicy as it looked.

She licked her lips.

A prickliness crawled across the nape of her neck, light and ticklish. She reached a hand around to push her hair away.

The creepy-crawly sensation transferred from her neck to the back of her hand. She pulled her hand down and stared in horror at the black widow spider inching across her skin.

She literally froze.

Her throat constricted. Her tongue turned to cement. Her brain locked.

Help!

The old spider-bite wound in her backside throbbed. Her hand blanched pale as bleached linen, highlighting the black spider's dark journey across her wrist.

She couldn't breathe. She couldn't scream. She couldn't move. She was trapped in a terrifying nightmare.

Help! Help!

Mason was staring out the window, the telephone receiver cradled against his cheek. She had to get him to notice her before the deadly spider sank her vicious venom into her bloodstream.

*Look at me, dammit!* she mentally willed.

No such luck.

Meanwhile Miss Arachnid strolled leisurely toward her elbow.

Help! Help! Help!

Charlee flashed back to that night in the Wisconsin woods. She recalled the painful sting as the black widow bit into her tender behind. She remembered, in vivid detail, the agonizing therapy at the hospital and the skin grafts that followed.

She could not, she would not go through that terrible ordeal again.

Act. Move. Do something.

Mason!

Galvanized by the same fear that a second before had frozen her, Charlee threw back her head and let loose with a bloodcurdling shriek.

Mason came up out of the chair as if he had been zapped in the butt with a blowtorch. He jumped to his feet, flinging the telephone away from him and jerking his head around to find Charlee lying on the floor, the hem of her miniskirt hiked up to her panties, a terror-stricken expression on her face.

"What is it? What's happened?" He sprang to her side, his blood pumping through his veins like a fire hose in a five-alarm blaze.

"Aaa-aaa-aaa."

"Charlee, speak to me." Good God, what was wrong?

She stared him in the eyes, then shifted her gaze to the small black spider crawling up her shoulder.

"The spider? You're scared of the spider?"

Vigorously, she nodded. Relief washed through him. Thank God. He couldn't imagine what had caused her to scream like Marie Antoinette at the guillotine.

So the tough P.I. from Vegas was afraid of spiders. He tried not to smile at her fear as he leaned over to scoop the spider into his palm.

"Noooooo," she wailed.

He blinked at her. "What?"

"It's a black widow!"

"No, it's not. See."

He opened his palm and she reacted as if he held a live hand grenade, covering her head with her arms in the fatalistic manner of a soldier in a fox hole.

"Charlee," he coaxed. "It's okay to look."

Tentatively she lowered her arms and peeked over the side of his palm.

"See, sweetheart," he spoke softly. "No red hourglass."

"Really?" Her eyes were wide and he spotted a tear glistening on her cheek.

He had never seen her like this, cowering defenselessly. Her unexpected weakness tugged at something inside him. He got up, walked to the window, opened it, and deposited the spider on the outside ledge.

When he looked up and glanced over the parking lot, he winced to see the Chevy Malibu parked across from the hotel. At some point he would have to deal with that threat.

But for now, Charlee needed comforting.

After closing the window, he came back, reached down, and tugged her gently up off the floor.

She cringed in his arms, trembling like a rabbit trapped in a coyote's lair. "I was so scared, Mason."

When she whispered his name, he realized it was the first time she had called him by his given name rather than Gentry.

What did it mean? More importantly, what did he wish that it meant? That she was drawing closer to him? Letting down her guard? Starting to trust him?

"I thought for sure it was a black widow. I admit I'm jumpy when it comes to spiders. I've been bitten and I know how bad it hurts."

He rested his chin against the top of her head, rubbed his hands up and down her arms. "Shhh, shhh. It's all right."

The sound of the phone off the hook buzzed its obnoxious message, but Mason ignored it. He held her close, comforting her, easing her fears.

The sweet smell of her invaded his nostrils and he marveled at his body's immediate response to their close contact. What was it about her that invariably brought out the horned, pitchfork-carrying devil in him?

If he kissed her, she would taste of expensive champagne, peanut butter, and ripe, delectable sin.

He wanted her.

Badly.

And it was all he could do to keep from carrying her to the bed and making love to her.

Before Charlee, he'd always been attracted to cool, detached petite blondes with an elegant style and impeccable breeding. But somehow, he found himself completely enchanted by this long-legged, black-haired dynamo with a tart tongue that covered up her tender heart.

She was the total opposite of everything he'd ever thought he wanted. She was bold when he'd thought he wanted demure. She was tall and muscular when he thought he wanted dainty and soft. She was sassy when he thought he wanted accommodating.

Charlee challenged him in ways he had never dreamed possible. She called to the wildness he'd buried along with Kip. She resurrected his lost sense of adventure and she had him questioning his blind insistence on following the straight and narrow path his parents had laid out for him.

For that gift he would be forever grateful.

He found her exciting and dramatic and totally captivating. He adored that she knew unequivocally who she was and what she wanted out of life. He admired the way she courageously stood up for what she believed in.

Most of all, he loved the fact that together they were an electric combination of will, drive, and determination. With her, he felt like more of a man.

And there was absolutely no way she would ever fit in with his world.

He struggled hard to imagine her entertaining his high-society friends or sipping tea with corporate wives, dishing idle chitchat or chairing charity auctions, and failed miserably.

He tried to envision her in designer outfits and diamonds instead of her neon blue cowboy boots and a battered straw Stetson. No. He couldn't see it. Not that she couldn't wear finery and jewels, those things just did not suit her.

In the soft cushion of his privileged world, safely cocooned from the realities of the rest of humanity, Charlee would either wilt like a hothouse flower or grow to hate herself for the compromises that life with him would force her to make.

Mason would rather die than risk ruining her zest for life.

No matter how much he wanted to have sex with her, to taste those delicious lips, to run his hands all over her naked body, to hear her whisper his name in the throes of ecstasy, he would not give in to his urges.

Charlee deserved far better than being a sexual conquest. She deserved someone who could love her for who she was and not expect her to compromise to meet some predetermined standard. She deserved the freedom to be herself.

And he simply could not offer her those things.

Reaching down deep inside him, he summoned the strength to ignore his driving biology. He could control himself. He would.

Tenderly, he brushed his lips across her forehead and then stepped back.

"I better finish making those phone calls," he said and turned away without meeting her gaze because he knew one look into those compelling green eyes and he was a goner.

# Chapter 14

Still light-headed from champagne, the adrenaline rush of spider freak-out, and the disturbing effects of being held in Mason's arms, Charlee had to take several long, slow, deep breaths before her pulse rate decelerated and her heart plunked back down into its regular place in her chest.

Easy. Steady. Calm.

*Breathe deep from your diaphragm. Let it out through your mouth.*

Her shoulders relaxed and she could hardly feel the lingering imprint of Mason's fingers on her skin.

Okay, good. Shake it off. Things were getting back to normal.

While Mason went to complete his telephone calls, Charlee inched over to the window and gazed out to study the black spider who was already busily spinning a web.

She admired the creature's capacity to adapt to her sudden change in environment and go about business as usual even though she had been rudely displaced. Bloom where you're planted.

Maybelline's insistence that they live in a travel trailer

had taught Charlee the importance of that lesson. If you wanted to last in this world you had to be ready, willing, and able to square your shoulders, pull yourself up by your bootstraps, and relocate whenever circumstances changed.

Her lifelong motto: Dust yourself off. Pick yourself up. Move on.

But she was tired of moving on. Tired of fighting her desire. Tired of being good. She was afraid of losing control of her feelings, not of sleeping with him. Actually, sex sounded really fabulous. It had been such a long time for her. Could she throw herself into physical pleasure while keeping her emotions at bay? Was she willing to roll the dice, take the chance for a night of exquisite pleasure?

Oh, yes, yes, yes.

*You can do it, Charlee. You can keep your emotions out of the fray. Go for it. Have wild circus sex and then discard him like those rich, handsome men have always discarded you.*

The idea excited her so much that she turned and raced into the adjoining bathroom with the intention of splashing her face with cold water to cool her ardor. She was startled to find a Jacuzzi tub big enough to hold an entire wedding party.

Plush, white matching his and her bathrobes were laid out on the mauve marble steps. More scented candles burned in gold and silver candle holders, scenting the air with Jasmine perfume. Another basket sat on the elaborate dressing table. This one was filled with toiletries, toothbrushes, toothpaste, and...*ulp*...were those Trojans?

A luxurious heat swept through her body along with the dreaminess of the champagne lingering in her bloodstream and she had an almost irresistible urge to strip off her clothes, settle right into that tub, and call for Mason to come join her.

Her yen for sin scared the bejesus out of her and Charlee back-pedaled from the bathroom.

Fast.

Mason was hanging up the phone. A frown creased his brow. "I couldn't get hold of anyone."

"What's up?" she asked nonchalantly, doing her damnedest to quell the erotic thoughts circulating through her brain with absolutely no success.

"According to the housekeeper my parents went to Paris for the weekend."

"What about your brother?"

"Hunter wasn't home and when I called his cell phone I got his voice mail. I left the number here. I'm hoping he'll check his messages and call back soon."

Her treacherous body throbbed, agreeing completely with the pleasure center of her brain.

Yeah, yeah, go for it.

Standing so close to him in this stylish suite, hearing him speak in that forceful businessman tone, smelling the tangy aroma of his cologne made Charlee's knees loosen.

She was terrified her lips might join her knees in rubberdom and she would say something truly frightening, like, "Let's get it on, you long-legged, brown-eyed, handsome, matinee-idol-smiling, beard-stubble-sporting stud you."

Oh, she was weak and stupid.

And she was more turned on than she'd ever been in her entire life.

High-caliber folly, rolling the dice and taking a chance that she could seduce him and then just walk away with her heart in check.

Charlee realized then she was breathing heavier than a greyhound after a race.

"You're panting," he said.

"No, no, I'm not," she denied.

"Still upset over the spider?"

"I already forgot about that."

"Charlee, you sound like you just ran up six flights of stairs. If you're feeling faint or something let me know. The last thing I want is for you to pass out and crack your head on the floor."

"Well, that's a sexy thought. *Not.*"

"Sexy?" He gave her an odd look.

Oh, crap! Why had she said that? She didn't want him knowing she was thinking sexy thoughts. Not when she was still so conflicted about said sexy thoughts.

"Did I say sexy? Not sexy. I didn't mean sexy," she babbled.

"How much champagne did you have?" Mason narrowed his eyes.

She held up two fingers. He glanced at his watch. "Two glasses in under forty-five minutes. You're drunk."

"I'm not drunk," she insisted, leaning in closer to get a better whiff of his Mason smell. "Just feeling a little..."

"Amorous?" he suggested with a raised eyebrow when she ran a finger over his collar.

"I was going to say horny, but yeah, okay, amorous will do."

"You're letting this honeymoon stuff go to your head, sweetheart," he said gently. "And although I find you sexy as hell, we both know this is neither the time nor the place to lose control."

"We're in the honeymoon suite of the Beverly Hills Grand Piazza. We have no idea where to start searching for our grandparents. And besides we can't go anywhere because the media and a Twilight Studios assistant are virtually camped outside our door, not to mention those two goons in the Malibu across the street."

She paused and studied his face. Stone wall. Nada. Zip. He was giving her nothing to go on. She took a deep breath and went on.

"We don't have any money or a car and we have no idea when your brother will call. Name a better time and place."

"I can't take advantage of you." He disentangled her arms from around his neck and stepped away. "I won't. You've had too much to drink."

"Such a gentleman." She clicked her tongue.

"You wouldn't think I was such a gentleman if you knew the thoughts spinning through my head, lady," he growled. "Some of them are downright illegal."

"Oooh. I like the sound of that."

"I can't do this," he repeated, although the distinct bulge in his pants argued otherwise.

"Open that bottle of champagne and catch up with me." She waved a hand at the bucket of Dom Perignon and lost her balance. "Oops."

He reached out and grabbed her before she fell and she smiled up at him.

"You did that on purpose," he accused.

"Who? Me?" She blinked innocently.

"Charlee," he said. "Please don't give me the full court press. I'm only human."

The look in his eyes sent her temperature blasting into the danger zone. Did she dare force the issue? Did she dare seduce him?

Was she brave enough to face her fears right here, right

now? Stab the vampire of her past rotten romantic experiences squarely in the heart and live to tell the tale?

Was she really as tough as she pretended or deep down inside, when push came to shove, was she all talk?

She leaned in close and kissed him, but because she was tipsy and wearing Violet's ridiculous stiletto ankle straps, her lips bounced off his mouth and skidded headlong into a dimple.

God, she was woefully inept at this sultry seductress stuff.

Luckily, Mason turned his cheek, removing the gouge of his dimple and presenting her with a second opportunity to capture his mouth.

He kissed her back, grabbing her shoulders in his hands and holding her steady on her shoes.

Eagerly, she ironed her body against his, reveling in the hard line of his muscles and bones.

Okay, this wasn't so scary. No big deal. Just hormones, right? Hormones and moving body parts and making each other feel good.

But a few minutes later, Mason pulled away, his breathing hot and spiky, a "what just happened" expression on his face. His hair was a sexy, disheveled mess, his lips damp with her moisture.

"That's enough, Charlee. This can't go any further."

*Seeze who?* She blinked at him.

"I can't. I won't do this."

"Okay." She shrugged and stepped away from him. "Suit yourself."

Then she slowly started undoing the buttons on her blouse as she turned and headed for the bathroom.

"What are you doing?" He sounded panicky.

"Taking matters in hand. If you catch my drift," she

called to him over her shoulder and dropped Violet's black blouse onto the tiled floor.

With a flick of her thumb, she unsnapped her bra and tossed it beside the blouse.

She shot a quick glance toward the mirror. In the reflection she could see into the bedroom. She could also see that Mason was craning his neck, getting a good view of her backside.

She bent at the waist to turn on the Jacuzzi and then wriggled her hips as she inched the skirt down over her thighs. She heard him inhale sharply and then cough as if he'd swallowed his tongue.

Pretending that she wasn't watching him watching her, she used her hair as a curtain to shield her face from him and sat down on the edge of the marble tub wearing nothing but thong panties and the scarlet high heels.

Her heart thumped against her chest gone tight with mounting anticipation. The whirlpool gurgled and churned and a fine mist rose to enshroud her.

With trembling fingers, she reached down to unbuckle the ankle straps. She heard footsteps and her pulse accelerated.

She thought she heard heavy breathing as well but she couldn't be certain over the noise of the hot tub.

Cocking her head to one side until a sheaf of hair slanted forward, she peeped cautiously through the opening and peered out at him with a coy look.

Mason stood in the bathroom doorway. His face had reddened and his chest rose and fell with hard, jerky movements.

Most definitely heavy breathing.

And he wasn't the only one.

The way his gaze caressed her skin made her tingle

with excitement. To think that she was responsible for that wild, lusty gleam in his eyes sent goose bumps bivouacking along her forearms.

She kicked off the stilettos. Then, with her head down and blood racing, shimmied out of her panties.

He made a noise of pure masculine arousal.

Charlee slid over the edge of the tub and into the hot, effervescent water. She leaned back against the headrest and closed her eyes tight but she was too tense to relax, too darned aware of Mason's blatant gaze roving over her body.

"That's not such a good idea," he said hoarsely.

"What's not?"

"Getting into the hot tub when you've been drinking." He clicked his tongue.

"I didn't drink that much."

"You drank enough to make you strip naked in front of me."

"If you hadn't been peeking 'round the corner you wouldn't have seen me naked."

She kept her eyes tightly closed. One look at him would send her scrambling pell-mell for that monogrammed bathrobe.

"You wanted me to see you naked. Otherwise you would have shut the door behind you."

"So how does that make you feel?"

"Angry."

"Angry?" She opened one eye at the testy note in his voice.

"Angry for not being able to resist you."

*Oh my, oh my, oh my.*

His fist grabbed for the front of his shirt and he pulled hard, sending buttons pinging off the tile floor. Charlee gasped and sat up straight, her eyes rounding in surprise at the feral, untamed look on his face.

Gone was the polished, controlled businessman. In his place stood a chest-thumping caveman, stripped naked of everything except the bare essentials.

Man. Woman. Biology.

Her pulse hammered.

He heaved his shirt flying and then his fingers went to his zipper.

She sucked in her breath as she watched the zipper slide down.

In one smooth move, he dropped his pants and a soft sound of pleasure popped from her lips. Ah, a silk boxer man. It figured.

His gaze was hot on her face and she felt her skin flush. She knew he was watching her breasts bob jauntily atop the water.

And when the silk boxers followed the pants and she got her first good, up close and personal view of him, Charlee just about choked.

Here stood a broad-shouldered, blue-blooded Texas businessman with chest hairs the color of dark Belgian chocolate and a very serious gleam in his eyes.

The sight of him left her nearly speechless.

"W-w-well," she stammered before getting hold of herself. "Are you going to strut like a proud turkey all day or shake your tail feathers and get in here with me?"

"Just a minute."

In two long-legged strides, he marched over to the dressing table, yanked the cellophane wrapper off the gift basket, plucked a condom from the plethora of products, tore the packet open, and rolled the Day-Glo green rubber onto his burgeoning erection.

"Now that's a picture."

"You haven't seen anything yet," he promised and strutted back over to the tub.

"Do those things work in water?" She was on the pill and she would bet anything he didn't have a sexually transmittable disease but still, no sense taking unnecessary chances.

"Don't know. Never used one in the Jacuzzi."

"Me either."

"So we're hot tub virgins together."

She liked the sound of that.

Mason slid down in the bubbling liquid and he looked across the tub at her, his breathing labored and his gaze turbulent.

The water churned and pulsated around them. She'd never been naked in a hot tub with a man before and that erotic reality along with the powerful water jets massaging and caressing sensitive areas of her body stoked her arousal.

"Come here," Mason said in a tone so husky it scraped her ears like sandpaper. He stared her right in the eyes and crooked a finger.

And just like that, every bit of courage she possessed drained from her body.

She shook her head.

"Don't make me come over there," he said, his voice a silky threat.

Her body trembled as if her temperature were a hundred and ten.

"You started this, now I'm finishing it." He reached under the water, found her foot, and trolled her toward him. Her head went under briefly and she came up sputtering, her hair fanning out around her. He hauled her closer to him until she floated above his knees.

"Is drowning me all part of your master plan?"

"I warned you."

She brushed the water from her eyelashes and looked at him. He rewarded her with his dimpled grin and she just about came undone.

He had one hand still clamped tight around her ankle and his other hand was... *oh, my.*

Charlee's eyes rolled back in her head at the sheer pleasure of what he was doing.

His fingertips lightly stroked her bottom in a tormenting technique that left her breathless, bewildered, and craving more.

"What's this?" he asked, his fingers finding the scar from her long-ago spider bite.

"Origins of my black widow terror."

He made a sympathetic noise and his touch lightened. He inched her closer toward him, slowly separating her legs with his knees while his eyes never left her face. He tilted his head and lightly ran his tongue across her parted lips. Licking first her top lip and then her bottom. He tasted salty yet sweet.

Letting go of her ankle, he reached up his hand to cradle her cheek as he kissed her and then she giggled.

"What's so funny?" he growled.

"You. Me. Everything."

"I'm glad I amuse you."

"Amuse me some more," she murmured.

She was in his lap at this point, her legs splayed on either side of his waist, her bottom bobbing against him.

"I love your breasts," he broke the kiss to murmur.

He scooted her bottom onto his knees and lowered his head to gently bite one of the stiff, pink nipples jutting hungrily forward.

"Oooooh," she exclaimed.

"They're beautiful," he pronounced, then went for the other nipple.

"Just like a peach."

"That's right."

His mouth was so hot against her tender flesh a fiery sizzle of electricity shot straight through her tense body. She ached for him. If he could cause this explosion inside her just by nibbling her breasts, she thrilled to think what else he could do.

Clutching his shoulders, she arched against him, pressing her breasts right into his face.

His tongue flicked across her nipples, initially slow, then gradually speeding up, building and building and building the pressure inside her.

Blindly, she reached down into the water, past their thighs, and found what she was looking for. The moment she cupped him in her palm, Mason gasped in shocked surprise.

"Your touch..." he rasped, "it's incredible."

She was smoldering, burning, simmering with heat and tension and desire.

"I want it now," she whispered. "I want you inside me. I want it hard and I want it hot and I want it fast."

"Yes, ma'am," he croaked. "Anything you want."

Mason spanned her waist with his hands and lifted her up in the water and then tried to settle her down on his erection, but she slicked off of him and he ended up crashing into her.

"Ouch."

"I'm sorry. Didn't mean to do that."

"'Sokay. Let's try again."

He carefully placed her over the throbbing head of him

and tried to ease her over his shaft. They made contact—he was butted up tight against her opening—but she couldn't slide down.

She was stuck.

*See what happens when you go years without having sex? Use it or lose it.*

"Now I know how a shish kabob feels," Charlee grumbled.

"Shh, don't make me laugh. Let me just wiggle around here for a better angle." He shifted his backside against the bottom of the hot tub.

He wriggled. She jiggled.

Nothing happened.

"You're too big."

"I have to say, no one's ever complained about that before."

"First time for everything."

"It's not my size," he argued. "It's the water. It swells the tissues and washes away moisture making it hard for things...to...er...fit."

"They make it look so easy in the movies."

"That's because it's simulated sex, not the real deal. Give me a minute to figure this out."

He tried a few maneuvers. Nothing.

"Maybe it's the condom," he said.

"This isn't working. Let's forget the whole thing." She tried to scramble out of his arms, but he held her locked in to place.

In a rush of panic, she remembered why all this scared her. Even their silly fumbling, especially their silly fumbling, escalated the intimacy between them. They were sharing and caring and laughing together and it was all too much to handle.

Charlee had thought that by getting naked with him,

having sex and enjoying it, that she could sate her biological needs without involving her heart.

She was wrong.

And now she was embarrassed. She ducked her head.

Mason crooked a forefinger under her chin and tugged her face upward, forcing her to look him in the eyes. He reached up and pushed back a strand of damp hair plastered against her cheek.

"Talk to me."

"What?"

"Something's going on in that sharp little brain of yours. Tell me what you're thinking."

"I'm not thinking about anything."

"Liar."

"Okay, I was thinking I suck at this."

"You don't."

"I do. I tried to seduce you and look." She spread her hands. "I can't even carry through."

"Sweetheart, it's not your seduction technique at fault here. It's the hot tub. We could move. Try it again on the bed."

"I feel like an idiot."

"You're not an idiot." He leaned in and kissed the nape of her neck, softly feathering his fingertips over her skin.

"Stop trying to make me feel better."

"Why? You like being miserable?"

"No," she said and smiled.

"There you go. That's my girl."

Then without any further discussion, Mason got out of the hot tub, scooped her into his arms, and carried her to bed.

# Chapter 15

What was he doing? Their failure to make a connection in the Jacuzzi had given him an out. They hadn't gone too far yet. He hadn't crossed the line.

Okay, he'd pulverized the line to dust, but theoretically, they hadn't joined bodies so the line, however invisible, still remained uncrossed.

But Charlee was in his arms, feeling wet and wonderful and smelling like heaven. He wanted her. And she'd wanted him. Sex between two consenting adults.

*Yeah, but you haven't broken up with Daphne yet.*

A mere technicality, the pitchfork-toting devil on his shoulder assured him.

Did Charlee really want to make love to him or was it simply the champagne, the excitement of their road adventures, and the thrill of winning the *Newlywed Game* motivating her? Mason didn't want her doing anything she would regret later.

She wrapped her arms around his neck and leaned her head against his shoulder, her long hair slapping wetly against his thigh as he moved. Strong feelings punted his gut. She looked so defenseless, so trusting.

Until that moment with the spider, until she said she was bad in bed, he had believed her completely invincible. Until now, the way she handled herself told him she was a woman who didn't need anyone.

Forget rough, tough, street-talking Charlee. This woman cradled against his chest was quiet and amiable and susceptible.

For the first time, she had really needed him and it made him feel big and strong and protective.

Then, when he laid her carefully on the bed, and she looked up at him with those exotic green eyes glazed with desire, he just about came unraveled. She pulled his head down to hers and kissed him tentatively, exploring the change.

He kissed her back, holding nothing in reserve. He gave her every ounce of the passion that had been building inside him from the moment they'd met.

She pressed herself against him, moaning softly, getting aroused all over again.

God, he wanted her so badly he could barely breathe. He hadn't been this shaken up about sex since that first time with Blair Sydney in the back of the Bentley.

*Take it easy. No hurry. You've got all night.*

He was dying to take her hard and fast and hot like she'd told him she wanted, but he would not. This felt too special. Too good to rush.

No matter how much the ache in his groin was killing him, he was bound and determined to make this a night neither one of them would ever forget. He owed it to them both.

He pulled back and gazed at her, his eyes tracing the lines of her body. Gorgeous. Simply gorgeous. Not small and petite and delicate but a sturdy woman, strong and capable and substantial.

She caught his eye and slowly ran a hand down her breasts over the flat of her belly to the soft curve of her inner thigh.

"Mason," she whispered his name. "I want you here."

Ah, hell.

He leaped onto the bed beside her and promptly slid off the slick satin and crashed onto the floor.

"Are you okay?" She leaned over the edge of the bed and peered down at him, mirth mingled with hot, frantic desire in her eyes.

"Fine," he mumbled.

"You're right, rich boy, there is an art to lying on satin. Unfortunately you don't seem to know the trick any better than I."

"Being around you makes me forget every damned trick I ever learned." He got to his feet and came back to bed.

"Oh, ho." She grinned when he crawled up beside her on the damp duvet.

"When I'm around you, Charlee, I can't think at all. You mess with my head, woman."

"In a good way or a bad way?"

"I'll let you figure that one out." He straddled her body with his and pushed her back against the covers.

For the first time in his life, Mason allowed his senses to run completely ungoverned, no holding back. He thrust his fingers through her hair, his skin exalting in the unfamiliar feel of her.

He plundered her mouth and air rushed from her lungs in a red-hot blast. He felt her breath against his lips, tasted her sumptuous flavor.

He didn't think about the consequences. He didn't think about his grandfather or the rest of his family or Daphne. He didn't think about the men in the Malibu. He didn't think about anything at all. He merely responded with every red-blooded masculine instinct inside him at the wonderfully erotic stimulus of kissing Charlee.

She wrapped her arms around his neck, spread her legs wide, and drew his body down on top of hers.

He sank into her, sweet and deep.

And then stopped, suddenly immobilized by the knowledge he wasn't going to last five seconds. Mason closed his eyes tight, gritted his teeth, and struggled for control.

*Think baseball scores. Think accounts receivable, think about anything except how good it feels to be inside her.*

Charlee arched her pelvis against his. "Please," she begged, "please."

She kissed him, hard and fierce, letting him know just how much she wanted him. She wrapped her legs tight around his waist and pulled him in deeper.

He moved against her, the sound of their panting breaths filling his ears, the taste of her exploding in his mouth, the smell of her charming his nostrils with her fragrant womanly scent. He tried to savor the moment, to take it slow and to make it last despite Charlee's whimpered urgings.

But she was so hot and tight and sexy he knew he simply could not hold out for long.

*There's always round two.*

She raked her fingernails over his back, wild to the core, and cried his name with escalating insistence.

Faster he thrust. Harder. His body ached and throbbed and quivered for release.

She met his rhythm, stroke for stroke. She bucked and writhed and wriggled in just the right way. Her breathing spread a thready heat across his shoulders, her muscles clenching him tighter and tighter still.

Then he made the mistake of opening his eyes.

Charlee's eyes were open too and their gazes met in a moment of pure surprised wonder. Her pupils widened and he stared deep inside her.

He felt as if he were slipping into an ageless abyss, dark and endless and wonderful. They made a connection far deeper than bodies joining.

His heart chugged sluggishly in his chest. All sense of time disappeared. Seconds could have passed or centuries. It was just him and Charlee there together.

Joined. One.

Something changed. He saw the shift in her eyes just before she closed them.

"Don't stop," she cried out and that's when he realized in the marvel of the moment, he'd stopped moving. "Please, don't stop."

She pounded lightly on his shoulders with her fists, urging him back into the tempo. "More," she whimpered. "More." She planted her feet on his buttocks and pulled him down to meet her thrusting pelvis.

The magical mist evaporated and they were back to raw primal sex.

He thrust and thrust and thrust. Giving it to her the way she wanted it. Hard and fast and hungry.

Not long now. He couldn't hold out much longer.

But, he suspected, neither could she. They hung on the verge of climax together, both seeking that sweet physical release.

Then she screamed his name low in her throat and her body went rigid. Her muscles gripped him and he knew she was coming.

Just as he was coming.

He felt the phenomenal energy rise up in both of them

as they tumbled over the edge together and pulsation after pulsation clenched their bodies. Mason shuddered as a blinding, red-hot heat blasted up him in a splendid splurge.

Gasping, they clung to each other as the last echoes of glorious ripples subsided. As they drifted down from the lofty heights of simultaneous orgasm, a rare headiness seeped through his spent limbs.

He rolled to one side, drawing Charlee into his arms as he went. She rested her head against his shoulder, her warm breath tickling his chest hairs damp with their combined sweat.

Like survivors of a siege they clung to each other, breathing in synchronized rhythm, happy to be alive and together. He didn't want to let her go. Ever.

He'd never felt this way with Daphne. Nor any of the other women he'd known. He'd never experienced such crazy, out-of-control feelings. Why was Charlee different? What was it about her that made him feel differently?

Why, until now, had his past love relationships been more of a convenience than anything else? He had considered marrying Daphne because she was everything he had thought he'd wanted. Polished, accomplished, with all the right connections and credentials. Blue-blooded and cultured and sophisticated.

And the sex had been lousy.

Nothing like this knock-your-socks-off romp.

*That's it, Gentry. It's the sex. That's why it feels different with Charlee.* Apparently, stupendous sex mucked up a man's thinking.

Charlee awoke sometime later and lay awestruck in Mason's arms. She'd never experienced anything like what they had just shared. She'd had good sex before, sure, but nothing like this mind-blowing, toe-curling, explosive crescendo.

Mason's breathing lulled her and she tried her best to stay wrapped in the warm romantic afterglow of post coital bliss for as long as she could, but eventually, reality reared its ugly head.

She had to go to the bathroom.

Regretfully, she slipped from his arms and out of bed. Once her feet hit the floor, she turned to gaze over her shoulder at him.

He was already asleep. Poor dear. Plumb tuckered out. After a performance like that, he deserved to sleep uninterrupted for a week.

This had been a first for her. Mindless, uncontrolled sex merely for the sake of mindless, uncontrolled sex. She felt cleansed, purified. Reborn.

Charlee grinned. This having sex for sex's sake wasn't half bad. She liked using a man to sate her physical desires while keeping her heart cleanly out of the fray. That was the ticket. Have sex with your eyes open and your mind locked down tight.

It had worked. She didn't feel that same agonizing tug of anxiety she had experienced after giving Gregory her virginity. No nagging questions like: why doesn't he take me out in public or introduce me to his parents? With her ex-lover she had waited for the other boot to drop, repeatedly wondering when he would realize she wasn't good enough for him.

Nothing to worry about. No commitment to fret over. Their mating had been about sex and putting her fears behind her and letting go of her unrealistic expectations about love and romance and intimacy.

Congratulating herself, she padded into the bathroom

and then caught sight of her reflection in the mirror from the flicker of candlelight.

She stepped closer for a better look. Her eyes sparked, her skin radiated with a satisfied sheen, her hair was a sexy, mussed mess.

*Casual sex looks good on you.*

But bedroom escapades aside, together they mixed like...*well*...caviar and peanut butter. She'd learned the hard way—thank you very much for that painful lesson, Gregory—the class caste system was alive and well in the good old USA. Hadn't Maybelline always sworn this was gospel? Mason came from the haves and she came from the have-nots and never the twain shall meet.

Outside of hot sex that is.

And even if he couldn't see that, Charlee most certainly could.

She finished up in the bathroom, blew out the candles, and then tiptoed back to bed. Mason lay on his side facing toward her, his features relaxed in quiet repose. He looked so darned handsome she caught her breath and held it. She studied him a moment. Thick lashes shadowed his cheekbones and strands of short black hair spiked straight up. His tanned skin contrasted sharply with the white cotton sheets and caused her pulse to jump crazily. God, but he was the most gorgeous thing she'd ever had in her bed.

She felt like a proud huntress who'd brought home the juiciest cut of beef. She felt like Aphrodite churned from the sea. She felt like Venus de Milo with arms.

She'd claimed her sexuality and liberated her heart. Triumphant, Charlee crawled up into the bed beside him, spooned her fanny against him, and for the sweet short moment before she fell asleep convinced herself that everything was going to be just fine.

A few minutes later his fingers reached out and he gently caressed her cheek. The fine hairs on the nape of her neck lifted and her body heated as quick as microwaved leftovers. She threw in the towel. After all, they'd already made love once. At this point, how much more damage could another round do?

A repeated pounding on the door tugged Mason from an exquisite dream about Charlee. He yawned, stretched, rolled over, and collided with a warm, soft body.

Blinking, he rubbed his eyes and then took another look.

Charlee. Snoring softly and totally oblivious to the racket outside their room.

That was no dream. The movie playing over and over in his slumbering brain was the real deal.

They'd made love.

Not once.

Not twice.

But three incredible times.

The insistent pounding continued. Probably an overly ambitious member of the Grand Piazza's housekeeping staff, he decided and slid out on the other side of the bed. If Charlee could sleep through that racket, more power to her.

Yawning again, he retrieved a plush terry-cloth robe from the bathroom, tied the sash around his waist, and ran his fingers through his hair to tidy it before he went to open the door.

It took a good two seconds to register that his fiancée-to-be was standing on the other side looking rather disgruntled. Quickly, he moved to block her view of the bedroom and Charlee.

"Skeet Hammersmitz, I presume," Daphne said, her voice as cold and sharp as an ice pick.

Every hair on her head was perfectly arranged. Not a speck of lint dared to rest on her tailored suit. And even at eight thirty-five on a Saturday morning, her makeup was artfully applied.

"D-Daphne," he stammered, guilty as sin. "What are you doing here?"

"What are *you* doing here?"

They just stared at each other, her ice blue eyes the temperature of an igloo.

"I'm guessing you saw the *Newlywed Game.*"

"Are you going to let me in, or do we have to discuss our relationship in the hallway?" Daphne raised one razor-thin eyebrow and crossed her arms over her chest.

"Mason?" Charlee called sleepily from behind him. "Is that room service? How sweet of you to order breakfast."

*Ulp.*

Every man's worst nightmare. The moment when your soon-to-be ex-girlfriend comes face-to-face with the woman you can't get out of your mind.

"Aren't you going to introduce me to your new 'wife'?" Daphne asked in a voice as frosty as a Siberian tomb at the same time Charlee came up behind him tying the sash to her robe.

"I hope you ordered Belgian waffles. I love Belgian waffles." Her tone was as light and airy as Daphne's was heavy and frigid. She touched his waist and peered around his shoulder at Daphne. "Oh," she said. "You're not room service."

Daphne glared at Mason. "Do we have to do this in the corridor?" she repeated. "You know how I hate a public scene."

"What's happening?" Charlee looked at him, bewildered.

Mason could not hold her gaze. The consequences of what he'd done whacked him in the gut with the impact of a wrecking ball taking down a Vegas casino.

*Must minimalize guilt,* his basic male instinct screamed. *Pretend this is normal. Pretend you haven't just made love with the right woman for all the wrong reasons while you're almost engaged to the wrong woman for all the right reasons.*

Mason ushered Daphne across the threshold. "Daphne, this is Charlee Champagne. Charlee, Daphne Maxwell."

"I thought her name was Violet."

"No. It's a long story."

"I'm all ears," Daphne said.

"Who are you again?" Charlee asked.

"How do you do?" Daphne extended her hand to Charlee. "I'm Mason's fiancée."

Since he was intently studying the wainscoting along the ceiling, Mason felt rather than saw Charlee's jaw drop.

"F-f-fiancée?"

He swallowed hard, jammed his fingers through his hair, and forced himself to look at her. The pain he saw reflected in her eyes just about killed him.

"Daphne and I are not officially engaged," he denied, knowing he sounded for all the world like a kid who was trying to have his birthday cake and eat it too.

"We've been dating for three years," Daphne said. "We've talked about getting married. We've even priced houses together. I call his parents Mother and Father. You, my dear girl, are nothing but a road-trip fling and if you were fantasizing about landing yourself a rich man, then honey, you were sadly mistaken."

Mason braced himself for Charlee's outrage. Would she go for his jugular? Scratch his eyes from his head? Pull out her gun and shoot him? Actually, shooting was too good for him. He'd behaved badly and he knew it. He'd led her on, he'd allowed himself to give into his lust, he'd hurt her and there was nothing he could say or do to alter that fact.

"You don't owe me an explanation. I'm just the one-night stand." She blithely waved a hand.

"Charlee..." He opened his mouth but he had no idea what he was going to say. He couldn't promise her anything. His own life was in turmoil. His grandfather was missing and he was more confused than he'd ever been in his life. "You weren't a one-night stand."

"Hey, listen." Charlee shrugged. "It's no big deal. I mean, I gotta confess, you took me off guard. You didn't strike me as the sort of guy to cheat on your fiancée."

"Honey," Daphne said sarcastically, "all men are the sort to cheat on their fiancées."

"She's not my fiancée," Mason protested feebly.

"This fight really needs to be between the two of you." Charlee picked up Violet's suitcase. She opened it on the bed and started rummaging through the contents. "Last night was great, Mason, I gotta confess. Really righteous. But if you thought it meant more to me than just sex, then you're dead wrong."

On the surface she seemed extremely calm. Impulsive, headstrong Charlee composed and in control?

That's when he noticed her hand was trembling oh-so-slightly. It was eerie to witness and that tiny tremor told him far more than a temper tantrum would have. She was hurt. To the quick.

He felt sick to his stomach. He disgusted himself.

She retrieved an outfit from the suitcase and marched

into the bathroom to get dressed. Mason watched her go, his heart sinking to his feet.

Daphne tapped him on the shoulder. He turned to look at her. She pursed her lips in a disapproving frown. He never noticed before how petulant she looked when things didn't go her way.

"If you come home with me to Houston right this very minute then I'm willing to forget all this ever happened. Every man deserves to sow his wild oats before settling down."

"Daphne, my grandfather is still missing."

"Well, that's not my problem now, is it?" She sank her hands on her hips. "I've already booked our return flight. The plane leaves in three hours."

"You had no right to do that."

"And you had no right to use your grandfather as a excuse for a quickee with trailer trash."

Mason fisted his hands. "Don't you dare call her that."

"What? The truth hurts? You go slumming, darling. Then you have to expect to acquire a few fleas."

Charlee popped back out of the bathroom wearing another one of Violet's short skirts, a very tight T-shirt embossed with the word "Hellraiser," and her own neon blue cowboy boots. Mason's eyes were immediately drawn to her long, shapely legs and his heart hitched when he saw her knees were trembling too.

What had he done?

"Good-bye you two." Charlee flung her purse over her shoulder. "Have a nice life."

"Charlee, wait." Mason started after her, totally forgetting he was in his bathrobe. "You can't go out there alone. Remember the armed men in the Malibu."

"If I can handle a night with you, I can handle those

two," she said flippantly and tossed her hair over her shoulder.

Her casual dismissal sliced into him and left him hemorrhaging. Had he meant nothing more than a sexual conquest? And why did that thought upset him so? Wasn't it what he thought he'd wanted?

No, he realized miserably. It wasn't what he wanted. Not at all. He wanted more. So much more he couldn't keep all the thoughts in his head at once.

He had to talk to her. Tell her what he was feeling. Hash this thing out.

"Come back here," he demanded.

She ignored him, squared her shoulders in that defensive little gesture of hers, and sashayed out the door. Mason grappled for the clothes he'd worn the day before, snatching Skeet's beige walking shorts up off the floor and trying to stuff both legs in at the same time. He ended up losing his balance and toppling over into the bed. The sheets still smelled erotically of the sex he had shared with Charlee.

"If you follow her," Daphne threatened, "not only is it over between us, but I'm pulling strings with Birkweilder. I have the influence to get him to cancel his account with Gentry Enterprises and you know it."

Mason met Daphne's cold, calculating stare. "You wouldn't dare."

"Oh, just try me. My contacts got you the deal, I can pull it whenever I want."

He clenched his teeth, surprised to discover he utterly did not care. "Do whatever you think you have to do, Daphne. I'm sorry, but it's over between us."

# Chapter 16

She'd done it again. She'd fallen for another wealthy, long-legged, brown-eyed, handsome man.

Stupid, stupid, stupid. Would she *ever* learn her lesson? Was she doomed to keep tumbling for the wrong guys? What in the hell was the matter with her?

The tears she'd managed to hold at bay back there in the hotel room tracked miserably down her cheeks. Angrily, Charlee scrubbed at them with the back of her hand.

Last night she'd deluded herself. Pretending that it was just physical between them, that she could keep her feelings in check, when she had simply been repeating her same old destructive patterns of getting involved with unobtainable men.

Secretly she had allowed herself to believe that Mason was different from the other men she had known and now she'd found out the truth. He was worse than the rest. The man was engaged.

*Well, not officially,* protested a tiny voice in the back of her head. The same stupid voice that had led her willy-nilly into his bed.

It didn't matter. He was a cheat and a liar. And he'd used her. Just like Gregory had.

Bastard.

*Ahem, you seduced him.*

Yeah but she'd been drunk on champagne.

*Excuses, excuses.*

She stalked down the palm-tree-lined street, her boot heels smacking against the sidewalk.

A group of guys in a Jeep drove by, honking at her and issuing crude catcalls, but she ignored them. Her anger was finely focused.

Jerk. Nimrod. Dillhole.

Her first impression of Mason had been the right one. Ruthless heartbreaker.

More tears streamed down her face. Dammit. Why couldn't she stop crying?

*Because you fell in love with him.*

No way. Nuh-huh. She was *not* in love with him.

In lust? Yes. Oh, baby, was she in lust. But she did not love him. She couldn't love him. She wouldn't let herself. She was not going through that kind of heartache again.

Not after being disappointed by her father and then treated badly by the likes of Tommy Ledbetter and Vincent Keneer and Gregory Blankensonship.

She was through. Done. Finished with men. Maybelline had the right idea all along. Men were worthless scoundrels, the lot of them.

Charlee was so busy mentally berating men in general and Mason Gentry in particular, she blocked out all external stimuli. She didn't hear the seagulls cawing overhead. She didn't smell the scent of coffee and pastries from the bakery she passed. She didn't taste the salt of her tears as they slipped over her lips. She didn't feel the breeze lifting the hairs on her arm.

And she didn't see the white Chevy Malibu slinking down the street behind her.

Mason tore out of the Beverly Hills Grand Piazza as if his hair had been dipped in kerosene and set ablaze. Charlee had a good three-minute lead on him. He swiveled his head right, then left, staring down the street in each direction for as far as he could see.

No sign of her.

Ah hell. Which way had she gone?

"Are you looking for your wife, Mr. Hammersmitz?" asked the ponytailed valet.

"Yes, yes. Did you see her?"

"Cute chick in the coolest blue boots and hot black T-shirt."

"That's her. Which way did she go?"

The valet held out his palm, the universal signal for you-want-information-it's-gonna-cost-you.

Mason stuck his hand in his pocket in search of a twenty-dollar bill to press into the man's greedy fist before remembering he was penniless.

"I'm sorry, man. I don't have any money on me."

The valet shrugged. "Dude, maybe I was mistaken. Maybe it wasn't her after all."

He was accustomed to money greasing wheels, making life easier. He'd never really thought much about it in his daily life. Money had always been a tool and he'd used it freely. It spoke for him so he didn't have to speak for himself.

The valet turned away.

Anger spurted through Mason. Anger at the system he

had helped to engender. Anger at the blasé valet. Anger at Daphne.

But most of all, Mason was angry with himself.

Without even thinking, he did something he would never have done even four days earlier. The dark wildness he'd kept hidden for so long burst free in an unstoppable torrent and he turned into a complete and utter Neanderthal protecting his own.

He grabbed the impertinent valet by his lapel, lifted him off his feet, and slammed him against the brick building. "Tell me which direction my wife went and tell me now," he growled with so much intensity he startled even himself.

"Hey, man, okay, okay." The valet's eyes rounded with fear. "Don't have an aneurysm. She was headed toward Rodeo Drive."

"Appreciate the information." Mason let go of the man's jacket.

As he hurried away he heard the valet mutter, "White trash."

His gut constricted and he managed to keep himself from whirling around and giving the guy an earful by reminding himself Charlee was in jeopardy. She was out there on the streets of Beverly Hills alone with those two goons who had followed them from Vegas. He had to get to her before they did.

He took off at a dead sprint and turned right. A woman walking her dog glared at him. He jumped over a hedge to avoid her, got caught in the spray from a sprinkler system and kept on running without missing a beat.

Dread filled his mouth and he knew with a horrible certainty Charlee was in trouble.

And then he saw her.

Relief washed through him. Thank God, she was all right.

She was a football field length ahead of him, marching with her head held high. Her coal black hair swaying provocatively just above her gorgeous butt. Those jaunty cowboy boots blazing a neon blue path across Beverly Hills as defiantly as a nose thumbing.

Something pinched inside his chest. Something tight and heavy. The stab of pain came not from running but from the very sight of her. Damn, he loved those neon blue cowboy boots.

And he loved the way that little skirt flounced sassily over her thighs. Since he was coming clean with himself, he might as well admit it. He loved a lot of things about her.

He loved her passion, her directness, her power. He loved the way she grabbed life in both fists and truly lived each moment to the fullest. But most of all he loved the way she made him feel like a better man for simply having known her.

Mason slowed to catch his breath, his heart thudding perilously loud in his ears. Charlee, Charlee, Charlee, his blood seemed to strum.

Mason was so compelled by the sight of her, his eyes feasting upon her luscious body, he didn't see the Chevy Malibu creeping along behind her until the back door was flung open.

"Charlee," he yelled.

But he was too late.

Just as she turned her head, one of the muscle-bound thugs tumbled from the car, slapped one hand around her waist and the other around her mouth, and then pulled her into the backseat.

Before Mason could react, the door slammed and the Malibu sped away.

"Oww!" the thick-necked goon cried as Charlee sank her top teeth into the base of his thumb. "Stop that."

"Get your hands off me, you big ape." She fought him but he held her tight against his lap.

"You're feisty," he said. "I like that."

She elbowed him sharply in the ribs.

"Oww! Sal, make her stop hurting me."

The guy behind the wheel raised a handgun and pointed it over the seat at her. "Behave."

Charlee settled down. Not because she was afraid of them—if she had a dollar for every time someone had pointed a gun at her she would be on vacation in the Caymans right now instead of stuck here with these two—but because she could think better if she wasn't having to battle Mr. Personality here.

"Who are you guys?" she demanded. "And where are you taking me?"

"You'll find out soon enough," grunted Sal the driver who thankfully lowered his gun and returned his eyes to the road. "Shit! Look at the freeway. It's backed up for miles."

"Take PCI."

"I can't turn around now."

"Well, take the next exit."

"We're gonna be stuck in traffic for hours," Sal complained.

The thug beside her had retrieved his handgun from his shoulder holster and held the nose of the thirty-eight pressed against her ribs. Charlee sighed and longed for her own gun.

"Who do you work for?" she asked him.

"None of your business."

"Why have you been following us since Vegas?"

He just grunted.

"You're the guy who shot through my grandmother's window, aren't you?"

"So what if I was?" he asked petulantly.

"Don't tell her anything," Sal commented.

"Did you ransack the trailer too? I saw your car at my grandmother's place."

"She had something we wanted."

"What?" Charlee demanded. "What's this all about?"

"Shut up." He prodded her with the gun.

"Were you the ones who set my father's apartment on fire? What was that about?"

"That wasn't us. We didn't start the fire. We were just looking for your old man."

"I said not to tell her anything," Sal snapped. "Are you listening?"

"He's right. Shut up." The other man dug the gun deeper into her side.

"Where are we going?" Charlee asked, figuring if she threw enough questions his way he'd answer some of them eventually.

"You don't take orders too good, do you?"

"Not from cretins who didn't finish high school."

"Hey! I got a GED, it's the same thing," the man beside her protested.

"Sure, go ahead, delude yourself," Charlee said.

"It is." He glared.

"Petey, she's giggin' you, man, don't fall for it," the driver said. "Just gag her and tie her up and be done with it."

Petey frowned. "You really think a GED isn't as good as a high school diploma?"

Frankly Charlee had no personal prejudice about anyone's level of education but Petey obviously had a problem with his credentials.

"Well, you did end up as hired muscle," she pointed out "Probably wouldn't have happened if you had stayed in school. Who knows? You might even be running your very own Subway sandwich shop today if you had just gotten that diploma."

So much for her smart mouth, Charlee decided five minutes later when they hadn't budged two feet in wall-to-wall traffic and she was trussed up with more tape than a Miss America contestant in the swimsuit competition and lying facedown on the seat.

On the up side, she hadn't thought about Mason in a good ten minutes.

*Mason.*

Ah, hell, why had she thought about him?

"Hey," Petey said. "Don't cry. We're not going to kill you, I promise."

Tears rolled down her face.

"Come on now." Petey patted her awkwardly on the shoulder. "It's going to be okay."

She must look pretty bad if her kidnapper was trying to console her. That made her cry all the harder. Damn Mason Gentry.

And just like that, all the fight left her. What did it matter if Sal and Petey did kill her? At least she'd be out of her misery.


Mason sped down the Pacific Coast Highway in the rental car he'd commandeered from a disgruntled Daphne. By some miracle, the Malibu had gotten stuck in a traffic jam and he'd managed to catch up with them. But he only saw the two men in the car.

What had they done with Charlee?

Savage vengeance, unlike anything he'd ever felt, coursed through his veins. If they'd hurt one single hair on her head, he'd wring their necks with his bare hands.

What had happened to the controlled, success-oriented businessman who'd walked into her office a mere four days ago? Where was the guy whose family name meant everything to him? Who was he now?

Something hard, solid, and certain burned directly to the left of his breastbone.

He was in love with her. Stone cold in love and he had no idea what to do about it.

Romantic love made no sense to his logical investment banker's brain or the fact that it had happened so suddenly, so unexpectedly. But there it was.

She was his soul mate. His better half. He knew it with a certainty that rocked his world.

He felt like cracked lightning. Raw, stark, dangerous. Charlee had done this to him. She stripped off his controlled exterior and exposed the man beneath. The man who'd been shambling through life without really living it. The man who'd been afraid to break free and go for what he really wanted. The man who'd been almost dead inside until he'd met her.

She'd changed everything and now he was about to lose her.

This whole thing was his fault. If he'd just told her about Daphne beforehand, they'd be safely ensconced in the hotel room waiting for Pam to come take them shopping for Oscar clothes.

Ha!

The thought of that leisurely afternoon spent watching Charlee try on designer outfits evaporated.

He gripped the steering wheel and moistened his lips. Once they'd gotten off the congested freeway and onto the Pacific Coast Highway, they'd been moving right along. Past Santa Monica, past Venice Beach, past LAX.

Where were they going and was Charlee still with them? And if she wasn't, what could they have done with her? Was she in the trunk of the car?

Was she dead?

Fear bit him. She wasn't dead. She couldn't be dead. He had so much to say to her, so much to explain.

He had to apologize and he had to tell her how he felt about her. It didn't matter if she didn't love him back. What mattered was that he was in love with her.

Steeling his jaw, he narrowed his eyes with resolve. He was sticking to the Malibu like Velcro. Nobody but nobody was going to abduct his Charlee and get away with it.

Nolan paced off the cramped confines of the mineshaft for the one-millionth time since Blade Bradford and his illegitimate son Elwood had abandoned them here the afternoon before. What in the hell were those two up to, he wondered.

A thin beam of light slanted through a hole in the ceiling, barely illuminating the constricted space. That dinner plate-sized hole was too far away to reach and every time he moved a fresh dusting of earth crumbled from the dirt wall.

What had once been two tunnels leading right and left from the underground room to the mines were now blocked with debris and rocks from a massive cave-in.

Elwood and Bradford couldn't have entombed them any
more effectively if they had actually buried them alive.

Come to think of it, this had all the makings of a Poe
short story.

"Nolan," Maybelline chided, "please stop pacing."

"I'm trying to erode the damned wall."

"More likely you'll cause it to fall in on us." She waved
at their precarious surroundings, then put the hand up to
shield her nose and sneezed.

He paused. She was right. Plus he was kicking up
enough dust to choke an asthmatic.

At first, Maybelline had been as antsy as he, pacing and
cussing both her offspring and her ex-lover for dumping
them here the day before. But during the last few hours
she had grown so calm Nolan got worried. Maybelline
wasn't the quiet type.

She sat with her back against the north wall, her eyes
tightly closed.

"Are you okay?" He squatted beside her and ignored
the creaking in his knees.

"I'm fine. I'm just trying to think."

Nolan exhaled sharply and sat down. He'd spent the
last sixteen hours wracking his brain for a solution and
he'd come up with nothing.

At gunpoint, Elwood and Blade had forced them into
the mine shaft, slammed and bolted the rusted but solid
metal door, and walked away. They'd had the decency to
leave them three two-liter bottles of Evian, four apples, a
bag of Doritos, and a Heath bar.

It wouldn't take long to go through their meager provi-
sions. Well, except for the Heath bar. His teeth not being
what they used to be, the chocolate-covered hard toffee
was not his candy of choice.

He got to his feet, unable to sit still, and squinted up at the shaft of light taunting him from overhead. He looked back over at Maybelline and watched her press her tongue to her lips.

A trickle of perspiration pearled at the hollow of her throat and the quick kick of lust that had him wanting to lick away her salty sweat startled him. He was as randy as a young buck. Go figure.

"Thirsty?" he asked, reaching for the Evian. They had been careful to ration the water, not knowing how long they had to make it last.

Maybelline shook her head. "We need to conserve."

"Your lips are dry."

She opened one eye to peer up at him through the thick haze of dust motes. "I'll live."

"One sip," he urged, fretting over how pale she looked. His gut clenched. He thought of how they'd made love in the back of the camper. How good she'd made him feel. How much he enjoyed being with her. "One sip won't hurt."

"Okay," she gave in. Obviously she was pretty darned thirsty if she acquiesced this easily.

Nolan untwisted the lid and the round plastic ring separated from the cap and came off in his hand. He passed the water to Maybelline but found himself staring intently at the white plastic ring.

Rings were symbols.

Of unity. Of eternity.

Of marriage.

Deep, long-buried emotions swept through him. From the time he could remember he'd been accused of being a hopeless romantic and now he knew it was true. He believed they would get out of here. He believed they had many long and lusty years ahead of them. He believed they would solve the Oscar dilemma facing them.

But most of all, he believed, with all his heart, that he was in love with Maybelline Sikes and had been for the last forty-seven years.

And he was going to ask her to marry him again. This time for real. Right here, right now, with the white plastic ring.

Holding the ring between his forefinger and thumb, he got down on one knee.

The sound of his knee hitting the ground resonated wooden, hollow.

He and Maybelline looked at each other in surprise.

"Wood floor under the dirt," she said.

Simultaneously, they began to dig.

# Chapter 17

Mason sat in Daphne's rented Mercedes next to a vine-yard outside Figero, California. It was a small town in the very corner of the state near the Arizona/Mexico border. He waited for the cover of darkness. The Malibu was parked in the driveway of a weather-scarred farmhouse a quarter mile from where he had stationed himself.

Apparently, the goons in the Malibu never realized they were being followed. When they'd pulled into the farmhouse, Mason had driven past, and then circled back. He'd caught a glimpse of the two men hustling Charlee inside.

Sitting still and doing nothing had never been so excru-ciating. The minutes ticked by. His stomach grumbled because he hadn't eaten since the seafood buffet at the hotel the night before, but he ignored the hunger pains. His own needs were inconsequential. Charlee was in trouble.

He wished for a pair of binoculars. He wished for a spy camera. He wished for a gun.

He'd thought briefly about going to the police but the idea of explaining everything and the fact that he had no identification on him, plus the terrible fear that if he left for even a moment the thugs might disappear with Charlee, kept him rooted to the spot.

He wished regretfully that he had commandeered Daphne's cell phone as well as her vehicle but unfortunately, the urgent need to follow the Malibu had overridden careful planning. He had to do the best with what he possessed.

Which meant he had his brains, his tae kwon do training, a tire iron, and the burning desire to make those guys pay for stealing his woman.

His woman.

He liked the sound of that. Liked it so much in fact that he grinned. He also liked the kick-ass, Vin Diesel attitude stoking through his veins.

He couldn't wait for nightfall.

Except he had no choice but to wait. Other than a dilapidated barn located a few hundred yards from the house, the surrounding field was vacant, barren land. They would see him approaching from all four sides. No bushes, no shrubs, no trees.

Darkness was his ally. Even though it was killing him, he would wait.

Briefly, he closed his eyes and saw Charlee. The way her face glowed when she laughed. The way she fit so snugly into the curve of his arm. The way she smelled like no other woman on earth. The way her lips tasted of honeyed sin. The way she teased and goaded him to fulfill his highest potential.

How had she managed to embed herself under his skin so quickly and so permanently? Instead of getting her out of his system as he'd hoped, making love to her had drawn him even closer to her.

He missed her with an ache so severe a fistful of Percodan wouldn't cure it.

His eyes flew open. Dammit. He had to see her. Had to touch her. He had to know she was all right. He clenched his fists to control his impulse to storm the farmhouse and risk killing them both.

Five minutes after sunset, he was out of the car, tire iron in hand, even though streaks of purple and orange still illuminated the sky behind him. The silence was eerie. He heard nothing except his pumping blood roaring through his ears.

Charlee. He had to rescue Charlee. Nothing else mattered. He'd die for her if he had to.

Driven by that one relentless thought, he crouched low and sprinted toward the run-down farmhouse. When he reached it, he paused to catch his breath and pressed his back flush against the wall.

Cocking the tire iron like a baseball bat, he waited, listening.

When enough time had passed so that he could be certain he hadn't been detected, Mason inched toward the bedroom window located a few feet to his left. Cautiously, he eased his head around and peeked through the curtainless window.

The room was empty.

Pulse strumming, he crept down the side of the house to the next window that turned out to be a bathroom with those watery panes you couldn't see through.

Sucking in his breath, he wiped his damp palms on the front of Skeet's purple hula girl shirt, reapplied his steel grip to the tire iron, and moved on.

Another bedroom.

He darted a glance inside the window.

And spotted Charlee.

Bound and gagged and reclining on her back in a pink and orange paisley plastic beanbag chair.

For one brief impossible second, his heart literally stopped.

She was alive. Thank God.

Now what? He paused to ponder his next move, his mind racing at a startling clip as he formed and rejected one plan after another.

"Ahem."

At the sound of a throat being cleared behind him, Mason froze.

Slowly, he turned his head and came face-to-face with one of his own ilk.

The tall, distinguished-looking gray-haired man wasn't one of the two goons who'd kidnapped Charlee. That much was clear. The man standing before him sported a hundred-dollar haircut, a thousand-dollar designer suit, and a very large handgun pointed right at Mason's head.

"Ah, the younger Mr. Gentry." The man gave him a cold, false smile. "I suggest you put down the tire iron and come with me."

Charlee had to pee bad. She'd been holding it for hours. If Sal and Petey didn't let her go to the bathroom soon she would have to wet her pants or suffer irreparable kidney damage.

Unfortunately, the two men were in the other room playing gin and she lay in the stinky beanbag chair that obviously had not been cleaned since 1975, her hands and feet bound and her mouth still covered with duct tape. Her captors had only been in to check on her once since they'd arrived at the farmhouse several hours earlier.

She knew she should be devising some clever plan

for escape, hatching some kind of brilliant detectivish scheme, but no matter how hard she tried she couldn't seem to concentrate on anything except the persistent ache in her bladder. Not even when she tried to evoke Mason's visage just so she could hate him.

About the time she had decided to surrender to nature and just pee her pants, she heard the front door slam and a new voice inside the house. Someone else was here.

Her pulse rate spiked. Who could it be?

She heard the sounds of an argument but couldn't make out what was being said.

Then came the footsteps. Several of them, headed toward the bedroom.

Oh, crap. This was it. They'd brought in the terminator. Would they let her pee before they killed her? she wondered idly.

The door flew open and Mason stumbled inside, pushed ahead of a dapper man with a thin mustache, cruel black eyes that belied his oily smile, and a nasty-looking forty-five in his hand. Petey and Sal stood in the doorway behind him.

Mason!

Their eyes met. She saw relief and a sweet tenderness swimming in his chocolate eyes.

Her treacherous heart leaped with joy at the sight of him when it should have been condemning the wretched scumbag. She'd never been so happy to see anyone in her entire life.

Even though she shouldn't be, she was glad, glad, glad he was here and she wasn't alone anymore.

"Mmghphm," she mumbled through the duct tape.

"You"—the man motioned to Petey with his gun— "take the tape off and let her speak. And you"—he frowned at Sal—"tie this guy up."

Sal went to fetch some rope while Petey squatted beside her and ripped the tape off her mouth.

"Ouch!"

"Payback's a bitch," Petey said. "That's for biting my thumb."

Oh, well, at least she'd gotten a free lip waxing out of the deal.

"I need to pee," she squawked. "Now."

Petey looked to the man with the gun. He nodded.

"But you go with her."

Charlee winced. She wasn't crazy about the idea of having Petey in the bathroom with her but at this point her eyeballs were swimming and her modesty had pretty much disappeared.

Petey untied the rope from around her ankles so she could walk, but the well-dressed man wouldn't let him untie her hands. She almost fell when she put weight on her feet but Petey caught her by the elbow and held her steady.

"How am I supposed to get my underwear down?" she grumbled.

"Just consider me your third hand." Petey grinned lewdly and wriggled his fingers at her.

Charlee wished she hadn't asked.

"If you do anything to her…" Mason started to threaten before the man in the suit shoved the gun against his temple and commanded, "Shut up."

When she returned from the bathroom with Petey, who'd actually been a perfect gentleman and averted his eyes after skimming her panties to her knees, she felt like a new woman. Pain-free and ready to start kicking some big thug butt.

Mason was tied up and sitting in the beanbag chair. Petey bound her ankles again and shoved her down on top of Mason.

She didn't want to take solace in his hard, masculine body but damn her, she did. Her short skirt exposed her thighs and the material of his shorts rubbed comfortingly against her skin.

The new guy was leaning against the windowsill, flanked by Petey and Sal. He cleared his voice. "Now that we have all the amenities taken care of, allow me to introduce myself. I'm Spencer Cahill, CEO of Twilight Studios."

Mason shifted beneath her and she sensed his confusion mirroring her own. Why had the head of Twilight Studios taken them hostage? Had he discovered they were masquerading as Skeet and Violet Hammersmitz and he was really pissed off about it?

But no, that couldn't be. His henchmen had been following them since Vegas. Spencer Cahill obviously knew who they were.

"Let me assure you, if you do as I say, you will come to no physical harm and following the Academy Awards tomorrow night you will be released."

"The Academy Awards?" Mason sounded as confused as she felt. What did the Academy Awards have to do with anything?

Cahill's eyes narrowed. "You don't know what this is all about, do you?"

"No."

"Ah, that's quite interesting."

"Interesting?"

"Humorous." Cahill laughed a dry laugh suggesting he wasn't the least bit amused.

"Let us in on the joke. We could use a good chuckle," Charlee said.

"I suppose I should take comfort in the fact your

grandfather has kept his mouth shut. It bodes well for your chances of getting out of this alive."

"What are you talking about?" Mason's muscles tensed beneath her fanny and his voice bristled.

"By the way, where is your grandfather?"

"You tell me, Cahill. You seem to be the grand Pooh-Bah around here."

Cahill studied Mason for a long moment. "For all your traipsing from Las Vegas to Arizona to California you haven't located your grandfather?"

"How could we with Frick and Frack over there riding our bumper?" Mason nodded at Sal and Petey.

"Hey," Petey started, "I resent..." But Cahill cut him off short with a quelling glance.

"Never mind. We'll find him."

"I don't get it," Charlee said. "What's the big deal about the Academy Awards?"

"This has something to do with Blade Bradford," Mason said flatly.

"You're an astute young man."

"So clue me in, fellas," Charlee said. "I wanna know what's going on."

Cahill pushed off from the windowsill, clasped his hands behind his back, and walked closer to the beanbag chair. "I see no harm in telling you what you're up against. In fact, it might insure your cooperation."

"Just tell us what's going on," Mason seethed.

"As you're probably aware, Blade Bradford is up for his second Oscar for *The Righteous,* a film produced by Twilight Studios."

"Yes, they kept yammering on and on about it while we were on the studio lot filming the *Newlywed Game.*" Charlee nodded.

"Oh, by the way," Cahill said. "I applaud your ingenuity. Getting yourselves on my *Newlywed Game* in order to elude my assistants." He shook his head. "Clever, very clever. And don't think I missed the irony. Here I was footing the bill for your stay at the Grand Piazza, which by the way runs a thousand dollars a night, and I couldn't touch you because of all the media coverage I'd arranged to promote the show."

She wasn't about to tell the guy they had stumbled into the deal. Let Cahill keep thinking they were brilliant strategists.

"A thousand dollars a night? You rich people are nuts." Charlee shook her head.

"Go on about Blade Bradford," Mason said. "What's this got to do with my grandfather?"

"Ah, yes. Last year, while going through some old records, I discovered quite by accident that Mr. Bradford did not legitimately win his first Oscar."

"No?"

"In fact, I've seen the original voting record from 1955. Your grandfather actually got the most votes."

"Someone cooked the books," Mason said.

"Of course," Cahill continued. "It seems the same year he was nominated for his first Oscar, Blade Bradford married Sheila Jenkins, the daughter of the man who once owned the accounting firm that audits the Oscars."

"The same accounting firm Gentry Enterprises now holds controlling interest in."

"Precisely. To make his new son-in-law's career, Max Jenkins cheated."

"What's that got to do with present circumstances?" Mason asked.

Cahill smiled. "I don't know if you're aware of this,

but Twilight Studios has not been particularly financially viable in recent years. As CEO, I've had to make a few executive decisions."

"Such as?"

Charlee could feel the heat of Mason's breath burning along the nape of her neck and she shivered.

"Convincing Sheila Bradford, who is still on the board of directors at the accounting firm and has a very strong influence there, that a second fix might just be the thing both Blade and Twilight Studios needed to boost our flagging sales."

"So that's what this is all about? Cheating on the Oscars."

Cahill smiled again, uglier this time. "Cheating to get what you want is as American as apple pie."

"Not in my America, buddy." Mason's voice was hard, unflinching.

"I applaud your gung ho, Boy Scout attitude, Mr. Gentry, truly I do, but really it shows an appalling lack of sophistication. I might have expected such lowbrow sentiment from someone like Ms. Champagne here, but from a man such as yourself?" Cahill clicked his tongue like a disappointed parent.

Hey! She bristled. Had that creep just insulted her? She glared at him.

"Listen here, Cahill," Mason ground out. "Don't you say disparaging things about Charlee."

"Ah, I see the lay of the land." Cahill pursed his lips and smirked. "You and Ms. Champagne have obviously bonded. I'm assuming you made good use of the honeymoon suite intended for Skeet and Violet Hammersmitz."

"That's none of your business. Leave Charlee out of all of this." *My hero.*

The words blazed across her mind like a neon billboard. Mason had defended her honor. Her chest swelled with pride, delight, and respect and then she got mad at herself for forgiving him so easily. She was not letting him off the hook without busting his chops first.

"I wish I could leave her out of it, but like it or not, Ms. Champagne *is* involved. You involved her when you left Vegas with her."

"I don't care what you say, I don't cheat and neither does my grandfather," Mason insisted.

*Except on your fiancée,* Charlee thought.

"And she's not my fiancée," he growled low in her ear, reading her mind so uncannily that Charlee jumped.

"I'm merely pointing out the obvious," Cahill continued "But you of all people, Mr. Gentry, should understand how the real world runs. Don't tell me you've never ordered the books to be cooked to make your company's bottom line look better to investors."

"Never."

"And you call yourself an investment banker?" Cahill shook his head.

"You're sunk, Cahill. I'm damn well going to the television stations with what you've just told me. It's over."

"If I believed that, then I would have to let Sal and Petey kill you. Fortunately, I'm confident you won't go to the media."

"How can you be so sure?"

The intensity of Mason's anger generated so much body heat Charlee feared he'd sear a hole in her fanny. She had the sense that if Mason wasn't hog-tied, he would be performing a few of his more advanced tae kwon do moves on Cahill.

"I'm certain you won't go public. If I wasn't I wouldn't

have told you a thing. See, we're now partners in conspiracy, you and I."

"The hell we are."

"Such vehemence. I remember what it's like to be young and passionate."

"I'm not like you. Not in the least."

"Perhaps you're right. However, one fact remains that ensures your silence and loyalty to my cause. Your family's auditing firm will be implicated if you go public with this information after Bradford receives the Academy Award."

"But you know my family wasn't involved," Mason protested. "We have no motive."

"It didn't matter with Arthur Anderson either. Only a few bad eggs were enough to topple one of the top four international auditing firms. Unluckily for you, Mr. Gentry, I'm your bad egg. You not only jeopardize yourself but your entire family fortune as well. Open your mouth and your life as you know it is over."

# Chapter 18

Mason didn't believe for a moment that Cahill would allow them to walk out of the farmhouse alive. The only reason he hadn't already killed them was because he was planning on using them as added leverage to keep Nolan quiet.

Cahill left the farmhouse, instructing Sal and Petey to watch over them. The two men had gone back to their gin game in the kitchen while Mason and Charlee remained piled on top of each other in the beanbag chair.

The weight of her body in his lap would have been uncomfortable were it not so erotic. Every time she squirmed, his body hardened.

"Sit still, dammit," he said, his teeth clenched.

"My leg is cramping up."

"That's not the only thing cramping up."

She gave a little gasp. "You're getting a boner."

"Yeah, so quit moving."

"I don't believe this. What are you, Gentry, some kind of sex machine? You've got two women and neither of us can keep you satisfied," she snapped.

"You're the only one who turns me on."

"I'm sure Daphne takes great comfort in that."

"Listen, Charlee, I'm so sorry about what happened."

"Save it for someone who cares."

Thank God, she stopped moving. They sat together in the darkness, her head tucked under his chin, her spine flush against his chest, his butt buried deep in the foul smelling beanbag chair. They breathed together in a raspy, sweaty, rhythm and it took a while for him to calm down.

"I should have told you I was almost engaged," he said. "It was wrong of me not to."

"I don't give a damn, Gentry. Honest."

"You lie."

"Oh, please, don't flatter yourself."

"You're going to tell me last night meant nothing to you?"

"That's right."

He clenched his jaw and all the hopes and dreams he'd been spinning in his head about a future with Charlee shattered. Had he been so wrong? Had he just imagined the chemistry—both physical and mental—between them? Or was she simply being stubborn, denying her feelings in order to punish him for not telling her about Daphne?

"I'm going to let this issue drop for the time being. We've got a serious problem on our hands." He kept his voice to a whisper just in case Sal and Petey were straining their ears to listen in on their conversation. "But don't think the discussion is closed."

"Yes it is, because the goons are going to kill us." The calmness in her voice gave him strength. She wasn't afraid. She wouldn't panic like she had with the spider.

"It's a distinct possibility," he admitted.

"Just my luck I have to die with Don Juan Gentry."

"Don't make jokes about this and I'm not a Don Juan."

"You coulda fooled me."

"For what it's worth, I wish you weren't here either."

"Yes, yes. I'm fully aware you're regretting ever having met me."

"Nonsense," he shouted, then remembered to lower his voice. "I don't regret meeting you! You're the best thing that ever happened to me."

Charlee snorted, sending a puff of warm air rolling over his cheek. "Oh, yeah, right. I'm betting you said something suspiciously similar to Daphne once upon a time."

"Dammit, Charlee," he snarled. "Will you let go of your anger for two seconds? Not that your wrath isn't justified. In fact, I wouldn't blame you if you never spoke to me again after the stunt I pulled. What I meant by my remark was that I wish you were far away from here and safe."

"Do you mean it?" she asked after a long pause. "That I'm the best thing that ever happened to you?"

"I never meant anything more in my life."

"Seriously?"

"It doesn't get much more serious than this."

"How am I the best thing that ever happened to you?"

"Since I met you I've come alive. You jostled me out of my doldrums. You're the breath of fresh air in my stale, studied world. You turned me on my ear. Woman, you made me forget Daphne even existed."

"You don't think it's just the excitement of the car chases and the goons waving guns at us and the hot sex do you?" She sounded as nervous as he felt.

"I'll admit these past few days have been a thrill ride but they've been exciting because of you."

"Oh."

He could hear in her tone that she wanted to believe him. Please, let her believe him. He gave her time to mull things over before saying, "I feel like an ass. I was supposed to be rescuing you, but I mucked things up and got caught by Cahill."

"Hey, I let myself get snatched by Dumb and Dumber. Doesn't make me feel particularly bright."

"This is all my fault. You were upset. If you hadn't just found out about Daphne, you wouldn't have had your guard down."

"Don't flatter yourself, Gentry."

"You can't fool me, Charlee. Last night was special I challenge you to deny it." He lifted his chin and nuzzled the curve of her neck.

"Well, I have to confess I enjoyed last night a little bit more than I'm enjoying tonight."

They fell silent.

That nasty old guilt nibbled at him. "I'm truly sorry I didn't tell you about Daphne before. I guess I never thought things between you and me were going to end up the way they did."

"I don't want to talk about this anymore. We need to concentrate on escaping. The sooner the better."

"You got any plans?"

"No, do you?"

"Not really."

"All rightee then."

More silence.

"I do have a rental car parked about a quarter of a mile away. If we could get loose we've got a ride back to L.A."

"Assuming Cahill doesn't find the car."

"Assuming."

"How did you get your hands on a rental car?"

"It was Daphne's."

"Oh, I bet that went over big."

"She's not an unreasonable woman."

"Which is what everyone looks for in a mate. Rich, sexy bachelor searching for wife. Must be sophisticated, beautiful, and oh, yes, above all, reasonable."

"You think I'm sexy?" he teased, grinning into her hair.

She poked him in the belly with her thumb.

"Ow, what was that for?"

"Being cocky."

"Babe, you have no idea."

"Knock off calling me babe. I'm not your babe or your sweetheart or your darling and I most certainly am not reasonable. If the tables were turned and Daphne had been kidnapped and you tried to borrow my car I wouldn't let you have it."

"You'd let the villains spirit her away?"

"Damned skippee."

"Lucky for you, Daphne's reasonable."

"No, lucky for you. If you were my fiancé and I caught you cheating on me, I'd castrate you with a pocketknife."

"For the last time, she isn't my fiancée. I never popped the question."

"Yeah, but you two obviously had an understanding."

"Things change, but I do regret the way it all transpired. I never meant to hurt either one of you." He lowered his voice, dipped his head, and blew on the back of her neck. Delight shafted through him when she shivered against the heat. "And if you were my fiancée, I would never cheat on you."

"Because I'd cut your balls off?"

"There is that. But mostly because I can't imagine any woman enticing me away from someone as spirited and exciting as you."

She said nothing for the longest moment but her breathing quickened. "Was that a compliment?"

"Yes."

"Well stop it."

"Why?"

"Because I don't want you to compliment me. I don't even want to like you."

"But you do."

"Yeah," she admitted after a long moment, "I do. Stupid me. I knew better, I warned myself, but I drank too much champagne and convinced myself I could separate sex from my emotions. I guess I was wrong. I've never been able to do that."

"What do you mean never?"

Charlee blew out her breath. She might as well tell him. She'd been avoiding facing her past for too long.

"It's a complicated story."

"I'm all ears."

She paused, searching for the words to begin. "When I was nineteen and working as a maid at the MGM Grand, I was courted by Gregory Blankensonship, one of the owners' sons."

"I've heard of the family," Mason said. "They're quite wealthy."

"I was leery. I'd already had a few bad experiences with wealthy guys. Including that senator I told you about, but Gregory was persistent. I would say I played hard to get, except I wasn't playing. I was attracted to him, oh, boy, was I attracted to him, but I was so scared of getting hurt that I resisted his attention."

"And that just escalated his interest in you."

"Uh-huh. He bought me gifts and took me on trips. I admit. He turned my head. It's an age-old story and foolishly I fell for it. When he told me he loved me, I slept with him. I gave him my virginity, Mason. I thought what we had was the real deal." Her voice caught and her throat clogged with tears at the painful memory. "I didn't care about his money, I swear. I was in love with him. Or the idea of who I thought he was."

"I hate the sound of where this story is going," he muttered darkly.

"The next day was Gregory's college graduation party. His parents were throwing him a huge shindig at their house in Tahoe. I thought he was going to introduce me to them at last. Even though I wasn't officially invited, I felt sure Gregory would want me there."

Charlee paused. Why did the memory still hurt so much? It wasn't the loss of Gregory that caused her so much distress. She'd never had him in the first place. What ate at her so cruelly was the humiliation.

"You don't have to go on, Charlee. It's none of my business."

"I just want you to understand," she said. "Why I came on to you last night and why I was so upset to find out about Daphne. Anyway, I bought a new outfit, purchased a plane ticket, and showed up at the party to surprise him."

"He wasn't expecting you to be there?"

"No. I walked into the party just as he was announcing his plans to marry this pretty young actress. I . . ." She couldn't go on. Tears splashed down her cheeks.

"Ah, sweetheart, don't cry," Mason said.

"I'm not crying," she denied, sniffling.

"It's okay to cry."

"Hell, I don't want to cry over that creep. I'm still just so mad that I fell for his bullshit."

"What did you do?"

"I thought about causing a scene. I thought about dumping his champagne over his head or knocking food off the buffet or just clawing his eyes out but a weird sense of calm came over me. I introduced myself to the actress and his parents. Gregory's face went white as a sheet. He told them I was some weirdo who'd been stalking him. Imagine. The night before he'd told me he had loved me and he had taken my virginity and now he was denying he even knew me. Gregory had security guards throw me out of the house. And I'm afraid I've held a grudge against rich guys to this day."

"You used me to get even with this Blankensonship guy," Mason said flatly.

Pressed against him in the darkness, Charlee couldn't see his face, but she felt his body tense beneath hers, heard his heart rate speed up. She'd hurt him and the knowledge pricked her conscience. Had she used him? Were her motives that shallow?

"Not intentionally."

"Face it. Whether consciously or subconsciously, you used me."

"I didn't say it was right. I'm not proud of myself."

He exhaled sharply, the sound of it echoed in her ears. "I suppose I deserve that. I should have told you about Daphne. I should have realized we were both feeling vulnerable after everything that had happened to us. I should never have made love to you."

"Mason, we didn't make love. We had sex. There's a huge difference." It wasn't true. Charlee *had* made love to him last night, even though she struggled to deny it.

*Reject him before he rejects you,* every protective

instinct inside her cried. *Don't, under any circumstances, let him know how you really feel.*

"Yeah." Mason swallowed hard.

She heard the pain in that gulp and knew she'd caused it. Feeling incredibly wretched, she closed her eyes and pretended she was asleep.

Charlee jerked awake sometime later. While they slept she and Mason had managed to shift around so she was off his lap and butted up against him. They were face-to-face, in the beanbag chair, both their legs spilling off onto the bare wooden floor. The rope bindings around her wrists hurt like the dickens and her fingers were numb but her mind was clicking.

She'd dreamed of escape and the dream had given her the answer to their dilemma.

"Mason, wake up," she whispered, her ears tuned for sounds from the rest of the house.

He mumbled.

"Psst, wake up." She raised her knees and bumped against his.

He opened his eyes and looked at her. Damn, was he ever adorable with his hair mussed and that impossibly sexy beard stubble. "What is it?"

"I've got an idea," she said, and then told him about her plan.

Two minutes later, Mason started groaning loud enough to wake the dead three counties over.

Right on cue Petey and Sal burst into the room, guns drawn, looking bleary-eyed and smelling of beer and cigarette smoke.

"What is it?" Sal demanded, waving his Glock at Mason. "What's going on?"

"He's bad sick," Charlee said.

Mason upped the groaning.

"Oh, yeah, like you expect us to fall for that."

"I'm not kidding." Charlee put her toughest tone into her voice. "The guy's a diabetic. If he doesn't get something to eat soon he'll go into a coma."

"He don't look like no diabetic to me," Petey said.

"Yeah, like you know what a diabetic looks like. You didn't even finish high school."

"I got a GED," Petey shouted. "It's the same thing. And they don't teach you about diabetes in high school."

"How would you know? You didn't go," Charlee asked.

Petey leaned over the beanbag and shoved his gun in her face. Charlee stared back at him unblinking. He looked a little rattled by her lack of fear. "I've had about enough of you."

Mason made retching noises and he was so good at it that for a couple of seconds there Charlee thought he was actually going to throw up.

"Ew, ew, get him away from me before he vomits in my hair," she said.

"You're not scared of a gun but you're scared of a little vomit?" Petey shook his head in disbelief.

"They're playing us, man," Sal exclaimed.

Mason kept retching. His face turned red and the veins at his forehead popped out. Damn, but he was his grandfather's progeny all right. Give that boy an Oscar.

"Oh, God," Charlee screamed. "He's going to have a seizure. Untie him, untie him. If he dies, you guys know Cahill will finger you for the murder rap. Who are the police going to believe? A powerful CEO of a movie studio or two hired guns who didn't finish high school?"

"I got a GED," Petey howled, but he did reach down to

cut the ropes binding Mason's arms with a knife he pulled from his pocket.

Sal put a hand to Petey's shoulder. "I'm telling you, it's a bluff."

"You willing to take that chance? She's right. The guy dies and Cahill's gonna have our heads."

Mason started bucking and his eyes rolled back in his head, then he flopped over onto his stomach.

"Shit, shit, shit," Petey exclaimed. "He is having a seizure."

"Untie him, untie him, untie him," Charlee repeated her mantra, hoping it would sink into Petey's thick skull and override Sal's objections.

Petey cut Mason's feet loose.

Mason's jerking intensified.

"His hands too! And turn him on his side," Charlee said.

"Yeah, man," Sal said. "If he pukes and inhales it he's gonna croak just like a rock star."

From the expression on Petey's face Charlee could tell he was relieved to have his partner backing him up at last. He clipped the twine binding Mason's wrists.

And Charlee figured Petey regretted that move for the rest of his life.

Like Bruce Lee and Jackie Chan and Jean-Claude Van Damme and Chuck Norris combined into one malevolent force, Mason leaped to his feet and he started kicking ass and taking names. His performance was a thing of beauty to watch.

*Blam, blam, blam.*

Three quick blows and Petey was out. He smacked facedown on the floor like a felled redwood.

*Timber.*

Completely unnerved, Sal pointed his Glock at Mason's heart but his hands shook so badly one roundhouse kick from Mason sent the gun flying across the room.

"Your turn." Mason smiled and put Sal on top of his buddy.

He retrieved Petey's knife while the two men lay groaning, then quickly sliced through Charlee's bindings. He grabbed her hand and dragged her toward the door.

"Wait, wait." She pulled away from him just long enough to snatch up Sal's Glock on the fly.

They tore through the house in a blind panic, through the back door and into the peaceful, cool predawn darkness. Charlee paused to tuck the Glock into the waistband of her skirt.

"Come on, come on." Mason took her hand again and hustled her across the empty field toward the vineyard lying like a dark oasis a quarter mile away.

Good thing they were both in good physical shape. Unfortunately cowboy boots didn't make for the best running shoes. Charlee's feet kept slipping in the sandy oil and she almost fell twice but Mason pulled her up and kept her from tumbling over.

"You can do it. We're almost there," he urged at the moment the first shot rang out.

"They're shooting at us."

"I noticed. Better get a move on."

"We're out of range."

"They have a car. Won't take 'em long to catch up with us."

"Oh, yeah."

He tugged her around the edge of the vineyard and into the road but stopped abruptly.

"What is it?"

He swore. "The rental car's gone."

More shots resonated from behind them and then they heard the sound of a car engine firing up.

They looked at each other.

"Into the vineyard," Mason said.

She was beginning to feel like a yo-yo the way he kept jerking on her arm.

"Get low, get down."

"Too bad it's not a cornfield," she grumbled, dropping to her knees and following Mason as he crawled through the rows. "They can spot us easily in here."

"At least it's still dark."

"Not for long." Yellow strips of sunlight were already staining the eastern sky.

"Shh, let's listen. Flat on your belly. Head down." He reached out and splayed a palm to her back and pushed her into the sand with his fingertips.

"We never tried that position."

"This isn't the time for jokes, Charlee."

"No better time than when you're about to die."

"Well, if I have to die, I can't think of anyone I'd rather die with."

What? He sounded completely serious. Charlee swallowed, not knowing how to take his declaration. "I know being dramatic runs in your family, Gentry, but I'm not about to let the likes of Sal and Petey do us in."

"Shh. Listen."

Charlee lay breathing in the dirt, every muscle in her body tensed, her ears sharply attuned to the sounds of the Malibu inching slowly along the road.

The car stopped, engine idling.

Oh, dear.

She ached to turn her head and glance behind her to see

how close the car was. Mason must have been feeling the same way too because he whispered, "Don't do it, Charlee. Don't move."

Like a kid playing statues, she froze. She didn't even blink. Blood rushed through her ears loud as a forty-piece tympani band. The Glock poked her uncomfortably in the ribs, but at least they had a weapon. Mason lay directly to her left, his fingers wrapped securely around her upper arm.

A car door shut.

"You see anything?" Sal's voice broke the silence.

She closed her eyes. Was Petey stumbling through the vineyard looking for them? Her pulse thumped in the hollow of her throat.

"It's too dark."

"Well, get the flashlight out of the trunk, dumb ass." They heard the sound of the Malibu's trunk being unlatched and then slammed back down. One set of footsteps echoed on the asphalt.

They were totally screwed. Petey was bound to see them. She didn't want to die in a gun battle in some god-forsaken spot in southern California.

*If I have to die, I can't think of anyone I'd rather die with.* Mason's words rang in her head.

It was the most romantic thing anyone had ever said to her, but she wasn't quite ready to die. Not yet. Not by a long shot. For one thing, she wanted more of Mason. Wanted more of his long, hot body in her bed. She wasn't going to let any half-brained thugs cheat her out of some seriously good sex.

*Or a once-in-a-lifetime love,* the little voice in the back of her head dared to whisper.

But Charlee wasn't ready to hear it. A panicky sensation

that had nothing to do with the trouble they were in and everything to do with the terrifying thought that she might be falling in love with Mason squeezed her stomach with a sharp pressure.

"Damn. Batteries are dead." Petey's voice wrapped around them in the darkness. It sounded as if he were standing close enough for Charlee to encircle his wrist with her hand but she knew sound carried. He couldn't be as close as it seemed.

"There're more batteries in the glove compartment."

"Dammit, my nose is still frickin' bleedin'," Petey complained.

"It's your own fault. I told you they were up to something."

"Who woulda thought a rich guy would know that kung fu shit?"

"You're just pissed 'cause he kicked your ass."

"Shut up. He kicked your ass too."

"My nose isn't the one that's broken."

"Oh, yeah? They got *your* gun."

"Crawl on your belly," Mason told Charlee. "Fast as you can while Dumb and Dumber are busy arguing."

Charlee started crawling but the Glock jabbed her so hard she lost her breath. Quickly, she shifted the weapon to the back of her waistband. Mason was already several feet ahead of her.

"Stay with me."

"I'm coming," she said and then added mischievously, "and I don't mean that in a sexual way."

He merely grunted.

By the time the flashlight beam played over the grapevines above their heads, they'd traveled another few yards from the road. The sun had edged up a notch and when she turned her head to the left, Charlee could see the outline of a dilapidated barn squatting in the field several hundred yards away from the farmhouse and directly parallel to their current location.

The flashlight beam returned, this time sweeping lower to the ground.

"I see something," Petey called out.

"Is it them?"

"Can't tell."

"Hang on."

The car door slammed again. Sal and Petey were now both in the vineyard.

Charlee grabbed the Glock with both hands, rose to her feet, and spun around. As Maybelline always said, the best defense is a good offense.

"Charlee!" Mason cried out in despair. "What are you doing?"

The flashlight beam hit her in the face, blinding her, but she pretended she could see. She kept her wrist locked, the gun extended out in front of her.

She was taking a huge chance that he didn't have his own gun at the ready. "Back off, Petey, or I'll blow your head clean off your shoulders, I swear I will."

She heard him moving toward her. He kept the flashlight trained on her face. "Sorry, but I don't believe you."

Moistening her lips, she cocked the hammer. "Hear defeat?"

"I hear it, but do you have what it takes to kill someone? Come on, put the gun down, and play nice."

"Freeze. Don't take another step."

Petey kept moving toward her. "Oh, and by the way, since you've got a light in your eyes you probably aren't aware that I've got my gun trained on your head too and lucky for me, there's no light in my eyes. Guess we have ourselves a Mexican standoff."

"I don't want to kill you."

She stood with her legs splayed. Her heart rate curiously slow. She'd never been so calm in her life. She was vaguely aware of Mason having gotten to his feet behind her. She had no idea where Sal was at and that bothered her.

"You're not going to kill me," Petey said.

Charlee squinted against the powerful beam. Petey was just a few feet in front of her and sure enough, she saw that he held the thirty-eight in his right hand, the flashlight in his left.

*Well,* she thought. *It's come down to this. I'm going to kill a man tonight.*

She'd never killed anyone before.

*First time for everything. It's either him or you and Mason.*

She had to do something to gain the upper hand. Think! Think!

Then from behind her Mason flung sand in Petey's face and followed that with a fistful of grapes.

Chaos erupted.

Petey howled, dropped the flashlight and the gun as he raised his hands to his eyes.

At the same time, Sal came from behind Petey and dived for his gun.

Mason, who'd somehow gotten around to her side without Charlee being aware of it, kicked Petey's gun away just before Sal grabbed for it. Mason's foot made a solid whacking noise as it contacted against Sal's hand. The burly thug screamed like a girl.

Now or never.

She had to act before Sal or Petey found the gun. Charlee stared down the sight, aimed at Petey's right shoulder, and pulled the trigger.

*Click.*

"Bitch!" Petey screamed, enraged, and lumbered toward her. "You tried to kill me. I'll strangle you with my bare hands."

Desperately, she squeezed the trigger again.

*Click. Click.*

The gun was empty.

# Chapter 19

Plan B." Mason grabbed her arm and she dropped the useless Glock.

"Plan B?"

"Tear ass for the barn."

"Right behind you."

They took off at a dead run, Sal and Petey cursing and hollering and thrashing around behind them. To Charlee it felt as if they were barely moving, slogging through syrup instead of sand. By the time they reached the barn door and shoved it open, they were panting so hard Charlee feared her lungs would leap right out of her chest.

"That..." Mason paused to heave in air, "was the most courageous, most foolhardy stunt I've ever seen anyone pull."

"See what happens when you live in an ivory tower? You don't get to meet many brave, foolhardy women."

"Charlee, I could search the world over and not find many women as bold as you."

"Me? What about you? Flinging sand and grapes in Petey's face. Stroke of genius, I might add."

"I certainly couldn't let him kill you and I didn't want

you killing him either. It's a terrible thing carrying the burden of blame for someone's death."

Charlee met his dark, complicated eyes. It sounded as if he spoke from experience, but she had no time to explore his unexpected testimony.

"We've got to barricade the doors."

Her gaze scanned the barn. The usual garden stuff. Rusted rakes, hoes, and shovels. A Weed Eater, a collection of weathered two-by-fours, and baling wire. In the middle of the barn sat something large covered with a heavy gray tarp. A tractor maybe?

Grabbing the hoe, Charlee jammed the handle through the door latch while Mason wedged two-by-four braces between the door and the floor.

Mere seconds later Sal and Petey slammed into the door from the outside. It shuddered beneath the men's combined weight, but the blockade held despite their repeated battering.

In unison Mason and Charlee turned and spotted a large sliding metal door at the rear of the barn. He lunged for the rake and she grabbed a shovel.

"We're trapped, you realize," she said to Mason as they worked frantically to shore up the back door. "There's no way out of here. We've bested them twice, they know what we're capable of, we won't catch them with their guards down again. They're gonna get serious."

As if to prove her point, a bullet whizzed past Mason's ear and smashed into a support beam.

Another shot and then another. Bullets ricocheted around the barn, zinging off the tin siding and spitting into the dirt floor.

Charlee covered her ears with her hands, eyed the tarp, and wondered if by some stroke of luck the tractor still ran. If they could get the thing started and crash through the back door . . . then what?

Petey and Sal had guns. They did not. And top tractor speed couldn't be more than twenty or thirty miles an hour. Not nearly fast enough to outrun a bullet.

But it was the only option her fevered brain could conjure. But what if it wasn't a tractor? Maybe it was a car. She could hotwire that puppy in sixty seconds flat.

Yeah, like what were the odds the thing would even run?

"Fine," Petey yelled at them. "I'm tired of wastin' my bullets on you. You can't get out. We've got you surrounded. We can wait."

Thank heavens. She could think more clearly without bullets bouncing around the room like pinballs.

"Charlee," Mason said, his voice gone deadly hollow, "do you smell gasoline?"

Their eyes met.

The air was hot and rich with the pungent odor of petroleum. Mason darted to the front door and peeked out through a bullet hole.

"They're pouring gasoline on the barn."

"Bastards," she said vehemently and stalked over to the tarp. Grasping the heavy gray canvas with both hands, she yanked hard.

And uncovered a single-engine Piper.

"Great. Just lovely. Isn't that our rotten luck?" She flung her hands in the air. "We find a plane and neither of us knows how to fly it. Why the hell couldn't it have been a car or a tractor? I'd have even taken a go-cart."

Mason didn't say a word.

The gasoline smell grew stronger, permeating the entire barn. It wouldn't take much to set this pile of kindling ablaze.

She looked over at him. His face was ashen and she was shocked to see his hands trembling. His gaze was fixed on the plane and he looked as scared as she'd felt when he had plucked the black spider off her shoulder.

"Mason! What is it?" She sprang to his side. "What's wrong?"

He swallowed hard.

"Talk to me." She grabbed his shoulders and shook him. "What is it?"

"I know how to fly that plane," he said.

"That's a good thing. Right?"

Mason shook his head and passed his palm over his chin. His pulse galloped a thousand miles an hour. Fear was a teamster's fist in his stomach. Just looking at the plane made him nauseous.

"I'm terrified of flying the same way you're terrified of black widow spiders."

"No."

"Yes."

"But that's crazy. If you're a pilot, how can you be afraid of flying?" Her voice pleaded for logic, for a lucid explanation.

"Crash," he said, his voice sounding eerily robotic. "College freshman. My roommate and I borrowed my father's plane without permission. Kip was at the controls but I was still responsible. My idea. A freak thunderstorm caught us. Brought the plane down. Kip was killed. My fault."

Charlee sucked in her breath. "I'm sorry for what happened to you, but we're wasting valuable time. You've got to fly us out of here or we're going to end up crispy critters."

"Can't."

He didn't want to be this way, but his limbs were

paralyzed, useless. He tried to step toward the plane but even the sound of crackling wood and wisps of smoke seeping through the barn could not propel him forward.

Every terrifying moment leading up to the plane crash flashed through his mind. The huge fight he and his father had had over Mason's career path. His father demanding he drop his aviation courses and study finance. The plot he'd hatched to steal his father's plane to get even. Kip's enthusiastic support for the idiotic scheme. The savage storm. Kip's bravado that he could handle the weather. The bone-jarring impact as they hit the ground. The pain that shot through his shattered leg. Kip's blood on his hands. The cold, hard rain in his face.

He simply could not get into that plane.

"Okay," Charlee said. "I'm going to let you wrestle with those demons, while I hot-wire the engine. But you don't have long to make your decision. Basically here are your choices. Fly us out of here or die."

She was right. Simple as that.

Forget about Kip. Forget about the past. Forget your fear. Think about Charlee.

Without another word she marched over to the plane and started to climb in. She flung open the door, and then froze.

"Black widow," she said.

"I'll get it." For the first time he was able to walk toward the plane.

She squared her shoulders, tossed her head. "I can handle it." Then she picked up her foot and crushed the spider beneath the heel of her boot.

He stared at her, awestruck. The woman was truly and utterly amazing. He would do anything for her. Fight to the death if he had to. Fly that damned plane.

"Hot-wire the sucker," he said.

"About time." She coughed against the rising smoke.

She tinkered with the engine. Seconds ticked by. Then minutes.

Smoke thickened, swirled.

The engine caught, sputtered once and died. Charlee swore and tried again.

Flames licked across the floor, spreading closer, ever closer.

The engine sputtered again and lasted a little longer this time before it died.

Hurry, hurry.

The third time it worked. The engine turned over and purred.

The room was unbearably hot, the smoke so thick they could barely breathe.

"I'll open the back door," she wheezed. "As you taxi by I'll climb on."

Mason nodded and slid into the driver's seat. *It's just like riding a bicycle. You can do it.* If Charlee could squash that spider, he could fly the plane.

She yanked away the garden tools and shoved the door open while he set the plane in motion. The minute he committed himself, his fear evaporated and his long-forgotten joy in flying lifted inside him.

Charlee climbed into the passenger seat, grinning like he'd just won the powerball lottery. Hell, he felt as if he had just won the powerball lottery.

He gave the plane more gas, it jolted forward and they shot out the door. He pulled back on the throttle and they were airborne.

A triumphant cry burst from his lips. Ha! He had done it.

"Oops, here comes Dumb and Dumber."

Sal and Petey charged around the back of the burning barn but they were too late. The plane had already climbed thirty feet.

"Bye!" Charlee leaned out the window and waved.

For a minute there Mason thought Petey was going to shoot the plane, but obviously he thought better of firing a bullet straight into the air, because he holstered his gun.

Sal screamed at Petey. Petey flipped Sal off.

Mason grinned and grinned and grinned.

And then he got a bird's-eye view of the barn completely engulfed in flames and his heart rocketed into his throat. Dark, oily smoke spiraled skyward. If they had waited very much longer it would have been too late to escape.

At the thought of losing Charlee, his chest constricted.

"Yahoo!"

He glanced at her. She leaned over and kissed him lightly on the cheek. The warmth of her lips branded the moment in time.

"You were totally and completely awesome. I am so proud of you," she said.

"I've got to confess, if you hadn't had the courage to stomp on that black widow I don't know if I could have snapped out of my terror."

"Oh, really?" She arched an eyebrow.

"You inspired me."

"I'm guessing this might be a bad time to tell you I faked it. There wasn't any black widow. I pretended to squash a spider. Pretty smart of me, huh?" She looked like a schoolkid who'd made the honor roll for the first time.

"Babe," he said, "you're unbelievable."

The sun was up and the sky was clear. Fire engines wailed in the distance. He spotted the Chevy Malibu tearing off down the road at a frantic clip. Sal and Petey on the lam.

Mason took the plane higher, ascending several hundred feet into the air and followed the road west, stunned at how good he felt. How alive.

He'd been taken prisoner, tied up, shot at, burned out, and forced to face his greatest fear. And he had never been happier in his entire life. How sick was that?

All thanks to Charlee.

She was the magnet that picked up the shattered, scattered filaments of the daring youth he'd once been and she'd put him back together again. He felt reborn. A new man. A new start. A new life.

A life he ached to share with Charlee. But was he in love alone?

Glancing over at her, he experienced the strangest tightening in his chest. He studied her profile, admired the way her cheek curved, the way her glossy black hair fell to her shoulders and beyond. She was dirty and soot-stained and her blouse was torn but he had never seen a prettier sight.

"You're gorgeous."

"Watch what you're doing, cowboy. From what you told me back there I'm assuming your flying skills are rusty."

"I mean it, you're drop-dead gorgeous."

"Ha. I'm not sleek and petite like Daphne."

"Thank God."

"What's that supposed to mean?"

"You're you. Every wonderful inch of you."

She gave him a look.

"What? You *are* wonderful."

"And you're drunk on courage. Fly the plane."

"Yes, ma'am." He couldn't stop grinning.

"You know what I wish?"

"What?"

"I wish I had a tall glass of sweet tea with lots of crushed ice." Charlee sighed. "I could suck down two gallons."

"I wish I had a cheeseburger and fries."

"No kidding? You?"

"It is my favorite food, remember?"

"It's Skeet's favorite food. Not yours."

"Fat and protein sound like heaven to me right now."

"I can do you one better. I'm so hungry I'd even eat some of those gross fish eggs you're so wild about."

"Better watch out, Charlee Champagne," he teased. "We're starting to rub off on each other."

"Egads!" She chuckled. "What is the world coming to?"

What indeed? In four short days everything in his life had changed. On the surface, it had changed for the worst. But why did he feel freer than he had ever felt in his life?

She cleared her throat a few minutes later. "You might want to consider not flying beside the road."

Mason looked down, saw the Malibu speeding along behind them and his grin disappeared. "They've got to be doing ninety to keep up with us."

"All this brouhaha for a rigged Oscar? I don't get it."

"Oscar wins are a big deal," he said, angling the plane north out across the desert. "Winning one can shoot an actor from unknown status to the exclusive twenty-million-dollars-a-picture club and it can mean billions of dollars for the studio involved."

"Do you suppose the accounting firm has been cooking the books on the awards ever since 1955?"

That was a chilling thought. Mason pressed his lips together. Since Cahill's revelation he'd been too busy dodging bullets and running for his life to fully consider the implications. But now, reality sank in.

His grandfather and his entire family's reputation hung in the balance. That's why Gramps had taken off alone. Somehow he'd found out about the bastardized accounting practices. That was why he had kept silent until he'd had a chance to investigate for himself. And that was probably why Nolan had taken the half-million dollars. He hadn't known ahead of time who he might have to bribe, hire, or hush up, so he'd taken enough money to cover any eventuality.

A spear of worry arrowed through him when he thought about Nolan and Maybelline. Where were they? If Cahill didn't have them, had Elwood recaptured them? And just where did Charlee's father factor in this whole Oscar scenario?

One thing was certain. They couldn't worry about Maybelline and Nolan. Not right now.

Top priority, they had to get to L.A. before the Academy Awards ceremony, audit the votes, and announce the real winner of the best supporting actor category. If he couldn't prevent Blade Bradford from getting the award, his entire family fortune would be destroyed.

But they had plenty of time. It wasn't even seven o'clock in the morning and L.A. was less than two hundred miles away. The Academy Awards didn't start until seven. That gave them a full twelve hours. No sweat. They would even have time for a meal, a shower, and a change of clothes.

And then the airplane sputtered ominously. Startled, his gaze shifted to the instrument panel.

The engine coughed. Once, twice, three times.

"Uh-oh," he said.

"What is it?"

"Look around. Quick. Help me find a good place to land."

"What's wrong?"

"We're out of gas."

Charlee ran a hand through her tangled hair and shook her head. She wanted to whine, but she was tougher than that. It seemed as if they'd been walking for weeks.

She was tired and hungry and thirsty. Her boots were rubbing blisters on her heels, her nose was sunburned, and she smelled of sweat and dirt and smoke and general run-of-the-mill funk. She wished for her cowboy hat and sunscreen and two dozen Band-Aids. She wished for toothpaste and a hairbrush and toilet paper.

But mostly, she wished for water. Cool, clear water.

So much for tough. Apparently, she was as soft as the next girl.

Mason had safely landed the plane, albeit in the middle of a cactus patch. Gingerly, they'd clambered out only to realize with despair they had no idea where they were.

It was long past noon, edging on toward one-thirty, she guessed.

"We've got to get to L.A. before the Oscars tonight," Mason said. They walked side by side, kicking up sand and dust behind them.

"So you told me. About a hundred times."

"I can't stress how important this is."

"I get it, I get it, but what can we do about it, Mason? We can't even find the friggin' highway and if we did, for all we know Sal and Petey are trolling it with orders from Cahill to shoot on sight."

"It's a big stretch of road between here and L.A. Sorry, but Petey and Sal just aren't that good."

"Hey, maybe even as we speak your grandfather is taking care of all this. Right now he and Maybelline could be at the accounting firm running roughshod on the number crunchers."

"We can hope."

"Boy, if that's your hopeful face don't let me see discouraged."

"Charlee," he said, "I'm on the verge of losing everything."

"That's gotta suck. Especially when you were on the verge of finding yourself."

He frowned at her. "What are you talking about?"

"When you were up in the air you were a completely different person. Relaxed, calm, confident. Now the old Mason is back. Anxious, controlling, argumentative."

"I'm not argumentative."

"You're arguing right now."

"This isn't arguing."

"What is it?"

"Charlee, I still don't think you get it. If we don't stop Blade Bradford from winning and it comes out after the fact that our accounting firm cheated, the Gentry name will be destroyed. In a business like ours reputation is everything. Companies will pull their accounts. Our stock value will plummet. The scandal will affect not only my family, but also all the people who work for us, or do business with us. You saw what happened to the stock market after Enron and WorldCom and Tyco."

"Your family has that much influence on the U.S. economy?"

"That's what I've been trying to tell you."

"Oh." She paused a moment. She knew Mason was rich and powerful. She had no idea he was *that* rich and powerful. Her secret lingering hope that things could work out between them all but evaporated. "Well, then walk faster."

"I'm glad you appreciate the gravity of the situation."

"So," she said, a few minutes later, "what would happen if, say, Blade did win and you and your grandfather just kept your mouths shut?"

"You mean cover up the accounting discrepancy?"

She slanted a glance over at him. "It seems like the easy way out."

"You mean just let Cahill and Bradford get away with their scam?"

"It's what most people would do."

Mason shook his head. "Let's concentrate on getting to L.A. so I'm not faced with that temptation."

Two hours later they finally reached the highway. Mason was so wound up about the time slipping away from them that Charlee thought she was going to have to put Valium on the top of her "I want" list behind food, sweet tea, and a long cool shower. The Valium was for him, not for her.

They hurried to the edge of the road.

It was empty. Not a vehicle in sight.

"Shall we?" Charlee inclined her head toward L.A. and tried not to limp. Her heels felt as if her leather boots had flayed the flesh to the bone. The only consolation, she hadn't been wearing Violet's ankle strap stilettos for the trek.

"You're hobbling," he said.

"It's nothing."

"Guess those boots weren't made for walking."

"Ha, ha. Normally they are very comfortable. They're rubbing blisters because I don't have on any socks. Violet apparently doesn't believe in them."

He stopped walking, turned toward her, and motioned with his index finger. "Come here."

"What for?"

"I'm going to give you a piggyback ride."

"No, you're not."

"Don't be so damned stubborn, woman. You can barely walk."

"Mason, I'm no little thing. I weigh a hundred and thirty-five pounds."

"I don't care. Get over here."

"You say you don't care now . . ."

Before she could finish her sentence he stalked over and slung her unceremoniously over his shoulder.

"Hey, wait, stop it. Put me down."

"Only if you agree to let me give you a piggyback ride."

"Okay, all right, I'll do it."

They trudged along the shoulder of the road, Mason carrying Charlee on his back, her bare legs wrapped around his muscled waist, her skirt hem flapping as he walked. She felt guilty, but man-o-man did her feet ever feel better.

Minutes passed, then half an hour. No car. No truck. Not even a motorcycle.

"Why don't we take a break," she said, fretting about his back.

He stopped and let her slide gently to the ground. "Where is this godforsaken place?" he asked. "I didn't think anywhere in America was this deserted."

"It's just a bad time of day. The later it gets the more likely it is someone will come along."

"Charlee, we're still three hours outside of L.A."

"Okay, let's not get off on the time issue again." *Or I'll have to strangle you with my bare hands.*

"Listen."

They stopped walking and cocked their heads.

"Sounds like an engine."

"Quick, stick out your thumb."

"Better yet, I'll strike a pose," Charlee said and imitated Claudette Colbert from *It Happened One Night*. It helped that she had on a skirt so short Barbie could have used it for a hanky.

They peered into the distance, waiting. Heat waves shimmered up from the ground like gasoline fumes, wriggling and crinkling and blurring the edges of reality.

Finally, an aging flatbed truck chugged into view over the rise. Charlee wriggled her leg provocatively. Mason stuck out his thumb.

*Please stop, please stop, please stop.*

The truck putt-putted leisurely over the asphalt. A smiling dark-complexioned woman sat behind the wheel, three hound dogs lolled on the front seat beside her. She waved at them and pulled over.

Mason and Charlee raced to the truck.

The woman gave them a dazzling smile and said something in Spanish. They shrugged. She pointed to the back of the truck stacked high with crates of strawberries. Apparently she wasn't about to dethrone her dogs for hitchhikers.

Who cared? It was a ride.

*"Gracias, gracias,"* they repeated and hurried around the truck, ready to hop in the back among all those delicious-smelling strawberries.

Only to be stopped by an unexpected but totally wonderful surprise.

There, curled up in each other's arms, looking just as grime-ridden and road-weary and hungry as Mason and Charlee, sat their grandparents.

# *Chapter 20*

Charlee flung herself into her grandmother's arms. "Maybelline! You're alive."

All four of them started hugging and laughing and talking at once with no one getting a word in edgewise. Charlee glanced over at Mason. He winked at her and gave the time-out gesture. "Okay, all right. One at a time. You start, Gramps. What happened?"

The attractive older man who shared a remarkable resemblance to Mason said, "Actually, the story starts with Maybelline. If she hadn't intervened, I might never have found out that Blade Bradford, his wife, and Spencer Cahill were rigging the Oscars."

Maybelline looked at Charlee with a happy glow in her eyes that she had never seen there before.

*She's in love with Mason's grandfather.* The thought hit Charlee out of the blue and when Nolan squeezed Maybelline's hand and smiled at her, she knew not only was it true, but that Nolan loved her grandmother in return.

Her stomach gave a funny little boot to her heart. Charlee slid a sidelong glance at Mason and her stomach kicked harder. Were she and Maybelline going to end up with dual broken hearts after all this was over? The women from the wrong side of the tracks falling for the guys far out of their league?

"Have some strawberries." Maybelline passed around an open crate of the juicy ripe fruit like the perfect hostess. "Angelina told us to help ourselves."

Charlee grabbed a handful of strawberries, leaned back against a stack of crates, and nibbled them politely instead of wolfing them down the way she wanted. Mason was sitting on the opposite side of the truck with Maybelline and Nolan sandwiched between the two of them.

Silly as it seemed, Charlee missed sitting next to him. For the past four days they'd been side by side almost constantly.

"It all started forty-seven years ago," Maybelline began, "when I first came to Hollywood, met a charismatic actor, and thought I'd fallen in love."

Charlee shifted her gaze to Nolan. He shook his head, denying he was the actor in question.

"It was only later, after I got pregnant with your father, Charlee, that I discovered the man was already married."

"Blade Bradford," Mason guessed.

"Yes," Maybelline admitted.

"How come you never told me this before?" Charlee asked her grandmother.

"I was ashamed. Embarrassed that I'd been taken advantage of. I never told anyone. Not even Elwood."

"You had nothing to be ashamed of," Nolan said gruffly.

Maybelline smiled at Mason. "Your grandfather was wonderful. In fact, he stopped me from flinging myself off the HOLLYWOOD sign."

Her grandmother had once tried to kill herself? Charlee

struggled to imagine her tough-minded granny as a young and vulnerable girl and finally gave up. The years had erased all traces of the naive innocent she had once been.

But then she caught Nolan looking at Maybelline. In his eyes, Charlee saw that young, troubled girl. How little she really knew about her own grandmother.

"Anyway, fast forward to the future," Maybelline said to Mason. "My son Elwood, who much to my unhappiness has always had trouble controlling his impulses, got in deep with gambling debts. He shoplifted cigarettes in order to get thrown in jail to avoid his creditors."

"I remember that," Charlee said. "I thought it seemed really weird at the time since he doesn't smoke, but he told me he'd planned on selling the cigarettes."

Maybelline sighed. "While he was in lock-up he met some guy who told him he could help him locate his biological father. Elwood got all excited. Not about the thought of meeting his father, but because it was another person he could put the bite on. I discovered all this after the fact of course."

"Let me guess," Charlee interjected. "Elwood blackmailed Blade Bradford."

The truck hit a bump and they all went sliding into each other. They righted themselves and Maybelline continued with her story.

"Elwood sent Blake a letter demanding five hundred thousand dollars or he threatened to go to the *National Enquirer* with what happened forty-seven years ago. But Elwood got more than he bargained for. In the blackmail letter, he was talking about his illegitimate birth. But apparently Blade thought he was talking about how he and his wife and father-in-law had rigged the Oscar votes so he would beat out Nolan for best actor."

"And Elwood's threats couldn't have come at a worse time," Mason said. "Considering how Blade was up for another Oscar again this year."

"Exactly."

Mason ate a strawberry and glanced at Charlee over the top of her grandmother's head. He had to fight the urge to drag her into his arms, kiss those rich, berry-stained lips and make all sorts of wild promises to her that he feared he could not keep.

"And," Nolan added, "unfortunately enough, Spencer Cahill stumbled across the records from 1955 and he was putting the squeeze on Blade's wife to put in another fix."

"So," Maybelline told Charlee, "this was when Cahill got involved and sent hired guns after your father with the intention of rubbing him out."

"We're quite familiar with Sal and Petey and what they're capable of." Charlee shook her head.

"Elwood had no knowledge of the Oscar fix until he went to confront Blade in person and tell him to call off his goons. He found Blade in the process of shredding documents. He and Blade had a fight and Elwood stole some of the documents. He didn't really understand what he'd uncovered but the date was 1955, so he brought a copy to me."

"Your grandmother knew I'd purchased controlling interest in the accounting firm for nostalgic reasons and she rightly supposed I had no idea I'd been cheated out of the Oscar in 1955. She called and asked me to come to Vegas and help her sort this out," Nolan told Charlee.

Then turning to Mason, he said, "I took the half mil from the company fund not only because I was going to pay Elwood's blackmail fee to keep him quiet about what had happened, but to get the family to send you after me." He grinned. "I knew they'd send you and not Hunter."

"You wanted me to come after you?"

"Of course. I needed help and I couldn't do this alone but I had to keep things quiet. Couldn't risk any of this leaking out."

"Why didn't you want them to send Hunter?"

Nolan laughed. "You've got to get over this second-son-in-the-Gentry-family syndrome, Mason. It held me back for too long. Kept me from my first love." He gazed tenderly at Maybelline. "Besides, Hunter couldn't find his ass in the dark with both hands."

Mason had to laugh too. "I can't take the credit for finding you. Charlee's the bloodhound."

"I'd say you make a pretty terrific team," Maybelline said.

This probably wasn't the time to burst their bubble and tell them that he and Charlee had found them purely by accident.

"Where's the money now?" Mason asked.

"I stashed it in a safe deposit box in Vegas," Nolan said.

"In the meantime," Maybelline said, "Elwood gets another visit from his creditors. He goes back to Blade, convinces him he's on his side, and offers to kidnap us and hold us hostage until after the Oscars are over."

Nolan continued the story, telling how Elwood had taken them to the vacant studio lot outside Tucson, how they'd escaped but been recaptured by Blade and Elwood working together after the camper broke down. He told them about being held prisoner in the abandoned mine shaft, how they'd found a false bottom in the floor, tunneled their way out, and hitched a ride to L.A. with Angelina.

Mason and Charlee then related everything they'd been through.

"What time is it?" Mason asked, after they'd finished their stories. "The Oscar ceremony starts at seven."

"But the Oscars drag on for hours," Charlee observed. "We can make it."

"Unfortunately, best supporting actor is one of the first nontechnical awards given out," Nolan said. "The sooner we get there the better."

"We have to get backstage," Mason continued. "Tell the presenters there's been a discrepancy. We can do major damage control if we can make it in time to stop the Oscar from being awarded to Blade." His eyes met his grandfather's.

"I know." Nolan nodded. "If we don't stop it beforehand, they'll think our family was in on the fix."

Maybelline consulted her watch. "It's five-thirty now and at the rate Angelina is driving, I'm afraid we're still a good two hours out of L.A."

They parted company with Angelina in Palm Springs and Mason's grandfather rented a Ford Explorer. Nolan drove hell-bent for leather, but the closer they got to L.A. the thicker the traffic grew. By the time they arrived at the Academy Awards venue, it was twenty minutes after seven and the place was swarming with security and media.

"How the hell are we going to get in?" Nolan gloomily asked him.

Mason pulled the crumpled tickets Pam Harrington had given him from his back pocket. "I've got it covered. Once Charlee and I get in, we'll identify ourselves, explain what's going on, and send someone out after you two."

"Sound plan." Nolan nodded. "Go, go, go."

Mason and Charlee tumbled out of the Explorer and rushed the red carpet.

After running a gauntlet of security checkpoints where the guards simply couldn't believe these two dirty, bedraggled wayfarers held VIP invitations to the lavish event, they finally stepped inside the theater lobby at seven forty-five.

*Don't let us be too late,* Charlee prayed.

An usher came forward, nose curled in distaste at their clothing, to escort them to their seats.

"We're not going to be sitting down," Mason started to explain but then Charlee spotted a tuxedoed Elwood leaving the men's room. She grabbed Mason's arm and whispered, "There's my father."

Charlee glared at Elwood. He looked like a convict caught scaling the prison walls at midnight in his underwear.

"Dad, you freeze right there," she growled.

Elwood raised his palms in a defensive gesture. "Now, baby girl," he said, "don't go jumpin' to conclusions." A split second later he turned tail and raced toward the theater.

"I can't let him get away," Mason said and sprinted after her father.

In ten long-legged strides, Mason tackled Elwood in the archway.

"Sirs, sirs," the usher chided. "No roughhousing at the Oscars."

Elwood threw a punch but Mason blocked it.

Then her father tried to head-butt Mason. He simply grabbed Elwood in a headlock and the two men went down in a heap of windmilling arms and legs.

"Dad, stop it!" Charlee yelled. "It's over. You're busted."

"You really don't want to mess with me, buddy," Mason

growled through clenched teeth. "I'd love to plow my fist into your kisser for the way you've treated Charlee alone, never mind blackmailing my grandfather."

"Stop fighting. Stop it right now or I'll get security," the usher cried.

Several elegantly dressed people seated near the entrance craned their necks to take a gander at the brawl, which was obviously more interesting than the thank-you speech of the guy who'd just accepted the Oscar for best theatrical lighting.

"And I want to thank my first grade teacher, Miss Dingleberry, and Phil, the guy who used to drive the Popsicle truck on my block, and my dentist, Dr. Purdy," the P.A. system resonated the award-winner's droning, endless speech.

Elwood flinched at Mason's cocked fist. "Don't hit me, man. It wasn't anything personal against your grandfather. I had debts to pay."

"It was pretty damned personal to Charlee. Imagine, her father is a blackmailing scumbag who kidnapped his own mother for money."

Elwood slanted a shamefaced look toward Charlee. "I was in trouble. I owed the wrong guys money. They set my apartment on fire."

"You're always in trouble."

"I didn't mean to hurt anyone. Sorry, honey, but you understand, don'tcha?"

"I understand all right. I understand you never cared about anything except yourself and money." Uttering the words had a liberating effect on Charlee.

For years she'd made excuses for her father, unable to believe he simply was incapable of loving her the way she loved him. She'd hoped and prayed and wished for things to be different but they weren't. Once she let go of her childish expectations, she understood he no longer held the power to break her heart. Elwood was Elwood and she could never change him. So be it.

"Get up." Mason snatched Elwood by his lapels and lifted him to his feet.

"And next," the dulcet voice of a famous actress resonated throughout the theater, "the award for best supporting actor."

The announcement jolted Charlee's focus off her father. They were about to give away the award for best supporting actor. To hell with Elwood, they had to stop the award presentation before it was too late.

She jerked her head toward the stage and that's when she realized they were surrounded by cops.

"And the Oscar goes to . . . Blade Bradford."

Mason grimaced. The minute the words left the presenter's mouth, his life changed forever.

Music swelled. The audience applauded. Stunned, Mason watched as Blade Bradford got to his feet and made his way toward the stage.

"You are under arrest," said the cop who was snapping handcuffs around his wrists. "You have the right to remain silent."

Mason tuned out the rest of his Miranda rights, every bit of his attention concentrated on Blade Bradford at the podium waving his statue over his head in victory.

He'd been unable to stop Bradford from accepting his bogus Oscar. Mason had lost. He'd failed.

And now he faced the greatest moral dilemma of his life.

Save his family from scandal by covering up the accounting discrepancies and thereby compromising all his deeply held values, beliefs, and principles, or go public with the knowledge the Oscars had been falsified and accept the fact his family would be financially ruined.

As the cops hauled him from the theater along with Elwood, his gaze met Charlee's. The tears glistening in her eyes sucker-punched him square in the gut.

He realized then that if he took the easy way out, kept quiet and allowed Cahill and Bradford and their henchmen to get away with their crimes simply to salvage his money and reputation, he would be just like all the other men who had betrayed her. From her shiftless father to that creep of a senator who groped her in the pantry to Gregory Blankensonship who'd taken her virginity, treated her like she didn't matter and made her question her own worth.

He could not let her down.

In that moment Mason knew what he must do, the consequences be damned.

# Chapter 21

The next morning Charlee paced the hallway outside the meeting room of the Beverly Hills Grand Piazza where Mason had scheduled a press conference.

After the fiasco at the Academy Awards, Nolan had booked her and Maybelline a room at the hotel while he'd gone to retrieve Mason from the county holding cell. For the time being, she and Maybelline had decided against posting Elwood's bond. Let him stew in jail.

Charlee hadn't seen Mason since he'd been arrested and she was nervous. Going before the press, admitting his family's company had been involved in an accounting scandal so huge it threatened to rock Hollywood to the core, could not be easy. She also felt at loose ends with herself, not knowing what to say to him, uncertain of her role in the outcome of the unfolding events.

They'd left so many things unsaid. So many important issues not discussed.

What did he need from her?

What did she want from him?

Where did they go from here?

The place buzzed with news media speculating on

the details of why they'd been assembled. Camera crews strung wires and cords throughout the conference rooms. A soundman checked the podium mike. Charlee forced herself not to chew her fingernails.

At five minutes before nine, a well-dressed middle-aged couple hurried down the corridor looking harried and concerned; beside them walked Mason's ex-fiancée-to-be, Daphne Maxwell. The man bore a striking resemblance to both Nolan and Mason.

And then she realized the couple must be Mason's parents.

Panic clutched her. Not wanting to be seen, Charlee glanced around for a place to hide, and spied the reprieve of a bronze metal modern art sculpture just a few feet from the open door of the conference room.

She flung herself on the other side of it and crouched down just in the nick of time. Her heart stabbed her chest. She heard the sound of footsteps on the terrazzo floor. Daphne and the Gentrys came to stand beside the sculpture. Daphne had her back to Charlee but she stood so close, Charlee could have reached out and wrapped her wrists around the woman's slender panty hose-clad ankle.

*Oh, crap.*

"Mason said he'd meet us here before he started the conference," Daphne murmured.

"I just hope we're not too late to talk some sense into our son," Mason's father said.

"I'm sure he'll listen to reason," his mother soothed. "If Mason absolutely insists on going public with this Oscar mess, then the least he can do is mend fences with Daphne. After all, she's willing to forgive and forget, which is very generous of her, and he owes the family that much consideration."

"You're absolutely right," his father said. "Our stocks are going to take a terrible hit in the fallout. We can't lose Daphne as both our publicist and future daughter-in-law too. Our son has got to listen to reason."

"Mason just went a little crazy, dear, but I'm sure once we speak with him, he'll see the error of his ways," his mother went on.

"It's that woman," Daphne said darkly. "She's corrupted his values. Once he's back home in Houston, surrounded by friends and family, he'll forget all about his little road fling."

Charlee's throat constricted. Road fling. That's all she was and she knew it. She could never be good enough for Mason and his family. She was no sleek, chic, high-society woman.

More footsteps echoed and when she heard Mason's voice she came completely unraveled. Her knees shook and her hands turned cold and clammy.

"Mother, Father." A long pause ensued. "And Daphne. I want to thank you for staying on as our publicist and agreeing to represent Gentry Enterprises in this matter."

"Daphne isn't here just as our publicist, son."

"She's willing to give you a second chance and for the good of the family business your father and I feel you should listen to what she has to say."

Charlee wished she could see Mason's face. What was he thinking? How did he feel about the pressure his parents were putting on him? Would he eagerly embrace a return to his old life and leave her in his rear-view mirror?

Before Mason could respond, she heard someone else approach.

"Mr. Gentry, Paul Stillson with KEMR news. Is the

rumor true? Has your accounting firm been rigging the Oscar votes for almost fifty years?"

"Please," Mason said. "Have a seat in the conference room with the other reporters. I'm on my way in. Mother, Father. Daphne."

Everyone moved away.

Charlee let out her breath without even realizing she'd been holding it. She waited a couple of minutes, then crept from behind the sculpture and slipped into the conference room.

It was standing room only. She waited just inside the door, spotted Maybelline and Nolan sitting beside each other up front.

Mason and Daphne stood at the podium together. Mason was sharply put together in an elegant navy blue suit, white shirt, and red silk power tie. He looked as if he'd stepped straight from the pages of *Fortune* magazine. Daphne was equally snazzy in a dove gray suit with pearl buttons and a pink lace blouse. His dark hair contrasted with her pale blondness. They looked tailor-made for each other.

Charlee swallowed hard and glanced down at Violet's short skirt and the Hellraiser T-shirt she'd washed out by hand the night before. She hadn't had the chance to buy anything new this morning and last night all the stores had been closed.

'Nuff said.

No matter what secret romantic thoughts to the contrary had been swirling around in the back of her mind, she and Mason were never going to get together. They were too different. Their worlds diametrically opposed.

The rich boy and the girl from the wrong side of the tracks.

Mason cleared his throat and began to talk. A murmur of shock undulated around the room as he told the reporters what he had discovered about the Oscar ballot discrepancies.

Pride filled her chest. She was so damned impressed with him. He wasn't like the other rich, powerful men who'd disappointed her. He sacrificed his family's reputation for what was right.

Mason looked up from the paper in his hands and his eyes met hers across the room. Charlee gasped as his gaze branded her. She felt the heat straight to her bones.

She blinked, trying to break eye contact to regain her equilibrium, but it didn't work. They were connected, seared, linked by something much more powerful than mere chemistry.

A blast of air from the open window cut through her cotton T-shirt and in that awful moment Charlee realized how much she was going to miss him.

And then she knew.

She'd lost her cool. She'd fallen and she was never ever going to be able to get up.

No matter how hard she'd tried to avoid it, no matter how she'd fought against her feelings, no matter how she'd struggled not to let him under her skin and into her heart, she was in love with a man she could never claim as her own.

The second his eyes met Charlee's Mason's brain shut down. He forgot about the reporters in the audience, he forgot about his parents, he forgot about Daphne pressing her palm against his lower back.

He stopped speaking in midsentence, his stare focused on the lone woman standing at the back of the room. The reporters turned their heads to see what he was staring at.

Daphne took the press release from his hand, stepped up to the microphone, and took over reading what he'd written last night while he'd been in jail.

At one time, Daphne was what he had thought he'd wanted. A woman to stand by his side as his business partner. A woman his family approved of. A woman with the right breeding, the right looks, the right contacts.

Mason realized that until he'd met Charlee, he'd had no idea what *he* really wanted.

To make amends for coming clean about the Oscar scandal and thereby causing deep financial losses to Gentry Enterprises, his parents were pressuring him to get back together with Daphne. But the old guilt trip no longer worked. For twenty-seven years he'd done what the Gentry name demanded, putting what was best for the family ahead of his own wants, needs, and desires.

What he wanted was Charlee Champagne.

But what did he have to offer her? Scandal. Shame. Dishonor. She deserved so much more than he could give.

These thoughts raced through his head in a matter of seconds. Daphne had finished reading the press report and the reporters were yelling questions at him but Mason didn't hear a thing they said. All he heard was the strumming of his pulse in his ears.

*Charlee. Charlee. Charlee.*

She was the woman he loved with all his heart. He'd known it the night he'd made love to her and looked deeply into her emerald eyes. She had given him his freedom and she had taught him to let go and just live. She was the toughest, strongest, most independent woman he'd ever met and he loved her for it.

Because of her, he'd taken chances he would never have taken. He'd faced his fears and come out the victor.

Because of Charlee he had learned to stop trying to live up to everyone's expectations and make the choices that were right for *him*. She'd taught him that a name didn't make the man but that the man made the name.

The realization sent his mind reeling. The liberty that a new belief in himself could bring opened up so many possibilities. He could be anything he wanted to be.

"Mr. Gentry," a reporter demanded. "Just how deep does this scandal go?"

Daphne nudged him in the ribs and Mason broke eye contact with Charlee to answer the man's questions. First he had to finish the press conference, but after this was over, he and Charlee were going to have a long, serious talk. He had to tell her how he felt. Question was, did she feel the same way?

He glanced at the back of the room again, hoping to find an answer in her eyes, but panic, much stronger even than what he'd felt the night before at the Oscars, knocked his world out from under his feet.

Charlee was gone.

Charlee's Band-Aid-covered blisters rubbed against the heels of her boots as she raced through the Grand Piazza, tears misting her eyes. Violet Hammersmitz's flouncy little skirt tail slapped the back of her thighs.

In the lobby, she stumbled through a crowd of curiosity seekers who'd gathered to hear the outcome of the press conference. People peered at her with prying eyes, escalating her sense of desperation. She had to get out of here. She saw Pam Harrington from Twilight Studios and Edith Beth McCreath among the milling throng. The women called out to her but Charlee ducked her head and just kept going.

Despair consumed her.

She lifted her thumb to her mouth to gnaw her fingernail but stopped with her hand halfway to her lips when
she saw the flash of shiny red polish.

Be Still My Heart.

What on earth had compelled her to get emotionally
close enough to a man that she would allow him to paint
her fingernails?

Her crimson nails taunted her. She yearned to soak
her hands in fingernail polish remover and eradicate all
evidence that she had foolishly let down her guard when
she'd known better.

From the minute she'd seen Mason Gentry in the parking lot outside her detective agency she'd known he carried the potential to break her heart. She hated this feeling.
She wanted her cynicism back, her detached aloofness, her
sharp-tongued defenses.

"Charlee!" It was Mason's voice and he was coming
after her.

No. No. She couldn't bear to look into his eyes again.
Couldn't stand knowing she must send him away.

"Charlee!" He was running to catch up with her.

She shouldered her way through the mob that was
growing thicker by the moment and hit the revolving glass
door that led to the sidewalk and freedom.

But she knew it was far too late for regrets. She'd
already fallen in love with Mason and he was out of her
league and out of her reach.

*Let go.*

A dissenting whisper started in the back of her brain,
low and seductive, rousing a rabble of contradictory
thoughts. Let go of what? The limitations of the past? Her
love for Mason? Her regrets? What?

*Let go.*

But she didn't want to let go. Holding on kept her sane. Clinging to her beliefs about rich men provided a safety net. But Mason was different and she knew it. He didn't fit the mold. He wasn't a stereotype. He hadn't hurt her on purpose.

*Let go of...*

Her boots slapped against the cement as she hit the sidewalk. She cupped her hands over her ears to drown out the noise in her head but it was no use.

*Let go of your...*

She did not want to hear this. Could not deal with the consequences of the statement. If she let go, then wouldn't she fly apart into a million vulnerable pieces? She didn't want to let go. She just wanted to be free. Free of the dread now strangling her heart.

*Let go of your fears, Charlee Champagne. Let go and accept the inevitable.*

But she could not.

"Charlee, wait."

She ran but he ran faster. She chugged a good four blocks from the hotel before he caught her.

Mason grabbed her elbow and spun her around to face him. He was breathing as heavily as she. Charlee studied his broad chest and refused to look him in the eyes.

"Let go of me." She tried to pull away.

"I won't. We've got to talk."

"There's nothing to talk about."

"Why did you leave?"

"I don't belong."

"You do belong. You belong with me."

"Daphne belongs with you. You're two of a kind. You're perfect for each other. Your parents want you to be with her."

"I don't give a damn what my parents want."

"Since when?"

"Since I fell in love with you."

She sucked in her breath. Had she heard him right? Mason was in love with her?

He crooked a finger under her chin and forced her head up. "Look at me, Charlee."

Reluctantly, she looked into his eyes. Every emotion she'd struggled to deny knotted her stomach. Love and hope and longing and desire snarled together and grew bigger by the moment.

She caught her breath at what she saw swimming in the warm brown depths of Mason's eyes.

"I know we're night and day," he said. "I know we come from completely different worlds. I know we've been acquainted less than a week. I know at times we irritate the hell out of each other, but I also know I've never felt this way about anyone in my entire life."

"Not even Matilda?"

"Not even Matilda."

"Really?"

"Trust me, I never expected to feel this way but from the minute I walked into your office you turned my life upside down."

"Ha. You turned mine into a roller coaster."

"You made me hunger for a life I'd always shied away from. You made me feel wild and free. You made me stop and consider who I really was and what I really wanted. Always being in control can get old and you showed me how to let go and live in the moment."

"I did all that?"

"You know you did. But I don't have much to offer you now except chaos. My family's fortune is in jeopardy, my reputation is shot, I just quit my job as Gentry Enterprises' investment banker. For the first time in my life, I don't know what's going to happen next and I feel freer than I've ever felt before. There, I've laid it all out for you. So now I've got to know, Charlee, how do you feel about me?"

Her heart thumped. He loved her. "How do I feel about you?"

"That's the question." He swallowed hard and she knew it was mean to leave him hanging but dang if she couldn't help but savor the moment.

"Hmm. You're pretty compulsive." She frowned and stroked her chin with her thumb and index finger.

"Yeah." A nervous expression hovered on his face.

"And you worry too much about what other people think of you."

"Uh-huh."

"You have an irritating habit of always doing the right thing."

"Is that so bad?"

"You're overly cautious and a stickler for the rules and have this annoying tendency of looking ten times before you leap."

"Yes, yes." He tightened his grip on her arm.

Oh, she was a rat for keeping him on tenterhooks. Relenting, she cocked him a sideways grin and he rewarded her with his dimpled smile.

"You're messing with me."

"Lucky for you I'm none of those things."

"What are you saying, Charlee?"

"I'm saying you balance me, Mason. We're two halves of a whole. And I love chaos and I have never placed much importance on money so if you lose your entire fortune

I could really care less and hey, you can always come work for me at the detective agency if you need a job."

He pulled her against him, lowered his head until his mouth was almost touching hers. "Say it, Charlee. Tell me what I need to hear."

Tears stung her eyes as the words leaped to her lips, words she feared she would never be able to say. "I love you, Mason Gentry, from the bottom of my heart, from the top of my soul, and everywhere in between."

# Epilogue

Tell me your most confidential fantasy," Mason whispered to Charlee in the darkness of her newly renovated office. He'd snuffed all the lights, locked the front door, and drawn the curtains. His disembodied voice floated disconnected, heightening the mystery of their true confessions and sending her senses reeling. "I want to know every intimate detail."

"I am Princess Charming," Charlee said, loving the fact she was sharing her most private daydreams with him. Six months ago she would have rather had her tongue plucked out than reveal herself so openly to a man. But six months ago, she hadn't been married to Mason. She marveled at the changes in her, reveled in the thrill and closeness such sharing had brought into her life. "And you are Cinderfella. You must do everything I command."

"Yes, Princess."

"Take off your clothes." She heard his belt slither through the loops of his pants, the rasp of his zipper going down, the whisper of denim. The sounds escalated her arousal.

"I'm naked."

"Come to me."

She heard his boots tread across the hardwood floor. The neon blue boots that matched her own. Her breathing quickened as she imagined his nakedness, except for those boots.

"I am here." His breath was hot on her neck.

She reached out with one long fingernail painted Be Still My Heart red and slowly tracked her finger over his bare skin, running down his shoulder to his chest and beyond.

He hissed in his breath.

She chuckled.

"And now?" he asked. She could feel his heartbeat thumping in rhythm with her own.

"Sweep my fireplace."

"What is that a euphemism for?"

"Guess."

He bit her ear. "Tell me or Cinderfella will have his fairy godfather turn him into one very excited prince."

"Sit on the desk."

He obeyed. Princess Charming shucked her dress and straddled him.

"No underwear?"

"A princess can never tell when she might need servicing by her Cinderfella."

"Ah," he said and pulled her body on top of his, taking their intimacy to the deepest heights of all with love and passion and secret whispers.

Later as they lay curled in each other's arms on the couch near the window, Charlee couldn't help thinking of all the things they'd overcome for their happy-ever-after ending.

The Oscar scandal had been front-page news. You

couldn't turn on the television or pick up a newspaper or listen to the radio without hearing about the infamous accounting dishonor.

People had gossiped about it at the beauty salons, over the water-cooler at work, in soccer carpools and doctor's offices. Online chat rooms had buzzed with rumors. Stand-up comedians had lampooned the Gentrys. The *National Enquirer* had a field day trying to guess which actors really had not deserved their Oscar for the past forty-seven years.

As Mason had predicted, the minute the news hit the Associated Press wire, the value of Gentry Enterprises plummeted. Actors had quaked in their boots wondering if their Oscar had been part of an illegal fix.

Cahill, Blade Bradford, and his wife were charged with conspiracy to commit fraud but their cases had yet to come to court. Nolan had been exonerated of all culpability in the accounting errors. Sal and Petey were currently serving ten-year sentences for kidnapping and attempted murder.

Maybelline had dropped the kidnapping charges against Elwood on the condition he go into treatment for his gambling addiction and surprisingly enough, while in treatment he'd found religion, become a preacher, and now officiated in his white Elvis jumpsuit at the Bells and Doves wedding chapel in Loflin.

It had taken several weeks but once the Oscar audits were completed and it was revealed the only cases of fraud happened in 1955 and then again this year, the stock of Gentry Enterprises began a steady rise.

The Gentry family forgave Mason for refusing to marry Daphne and for quitting the firm. Daphne and Hunter started dating. Nolan and Maybelline, and Charlie and Mason had a huge double wedding in a fancy Houston church. Maybelline and Nolan were currently on a world tour honeymoon.

Mason was working on getting his pilot's license and he helped out at the detective agency. And every day Charlee thanked God for bringing him into her life.

"I love you, Mrs. Gentry," Mason whispered.

"I love you, Mr. Gentry," she murmured drowsily, and just before she fell asleep, Charlee realized that with her own rich, long-legged, brown-eyed, handsome, matinee-idol-smiling, beard-stubble-sporting man at her side, nothing but nothing scared her.

Especially, not love.

# You Only
# Love Twice

*In memory of Warren Carl Norwood, 1945–2005*
*Writer, mentor, friend*
*I'll miss you. Blessed be, Warren.*

# Special Acknowledgment

I wrote this book while on my first cross-country book tour. Writing amid conferences and book signings and traveling is an exciting but overwhelming task. A hearty thank you to the following people who made the journey easier.

Carol Stacy and the staff of *Romantic Times*.
My writer buddies, Kelley St. John, Kathy Caskie, Jennifer St. Giles, and Rita Herron, who gave me a place to crash at the RT conference.
Booksellers Kathy and Ashley Ross at Half Price Books of the Ozarks. Tracy Smith and Lisa Watford from the Booksmith in Del City, Oklahoma. Jackie at Borders in Oklahoma City. Steve at Page One in Albuquerque. Writers Gabriella Anderson and Judy Ballard from LERA, the New Mexico Chapter of Romance Writers of America. Booksellers Nancy and Robyn and the rest of the gang at Sunshine Books in Cypress, California. And to my dear friends at The Book Ladies in Corona, California—Sherrie, Miriam, and Jackie. You rock!

And most of all, to the wonderful readers who came out to buy books and support the tour. You guys are the greatest readers any author could hope to have. Thank you from the bottom of my heart.

# Chapter 1

Marlie Montague was right smack-dab in the middle of exposing a massive government cover-up when her front doorbell chimed, playing the *Mission: Impossible* theme.

Although she heard the bell, Marlie was so deeply engrossed in the comic book she was illustrating that the sound didn't really register in her brain. She sat tailor-style at her white drawing board, black charcoal pencil in hand, surrounded by a bank of computer equipment, some ivory, some ebony, all Macs. She drew Angelina Avenger with her eyes blazing and her guns drawn as she confronted a top-ranking CIA agent about his part in a global oil conspiracy.

Her pencil hollowed the lines of Angelina's cheek-bones, accentuating her haunting beauty and steely inner toughness. She employed the eraser to perfectly arch her heroine's auburn eyebrows. Angelina might be the most kick-butt crime fighter in the comics, but she never neglected her grooming. The woman was serious trouble in high heels.

Quite unlike Marlie.

She glanced down at the rumpled black track suit that

she'd never once run track in. It was two o'clock in the afternoon and she realized she'd been toiling for almost nine hours without a shower or anything more to eat than her morning bowl of Froot Loops, and only her trusty tweezers knew for sure the last time she'd plucked *her* eyebrows.

The doorbell played the *Mission: Impossible* theme again.

Irritated by the interruption, Marlie sighed, laid her pencil down, and pushed back from the storyboard.

Maybe it was UPS with a box of free author copies of her twenty-eighth comic book "CIA Zombie Recruits," the upcoming March issue of her heroine's exploits, in which Angelina uncovers a secret government brainwashing experiment using the news media to subliminally program the masses.

When she reached the front door, she had to go up on tiptoe to peer through the peephole. Being five-foot-two was a hindrance at times; little wonder she had created Angelina as a six-foot Amazon.

It was a man.

A stranger.

The hairs on her forearm lifted. Who was he?

He stood with his back to the door, gazing out at the moderately priced homes that comprised her cozy little corner of Oleander Circle just a mile from the Gulf of Mexico. He looked displaced in suburbia. Like a cactus in a petunia patch.

Pushing her glasses up on the end of her nose, she squinted to get a better view. He wore a sweat-stained navy blue T-shirt and gray cotton workout pants that in spite of their bagginess did not camouflage his strong, muscular butt.

In one hand he held, of all things, a Pyrex measuring cup. Could this be her new next-door neighbor come to borrow a cup of sugar?

More likely a cup of egg whites. Clearly, this guy, with his no-flab body, never put a bite of the sweet stuff in his mouth.

If this was indeed her new neighbor, then she had watched him from her office window two weeks earlier when he'd moved in next door. Her imagination went off the chain as she remembered him lifting those boxes with bulging biceps, stripping off his shirt when he got over-heated, and dazzling Marlie with a righteous view of his late-night-infomercial abs.

He wore his hair cropped close to his head. Not quite a buzz cut, but almost. More like Richard Gere in *An Officer and a Gentleman*. She knew the look.

Precision military.

Was he military? She hoped he wasn't military. She didn't trust military men. Not even ex-military. Not even sexy ex-military.

*Don't sweat it, babe,* Angelina whispered inside her head. *He's much more my type. You should have hooked up with Cosmo when you had the chance.*

But she had never been physically attracted to Cosmo. They'd been best friends and close confidants; that is, before Cosmo sold out his scruples and left Corpus Christi to go to work as a civilian computer cryptologist for the Office of Navy Intelligence in Suitland, Maryland. She still missed her buddy and wished she could have been more accepting of his career path.

The riveting man on her doorstep pivoted, giving her a breathtaking view of his ruggedly handsome profile. He looked as if he should be gracing the cover of one of those outdoor adventure magazines. A provocative five o'clock shadow encircled his angular jaw, and his hooded eyes were an intriguing shade of blue-gray-green, like the Gulf of Mexico in turbulent weather. And like a storm-swept sea, he looked both demanding and resilient.

And as treacherous as a downed power line on a schoolyard playground.

She was mesmerized.

Her fingers tingled to draw his face, to capture his effigy in charcoal. Her eyes studied him as if she were actually seeing him on canvas and tracing his exquisite form with her art pencil, forever trapping him on the page. Her brain cast him in geometry; a circle for his head, an inverted triangle for his torso, a right-side-up triangle for his lower body, and rectangles for his legs, which she mentally lengthened and shaded until they were long, strong pillars.

Leaning in, he rapped hard against the door.

Caught off guard by the unexpectedness of the sharp sound, Marlie gasped. She jumped back and almost fell over her black-lacquered coffee table. He was persistent. She'd give him points for that.

But what if she was wrong? What if this guy wasn't her next-door neighbor?

Her underground comic books were considered controversial by mainstream publishers. Just last week she'd gotten a death threat mixed in with her fan mail. It wasn't the first. She'd received them a few times before and she'd even notified the police with the initial one. But they'd blown her off, pooh-poohing her fears as unlikely. She hadn't bothered phoning again. In the best of times, Marlie wasn't a fan of authority figures.

Seven years spent researching, writing, and illustrating

her conspiracy theory comic book series had given her a suspicious mind. That and the fact that her father had been a government whistle-blower killed under mysterious circumstances by the naval officer who was supposed to have been his trusted friend. To top it off, the Navy had framed her father and proclaimed him a traitor, asserting that he'd been selling Mohawk missiles to terrorists.

*You're being paranoid again,* Angelina chided. *This guy has nothing to do with those death threats or what the Navy did to your dad. Open the door.*

"Easy for you to say; you're a fearless crime fighter."

*Don't give me that b.s. You're not afraid that Mr. Hunka Man came over here to do you harm. You're just too chicken to talk to him.*

There was that.

Marlie's natural impulse urged her to slink back to her office and pretend she'd never heard the *Mission: Impossible* theme summoning her to the front door. She had a deadline looming and three pages left to illustrate before tackling the computer phase.

*That's right. Go ahead. Blame it on your work. Never mind that you're hiding behind your shyness as an excuse to avoid getting a real life. And maybe, just maybe, a real man.*

"I'm not sticking my head in the sand." She knew she had a bad habit of talking to her own fabrication. It was one major drawback to living alone and working out of her home.

*Prove it.*

"I am not the slightest bit interested. He's military."

*You don't know that.*

"Girlfriend, check him out. His posture is so perfect it looks as if someone nailed a two-by-four into his spine."

*What's wrong with military?*

"Come on, you of all people? Asking me a question like that."

*You think the dude's got a submachine gun stashed down the front of his sweatpants?* Then Angelina started humming the old Beatles song "Happiness Is a Warm Gun."

"I can't open the door looking like this." Marlie's hair was unkempt, she wore no makeup, and there was a coffee stain on her white T-shirt at a strategically embarrassing spot.

*Excuses, excuses.*

"Hello? Anybody home?" The hypnotic sound of his voice, all sinful and chocolaty, lured her.

*Double dare you to introduce yourself,* Angelina challenged.

"Okay, fine, all right. Just give me a second to freshen up."

*Hurry before he leaves.*

What suddenly compelled her (besides Angelina's big mouth), Marlie couldn't really say. It was an odd sensation, pushing up from somewhere deep inside her, daring her to open the door.

Maybe it was nothing more than the urge to get a better look at the supreme hottie. Maybe it was because she'd been feeling a little too isolated since Cosmo left. Or maybe it was because if this man was going to be living next door, she had to know exactly who he was and what he was about. When push came to shove, Marlie valued information over safety because the right kind of information could ensure her safety.

Stripping off her coffee-stained shirt as she went, Marlie dashed into her bedroom. She pushed back the black-beaded curtain that served as a closet door and somehow, in the process, managed to dislodge her bowling ball from its place. The ball escaped, bumping away across the hardwood floor. She ignored the fugitive, snatched a clean T-shirt from a hanger, and hurried into the bathroom.

He rang the doorbell again.

*This is your mission if you choose to accept it.* Angelina snickered. *Open the door to your mystery date.*

"Hush," she told Angelina and then sang out, "Coming, coming."

Marlie rinsed her mouth with Scope, while simultaneously releasing the elastic band that kept her unruly brown hair pulled back. She ran a brush through the tangles and then dabbed on a subtle shade of pink lipstick. Semipresentable.

She turned and rushed down the hall. She was so focused on her goal that she did not see the bowling ball. Her ankle clipped it and the ball rolled between her legs.

Marlie ended up sprawled facedown on the floor, staring underneath the sofa. Ouch. That was gonna leave a mark.

*Wow,* Angelina said, *check out those dust bunnies.*

The doorbell rang again.

*Hustle, hustle. This mission will self-destruct in seven seconds.*

"Hang on!"

Dragging herself to her feet, she hobbled to the door and flung it open, only to discover that her sexy neighbor had vanished. In his place stood the UPS man.

"Where'd he go?" She cocked her head, craning for a look around the man's body, but all she could see was the boxy brown delivery truck parked at the curb.

"Where'd who go?" asked the UPS man.

"The guy who was just here."

"What guy?"

Marlie sighed. At some point between the Scope gargle and the bowling ball mishap her neighbor must have given up and gone home, and the UPS man had come up the sidewalk in the meantime.

Oh, well. Perhaps it was for the best. At least Angelina couldn't accuse her of not trying. She blew out her breath, surprised to find she felt disappointed. Shaking her head to dispel the sensation, she reached out to take the box from the UPS man.

Only to discover that he was also clutching a wicked-looking semiautomatic weapon.

With a silencer attached to the end of it.

Naval Criminal Investigative Service Special Agent Joel Hunter took the measuring cup and strode back into his house. So much for his brilliant may-I-borrow-a-cup-of-shampoo ploy.

Apparently, Marlie Montague wasn't about to open her door to a stranger. Not that he could blame her. She was a young woman living alone and engaged in antigovernment activities. He'd be leery too if he were in her shoes. But he knew she was home. Her white Toyota Prius with the black interior was parked in the driveway in front of her white craftsman-style home with the black trim. Plus, when he'd returned from his run he'd checked the surveillance equipment that covert ops had installed in her home two weeks earlier, and Marlie had still been holed up in her office, working on her comic book.

Joel had retrieved the measuring cup from the kitchen cabinet of the house he'd rented fully furnished and trotted over to carry out his new orders. Initially, his assignment had been simple. Keep her under surveillance. Then while on his jog he'd gotten a cell phone call from Camp Pendleton with additional instructions. Befriend the suspect and gain her trust. But under no circumstances was he to allow her to uncover his true identity.

But of course. *That* was a given. You couldn't exactly expect to get chummy with the daughter of the man your father had killed.

Time for a new angle of attack. He wanted off this detail. The sooner the better. He opened his flip phone and gave the voice-activated command to call Camp Pendleton.

"Special Agent Dobbs."

"Hunter here."

"Have you made contact?"

"Sir." Joel stalked into the kitchen and set the measuring cup down on the counter. "If I may speak freely, I don't believe I'm the right agent for this particular assignment."

"You haven't made contact yet? What's the matter, Hunter?" Dobbs scoffed. "You're male, she's female. Your charm slipping?"

"My charm isn't the issue, sir." Joel headed for the bathroom.

"No? Then why aren't you out there getting her to fall head over heels for you and spill all her secrets?"

"Honestly, sir?"

"Speak your mind."

Joel swapped the phone from one hand to the other as he wrestled out of his sweaty T-shirt. "This assignment is a waste of time."

"How so?"

"The woman is no more subversive than Little Orphan Annie. She stays to herself, gets very few visitors, and rarely goes anywhere except to the grocery store and her bowling league on Wednesday nights. She's downright mousy, and I've seen no signs of seditious activities. In fact, I think she may be agoraphobic."

"I get it," Dobbs said. "You're bored because she's not a hottie with an interesting sex life."

"I'm wasting my time and my talent. I don't even know why I'm here. If you could give me a little more to go on, that would help." Joel tossed his shirt in the laundry hamper and toed off his sneakers. "What is it that Marlie Montague is supposed to be up to? Why is she under such close scrutiny? What exactly am I supposed to be finding out?"

"Sorry. Top secret info. You don't have the clearance."

"So reassign me and get someone with the right clearance."

"No." Dobbs's tone was anything but friendly.

"Look, I know her. Or at least I knew her when I was a kid. Don't you think that's some kind of conflict of interest?"

"Would she recognize you if she saw you?"

He sighed. "I doubt it."

"Then you're not getting out of it."

"Come on, Dobbs, cut me some slack. I do a good job for you."

"No can do."

"Why not?"

"You were personally requested for this mission by someone very high up."

"Let me guess. Admiral Delaney stuck me with this crappy babysitting gig."

"I'm not at liberty to say."

"Why?"

"It's not yours to reason why, but to follow orders. Now, quit your bellyaching and get back to work."

"Do I have to?" He gritted his teeth.

"Either that or you can hand in your resignation. Take your pick." Without another word, Dobbs hung up.

*Well, fuck me running.*

Joel had the urge to punch something hard, but managed to satisfy himself with savagely kicking his sneakers across the bathroom floor and into the bedroom, wishing it were his ex-father-in-law's head instead. He was certain Chet Delaney was behind this.

Joel's ex-wife Treeni was due to return to Washington any day and she'd been calling him, hinting at getting back together. He would rather set his hair on fire than reunite with Treeni, but he didn't appreciate Chet's running interference for his precious daughter, shipping him out of D.C. on some bullshit job.

He was stuck with being the stringed marionette to Chet's puppeteer. And there was nothing Joel hated more than being beholden to someone with power over him.

After Joel had been expunged from the Navy SEALs following a sordid incident in Iraq involving Treeni, one of Saddam Hussein's top-ranking officials, and the search for weapons of mass destruction, his ex-father-in-law had pulled strings and gotten Joel the job at NCIS. It had been a bribe of course, to keep him from telling the truth about what had gone down over there.

Chet had just stepped down as director of ONI so he could declare his candidacy for President of the United States. He was considered by many as his party's front-runner to secure the nomination in the upcoming primary, although his warmongering and hard-line stance had earned him almost as many detractors as supporters.

At this point, Chet's main concern was keeping all his skeletons locked up tight.

Joel was one of those skeletons.

But his ex-father-in-law needn't have worried. Joel's lips were forever sealed. It hurt too much to think about what had happened, much less speak of it. He'd taken the blame for what Treeni had done and he'd accepted the consequences, but losing his place in the brotherhood was like losing a chunk of his soul. Being a SEAL was the first time he'd ever felt like he'd truly belonged anywhere. He'd been with like-minded men who pushed themselves to extremes.

Joel twisted the shower faucet to a tepid temperature, climbed inside the tub, and yanked the shower curtain closed. He didn't know the real reason why the Navy wanted Marlie under surveillance, but he felt sure they were barking up the wrong tree. The hush-hush, top secret instructions just didn't jibe with what he'd learned about her.

For God's sake, Montague looked like somebody's wide-eyed kid sister. The kind of wholesome girl-next-door so valued in 1950s and '60s sitcoms. *Gidget* and *Donna Reed* and *Father Knows Best*. She even wore her hair in a ubiquitous ponytail.

A dissident innocent?

Was there such a thing? The only time he'd seen her act the least bit feisty was when he had spied on her at the Starlight Lanes. She mowed down bowling pins as if they were dandelions and she were a John Deere lawn tractor, racking up strike after strike with deadly precision. So what if she'd written a couple of conspiracy theory comic books with antigovernment themes. Big deal. It was fiction.

Joel lathered his hair. See, that's where he kept getting hung up. If her comic books were strictly fictional, why did the Navy consider her a threat to national security?

It made no sense.

He blew out his breath. Like it or not, he was stuck with his circumstances. He'd already gotten kicked out of the SEALs over one woman. He wouldn't lose this job over another. For whatever reason, his orders were to get friendly with Montague, and that's what he would do.

But Joel sure as hell didn't have to be happy about it.

# Chapter 2

Aw, hell, Marlie thought, what a day to get whacked.

She needed a shower, her Visa bill was three weeks over-due, and worst of all she hadn't had sex in the past two years. *I'm going to die broke, manless, without clean underwear on, and living in a house that I rent from my mother.*

"Step back," the man said and kicked the door closed.

In a weird way, she'd been waiting for something like this her entire life. As if deep down inside she'd always known she would come to a disastrous end.

She felt at once both calm and panicked. She was terri-fied, but being a worst-case-scenario kind of gal from way back, she'd frequently planned out how she would react in just such a situation.

Yeah, well, best-laid plans. She'd always imagined she'd smack a male attacker in his man parts and run like hell, but this guy wasn't standing within gonad-smacking distance.

He was a bland, nondescript sort of fellow. Young but with blond hair already thinning at the temples, ordinary features, medium build, steady hands. A perfect killer. Calm, cool, and unmemorable.

"Who are you?" she squeaked.

He casually tossed the box aside and raised the gun. "I'm your assassin."

Had he actually said that? This couldn't really be happening. It seemed too surreal. Too laughably Hollywood-esque.

He stood there, as deadly as a coiled rattlesnake, staring at her with absolutely no expression on his face, but his blue eyes…dear God…his calculating eyes were unforgiving.

Marlie's heart pounded and her lungs felt white, squeezed of air, constricted by fear, dread, and oddly enough, curiosity. Her head throbbed and her ears rang with Madonna's version of "American Pie," telling her that this would be the day that she died. Great. She didn't even care for Madonna. She was much more of a Sheryl Crow fan, but she didn't think Sheryl had done any songs about dying.

"Shhh." His voice was low and steady. "Don't worry. It won't hurt."

Reality slapped her hard. This guy wasn't bluffing. He was going to kill her. Game on.

Everything happened so rapidly.

In a rolling dive, Marlie hit the floor at the same time the gunman fired.

*Keep moving, get behind something.* It was Angelina's voice, firm, commanding.

Marlie scrambled behind the coffee table. Rapid-fire bullets decimated it. Wood chips flew everywhere. Amazingly, she hadn't been hit.

*But you soon will be if you don't do something. Move it!*

That's when Marlie's gaze locked on the bowling ball. There was no time to think. One-handed, she stuck her fingers in the holes and raised the ball up to her head just in time to block the shot.

The bullet struck the bowling ball and ricocheted off.

The force of the impact vibrated all the way up Marlie's arm and into her shoulder. For a moment she was dazed, unsure what had happened.

The gunman yelped, dropped his weapon, and clutched his hand. Apparently the stray bullet had struck him.

All rightee, if she couldn't kick him in the balls, she'd hit him with one. Marlie leaped to her feet and slung it as if she were bowling a perfect game. The ball bounced once and caught him in the shins.

He went down hard, turning the air blue with a string of vile curses.

Blindly, she ran, bracing herself for the earth-splitting pain of a bullet slicing off the top of her head. She flew across the kitchen floor, threw herself out the back door. The brick patio was rough and cold beneath her stocking feet.

As she sprinted around the corner of the house, her shirt caught on the bare branch of a peach tree. Chilly January air bit into the skin of her armpit as the material ripped. Her breath came in raspy gasps and her heart hammered like a NASCAR piston. The fifteen extra pounds she was wagging around suddenly seemed like a hundred and fifteen.

She panted, her mouth dry. She ran full throttle, her lungs crying out in pain, and yet it was as if she were moving in slow motion, her feet mired in invisible syrup, her life flashing before her eyes.

Marlie, age three, the first Christmas she could remember, clutching the little red wagon that Santa had brought and crying because the handle had flown up, struck her in the nose, and broken it. Proving that you couldn't even depend on old St. Nicholas to bring a safe toy.

Marlie, age eight, at her very first dance recital, tripping and falling on her chubby white tutu-clad butt in front of a tittering audience, thus figuring out early on that she simply wasn't prima ballerina material.

Marlie, age eleven, dressed in black at her father's funeral, clinging to her mother's hand. Learning for the first time that the man who'd killed her daddy had been his best friend, teaching her you couldn't trust anyone. Ever.

Marlie, age nineteen, tearing open the envelope containing a check from Underground Press for three hundred fifty dollars for her first *Angelina Avenger* comic book. She'd been so proud of herself, so happy.

It was all there in a microsecond; her memories tumbled in and then were gone quicker than the time it took her to blink. Any second her world would go black forever. Her life cut short at twenty-six.

And she'd never really lived.

Why had she been so scared to live?

She could hear the hit man thrashing around the peach tree behind her. She heard him grunt. Heard the deafening sound of her own blood whooshing in her ears.

Something hot and fast and quiet whizzed past her head.

Another bullet.

Yipes!

It ricocheted off the bricks on the house and a piece of mortar struck her cheek.

*Get moving. Over the fence.*

Marlie didn't exactly know how, but she managed to scale the six-foot wooden privacy fence and fling herself into the yard next door without getting killed. Up and over. A mindless plunge. It was a tough scramble and wood splinters scraped her knees, but she negotiated it in one piece.

Dizzily, she stumbled, fell down in the straw-colored grass but quickly jumped up again. She risked a glance over her shoulder and saw that the hit man wasn't climbing the fence after her.

He must be hurt.

A perverse sense of glee overtook her. Woo-hoo. She charged up the steps of her neighbor's porch. Inside her head, Madonna had abandoned "American Pie" for "Die Another Day."

She turned the door handle.

Locked.

No big bad tough macho man was at home to save her. Marlie cried out, but it was a small sound, soft and helpless.

*Don't admit defeat,* Angelina growled. *Not yet. No matter what, you have to get inside. Have to find a phone and call 9-1-1.*

Stripping off her shirt, she bunched it around her fist and punched a hole through the paned glass of the upper part of the kitchen door. Heedless of the shards, she stuck her hand through the opening, twisted the lock, and pushed the door inward.

Marlie shoved her way over the threshold. Her feet, covered only by black-and-white toe socks, glided over the glass, miraculously unscathed. Her heart was a smashing weight inside her chest, shooting blood through her body with the force of a pulsating projectile.

At that very moment a disturbing notion occurred to her.

What if her neighbor and the UPS man were partners

in crime? They'd both been at her front door just minutes apart.

Coincidence? Or design?

*There you go with the conspiracy theories again.*

"What the hell is going on here?"

Startled, Marlie raised her gaze and met the sharp-eyed stare of the muscular man standing in the kitchen entryway. Yep, this was her new neighbor, the one who'd been on her front porch just minutes earlier.

And he was wearing nothing except a scowl and a skimpy bath towel cinched around his gorgeous waist.

On what would have been her twenty-seventh wedding anniversary, Penelope Montague poured a glass of moderately priced merlot, collected the family photo albums and a box of tissues, and climbed into her lonely four-poster canopy bed for a prolonged sobfest.

She missed Daniel. As much now as the day she'd learned he'd been murdered. Maybe even more so.

Their love had been the real deal. Soul mates. Sweethearts. Truly each other's better halves. There'd never been anyone else for either of them.

Fifteen years ago a phone call had shattered her world forever. If it hadn't been for Marlie, Penelope knew she would not have survived. She hadn't wanted to survive, but her daughter had been only eleven years old and there'd been no one else to look after her.

So Penelope had refused to give up. She'd put one foot in front of the other, gone to work in her job as head bank teller, cared for her daughter, done what had to be done, and miraculously enough, the time had passed.

And while her aching heart had never fully healed, the pain had become more bearable.

Except on days like today.

She settled back against the pillows, took a sip of wine, and opened the first album.

Their wedding.

Daniel's smiling face hit Penelope like a fist to the gut. She would go to her grave missing that dashing grin. With a shaking hand, she traced an index finger over the couple in the photograph. They were so young, so far away. They looked so hopeful, so full of plans. It seemed now as if they'd hardly existed at all, those optimistic, idealistic youths.

She remembered the day Daniel had asked her to marry him. He'd taken her out on his sailboat at sunset—how that man had loved the sea. They'd rocked on the water, talking, drinking champagne, and eating plump, sweet strawberries, feeding each other. Speaking of their hopes and dreams for the future. Holding nothing back. The moon had only been a thin sliver of cheese in the inky black night. Shooting stars hurled across empty spaces, burning themselves up, just for the fun of putting on a show.

And when Daniel got down on one knee and asked her to be his wife, Penelope could have eaten the whole sky. She felt that damned happy.

She flipped the pages.

More smiles. More laughter.

Their honeymoon on Maui. Their first home in Navy housing. The day, just a month later, when they found out she was pregnant with Marlie. A picture of the three dozen roses they could ill afford that Daniel had bought in celebration.

She gulped back a mouthful of merlot. Inside her head, inside her heart, Penelope horded a storehouse of memories, a cache of bright, good times.

Daniel holding her hand while they strolled through the park. Daniel gazing in awe at their newborn daughter, cradling her tiny body snug in his big burly arms. Daniel cooking her breakfast in bed on that first Mother's Day and burning the eggs, and then taking her to brunch at the fanciest restaurant in town. Daniel, looking so handsome in his Navy uniform, his white shirt starched, his shoes polished until they gleamed.

But there had been other memories as well.

Dark, moody memories. The secrets Daniel's job forced him to keep. The months he was away on missions, leaving Penelope alone with Marlie.

Ah, dear sweet Marlie, who was just a little bit strange. The girl lived too much inside her head. She had always been an introvert, preferring to make up imaginary friends rather than playing with real kids. She and Daniel had wanted other children. Penelope knew that having a brother or sister would cure Marlie's flights of fantasy, but they'd tried and failed to get pregnant a second time.

Then Daniel had been killed.

His death had affected their daughter in irrevocable ways, and Penelope despaired that Marlie would ever stop being at odds with the world around her. She was afraid to trust people she hadn't known for a very long time, and even then, her allegiance was hard-won.

And yet Marlie always seemed to be searching for a hero. Someone that she could look up to. Someone she could believe in. Penelope watched her daughter's beliefs play out in comic books she created. The lone, strong woman fighting against the masculine tenets of power and authority. She wanted to be like Angelina Avenger, but she was too scared to trust herself, too blinded to her own inner strength. She couldn't seem to see that if she would just dare to look inward instead of outside herself for validation, she would find the hero that she was searching for right there in her own mirror.

And if Marlie didn't learn to trust others, she was never going to find the unity that only love could bring. And how could she love if she couldn't trust?

Penelope knew she nagged Marlie too much about finding a man. Of course, she didn't want her to have just *any* man. What she wanted for her daughter was the grand, sweeping passion that she'd had with Daniel.

A violent, headlong rush of emotions stormed her, stomped her heart. Guilt and grief, pity for herself, for the happiness that had slipped through her fingers. Anger, betrayal, hurt, loss.

Throbbing, aching, burning, raw loss.

It was too much to bear.

Penelope broke down. Crushed underneath the racking sorrow, she drew her knees to her chest. Wave after wave besieged her until she was left limp and shaking. Finally, when she could cry no more, Penelope wiped her eyes, polished off the wine, and poured herself a second glass. From the middle drawer of her bedside table she took out a bottle of sleeping pills.

How many times in the past fifteen years had she seriously considered taking her own life?

A dozen? Two dozen? Only her love for her daughter had kept her from swallowing those pills.

But Marlie was grown now and no longer needed her as much as she once had, and Penelope missed Daniel so desperately. How easy it would be to slip into a deep, dreamless sleep and embrace death.

What bliss.

Silence.

She opened the bottle and poured the fifty white oblong pills into the palm of her hand. They were so small it would only take a couple of mouthfuls to get them all down. Hand trembling, she brought the tablets to her mouth.

The telephone rang.

Penelope closed her eyes. *Swallow the pills, ignore the telephone. Do it. End your misery. Go be with Daniel at last.*

But what if it was Marlie on the other end of the line?

The phone rang again.

Penelope couldn't do it. Reluctantly, she put the pills back in the bottle and reached for the telephone.

"Hello?"

At first she heard nothing except an odd crackling as if there was disturbance on the line.

*Or as if it was bugged.* Her daughter wasn't the only one with a suspicious mind.

"Who's there?" Penelope demanded.

More crackling.

Static. Like a ship-to-shore call. Daniel had made enough of them for Penelope to recognize the sound. She pressed the flat of her hand against her heart and held her breath.

The crackling continued and sudden fear swept through her. She started to hang up when she heard someone inhale sharply.

"Yes? Hello? Who is this?"

And then the caller said the word that no one had spoken to her in fifteen years. A word resonant with double meaning. The sound of it dropped Penelope to her knees.

"Rendezvous."

Their eyes met over the smashed glass of the broken pane from his back-door window.

Time stopped.

They were locked, frozen in the moment. Her startled. Him stunned.

It was like they recognized each other in a significant but inexplicable way. In that suspended second, their eyes spoke, saying what a man and a woman don't say until they've known each other for years…things a man and a woman might never tell each other, not even in the bliss of their marriage bed after decades together.

It was as if they'd known each other beyond forever, beyond time.

*Hogwash.*

What in the hell was wrong with him?

Joel had been caught with his pants down. That's what had happened, and he was furious with himself. He'd had one job. Keep a close eye on Marlie Montague. And he'd fucked up.

Major.

For a fraction of a second, Marlie stared at him as if he'd just saved her life. Her eyes overflowed with gratitude and relief that barely hid a lurking dread. The pallor of her cheeks, her rapid shallow breathing, and her quivering bottom lip told him something terrible had just happened.

But what?

"I…I…," she stammered and swayed.

And that's when Joel noticed the blood and realized her knees were about to crumple.

She was in shock.

He moved toward her, barely recognizing that the knot at his towel could come unraveled at any minute, and he caught her just before she plowed face-first into the broken glass.

His lingering high school football locker-room fear of athlete's foot had instilled in him the habit of wearing rubber flip-flops whenever he got out of the shower. Otherwise, his feet would have been shredded. He scooped her into his arms, carried her into the living room, and laid her on the davenport. She looked up at him, wide-eyed and terrified.

"Stay put," he commanded. Storming into the bathroom, he retrieved his first-aid kit.

Joel felt slightly off balance, as if his brain were a little sticky, but he couldn't say why. He'd been trained to rapidly adapt to changing circumstances and not only survive, but thrive. Was he losing his touch already? Only eighteen months after leaving the SEALs? He didn't like thinking that might be the case.

He returned to the living room to find Marlie staring blankly off into space. She was definitely in shock. He knelt on the floor next to the davenport, opened his first-aid kit, and then gently reached for her injured hand. Her skin felt cold beneath his fingers. She sucked in her breath.

"I'm sorry to hurt you," he said, "but this needs attention."

"I know," she mumbled.

She'd sliced a two-inch-long gap from the fleshy part of the pad underneath her thumb to the top of the wrist, very narrowly missing the artery. A fraction of a millimeter in the wrong direction and the wound could have been life-threatening.

Joel felt something fierce build inside him. He recognized his internal drive to protect a woman in need. He didn't like feeling this way, but there it was.

Whenever a vulnerable woman's face beseeched, "Can I get a hero?" Joel could never refuse the call.

Tightening his jaw, he relied on his basic first-aid training and tried not to notice that her T-shirt was wrapped around her arm and not her lush body. But while his fingers applied pressure to the wound, he couldn't help casting a quick glance at her chest.

Wow.

Ashamed of himself, he snapped his gaze back to her face.

She was much prettier than he'd initially thought. From a distance and on the surveillance camera all he'd seen of her were those oversized black-framed glasses and baggy clothes. But up close and personal, Joel could see beneath the surface facade.

Her cherubic cheeks gave her the appearance of a friendly angel, the kind on Christmas plates that old ladies collected. Her skin was flawless, her hair a silky dark brown mass, and her eyelashes long and thick. Her lips were small, but shaped in a perfect bow.

Only her nose seemed out of place.

It crooked at the bridge as if she might have broken it once upon a time. Yet it was that crooked little honker that lent an air of unexpected pride and dignity to her face.

Their gazes met again. He spotted a mixture of emotions behind her glasses. Confusion, worry, fear, and something else.

Awe? Curiosity?

No, that wasn't quite it. Rather, it was more like she'd looked into his eyes and knew him instantly both inside and out.

Weird. Joel shook off the unsettling thoughts. Suddenly he felt winded, exposed, his nerve endings raw. Yep, he'd been caught with his pants down all right, and there was nothing to be done about it. Except ignore the feeling and find out why the woman who wouldn't let him into her house minutes before had just come crashing through his back door.

# Chapter 3

Admiral Augustus Hunter had gotten everything he'd ever wanted. An oversized office at the Pentagon. Fancy house in Maryland. Two top-of-the-line Mercedes Benzes. A pretty young trophy wife sporting bought-and-paid-for tits twice the size of her waist. And a second chance to be a better father to his three-year-old daughter Amy than he had been with his son Joel. Although at Gus's age, taking into account his heart condition, it was unlikely he would live to dance at Amy's wedding.

Gus had come up the ranks the easy way, covering his bosses' asses, keeping secrets, playing politics. He'd just finished a three-hour lunch that included Russian caviar at a five-star restaurant with two of the most powerful men in Washington. He retrieved his tailor-made overcoat from the cloak-check girl, flipped up the collar, and shrugged into it as he stepped through the revolving door.

"Silver SL500," he said, palming his claim ticket and a twenty-dollar bill to the valet who greeted him on the sidewalk. "Careful with her."

Beaming, the valet bustled away.

Gus stuck his hand in his pocket in search of a cigar

and found instead a rolled-up magazine. Aw, hell. Nobody could get anything right these days. He went back inside, the magazine still clutched in his hand.

"You gave me the wrong coat," he said to the cloakroom girl, who had a blowsy Monica Lewinsky look.

"No, I didn't," she denied.

"Yes, you did," he argued. "I found this in the pocket." He shook the magazine at her. "It isn't mine."

"One," the girl said, raising a finger to tick off her points. "Yours was the only navy blue coat I've had in the cloakroom all day, so no mix-up there."

Gus stared at her hands. At first he thought she must have shut all her fingers in a car door, but then he realized she wore black nail polish, her petulant Goth attitude barely covered by her crisp maroon-and-white work uniform. Young women hadn't been so sassy in his day. He hoped Amy would have more respect for her elders when she was twenty.

"And two," she continued. "The comic book was in your pocket when you gave your coat to me. I know because as I was hanging it up, the comic fell out, and I remember thinking how weird it was that an old Republican geezer would be reading *Angelina Avenger*."

Gus ignored the old-geezer part and unfurled the magazine. It was indeed an *Angelina Avenger* comic book.

He frowned. There was a paper clip marking a particular page. He flipped it open and read the cartoon frame. And then his greatest fear was upon him.

For fifteen years he'd been looking over his shoulder, waiting for disaster to strike, and now it was happening. The sins that he'd thought he had buried deeply enough that no one would ever find them had risen from the grave.

And his only son was caught in the cross fire.

The sins of the father.

Gus gritted his teeth and stared at the comic book again. It was put out by some cheesy underground press and written and illustrated by Daniel's daughter, Marlie Montague.

The young woman had no idea what she'd wrought.

His pulse beat erratically. Son of a bitch, he'd forgotten to take his Inderal that morning.

Unwittingly, Joel had been dropped into the middle of a complex cover-up fifteen years in the making, and he would have no inkling what he was up against.

Agitated, Gus spun away from the cloak-check girl and hurried back outside to find his Mercedes waiting at the curb. He climbed in but did not put the car in gear. Instead, he whipped out his cell phone and called his assistant on his private cell number rather than the office extension. Gus knew well enough the CIA bugged the Pentagon land lines, and he rarely used his office phone for anything more than phoning home. He also changed his cell phone number often and made sure his assistant did the same. Call him paranoid, but he had too much insider knowledge not to be ultracautious when discussing sensitive matters.

Petty Officer Third Class Abel Johnson answered on the second ring. "Yes, sir?"

"You picked up my coat at the cleaners yesterday."

"Yes, sir."

"Did you notice if there was anything in the pocket?"

"No, sir. I did put your cigars and lighter in the right-side pocket as usual after I brought it into the office."

"And you didn't see anything else in the pocket?"

"No, sir."

Gus cursed and flung the comic into the backseat. Who and where had the damn thing come from?

"Are you all right, Admiral?"

"Fine." He was anything but fine. He felt desperate and unwell. Someone knew his secret, and they had sent him the comic to let him know that they knew.

"Is your heart acting up?"

"I said I'm fine, dammit." Gus had made some bad choices in his life, and they were coming back to haunt him. The Navy had cost him not only his best friend, but his first marriage and his relationship with his son.

And it wasn't over yet.

Mentally, Gus closed down his emotions. His ex-wife, Deirdre, claimed he was a master at shutting off his feelings, and she was right. The ability to do just that had made him the consummate commander. In his job, with the secrets he kept, he had no option. Feelings were for females and fools.

Luckily, Amber didn't care if he expressed his feelings or not, just as long as he kept her in designer clothes and Amy in a chichi private preschool. But the grinding in his gut was caused by much more than just strong coffee and rich food. Gus Hunter was afraid.

Very afraid.

He couldn't undo the past, but he could definitely change the future. He had to warn Penelope Montague.

They hadn't spoken since Daniel's funeral when she'd spit in his face and called him a heartless murdering bastard. He'd never blamed her. He understood how she felt. Things couldn't have played out any other way. He just prayed she would listen to him now.

"I have to leave D.C.," Gus said to Abel. "Right away."

"How long will you be gone?"

"I don't know."

"What about your afternoon appointments?"

"Reschedule them."

"Until when?"

"Until I tell you otherwise." Gus switched off his cell and drove to the nearest pay phone. He called information for Penelope's number. Her phone rang. Once, twice, three times.

Finally, her voice mail answered. Gus hung up when it occurred to him that her phone might be bugged as well. Dammit. His pulse beat a couplet. Where had he put that Inderal?

He searched in his glove compartment, found the bottle of heart medication, and dry-swallowed a tablet. Penelope was in Corpus Christi, Texas, and he had to get to her before the wrong people did. He had to find her.

Today.

He would take the next flight to Corpus. He'd tell Amber he was going out of town on business. She never questioned him. In fact, he'd tell her to take Amy and visit her mother in upstate New York for a few days. Get them out of the vicinity. Just in case there was any collateral damage.

Because Penelope's very life depended on him. As did the lives of his son and her daughter.

And, quite possibly, the fate of the free world.


Momentarily, Marlie forgot all about what had brought her to this man's house.

Assassin? What assassin?

Who could even think rationally with such a big, strapping, handsome man nestled so close?

The flat of his masculine thumb was pressed against the cut at her wrist. Her heart thumped and her stomach flip-flopped, heat pulsating beneath her flesh. Oddly enough, his presence made her feel secure in a way she hadn't felt since her father had died.

*Watch out.*

She knew better than to blindly trust anyone. She didn't even trust her own ability to tell if a man was a good guy or not. It was always safer to assume the worst. That way you were never surprised or disappointed by anything or anyone.

His head was down, his attention focused on tending her cut. His lean jaw was clean-shaven now, and there was a small dot of blood on his upper lip where he'd nicked himself shaving.

Beads of water from his interrupted shower clung to his earlobes like dewdrops. His broad shoulders were tensed, his mouth sensual, and his breath tickled deliciously warm against her heated skin. Her gaze fixed on his long, strong fingers, the heavy tendons, the etching of thick blue veins.

Pulling her gaze from his hands, she peeked at his face.

The minute beginnings of smile lines feathered lightly out from his eyes, giving him character. He probably wasn't much more than thirty, although the severe haircut made him seem older. His lips were softly curved, full but not girlie voluptuous.

Naughtily, she lowered her lashes and allowed her gaze to rove downward past the uncompromising lines of his chin to the taut column of his throat to his angular collarbone and beyond.

She caught her breath.

He plucked a pressure bandage from the first-aid kit and applied it to her wrist. He looked up and caught her staring.

It was only then that Marlie realized her bloody T-shirt

was still bunched around her wrist and she was naked from the waist up except for her white cotton bra, her plumpness exposed for this stranger to see.

Her cheeks blazed hot.

She felt vulnerable and nervous and incompetent. The exact opposite of tough, cool, accomplished Angelina Avenger. She wished she could stop feeling so faint of heart and be more like her cartoon heroine.

Marlie's saving grace was that he looked as disconcerted as she felt. She covered her chest as best she could with her hands as he leaped to his feet. She cut them both some slack and squeezed her eyes tightly closed. She heard him pad away into another room and return a moment later.

He cleared his throat.

Tentatively, she opened one eye to find him wearing snug-fitting blue jeans, a colorful Magnum, P.I., Hawaiian-print shirt, and a pair of old running shoes without socks. Over his arm he carried a man's long-sleeved white dress shirt.

She opened her other eye.

"Put this on," he said without preamble—she'd already noticed he was pretty bossy—and tossed the shirt to her. His face was inscrutable.

Scrambling to sit up, Marlie poked her arms through the sleeves and quickly buttoned it closed. The garment was overly starched—more indication he might be military—and scratchy against her skin, but at least she was covered.

The stiff hem of his shirt hung well past her knees, and she had to roll up the sleeves that extended a good five inches below her fingertips.

"Who are you?" he demanded sternly, coming to stand

right in front of her so that she was forced to stare at his waist. "And why did you break into my house?"

He was covered up now, but Marlie remembered all too vividly exactly what the man looked like underneath that garish hibiscus-and-parrot-print shirt.

She gulped. Forcing a smile, she did a Princess Di, ducking her head while casting a surreptitious glance up at him. She had trouble socializing with good-looking men under the best of circumstances, and this most certainly was not that.

"I'm your next-door neighbor, Marlie Montague," she said, trying to sound chirpy. "And you are…"

"Joel…" He hesitated, scowling. "Joel…Jerome. And please don't try to tell me that knocking the windowpane out of someone's back door is how you folks in the 'burbs welcome new people into the neighborhood, because I'm not buying it."

Was that a joke? She cut her eyes to his face. With him it was impossible to tell.

Marlie opened her mouth to explain that she'd been chased by a hit man, and then closed it again. How did you explain something like that?

The reality of what had happened finally hit her. She couldn't explain it, because she couldn't talk about it. That was why she had allowed herself to get sidetracked by Joel's sexiness.

She was in serious denial.

It had been so much easier to ogle Joel than to face what had just happened. The notion that someone had tried to kill her—hell, had nearly killed her—was too much to bear. She wasn't ready to ask herself the hard questions that needed asking.

Like who? And what? And why?

"Lady," he growled, "you better start talking, because I'm this close to calling the cops on you for breaking and entering." He measured off an inch with his thumb and index finger. He was tall and broad-shouldered, and he scared the bejeebers out of her. His eyebrows were pulled downward in a dark frown. From his point of view he had every reason to be angry and suspicious, but the last thing she needed right now was his disapproval.

"I...I..." Tears pushed against the corners of her eyes.

*Oh, swell,* Angelina muttered inside Marlie's head. *Here come the waterworks. Suck it up, Montague. Don't bawl, for God's sake. He'll think you're a big baby.*

Marlie tried so hard not to cry that the tears backed up into her sinuses and burned her nose. She'd been able to block out the UPS man's face (although she was seriously beginning to doubt that he really worked for UPS), replacing it instead with the sight of Joel's handsome mug, but now she could not stop remembering.

She trembled, from the top of her head to the tip of her socks still embedded with pieces of Joel's window glass, but to her credit, she did not cry.

*Nah, nah, Angelina.*

"What's wrong?" Immediately he was beside her on the sofa. "Are you sick?"

She shook her head. For a minute Marlie thought he was going to slide his big strong arms around her and hold her tight, and she found herself praying that he would, but then his tone turned suspicious and she was glad that he hadn't.

His eyes narrowed. "Is this just a ploy to keep me from calling the police?"

"Call them," she whispered. "Call them now." Marlie looked into the depths of his dark eyes and was desperately relieved to see compassion reflected back at her. He wasn't such a hard-ass after all. "Please."

She kept shaking. Why couldn't she stop shaking? It was over. She'd survived. To distract herself, she picked at the bandage on her wrist.

"Leave that alone," he scolded. "I don't think the cut is deep enough for stitches, but the pressure dressing will keep it from bleeding."

"It's too tight."

"That's the point of a pressure dressing."

"So go ahead, call the cops." She reached up to tuck a lock of hair behind her ear, but her hand was quivering so much she couldn't accomplish even that simple task.

"Something traumatic happened to you. That's why you broke in. To get help."

Marlie nodded. "I tried knocking, but you must have been in the shower."

Suddenly those big strong arms did go around her. She appreciated his comfort and yet hated her need for it all at the same time.

"What happened?" His lips were pressed close to her ear. She felt his speech vibrate deep inside her. The clean, fresh, soapy scent of him filled her nose.

"It...he..." Her teeth chattered, not from cold, but from fear.

"Take your time. No rush." He tightened his arm around her and pulled her closer.

She clung to him. It felt both scary and exhilarating to be held in a stranger's embrace. She'd actually had a few sexual fantasies about him as she had watched him move his stuff into his house. Once or twice she'd lain awake thinking about all the ways they could pleasure each other. It had been a titillating dream.

But there was nothing titillating about the way Joel was holding her now. Nothing erotic or sensual. It was a comfort hug and nothing more, and it was exactly what she needed.

Empowered, she pulled from his arms and met his eyes again. "The UPS dude tried to snuff me."

"What?"

Joel wasn't sure he'd heard correctly, but he wanted answers and he wanted them now. Someone had tried to kill her? On his watch? Impossible.

*Don't push. Wait for details.* Act first and ask questions later might have served him well as a SEAL, but he was with NCIS now. He was learning the hard way that patience went much further in this job than aggression. It was a hard lesson for a man with a deeply ingrained belief that a good offense is the only defense.

Solemnly, Marlie nodded, her big brown eyes growing wider, the tiny flecks of green catching the light and making her look even more like a 1950s ingenue.

Regardless of his briefing, Joel couldn't reconcile her wholesome poodle-skirted-bobby-soxer image with the antiauthoritarian extremist who penned the *Angelina Avenger* comic books.

"He tried to *snuff* you?"

"You know, bump off, waste, send to meet your maker, dispatch, do in, slay, murder, kill." She sounded irritated.

"Someone tried to kill you?"

"I know it's hard to believe," she said. "I wouldn't even believe it myself if he hadn't shot at me."

"He shot at you?"

"Is there an echo in here, or do you have an obsessive-compulsive disorder where you have to repeat everything someone says?" she asked tartly.

"Oh-ho, so you're something of a brat," he teased.

He'd never suspected she had a smart mouth. That tidbit hadn't been included in her dossier, and he'd been studying it nightly for the past two weeks because he hadn't had anything else to do. The file listed her birthday. She was a Pisces. It detailed her education, which included a bachelor's degree in graphic design from the University of Texas. It described her medical history. She'd broken a wrist falling out of a tree while reading a book when she was twelve, and her blood type was A-positive. But there hadn't been a word about a tart tongue.

Joel eyed her.

Was her story true? Or was she merely a superb actress putting him on? But why would she do that? Besides, he knew real fear when he saw it, and this woman had been terrified. Even though she was struggling to hide it by giving him lip and sitting on her trembling hands.

"I am telling you the truth," she declared belligerently, crossing her arms over her chest.

How had this happened? If someone really had tried to kill her in the few minutes between the time he'd walked away from her house and the moment she'd burst into his, then that meant someone had *him* under surveillance.

But who?

He was pissed.

His gut squeezed, a visceral and immediate response to this new information. He wanted to hunt down the bastard who'd tried to kill Marlie and strangle him with his bare hands.

Carefully, he schooled his features. He hated lying, even when his job necessitated it, and he had to concentrate in order not to inadvertently give himself away. How would a civilian respond under similar circumstances? What would a normal next-door neighbor do?

He would call the cops.

Without another word, Joel stalked to the phone mounted on the wall between the living room and the kitchen. He cocked his head so he could watch Marlie while he dialed 9-1-1.

She huddled on his sofa, shivering like a wet French poodle. Post-traumatic stress, he diagnosed. He had seen this reaction in inexperienced soldiers in Iraq.

"Nine-one-one, what's your emergency?"

He told the dispatch operator where and why he needed a patrol car and then Joel hung up. He went back to stand beside Marlie.

Nervously, she worried the hem of the shirt he'd given her to wear, furling and unfurling the material around her index finger. He also noticed she'd bitten her thumbnail to the quick.

"The police are on their way."

"Thank you for believing me. I know it sounds far-fetched. But it's what happened."

"Why would anyone want to kill you?"

"I write controversial comic books. I've had death threats."

"And you didn't hire a bodyguard?"

"I never really took the threats seriously."

"And now you're in trouble."

"You believe me?"

"It's obvious something disturbing happened to you," Joel replied.

So far he'd fooled her. He had acted like an offended home owner in the process of being burgled and then he'd adopted the concerned neighbor act at just the right time, but where did he go from here?

His mission was covert and much more complex than

it had seemed on the surface. He had been careful to give her his middle name instead of his last. When she'd known him he'd been ten years old and he'd gone by his initials. Clearly she didn't remember him at all, and to be honest, he barely remembered her. But while Joel Jerome hadn't provoked a response in her memory banks, he knew the name Hunter certainly would. It'd be like telling a Hatfield that she was face-to-face with a McCoy.

"You've been very kind. I appreciate you bandaging my wound." Marlie held up her right wrist. She looked so damned vulnerable that it was all he could do not to wrap his arms around her again.

"You're welcome."

"May I have something to drink?"

"I've got whiskey."

"I was thinking more along the lines of a glass of water," she said.

"I'll get you whiskey," he said. "It'll help."

"Okay."

Joel went to the kitchen. Chilly wind whistled through the broken windowpane in the back door. Droplets of Marlie's blood lay drying on his floor. The evidence of what had just happened to her hit him like a brick to the head. As soon as he could, he would review those surveillance tapes and find out exactly what had gone on over at her house.

He turned to get a tumbler from the cabinet and jumped a good six inches when she reached out and touched his shoulder. Some spy he was. He hadn't even heard her pad into the kitchen behind him.

"What do you want?" Joel knew he sounded testy, but she'd sneaked up on him and caught him off guard again. She was developing a really bad habit of messing with his equilibrium.

Her ink-black lashes fluttered behind the lenses of her glasses as she struggled to hold his gaze. He could see the tug-of-war in her face. She was scared of him, but she didn't want him to know.

"I didn't want to be alone," she murmured.

He felt like an ass. Her nervousness touched a soft spot deep inside of him that he didn't want to think about. He couldn't help remembering what she'd looked like stretched out on his sofa with no shirt on. She had a womanly body, curvy and full, and she made him feel hot and edgy inside.

Why?

She was not his type. She was too quiet, lived too much in her head. He liked his women rowdy, physical, and adventuresome.

Like Treeni.

*Yeah, and that had worked out so damn swell.*

Joel clenched his jaw, forcefully shutting off his attraction. He swept his gaze over her, noticing that she'd stripped off her incongruous black-and-white toe socks and was standing barefooted beside the stove. He had the strongest urge to pick her up and carry her back to the davenport.

It irritated him that she provoked his caveman instincts. He was breathing too hard, reacting to her on a primal level. It had to be the damsel-in-distress thing she had going on.

"Be careful not to step in the broken glass," he said kindly. Expressing concern for her feet was his way of apologizing for snapping her head off. He poured a splash of whiskey into the tumbler and passed it to her. "Drink this."

Her lips were full and slick with a subtle salmon shade of lipstick. She licked them nervously, and then tentatively brought the tumbler to her mouth and took a timid swallow.

Immediately her face contorted. Sputtering, she raised a hand to her throat and thrust the tumbler back at him.

"Gawd, that's awful."

"It's whiskey. Don't tell me you've never had any before."

"Okay, Chug-a-lug," she said, her big brown eyes flashing with sudden feistiness. "Not everyone has spent their life in a bar."

There was that smart mouth again. Joel grinned. "What makes you think I've spent my life in a bar?"

She waved a petite hand at him. "You've got that special missing-link quality about you."

"Missing link?" Bemused, he arched an eyebrow.

"You know, the chest-thumping, cave-dwelling, bonking-women-on-the-head-with-a-club-and-dragging-them-off-to-your-lair troglodyte thing that you've got going on."

The fire in her eyes stoked his inner Neanderthal. Damn if he didn't have a sudden urge to drag her off to his lair. He took two quick steps toward her, hemming her in between him and the kitchen counter just to see how far she'd take the flirtation, and instantly her spunkiness evaporated as quickly as it had emerged.

She dropped her gaze, ducked her head, and shrank into herself. The woman talked a good game, but she rattled easy. Joel backed up, realizing he'd crossed into dangerous territory.

The sound of sirens pulling onto Oleander Circle ended the awkward moment, but left Joel wishing he could provoke more of her spunk. Because if there really was a killer on her tail, she'd need all the spunk she could muster, and he'd need every bit of military cunning at his disposal. He wondered again about the true nature of his assignment and if Admiral Delaney was indeed the one who'd sent him here.

Was it just to get him out of Washington and away from Treeni? Or was there something else going on?

One thing was for sure, his boring babysitting assignment had suddenly morphed into a very dangerous mission and all bets were off.

# Chapter 4

The minute Marlie spied Officer Kemp her heart sank to the soles of her feet. He was stocky, cocky, and walked like the Penguin from the old *Batman* television series. He had scars on his knuckles, and his face was something of a liability with a big thick nose and an unattractive cleft in his chin.

Out of all the cops in Corpus Christi, why did the patrolman who'd answered Joel's 9-1-1 call have to be the same cop who'd arrested her three months earlier?

"I know you," Officer Kemp said the minute he stepped inside Joel's house.

"Yeah?" She acted like she didn't know him from an ice hole in a fishing pond in eastern Siberia.

He pointed the tip of his pen at her. "You're that hippy, dippy, freaky chick who tried to bite me at the Save the Shrimp rally last fall."

"You maced me," she protested.

The butthead. It had taken two days for her eyes to get back to normal. Well, actually, Angelina had been the one he maced. Marlie would never have bitten anyone, even if they were touching her inappropriately, the way Kemp had grabbed her butt.

"Only because you wouldn't get out of the middle of the oncoming traffic," Kemp said.

"I'm sick of shrimp habitats being destroyed just so greedy corporate restaurants can get rich." She flipped her hair in a dismissive gesture.

The blue vein at Officer Kemp's forehead bulged. "Hey, my old man is a shrimper, and you bleeding-heart liberals are ruining his business."

"Excuse me," Joel interrupted, "but we have bigger issues than your ongoing shrimp feud."

We?

Marlie studied him a long, empty second as she tried to process why Joel would be willing to get involved in her problems. She didn't trust guys who were too helpful.

Kemp eyed her tousled hair and bare feet and the fact she was wearing a man's shirt. He snapped a quick look at Joel. Marlie could see him jumping to the wrong conclusions about their relationship. She didn't know if it was worth the trouble to set him straight or not. He probably wouldn't believe her anyway.

"So tell me exactly what happened."

Trying her best to remain unemotional, Marlie detailed her run-in with the UPS-man-turned-deranged-psycho-killer.

"Let's go see this alleged crime scene." Kemp nodded tersely, his boots crunching across the broken glass as he headed for the back door.

Marlie looked from her bare feet to the door, but before she could say a word, Joel's arms were at her waist. He picked her up off the floor as easily as if she weighed thirty pounds instead of a hundred and thirty.

"Hey," Marlie said breathlessly. "What's this all about?"

"Put your arms around my neck so I don't drop you." He toted her over the threshold and out onto the back porch before pulling the door closed behind them.

"There's no need." She resisted, amplifying their closeness by keeping her arms folded over her chest. "You can put me down now; we're clear of the glass."

"Nope." His chest rose in a slow, I'm-being-patient-with-you breath.

She controlled herself with effort and spoke in a terse, coiled voice. "I don't like the way you take control without asking my permission."

"Tough. It's winter, you're shoeless, and you've had an unpleasant shock."

"Who died and made you God," she grumbled.

"If you don't like it, break into someone else's house next time. Now, put your arms around me."

Reluctantly, she slid her arms around his neck. His shoulder muscles corded at her touch. Her body flushed with heat against his reaction.

"I want to be clear about this," she whispered.

"About what?"

"About...about..." She snorted indelicately, trying to find the words to express what she was feeling, but Kemp interrupted before she could even decide what she meant to say.

"This the fence you climbed over?"

The cop stopped beside the six-foot privacy fence separating her property from Joel's. He eyed the boards as if they were suspects in a lineup.

"Yes."

"You're claiming you scaled this fence barefooted

while there was a semiautomatic-wielding assassin chasing after you?" Kemp frowned.

What was this guy's problem? Just because she was against overfishing the sea and his father was a shrimper didn't give him the right to act like she was guilty of something, especially when she was the victim here.

"I had socks on," she said, knowing full well she sounded defensive.

"He just let you get away? Some hit man."

"I told you he was injured." Marlie felt like a lapdog addressing Kemp from the circle of Joel's arms. She was at a distinct disadvantage. She wriggled, wanting down.

"You said that he was hit by a ricochet bouncing off your bowling ball."

"That's correct."

Kemp stroked his chin. He had that something's-not-adding-up look in his eyes.

Marlie squirmed harder against Joel and accidentally poked him with an elbow, but instead of putting her down he just tightened his grip. Her irritation sat big inside her, a disgruntled elephant. She didn't like being manhandled, even though in a bizarre way it felt very pleasant.

Kemp made a noise of disbelief, shook his head, then opened Joel's gate and led them around to Marlie's side of the fence. The closer they got to her back door, the faster her heart pumped.

"What if the killer is still in there?" she murmured.

"Stay back until I clear the house," Kemp instructed.

Joel surprised her by stopping and waiting at the corner of the house beside the peach tree—which still wore a swatch of Marlie's white T-shirt. It fluttered in the breeze like a truce flag. Kemp drew his duty weapon, cautiously twisted the doorknob, and then disappeared inside.

Two minutes later, he was back, holstering his gun. "The place is clear."

"Put me down," Marlie said to Joel through clenched teeth as soon as they were inside her house.

Slowly, he let her slide to the floor. Her bottom skimmed lightly over his hard masculine thigh. The glide down his leg seemed infinite, an endless slip out of time and space. She ignored the resulting tingle and resolutely turned her back on Joel to find Officer Kemp studying her intently.

"You said this unknown assailant shot up your coffee table. That right?"

"Yes, that's what happened." Marlie hurried from her kitchen to the adjoining living area to show him the evidence and stopped dead in her tracks.

Her mouth dropped open. Unable to believe what she was seeing, she blinked and rubbed her eyes.

The coffee table was gone.

Cosmo Villereal loved his new job at the Office of Navy Intelligence.

He was working as part of a dedicated team that made a difference in his country's national defense. What could be more fulfilling than that? Granted, the job was extremely challenging. The ONI held him to the highest of standards and he put in eighty-hour workweeks, but there was nowhere else he would rather be.

Not even back in Corpus with Marlie.

Since he'd been away from his old friend, Cosmo had come to realize Marlie had been right about their relationship. That while the mental connection they shared was intense, the physical spark just wasn't there. For years he'd tried to take their friendship beyond the platonic, but Marlie had resisted.

Now, since Treeni Delaney had come strolling into his life, Cosmo understood why.

His feelings for Marlie were more brotherly than loverly. He just hated that they'd fought over his job and that he'd left town before they'd resolved things between them.

Treeni Delaney.

She was pure vixen, and you never knew what she would dare do next. She was nothing like sweet, predictable Marlie. Treeni was tall and lithe and muscular, and he certainly wouldn't mind being trapped between those powerful thighs. Plus, she was a hellacious beauty with a face that could stop traffic and a body to match. Part Jordanian, part American, dual citizenship. And according to the office watercooler gossip, the best damn spy the U.S. Navy had in the Middle East.

The olive-green color of her eyes she'd inherited from her father, Chet Delaney, former director of the ONI. The slight exotic tilt of those sharp green eyes came strictly from her mother, Nyra, who claimed direct lineage to the Jordanian royal family. Treeni's nose was regal, a perfect complement to those striking eyes. She had a wide teasing smile that she wielded like a weapon and silky smooth skin the color of toasted almonds. She had a bold, uninhibited voice that made everyone around her sit up and take notice. Her hair was chestnut brown and she wore it in a sleek, straight style. Her breasts weren't too big nor were they too small; in fact, they were perfect.

Treeni was perfect. Not that he had a ghost of a chance with a woman like her.

Cosmo had heard the rumors. She was the talk of the ONI. He knew that in her line of work she had to be a master manipulator. She'd brought down some very powerful men using questionable techniques, but the bottom line was that she got the job done when few others could.

But rather than scare him off, her reputation fueled his desire, and now he arrived early to work every morning just so he could stand by his desk and watch her saunter in.

And here she came, strutting her stuff in boots and a chain-mail micro-mini. Fifteen minutes late as usual. But Treeni could get away with tardiness. It had as much to do with her crackerjack spying abilities as her stunning beauty or her father's executive position.

She had two cups of Starbucks coffee in her hands, and instead of walking on past as usual with a glib, teasing greeting, she sidled over to him, a thousand-kilowatt smile on her face.

Holy smokes.

Cosmo had fantasized about this moment a hundred times, but he'd never really believed it would ever come to pass. His heart somersaulted. No way was this really happening. He had to be dreaming. It was too surreal to think otherwise. The luscious Treeni Delaney, soon-to-be first daughter of the White House, bestowing her attention upon him.

*Don't wake up, don't wake up, don't wake up.*

" 'Mornin', Cosmo." She gave him a sultry wink.

*She knows my name!*

Treeni rested her shapely butt against his desk and leaned over. She extended one of the Starbucks cups toward him. A quick look down told him that she was wearing one of her infamous low-cut blouses and giving him an exceptional view of her cleavage.

On purpose.

He snapped his gaze back to her face and found her smirking smugly. "Like what you see?"

"I...uh..." *Don't stutter, you idiot.*

"Relax," she said. "I don't mind. Here, I brought you an espresso."

"Thank you." He didn't drink espresso, it made him jittery, but Cosmo reached for the cup as if she were offering him the elixir to immortality.

Treeni scooted closer, one lean thigh edging up over the corner of his desk. "My father tells me you've got an IQ of one eighty."

Cosmo pulled at his collar with an index finger. "Actually it's one eighty-three."

"My, my, my." She walked two fingers up his tie.

Cosmo gulped and simply let her walk all over him.

"Aren't you precise? I find brainy men a real turn-on. My father also tells me you're very thorough. I hear that your first day on the job you found a computing error that was costing us thousands of dollars a year."

"I try," Cosmo said, doing his damnedest not to blush and give his feelings away.

She kept leaning in closer until her lips were just inches from his. He knew without looking around that every eye in the vicinity was on them. Every eye in the vicinity was always on Treeni.

"You know what?" she said in a voice as breathy and seductive as Marilyn Monroe's.

"What?"

"I married the last man my father told me was very thorough." Treeni gave a husky laugh that sounded the way date palm fruits would sound if they could laugh— dry and rich and exotic.

"You're married?" Cosmo gulped. He was more disappointed than a kid who'd just learned Santa Claus didn't exist.

"Not anymore." Treeni's green eyes twinkled and she slid to her feet.

His hopes rebounded.

They were standing toe-to-toe and nose-to-nose. She smelled intoxicatingly of lotus flower and tangerines. She was so close he could feel the heat radiating off her body in sensuous waves.

*I've died,* Cosmo thought. *I've died and gone to heaven.*

"Here's the deal," she said.

"Uh-huh." He was scarcely breathing. Scarcely thinking. At least not with anything above the waist. It felt as if his heart had been shot from a cannon. If Mensa could see him now, they'd permanently revoke his membership card.

"I need you to do me a favor."

"Sure, Ms. Delaney, whatever you need."

"Call me Treeni."

"Yes, Treeni." He cleared his throat. God, she was going to flatten him like a pancake, but he didn't care. He was that wowed by her. Better to take a chance and regret it than never to take a chance at all.

She fished in her cleavage for a business card and pressed it into his hand. "This is my address. Be there at eight o'clock tonight, bring your laptop, and don't disappoint me."

"So, Nancy Drew," Officer Kemp taunted Marlie, "is it the case of the missing coffee table, or did you just make up the assassination attempt crap? Are you aware that it's a crime to file a false police report?"

"Where did it go?" Unable to believe what her eyes were telling her, Marlie turned in circles in the middle of the living room.

"Tell the truth. Do you even *own* a coffee table?" Kemp challenged her.

She wasn't paying him any attention. She was trying to figure out what had happened. "There's got to be wood chips, bullet casings, something."

Frantically, she dropped to her knees and began searching the carpet, even though she knew it was futile. From the uniform direction of the pile it was clear the floor had been vacuum-cleaned. Even the clump of dust bunnies underneath the couch had disappeared.

Say what you would about the assassin, he was very clean.

Marlie nibbled a thumbnail as anxiety pushed against her. She sat down hard on her bottom in the middle of the floor. Desperate for an ally, she looked up at Joel.

He stood silently in the corner, his eyes sharp and alert, arms crossed over his chest. She could see him assessing and analyzing her, but she could not tell what he was thinking.

Did he believe her? Or was he on the side of the skeptical lawman? Perhaps he merely felt that he'd gotten caught up in something that was none of his business, and he was trying to figure out a classy way to make an exit.

Briefly, he made eye contact with her but then glanced away as if he regretted even that small connection. The hard angles of his profile made him seem very out of place in her living room.

All rightee then.

His position was clear enough. Except for Angelina, she was on her own. No problem. She was used to it. Hell, she preferred it that way. She really did. She didn't need anybody. Not even Cosmo. She had Angelina. That was enough.

*But I'm just a cartoon character,* Angelina pointed out.

Yeah? So? What was wrong with that? Lifting her chin, Marlie hardened her heart against the attraction. Never mind the quaking in her knees. She'd survived a lot worse than this. Mentally, she stuck her tongue out at her fear. Do your worst.

The two men were standing around staring at her as if she'd lost her marbles, and then Marlie remembered the bowling ball. She scrambled to her feet.

"My bowling ball! Find my bowling ball. The UPS guy shot my bowling ball. That should prove I'm telling the truth."

Kemp and Joel glanced around the room. No bowling ball.

"Maybe it's in the kitchen," Joel said. "I'll go check."

"I'll search the bedroom," Kemp volunteered and took off down the hall. Marlie didn't like the idea of him rummaging around her bedroom, but what could she say? He was a cop.

Too bad Joel wasn't the one searching her bedroom.

*What? You want him to go through your underwear drawer and find out that you're more of a Wal-Mart ten-pack-of-cotton-undies-for-five-dollars rather than a Victoria's Secret fifteen-dollar-a-pair-handwash-in-Woolite-only kinda gal?*

Excellent point. Okay, she officially didn't want any men in her bedroom.

*And that's different from the usual state of affairs because... ?* Angelina challenged.

Shut up.

Maybe she did need to make flesh-and-blood friends after all. Ones who would not deride her taste in underwear or her lack of a love life.

Joel returned from the kitchen shaking his head. "No bowling ball in there." But he did give her a small smile that made her feel better.

"You must have the Bermuda Triangle of living rooms," Kemp said sarcastically upon his return. "First a coffee table, now a bowling ball. Quick, call News 5."

The guy was a bullying asshole. In high school he had probably been one of those swaggering jocks who terrorized the kids from the chess club. Marlie had been in the chess club.

"No, no," she said, struggling to keep a lid on her hysteria. She had to make him believe her. "Don't you see? The assassin took them away."

"Yeah," Kemp said. "That's real likely."

"He took them," she insisted. "The coffee table, the bowling ball. In his UPS truck. Then he must have vacuumed up the wood chips and picked up the bullet casings while I was next door at Joel's. He's trying to set me up, make me look like I'm crazy."

"You are crazy. Whatcha been doin'? Smokin' crack?" Kemp asked. "Or droppin' acid?"

"Stuff it where the sun don't shine, Porky." Marlie's lips said the words, but it was Angelina's sassy voice doing the talking.

Joel's eyebrows shot up on his forehead, and Marlie could have sworn he grinned. It was quick but unmistakable. Mortified, Marlie slapped a hand over her mouth.

Way to go, Angelina. Piss the cop off enough to toss you in the slammer.

*I'm not going to let that meathead treat you so rudely.*

*You might put up with that kind of crap, but I don't.* Angelina sniffed.

Kemp pulled handcuffs from his pocket. "That's it; you're going downtown."

But Angelina wasn't the only one jumping in to defend her. Joel stepped between Kemp and Marlie. He raised a palm at the patrolman's chest.

They stared at each other like gunslingers squaring off on the dusty main street of a one-horse town. Marlie half expected to hear the theme from one of those spaghetti westerns her dad used to watch. Their posturing was fascinating, two alpha dogs warring over the same bone.

Why did she suddenly feel like a pork chop?

Joel's energy permeated the room. Or maybe it was just Marlie's skewed perception. She wasn't the kind of woman who fell easily into lust, but there was something about her new neighbor that tripped her sexual trigger. Not that she was happy about it.

Or maybe it was just the combination of whiskey, adrenaline, and fear. She prayed that was the case. Those things wore off quickly. It took a lot longer to lose a bad case of infatuation.

"You instigated this, Kemp," Joel said. "Just step off if you don't want me to report you to the police commissioner, who just happens to be a very close friend of mine."

Kemp eyed him speculatively. "You know Jonas Barnhill?"

"Hunt with him every deer season at Rocky Ridge Ranch. Jonas brings the Jim Beam; I bring the sirloins and the Sterno."

Slam-dunk!

Was Joel telling the truth? Marlie searched his face, but

his eyes were inscrutable. If he was lying, he was damned good at it. She was glad he was on her side.

*Maybe,* Angelina said, *rather than getting so impressed with Mr. Sauntering Sinew and Bulging Biceps, you should ask yourself why he's on your side.*

Kemp sniffed at Marlie. "She's been drinking. I can smell it on her breath."

"You ever been shot at?" Joel asked him.

Sliding one hand onto the butt of his holstered gun in a cock-of-the-walk stance, Kemp met Joel's eyes. "What's it to you?"

"I'm trying to prove a point."

"No," Kemp admitted.

"Well, I have." Joel thrust out his chest and stepped closer.

That statement instantly piqued her interest. How had he gotten shot at? Was he law enforcement? Was he military? Had he been in Iraq? Or had his experience with guns been something of a more notorious variety?

"So?" Kemp grunted.

"First thing you want to do after staring down the barrel of the gun of some crazy-eyed bastard and living to tell the tale is to have a strong belt of the hard stuff. That's why I gave Miss Montague a shot of whiskey. She was stone-cold sober when the attempt was made on her life. I'm a witness to her state of mind at the time."

Marlie's heart fluttered. *My hero.*

*Get rid of that thought right now. This guy is not your hero. He's not your anything. You don't need a man to defend you. Tell him to butt out. You've got it under control.*

"Hey, what are these?" Kemp asked, leaning over to pull a stack of her research books from the end table.

He read from the back-cover copy of a book with a particularly lurid cover. "Brainwashed by patriotism, why gullible Americans swallow blatant military deception."

*Here we go*, Marlie thought. It was't the first time she'd been ridiculed for her interest in conspiracy theories. Occam's razor aside, she and her family had suffered firsthand from a government cover-up. She knew such things went on.

Kemp tossed that book onto the couch and went on to the next one in the stack. "The U.S. government's plan for world domination." He chortled. "Yeah, right. Whoever wrote that was obviously never a public servant. Politicians can't even dominate their own sex drives."

"For your information, that book was written by a former head of the FBI," Marlie said crisply, even though she knew she was only adding gasoline to the flame.

"Beyond the veil of secrecy, exposing clandestine brotherhood sects." Kemp howled. "Learn the truth! Evil lizard people disguised as monarchy control the world's banking system."

Marlie cringed as the arrogant cop kept reading from the backs of the books. Taken out of context, her reading material did make her look a bit unbalanced.

"Lady," Kemp said, dumping the remainder of the books back onto the end table, "you're a certified whack job and anti-American to boot."

"That's enough, Kemp," Joel barked. "Back off."

Marlie's eyes widened.

Joel was in battle stance. Fists hardened into lethal weapons, jaw jutting forward, legs spread a shoulder's width apart. His tone was challenging, the sharp expression in his green-gray-blue eyes commanding.

*You've finally found a real alpha male, and he is yummy.* Angelina sighed.

But Marlie didn't want an alpha male. Guys like that scared her. While she admired Joel's bluntness and bravery, his confrontational style made her want to turtle up inside herself.

*Grow a backbone, woman.*

*Easy for you to say,* Marlie mentally retorted. *You're just a cartoon character. You take a risk and get into trouble, and I'm the one who writes you out of it.*

Joel's eyes locked with Kemp's.

Marlie looked from Joel to the policeman and back again. Even though the officer was taller than Joel, he was overweight and so full of himself he apparently didn't recognize how quickly Joel could take him out. Joel shot him the most bloodcurdling, Clint Eastwood, go-ahead-make-my-day look Marlie had ever seen.

Kemp suddenly backed down. "I'm out of here."

"Wait a minute. You're leaving?" Marlie protested. "Just like that?"

"There's no evidence that a crime's been committed," Officer Kemp said, edging cautiously around Joel in his break for the front door.

"But what if the guy returns?" Marlie anxiously knotted her hands.

"I don't believe there was a guy."

"I've been receiving threatening letters. I even filed a report about it last year."

"I'm aware of your report. I'm also aware that the officer on the case concluded you wrote the letter to yourself."

"I did not," she declared hotly.

Kemp stopped at the front door and issued his last

threat. "Dare to file another false police report, and I promise that you'll find that cute little butt of yours locked up in jail so fast it'll make your head swim."

"Hey!" Marlie's lips moved, but it was Angelina who shouted as Kemp walked out the door. She punched an index finger in the air for emphasis. "That comment is sexual harassment, buddy, and I'm going to report you to Jonas Barnhill."

Her threat fell on deaf ears. Kemp kept walking and never looked back.

# Chapter 5

W hat in the hell did you do that for?" Marlie spun around to scowl at Joel. He was surprised by the vehemence in her eyes as she turned on him the minute the front door shut behind the policeman.

"Do what?"

"Butt into my business. I didn't need your meddling interference."

"Yeah? Then how come you broke into my house? What was that all about?" He stepped forward, encroaching on her space.

"I had to get away from a killer, and your house was handy. It had nothing to do with you."

"No? Then why didn't you break into the house on the other side of yours?"

"Mrs. Whittaker is an eighty-three-year-old widow and she's half blind."

"My point exactly."

And then Joel realized why Marlie had jumped down his throat rather than thanking him for helping. She was scared spitless, but loath to show it. In spite of the tough image she hoped to convey with her narrowed eyes, clenched fists, and determined chin, she could not hide the telltale throbbing of her pulse. It fluttered frantically at the base of her throat. The evidence of her vulnerability caught him low in the gut. Aw, damn. Her bravery in the face of fear notched his respect for her tenfold. Dobbs had to be wrong. She could not be involved in antigovernment activities, in spite of her kooky conspiracy theory books.

"You had no right to interfere," she insisted, stubbornly hanging on to the issue.

The best way to handle this situation was to let her believe that she'd won. She had her arguments settled in her head, and he could see she wasn't about to change her mind. Joel held up both palms. "You're absolutely right. Just because I have a thing about bullies pushing people around doesn't mean I had a right to step in on your behalf without your permission. Even if you were getting bullied."

"Darn straight." She flicked a lock of hair back over one ear.

"You don't need some chauvinistic guy telling you what to do."

"I don't."

"You're an independent woman living happily on her own."

"Now you're just patronizing me."

"I'm not, but if it makes you feel any better, I apologize," he said.

"What? I didn't catch that."

Apologies weren't his thing, but if she needed to hear it again in order to feel better about herself, he could suck up his pride and give her one. "I said I apologize."

"Well," she relented as she thought about it for a minute, "you were just trying to help."

"Absolutely."

"But why would you take up for me with Kemp?"

"Do I need a motive beyond common courtesy?"

"It makes no sense."

"Chivalry makes no sense?"

"You don't even know me."

"I know you have issues. A guy tries to do something nice and you crawl down his throat."

"Why do you want to defend me?"

"You mean besides the fact I think Kemp is a giant asshole?"

"Ah, so that's what this is about. Can't have two bulls in the same pasture, huh?"

"That's not it. Kemp reminds me of one dickhead stepfather too many." She was starting to tick him off the way she kept badgering for answers. "Guys like Kemp are all cowards inside. They're afraid of getting pushed around, so they do the pushing first. I hate cowards."

He thought of his father when he said it. Of how Gus had stood on the courthouse steps during the custody hearing but never worked up the courage to go inside. Without Gus there to stand up for his rights as a father, Deirdre's lawyer had mopped the courtroom with him and his mother had gotten full custody. Joel batted the thought away. Why was he thinking about Gus now?

"How many dickhead stepfathers did you have?"

Joel wished he hadn't said a damn word about this to her. He wasn't one of those people who whined about a tough childhood. And he didn't like the "you-poor-baby-tell-me-all-your-troubles" expression in Marlie's eyes.

"More than one," he said lightly.

Joel was surprised that she let it go, but he was grateful. When most women found out he came from multiple broken homes, they immediately wanted to mother him. Treeni was the only woman he'd ever known who had not.

"Was that story about knowing the police commissioner true?" she asked.

He shrugged. "Not a word of it."

Her frown deepened. "Do you lie often?"

"No more than necessary."

"I don't like liars. Can't trust 'em." She tilted her head and studied him. "I suppose I was rude to you just now."

"You had a right. You've had a big scare."

"Do you believe me?"

"I don't know exactly what happened here," Joel said, "but I believe that you believe it."

"I *was* shot at," she said obstinately. "I didn't hallucinate."

"I never said you did."

"I saw your face when Kemp dragged out my books. I know what you were thinking."

"So now you're a mind reader?"

"FYI, I don't believe all those conspiracy theories," she said. "They're just research for the comic books I illustrate."

"But you do believe some of them."

"I don't take anything on faith. Not even conspiracy theories."

"A suspicious mind isn't necessarily a bad thing," he said.

"Try telling that to the rest of the world."

"Considering what happened, you shouldn't stay here alone tonight. Do you have someplace else to go?"

She nodded. "My mother's house."

"That's good."

"Thank you. You've been very nice. And tolerant." She moved toward the door.

"I'm being dismissed?"

"You've been great, but I'd like to be alone now. Good-bye."

"All right, I'm going. But if you need anything, feel free to drop by. The window's already broken out of the back door so it shouldn't be so hard getting in the next time."

"Thanks." Her smile was tight.

He saw the longing in her eyes and knew she wanted to trust him but simply couldn't bring herself to do so. She wasn't one to let down her guard easily. Getting close to her was going to take time. Lots of time.

Time he didn't possess. He had to find a way to accelerate the process and overcome her jitteriness with strangers.

Joel left her place via the backyard gate. He paused in the narrow strip of lawn between her house and his. Part of him admired her internal vigilance, but another part of him was irritated. He wasn't accustomed to working so hard to prove himself to the opposite sex. Normally, he just cocked a grin and women melted in his embrace.

But not this one.

Marlie was a challenge. She required a bigger push, an added incentive to rush into his arms and ask him to slay dragons for her.

Joel grinned. Unluckily for her, he thrived on challenges.

What would force her to ask for his help?

Well, if her car wouldn't run, she'd need a lift over to her mother's house.

It was sneaky and underhanded. He didn't like the idea of scaring her more than she already was, but sometimes for the good of all concerned, you had to make tough judgment calls.

Nonchalantly, Joel sauntered over to Marlie's Prius. He cast a glance around the neighborhood. No one appeared to be watching. He darted a look back at her front window. If she caught him, he'd better have a cover story she would believe.

Okay, he had it. He'd just tell her he was thinking of trading in his Durango for a Prius and he'd stopped by to take a look at hers. That should not only allay her mistrust, but earn him brownie points for being an environmentally conscientious consumer.

Joel hunkered down on the side of the Toyota facing away from Marlie's window and removed the valve stem cap from her rear tire. He found a slender twig, about the diameter of a toothpick, in the grass. He broke it into four sections, lodged one piece of twig against the valve stem core to make the tire go flat, and replaced the cap. He quickly repeated the procedure with the three other tires. He used the twigs to flatten the tires because if he did it by hand, it would take too long, and it upped his risk of getting caught. Later, when he had a chance, he'd come back and retrieve the twigs so no one could trace the flats back to him.

Then he straightened and strolled home. He didn't feel guilty. He'd done what he had to do.

Three minutes later, he settled into the chair in front of the security monitor set up in the spare bedroom and ran the tape back to fifteen minutes before the time Marlie had broken into his house. Two weeks earlier, the NCIS covert ops team had installed the cameras, getting her out of the house by posing as city workers looking for a leaking gas main. Joel hadn't been involved because they hadn't wanted to risk her recognizing him again later.

On Camera One Joel zeroed in on her empty living room. It looked no different on the color camera than it did in person. Black leather davenport with white pillows.

Alabaster wicker rocking chair with ebony cushions. Ivory carpet, black-lacquered end tables. Black-and-white-striped curtains. The lamp shades were yin and yang symbols. The effect created a feeling of distance and aloofness.

Marlie Montague isolated herself even in her own house. He could almost touch her loneliness.

He switched to Camera Two, which was mounted in the air vent in her kitchen. The room resembled a 1950s diner with the black-and-white-checked linoleum flooring and the chrome dining table. The countertops were black granite, and the cabinetry was painted a high-gloss pure white. All the appliances were black except for the stainless-steel refrigerator. He liked the art deco style, but this room also felt empty.

Joel went back to Camera One and eyed the coffee table. Yep. There it was, completely unharmed. He fast-forwarded the tape.

Here came Marlie on-screen. She went to the door, stood on tiptoe, and peered out the keyhole. She hesitated and stepped back. It looked like she was mumbling to herself, but there was no audio.

Did he have the mute on?

Suddenly the camera went blank, as if it had been switched off at the source. He futzed around with the controls.

Nothing.

He changed the batteries in the remote.

Nada.

He jiggled the cords to make sure they hadn't come unplugged but the screen remained blank.

He switched inputs.

Zip.

He triple-checked everything, but the problem wasn't with his equipment. Someone must have tampered with the camera.

Had the assassin used some specialized electronic device to disable the video while he was still outside the house?

Or—and he hated to think this because it would mean she was one hell of an actress and the entire assassin thing had been a ruse and she was onto him—had Marlie herself disabled it?

When her mother didn't answer either her home phone or her cell, Marlie flipped out. She paced the living room, mentally conjuring every horror imaginable.

In the primary scenario, the hit man had left Marlie's house—bowling ball and damaged coffee table in tow—motored over, and murdered Mom.

*But why would he want to kill your mother?* Angelina reasoned.

"I don't know. Why was he trying to kill me?"

*There are several options.*

"Yeah? I'm all ears."

*It's the guy who wrote you the latest death threat. "Love America or die, bitch." Weren't those his exact words?*

"Something along those lines, yes. What if it's not the eloquent letter writer? Who then?"

*I'd say you finally hit upon a real conspiracy theory. You landed an arrow in someone's Achilles' heel. Remember Mel Gibson in* Conspiracy Theory?

What if she had? But then which conspiracy theory was it? Had the government been hiding space aliens in plain sight since Roswell? Were lizard people in control of the banking system? Had LBJ really hired marksmen to gun down JFK in the motorcade because he'd secretly wanted to sleep with Jackie?

Oh, shit. Oh, shit. Oh, shit.

*Try to call your mother one more time before you completely lose it.*

Okay, okay.

Marlie took a deep breath and picked up the phone. She heard an odd rustling sound on the line and her stomach roiled.

Was she being bugged?

Compelled by years of conspiracy theory thinking, Marlie went to the kitchen, plucked a butter knife from the silverware drawer, and then marched back into the living room. She picked up the cordless phone and set about prying the cover off. The butter knife slipped a couple of times and rapped against her bandaged wrist.

Ouch.

Grimly, she gritted her teeth and kept chipping away at the plastic until she finally levered it open.

In all honesty, she really hadn't expected to find the small black microphone imbedded in the circuitry, but when she did, for one monumental millisecond, her heart stopped. Slowly, Marlie extracted the device and brought it to eye level.

Her assassin was no simple do-it-yourselfer. The bug was military issue. She was familiar with the style. Cosmo had fully indoctrinated her in electronic spyware after they'd met at a spyware convention five years earlier where Marlie had been researching "KGB Killers Gone Capitalist" for comic book number thirteen.

All the breath left her body. She felt as if she'd been sucker-punched. Here it was, the very thing she'd spent half her life fearing. She'd been violated. Her home and her sanctuary encroached. Truly, there was no safe place.

Her initial impulse was to destroy the wiretap, jump up and down on it with both feet, and then slam it against the wall a few times before flushing it down the toilet. But Angelina stopped her.

*Put the bug back. In case he's still recording you. So he won't suspect that you're on to him.*

Him. Or them. Whichever the case might be.

Her fingers automatically replaced the bug in the receiver while her mind raced. She had to get out of here. Had to find Mom.

She slammed the phone back in its dock, grabbed her purse, and rushed out into the twilight.

At that hour her neighborhood smelled of all those delicious "Honey-I'm-home" aromas. Sautéing onions, grilling meats, and roasting garlic mingled with the aromatic scent of delivery pizza called in by working moms too weary to cook.

Marlie eyed the Domino's guy long and hard as he drove around the cul-de-sac. She'd seen him before. He'd brought many extra-cheese pepperoni pies to her front door over the past several months, but she'd never learned his name. He didn't make eye contact as he motored past, and she hadn't realized she'd been holding her breath until his car turned off Oleander Circle.

Anxiety pushed at her like an open palm. Hurriedly, she unlocked the Prius's driver's-side door and tossed her purse inside. She was about to climb in when she noticed the tires.

Pancakes. All of them.

Four flats?

She bent to examine the tires. It couldn't be a coinci-

dence. They hadn't been slashed. Someone had intentionally leaked the air out.

But who?

And why?

How long had they been flat? Minutes? Or hours? Or
maybe even days?

She hadn't been out of the house since her bowling
league on Wednesday night. Had the assassin deflated her
tires before he'd come to the door to minimize her chance
of escape? Gulping, she cast another glance around the
neighborhood.

Nothing seemed out of the ordinary. Nine-year-old
Jenna Knightly was twirling her baton in her front yard
across the street, and two houses down from hers, a group
of teenage boys were shooting hoops in their driveway.

Maybe it was just kids up to skulduggery.

Or maybe not. She wasn't taking any chances.

Marlie marched inside the house, retrieved a Ziploc baggy
from the pantry, slid on a pair of yellow kitchen gloves, and
stalked back outside to remove the valve stem caps.

When she found the broken-off pieces of twig wedged
against the valve cores, a fearful edginess curled around
her heart. Seeing actual proof of sabotage made it too
real. She'd been spied on, watched, and targeted. Marlie
stuffed all four of the valve stem caps and the twig pieces
back into the baggy.

"Gotcha, you bastard," she muttered.

Except for the fact that the assassin had been wearing
gloves when he'd shouldered his way into her house with
his semiautomatic. It was a long shot that he would have
put them on after he'd flattened the tires on her car.

Her temporary cockiness sagged. Marlie almost threw
the baggy away, but it was her only hope of finding out

who'd vandalized her tires. Besides, no prints at all would be a pretty solid indication this was indeed the handiwork of her assassin.

She returned to the house, went to her office, and wrote Cosmo a short note explaining that she desperately needed him to pull strings and find someone who could dust the evidence for prints and why.

And then she added a heartfelt note of apology for the way she'd acted when he'd told her he was moving to Maryland and taking the job with ONI.

If nothing else, maybe this would mend fences between them. Cosmo would do anything to help her, even if he was still miffed because she hadn't supported his career decision. She realized how shortsighted she'd been. She didn't know if Cosmo would even be able to get the valve stem caps checked for fingerprints, but he was the only person she trusted.

Slipping the note and baggy into an express mail envelope, she slapped the exorbitantly priced stamp on it—luckily she kept a supply of express mail packaging supplies on hand for tight deadlines—and then went outside to drop it into her letter box and raise the red flag, but before she got to that step a voice from the gathering gloom reached out and slid an invisible hand up her spine.

"Need a ride?"

He was lounging insouciantly with one shoulder propped against her garage door, his sneaker-clad feet crossed at the ankles, the picture of a classic bad-boy rebel. Sex, muscles, and attitude.

Where had his G.I. Joe posture gone? Was he trying to be provocative? Doing his best Colin Farrell imitation, all slouchy and sexy?

He didn't move, just kept lounging as if he didn't have

the skeletal structure to hold himself upright. He didn't say anything else. Just waited for her to answer his question.

Shadows cloaked his face. She could not see his eyes or read his expression, but the tilt of his head left no doubt in her mind that he was assessing her.

And in a very sexual way.

Marlie raised a hand to her throat. She hadn't taken the time to change from her well-worn track pants and the white dress shirt he'd given her to wear.

"You need a ride?" Joel repeated in a deep-throated drawl that made her forget absolutely everything that had brought her to this point.

It was a defense mechanism and she knew it. The way her mind would semi shut down on information overload just as it had when she'd broken into his house. There were so many dreadful, frightening things to think about that all she could focus on was the moment.

On her breath. On this man.

Coming toward her.

He moved with a controlled, powerful, no-bullshit stride. The way of the warrior. The prowl of a protector. The gait of a guardian. He looked at once like both sinner and savior.

She could make out his features now. Slightly sinister but yet strangely soothing too. The hollows below his high cheekbones, his angular jaw, his tanned skin.

He was on the porch beside her, crowding her space, and Marlie gulped, disoriented by his nearness and the strange feelings he stirred. In such close proximity, he looked and sounded as dangerous as hell.

"You need a ride." This time it was a statement, not a question.

She wanted to say no, to refuse his offer. She would call a cab.

*It'll cost you forty dollars to go out to North Padre,* Angelina said. *I've seen your wallet. You don't have that kind of cash.*

But she couldn't get into a car with Joel. She knew next to nothing about him, and she didn't take rides from strangers.

*Which is more important? Your peace of mind or your mother's safety?*

He reached out a hand and cupped it under her elbow, but stopped just short of touching her. He didn't have to touch her for Marlie to feel him.

He was that potent. That masculine. That decidedly male. Energy jumped off him in a thousand different directions.

His eyes met hers.

*Trust me.*

Wasn't that what the devil said to Eve when he was tempting her with a juicy Red Delicious?

Think about Mom.

Marlie opened her mouth and said the thing she most did not want to say. "I need a ride."

# Chapter 6

A minute later Marlie was clinging to the passenger-side door handle of Joel's gas-hog SUV, preparing to fling her body out of the moving vehicle if he made any untoward moves. When she thought he wasn't watching, she stealthily unbuckled her seat belt. Just in case she had to jump out on short notice. She might have been forced to accept a ride from him, but she wasn't letting her guard down, no sirree, not for a second.

Finding that listening device in her telephone brought home just how susceptible she really was. How could she not have had Cosmo sweep her house for bugs before now? She was ashamed of herself.

"Could we drive by the post office?" she asked and held up the express mail envelope. "I need to overnight this."

"Sure thing."

He seemed affable enough. At least for now. But she'd keep a close watch on him. He detoured to the post office and dropped her package in the express mail box.

She gave him directions to her mother's house on the shores of North Padre Island, but then the silence stretched out so long it unnerved her. All kinds of "what-ifs" crowded in until her brain felt like a Mini Cooper stuffed with college kids trying to break the Guinness Book world record for the most sophomores in a compact car.

What if Joel were a government operative sent to spy on her? What if he were actually a space alien in a very good disguise? What if he and the hit man were tag-teaming her and he was at this moment driving her to her death? What if...?

Okay, she had to put a stop to this or she'd drive herself insane.

"What do you do for a living?" Marlie asked, as much to fill up the awkward silence as to find out more about him.

He was clearly the strong silent type, and she was shy around people she didn't know. She could have let Angelina do the talking, but that tended to get her into trouble, as it had with Officer Kemp.

"What's your guess?" He slid an assessing glance her way.

"You military?"

"What makes you think I'm military?"

"You have that tilty cock to your walk," she said.

"Tilty cock?" Joel laughed.

"Cocky tilt, cocky tilt, cocky tilt. I meant cocky tilt."

"Sure you did."

Oh, God. Marlie's face flamed. Distressed, she wanted to crawl into a fetal position on the floorboard and breathe her last.

His eyes gleamed with amusement and something else. Something dark and heavy and sensual. Marlie gulped. Was it desire?

For her?

Joel winked.

It was! Oh, geez.

He didn't seem the least bit embarrassed to show that her statement, however misconstrued, had aroused his interest. She wasn't accustomed to such unabashed masculine appraisal or approval, and she wasn't certain how to handle it.

*I do; let me at him,* Angelina volunteered.

"I meant cocky tilt, I really did," Marlie said, only making things worse. Why couldn't she just shut up?

"That might have been what you meant to say, but what you did say was a classic Freudian slip."

"Listen, buddy, you don't even know me, so buzz off with your pop psychology."

"Now you're being defensive."

"So what? I'm allowed to be defensive if I want to be. No law against it."

He grinned at her, slow and teasing. "FYI, my cock is anything but tilty."

She clamped her hands over her ears. "I'm not listening." But she heard him anyway.

"Ah, come on, don't let a little thing like a tilty cock upset you."

The next words that shot out of Marlie's mouth were pure Angelina. "Aren't you lucky," she purred. "Little cocks don't upset me."

Joel guffawed.

All rightee. There was officially no way she could make this any worse. Thankfully, he'd just turned onto her mother's street.

"Third house on the left." She pointed to her mother's bungalow.

The air smelled of the winter sea. Overhead, gulls circled, making one last pass over the water before settling in for the night. A pelican, roosting on a piling, was busy gulping down a grouper. In spite of the lingering rush-hour traffic, they made good time, probably because he'd exceeded the speed limit by quite a clip.

Marlie had the door open before he'd even pulled to a complete stop. She wanted out of here and away from the source of her humiliation.

"Whoa." He sounded jovial and neighborly and nothing else. "Where's the four-alarm?"

"You don't have to come in with me," Marlie said in a rush. "I'll be fine. Thanks for the ride."

"What? Are you too ashamed to introduce me to your mother?" He grinned.

"No." Marlie surprised herself by smiling back. At this point, she hadn't known she had any levity left. "Too afraid my mother will play matchmaker." Assuming of course that Mom was home and out of danger. "I've never brought a guy home before."

"Never?" Joel arched an eyebrow.

"Well, Cosmo." She pushed her glasses up on her nose. "But he doesn't count."

"Who's Cosmo?"

"My best friend."

"Why doesn't he count? He gay or something?"

"No, he's not gay. We're just friends."

"Men and women can't be just friends."

"Yes, they can."

"Women think they can, but it's usually that the guy has just settled for not having sex with the woman he wants just so he can still hang around with her and keep hoping her feelings for him will change. But they rarely do."

Marlie opened her mouth to deny it but realized Joel was right. Cosmo had settled for friendship when she wouldn't give him anything else.

"So how come you never brought a boyfriend home to meet your parents? You can't tell me you've never had a boyfriend, because I'm not buying it. A woman as cute as you, guys are bound to be knocking down your door."

*Cute.*

There was that word she hated.

She supposed Joel thought he was paying her a compliment. People often called her cute or adorable or cuddly. Elderly ladies had literally pinched her chubby cheeks. Marlie didn't want to be cute or adorable or cuddly. She wanted to be tall and beautiful and striking. She wanted cheekbones like Halle Berry's. She wanted a face like Helen of Troy's. Not a Keebler elf's.

*Yeah, well,* Angelina said, *sinners in hell want ice water. Ain't happenin'.*

"Believe it or not," Marlie said drily, "when you're *cute,* guys are more likely to ask you to bake them cookies or babysit their dog instead of asking you out."

"Stupid guys." He shook his head.

She felt another flush rise to her face. Why did she have to blush so easily? Joel waited, saying nothing. Not really knowing why she did it, Marlie rushed to fill in the void and ended up spilling her guts.

"Mom's pretty desperate for me to find the love of my life."

"Anxious for grandkids, huh?"

"It's more than that. She's convinced I'm missing out on something spectacular by not being attached at the hip to some guy, yada, yada. She goes overboard with the matchmaking thing. She and Dad had this very special relationship. They were soul mates. If you believe in that sort of stuff."

"You don't?"

"No."

"Why not?"

"I saw what happened to my parents' fairy-tale marriage."

"Bad divorce?"

"No, Dad died when I was eleven." Why was she running off at the mouth? Telling him private things? This wasn't like her. What was it about him that loosened her lips? Why didn't she just get out of the car, tell him thanks for the lift, and sprint into her mother's house?

"Tough break," he said.

Was that sympathy in his voice? Surprised at his sincerity, Marlie raised her head and looked him straight in the eye.

*Clam up, keep your lips zipped, don't you say another word.*

Maybe it was because she'd kept her feelings bottled up for so long and they just had to get out. Maybe it was the genuine expression of concern on Joel's face that chipped away at her reserve. Or maybe it was that almost getting killed had skewed her ability to keep her emotional distance.

Whatever the cause, Marlie couldn't stop the words from spilling out of her mouth. "My father was murdered, and his death tore my mom to ribbons. I thought she was going to die from despair and loneliness. Either that or commit suicide."

Shut up, shut up, shut up.

Joel didn't ask for details. He simply reached out and touched her hand. Lightly, briefly, and then pulled away. The gesture surprised her. He seemed more the suck-it-up-and-buck-up type than a shoulder to cry on. Thank God, he moved his hand away before she burst into tears.

"What about you? How did his death affect you?"

Marlie snorted to keep from crying. She'd already broken down one time too many in front of him. "It makes me want to steer very clear of soul mates. Who needs that kind of heartache?"

"You don't think it's better to have loved and lost than to never have loved at all?"

"Hell, no." She hadn't meant to sound so vehement, but she'd actually given this a lot of thought over the years. "I'm in the 'can't-miss-what-you-never-had' camp."

"No kidding?"

"What? You think it's wrong that I'd choose to avoid pain when I know it's an inevitable component of love? I think it's a rather smart position."

"No," he said. "I think it's a shame that you believe love isn't worth the pain."

"I suppose you've been in love."

"Yes."

"And you got your heart broken?"

"I got my heart broken."

"Was it worth it?"

"Oh, yeah." The way he said it made it seem as if he was remembering some very fine times. Marlie felt a twinge of jealousy.

"How many times have you been in love?"

"Just the once."

"And you're willing to try again? Don't you think that once was enough?"

"I'm willing to give it another shot. Why not? That's

what life is about. Getting knocked down and slugging your way back up again."

"Masochist."

"Hey, at least I'm out there swinging. Come on, tell the truth. You've never ever been in love?"

Marlie hesitated. "Well, I did have a mad crush on a boy when I was little. Does that count?"

"How little?"

"Five."

"Who'd you have the crush on?"

"Ironically enough, it was with the son of the man who murdered my father."

"What?!" Joel coughed as if he'd swallowed wrong.

"You okay?"

"Fine," he said, but his voice sounded strangely tight. Marlie eyed him apprehensively. "Go on."

"I had the biggest crush on J. J., but it was long before his dad killed mine. J. J. was five or six years older than I was. He considered me a pest because his parents made him play with me, but I was besotted." Marlie sighed wistfully. She hadn't thought of J. J. in years. Which was a shame because it was a sweet memory. One of the few good ones she cherished from her childhood.

"Yeah?"

"He was so cute. Tall and dark-headed, and he had these amazing gray-green-blue eyes that looked a lot like yours. They're an unusual color you don't often see. He loved baseball, and he always had a pack of baseball cards stuck in his back pocket. He would buy them and then give me the gum out of the pack. I pretended to like baseball just for the gum and to hear him talk about his favorite team, the Texas Rangers."

Maybe that's why she was so intrigued by Joel. On a

subconscious level, with his dark hair and ocean eyes, he reminded her of J. J. Hunter.

"Whatever happened to this kid?"

Marlie shrugged. "His parents divorced and his mom got full custody. I never saw him again."

"When was the last time you thought about him?"

"Oh, not for years and years. I wouldn't have thought of him now if you hadn't brought it up."

"Then no." Joel shook his head. "That crush doesn't count as being in love. You were too young."

"Maybe, but in my five-year-old brain it was pretty intense."

She might have been young, but her feelings for J. J. had run deep. She could still remember how he'd given her piggyback rides up and down the beach that summer. How warm the sun had felt on her face, how light her heart had soared. And there was the time he'd stood up for her when a couple of bullies had tried to take her ice-cream cone from her when they'd cornered her on the boardwalk.

Why was there a lump in her throat? She stared out the window at her mother's house. For the first time she noticed every light was on in the bungalow. That was odd. Mom was compulsively frugal. She never left a room without turning off the lights.

"Marlie? You okay?" Joel touched her again. This time she felt much more than mere sympathy in his contact. His touch was firmer, lingering, his thumb brushing against her knuckles.

She jerked her hand away and stared into the turbulent depths of his eyes. Unbidden, she found herself wondering what it would feel like to look into those eyes as he made love to her. Startled by the thought, she dropped her gaze, hoping he hadn't been able to see the irrational fantasies written on her face.

Mom. Concentrate on Mom.

But she couldn't concentrate on Mom, because if she did, she would start visualizing all kinds of horrors that she wasn't prepared to deal with.

"I'll walk you to the door," he said.

"No need." She was out of the SUV, but so was Joel, and he was already halfway around it.

Lovely.

Before she could tell him to beat it, he'd locked his fingers around her elbow and was escorting her up the walkway.

It was totally dark now, all twilight gone. The security lamps had come on, adding to the electrical glow from her mother's bungalow. The house hunkered on a sandy bluff; the air was thick with the smell of sea and the sound of the surf crashing against the shore.

Fear bloomed on her tongue. It tasted sharp and sour.

Something was very, very wrong. Her mother would never leave all the lights on.

Marlie broke free from Joel's grip and ran up to the porch. She jiggled the knob and the door flew open.

Recoiling at the sight before her, she turned to bury her face against Joel's chest and took in a few deep calming breaths before she could bring herself to look again.

Mom's normally immaculate house was trashed. Pictures were ripped from the walls, furniture overturned, papers scattered across the floor. Panicked, Marlie tossed her purse onto the bar and tore through the rooms, screaming her mother's name, flinching at each new scene of destruction.

A shattered mirror in the bathroom, smashed plants in

their clay pots in the sunroom, and in her mother's bedroom family photographs strewn everywhere. Some torn, some stepped on. Most of them ruined.

Marlie let out a shriek of despair and dropped to her knees. She snatched up the pictures, clutching them to her chest with trembling fingers.

Joel crouched beside her and placed a comforting hand on her shoulder, but she wrenched from his touch, inconsolable. *Stop relying on this man. You don't know him. Can't trust him.* She glanced down at the carpet and saw a dark stain and several droplets on the floor leading away from it.

Blood.

"Mom," she whimpered. "Mom, where are you?"

The bouncy hip-hop sound of the Black Eyed Peas vibrated from behind the door of Treeni's trendy Georgetown condo. Cosmo stood on her front stoop, his laptop in one hand, a boxed cheesecake in the other.

He had thought about bringing her flowers, but that seemed too romantic for a woman like Treeni. He had finally decided on the cheesecake because he lived two blocks from The Cheesecake Factory and besides, who didn't love cheesecake?

Cosmo was so excited about seeing her tonight that he'd even made a couple of mistakes at work, his first since starting at ONI. Nothing major, but his boss had noticed and commented on the errors. Then, just as Cosmo was leaving for the day, Chief Peterson had stopped by his desk and said ominously, "Don't let Treeni Delaney ruin you too, Villereal."

What had he meant by that?

And why had Peterson's forbidding statement made him want Treeni all the more?

Cosmo took a deep breath and prepared to knock, but he'd no sooner raised his fist to the door than Treeni yanked it open from the inside.

"Get in here, quick." Treeni grabbed him by the belt loop and tugged him over the threshold.

Her touch was like an electrical current, shocking him with a perverse thrill. He cast a glance over his shoulder as she slammed the door behind him.

"Were you followed?" She lifted back the roman shade and peered out at the street.

"Followed?" Cosmo blinked.

She was wearing a slinky fire-engine-red dressing gown and matching mules with feathers on them. She'd combed her hair down loose, and it cascaded over her shoulders in thick, fetching chestnut waves.

Cosmo swallowed hard as his gaze fixed on her bottom. Her attire left no doubt as to her intentions. He was here to be seduced. Frankly, he didn't know if he was ready for this step or not, even though he wanted her more than he wanted to breathe. Wanted her so badly that he'd stuffed three condoms in his laptop case and prayed he'd get to use at least one of them.

It wasn't like him to be so bold, so calculating, but he'd grown tired of always watching and waiting, hanging back and letting other men take the lead and reap the spoils for their effrontery. It was his turn now, and he wasn't backing down. He'd snagged the job he'd always wanted, and now he wanted Treeni.

Treeni turned back to look at him, letting the shade drop. "You didn't check to make sure you weren't being followed?"

"No. Was I supposed to?"

"You work for ONI. You're always supposed to check

to see if you're being tailed. Didn't they teach you anything in orientation?" Treeni looked at him as if he were a
not-too-bright Labrador retriever, and Cosmo was immediately plunged into self-doubt. He wanted her to look at
him with reverence and respect.

"I'm civilian," Cosmo reminded her and shook his
head. "Not a Navy spy."

"You're always vulnerable," she scolded. "Nefarious
forces could kidnap you and torture you for the things you
know."

Was she kidding? Cosmo stared at her. She didn't look
like she was kidding.

"ONI is serious business," she said. "Don't doubt it for
a minute."

"I know, I know. They did cover security measures
in the orientation briefing. Who's supposed to be watching me?"

"They're not watching you. They're watching me,"
Treeni said.

"Who's watching you?"

Treeni sighed. "My father's minions."

"Your father has people spying on you? What for?"
Cosmo asked.

"Dad's bid for the presidency is a royal pain in my
butt. He's got his yes-men out making sure I don't do
anything to embarrass him." Her tone changed when she
caught sight of the box he was holding. "Oh, you brought
me Cheesecake Factory. How sweet. What kind didja
get?"

"Turtle."

Her eyes lit up. "Yum, my fave."

She took the box into the kitchen. Cosmo followed
after her, still feeling like that dumb Labrador. So much

for being strong. She waved at her kitchen table. "You can go ahead and set up your laptop."

Cosmo did as she asked. Plugging it in to save on the battery, booting up, and then looking to her for further instructions. He didn't know what this was all about. Was it a date? He eyed her attire. She was dressed as if this was far more than a simple date. But then why had she asked him to bring his laptop?

Was she one of those people who loved to have sex on camera and upload it live onto the Internet? Or did she get her thrills by watching other people who were uploading their live sex acts?

He hadn't bargained for this. What would he do if she asked him to log on to a swingers' Web site? He remembered what Peterson had said. *Don't let Treeni Delaney ruin you too.*

"You're wondering what this is all about," Treeni said.

"Well, yeah."

While he'd been getting his laptop up and running, she'd uncorked a bottle of Moscato d'Asti and poured two glasses. She brought the dessert wine to the table along with a huge slice of cheesecake and two forks. She positioned the cheesecake plate between them and scooted her chair closer to his.

She smelled so good he could hardly think, and her elbow rested just an inch away from his. If he moved his arm to reach for one of the forks, he could touch her. The very thing he'd been dreaming of doing from the moment he'd first set eyes on her.

*You and every other heterosexual male on the planet.*

The chemical roller-coaster ride carried him at a supersonic clip over rickety wooden tracks. He ached to blend his body with hers, to mate and mix their genetic codes.

God, he'd never been so infatuated. He was completely miserable and loving every minute of it.

"Log on to ONI's Intranet," she said.

Cosmo studied her, heart thumping madly. "Are you and I up to something illegal?"

"Pretty much."

"We're hacking?"

She grinned. "Yep. That scare you off?"

He grinned back. He didn't care. She was smiling at him. It felt like sunshine and rainbows and four-leaf clovers. "Hell, no. I live to hack."

"I know. It's how you got your job at the ONI."

"You've done your research."

"You're not the only one who's thorough, Cosmo Villereal."

"What are we hacking into?"

"My father's personal journal entries."

"Do I smell an Electra complex?"

"Freud was full of crap on so many levels, but I will admit that my father and I have an adversarial relationship. Is that Electra enough for you?"

"Am I going to lose my job over this?" Cosmo wasn't sure a night with the sexiest woman he'd ever shared cheesecake with was worth losing his job over, but it came pretty damn close.

"Not if you're as good at this as everyone says you are."

"Are you using me?" he asked her.

"What do you think?" Her look was inscrutable.

They stared into each other's eyes over the top of his computer. The air was thick with the vibration of their hormones rising and colliding.

Treeni sliced off a chunk of cheesecake, leaned over and lightly touched it against his lower lip. "Come on,

Cos. Take a walk on the wild side." She winked. "Have a bite."

Ah, the war zone of the heart. With that sultry look she offered him eternal damnation.

And like Adam to Eve's fateful, fabled apple, Cosmo bit.

# Chapter 7

Drink this."

Not knowing what else to do or how else to calm Marlie, Joel had left her grieving over family photographs, gone out to his SUV, retrieved the silver flask he kept in his glove compartment for emergencies just like this one, and brought it back into the house to shove under her nose.

She put up a hand to block the flask. "I don't want any."

"Drink it, dammit."

"What is it with you and whiskey? Are you an alcoholic or something?"

"No," he growled. "I'm not an alcoholic. Now swallow the stuff before I get a funnel and pour it down your throat."

He was being an ass and he knew it. But Joel was scared. He had no idea what had happened in Penelope Montague's house, but he was very afraid it had been fatal.

For some reason, he felt guilty about her mother's disappearance, as if he were responsible. And feeling guilty made him defensive, and feeling defensive made him aggressive. It was a throwback habit to the days when he had to battle stepfathers in order to survive, and it was a habit he'd never tried to shake.

Plus, he was still feeling unnerved after Marlie's story of having had a crush on him when she was a kid. What would she say, he wondered, if she knew that he was J. J. Hunter all grown up?

Would she remember him so fondly then?

"Drink it." He figured if he made her angry enough, he could get her mind off her mother's fate for a few minutes.

The ploy worked but quickly backfired.

"You want me to drink it, fine." She shot to her feet, fire blazing in her eyes, slung the photographs onto the bed, and snatched the flask from his hand.

He admired that flash of spunk, loved how it showed up unexpectedly under pressure. She was like a powerful muscle-car engine couched deceptively under the hood of a Volkswagen Beetle. This was a woman you could count on in a crunch, whether she even knew it herself or not.

Marlie twisted the cap from the flask and took a long, inhaling gulp. Coughing, she brought a hand to her mouth. Her face reddened, but when Joel reached for the flask, she batted his arm away and took another swig.

"Easy."

"You want me calm, I'll give you dead calm." She took a third swallow.

"Marlie." He held out his palm. She was beginning to scare him. "Give me the flask."

Her face went from red to green-tinged. She groaned and splayed a hand over her belly. Belatedly, Joel realized that he was standing between her and the bathroom door. He sidestepped out of the way just in the nick of time.

She barely made it to the toilet before she threw up.

The sounds of her retching stirred his sympathy. He'd worshiped the porcelain god a time or two himself and knew how miserable it was.

She kept heaving long after the alcohol emptied from her stomach.

Aw, hell. He hadn't meant to make her upchuck. Poor kid.

He wasn't too good at this nursemaid stuff, but since it was his fault she was puking, he felt obligated to do what he could to soothe her. Joel stepped to the bathroom cupboard, located a washcloth, doused it in cold water, and then squatted beside her. Awkwardly, he lifted her chin, brushed back her hair, and bathed her face. He could hear her ragged breathing, feel her rib cage rise and fall with each jagged respiration.

God, he *was* an overbearing ass, pushing too hard, forgetting that adversity didn't bring out the best in everyone the way it did him.

Uncool. The things he was feeling. Sympathy, guilt, tenderness. Definitely uncool. He remembered something Gus used to say to him whenever he let tender emotions show. *Feelings are for females and fools.*

She rocked back on her heels away from him, pressing the back of a hand against her mouth and glowering at him. "Happy now?"

He brought her a plastic cup of mouthwash from the bottle perched on the bathroom sink. Apologies didn't come easy for Joel. Normally he viewed them as a sign of weakness, but he was working on reaching down deep inside and chiseling one out when they heard a crash from another room.

It sounded like something had fallen or had been knocked to the floor.

Their eyes met and the silent question arced unspoken between them. Was there someone else in the house?

"The assassin." Marlie whispered the very same thought that was circling Joel's brain.

A split second later, the kitchen smoke alarm began to shriek.

Dear God. What now? The plastic cup of Listerine that Joel had brought her dropped from Marlie's hand.

"Stay here," he said and whipped a gun from the waistband of his pants.

Marlie's eyes widened. He had a gun!

Who was this guy? And what had she gotten herself into? She'd known better than to accept a ride from him. Why oh why had she gotten into his SUV? Why hadn't she listened to her gut? She'd known better. She didn't need him. She could take care of herself. She had a canister of Mace in her purse and she had smoke bombs.

Um, yeah. Smoke bombs.

"Hold on a minute." She had to shout over the noise and grab onto Joel's belt loop to snag his attention. "I think maybe it's not an intruder after all."

He glanced at her over his shoulder. "Then what is it? Your mom have an arsonist cat?"

"The noise we heard could have been my purse falling off the bar."

"And this stuff?" he asked, indicating the tendrils of smoke invading the bathroom.

"The smoke bomb in my purse could have accidentally detonated when my purse fell off the counter. The bombs are pretty old. They're left over from Desert Storm."

"You carry smoke bombs around with you in your purse?"

Marlie shrugged. "What can I say? I like to be prepared."

"How would a smoke bomb help you be prepared?"

"Never know when you're going to get caught in a riot or need to create a smoke screen so you can escape."

"Escape from what?"

"Kidnappers, hired assassins, government operatives, the usual suspects."

"You're weird, you know that?"

"So I've been told."

"Where did you get smoke bombs?"

"They belonged to my dad. That's why they're old."

"I'll check it out. You stay put." Hunkering low in a crouching position, Joel scuttled from the bathroom.

Marlie drew her knees to her chest and clamped her hands over her ears in an attempt to shut out the deafening noise. She couldn't get over the fact he'd been carrying a concealed weapon. Fear did a dance in her gut.

Just who in the hell was he?

Until he'd appeared on her front porch that afternoon, her life (with the exception of her tiff with Cosmo and an occasional death threat or two from disgruntled wackos) had been perfectly normal. Okay, maybe not normal in the traditional sense of the word, and maybe not so perfect either. There were the occasional death threats, the date-lessness, that three-week-late Visa bill, and she did rent from Mom. But until now, no one had been shooting at her or bugging her phone or letting the air out of her tires or ransacking her mother's house.

What wasn't he telling her? Could Joel somehow be tied to all of this?

*He is rather Johnny-on-the-spot,* Angelina said. *Be careful.*

"I thought you liked him," Marlie muttered.

*I do, but it's not smart to trust strangers. Strange men in particular. Especially gorgeous strange men. Now get up and go see what he's up to.*

"He said to stay here."

*And you're going to listen? Remember your tendency to idealize anyone who champions the underdog? And remember what invariably happens when they turn out to have feet of clay?*

Angelina was making a lot of sense for once.

The smoke in the bathroom was growing thicker, darker. Marlie grabbed hold of the towel rack and pulled herself to her feet. Tentatively, she crept into the bedroom.

More smoke billowed in from the hallway. Coughing, she dropped to her knees and crawled for the door. She heard a soft hiss of apprehension and realized the sound came from her own lips.

"Joel," she called out, "where are you?"

Smoke filled her lungs.

She could barely see a foot in front of her, it was that thick. Her nose burned and her eyes watered. She had to get out of here.

Now.

But what about Joel?

In the hallway, she staggered to her feet, calling his name and sucking in more smoke. Her coughing turned severe, her lungs fighting to expel the pollutant. This was no smoke bomb.

*Keep moving.* Angelina's voice was in her ear. *You can do it.*

Tears streamed down her cheeks and she blinked hard, trying to see beyond the blur.

"Joel!"

She'd made it to the living room. The front door was just a few yards away but her legs felt heavy, mired in invisible syrup, and her head was as light as cotton candy. She tripped over something and stumbled, then realized it was her purse that had fallen off the bar onto the floor. She felt for it amid the swirling smoke, found the strap, and slung it around her neck.

Her eyes burned. Her head ached. She coughed again, choking.

*You can make it,* Angelina said. *You already escaped a hit man today. Getting out of a burning building should be a piece of cake.*

Marlie dragged herself to the door by sheer mental will, grabbed the heated knob, and twisted.

It was locked.

No!

Panic was a living thing, clawing at her chest. *Out, out,* she had to get out. Blindly, her fingers grappled for the locking mechanism. She flipped it to the unlocked position and tried the knob again, but it still wouldn't budge.

She yanked harder, but to no avail. Someone had tampered with the locks, sealing them inside and then setting fire to the place. Someone had intended to kill them.

*This is it. Second time today I'm going to die,* Marlie thought. *And I still don't have clean underwear on.*

Joel caught Marlie just before she fell and threw her over his shoulder. The heat was intense. Flames licked up the wall between the garage and the kitchen; the pungent odor of gasoline was overpowering.

This wasn't the result of a smoke bomb. This was arson. He should never have left Marlie alone in the bathroom. He'd abandoned her, the same way he'd abandoned Treeni in Iraq. He'd never seen a fire spread so quickly, and in the chaos of war he'd seen many fires. By God, he wouldn't let it happen again.

Fire engulfed the room in a series of liquid snaps that sounded like bones cracking. The air, what was left of it, vibrated with a wavery hum. The smoke alarm kept screaming—why hadn't it melted in this heat?—and mingled with the wail of fire truck sirens.

He tried the front door even though he'd seen Marlie struggle to open it and fail.

But the knob wouldn't budge.

Eyes burning from the smoke, Joel hurried to the window and tried to pry it open. The windows were nailed shut from the outside. There was no doubt in his mind. Someone had planned this arson to the last detail.

He let Marlie slip off his shoulder and gently leaned her against the wall. She could barely stand. Smoke obliterated everything.

*Get out. Get her out of here.*

Sweat rolled off his body. He could barely see, but he could make out the shape of a chair rising ghostlike from the corner of the room. He snatched the chair up and, putting all his weight into the effort, tossed the piece of upholstered furniture through the window.

He went back for Marlie, slinging her over his shoulder once again and stumbling a little on his way out the window, her weight throwing him off balance.

"Marlie," he murmured, "are you okay?"

She didn't answer.

Alarmed, he blinked in the light from the blazing fire and looked up to see a crowd of somber bystanders ringing the lawn. Reeling like a drunkard, he moved as far away from the fire as his legs would carry him, then dropped to his knees and laid Marlie on the ground.

"Give her some room." He shooed back the throng. Respectfully, they stepped away.

He was vaguely aware of the arrival of fire trucks, but his eyes were trained on Marlie's chest. She wasn't moving air. He placed two fingers against the carotid artery in her neck.

Thank God, she had a pulse, but it was weak and thready, and she still wasn't moving any air. If he didn't give her artificial resuscitation immediately, her heart would soon stop.

Sliding his thumbs underneath either side of her jaw, he carefully tilted her head back and positioned himself at her side. He gently pinched off her nose with a finger and thumb and then lowered his lips to hers and blew two quick puffs of air into her lungs. He turned his head to watch her chest.

No spontaneous respirations.

Dammit. He refused to lose her.

He continued to do mouth-to-mouth resuscitation. Her lips were cold, her skin pale.

Time evaporated.

It might have been a few seconds. It might have been an hour. Joel had no sense of any reality except the feel of Marlie's mouth beneath his as he frantically tried to breathe life into her inert body.

He was consumed. Every conscious response concentrated on saving her life. He didn't hear the noises around him, didn't see the people, didn't smell or taste or feel anything except Marlie.

A deep miasma ensnared him, the drone of the fire truck engines and the sympathetic murmurs of the crowd blurred and blended into an acoustical resonance that throbbed and urged, *Breathe, dammit, breathe.*

A firm hand clamped him on the shoulder and a man spoke. "Mister, you can stop."

No, no. He would not stop. She could not die. He refused to let it happen.

"She's breathing, mister," the man said. "You can stop mouth-to-mouth."

Joel rocked back on his heels. Marlie looked up at him, her eyes red-rimmed.

Their gazes met and stuck.

She was reborn.

Tentatively, Marlie licked her lips. Her gaze, wide and innocent, said it all. *Thank you.*

Joel stood. His legs as heavy as sandbags.

"Need a boost up?" he heard himself say casually, as if nothing monumental had just happened. He'd spent years playing the tough guy. He wasn't about to turn soft now just because she'd almost died. No matter how much his gut quivered like jelly.

"Joel," she whispered.

"Yeah?" He knelt beside her again.

She reached out and tightly curled her fingers around his bicep. "See that man at the back of the crowd? The one in the green windbreaker?"

Joel lifted his head and searched the collected group bunched together underneath the streetlight. "I see him."

"It's the guy."

"What guy?"

"My assassin."

When Gus Hunter saw the crowd gathered outside Penelope Montague's burning house, he knew that he was too late.

Bad news. Really bad news.

He slowed the silver Ford Taurus he'd rented at the airport and cruised past the house at a crawl, rubbernecking around the spectators to see what he could see.

Smoke billowed from the shattered front window. Orange

flames licked the roof. The rising wail of more emergency vehicle sirens vibrated the air. Something was going on in the middle of the lawn, but Gus couldn't see what it was.

He felt sick to his stomach and a sour taste rose in his mouth. Had a passerby managed to drag Penelope from the burning bungalow in time to save her life? Gus gulped back the bile and prayed that was indeed the case.

Before he could decide what move to make next, his cell phone rang. Distracted, he guided the Taurus to a stop beside a culvert several houses to the right of Penelope's. The crowd was growing larger, people running in from the beach, cars pulling over willy-nilly.

He flipped open his cell phone and recognized Abel Johnson's number on the caller ID.

"Yeah?" Gus grunted.

"Admiral?"

"You were expecting Frosty the Snowman?"

"No, sir. It's just you sound a little...um...I don't know, sir, not yourself."

"I assure you that I am one hundred percent myself, Petty Officer Johnson," he said, never mind that he was anything but. Admirals didn't get to be admirals by admitting the truth about how they were doing. "What do you want?"

"Where are you?"

"That's none of your damn business."

"With all due respect, sir, I withdraw the question. I was merely concerned and wanted to give you a heads-up," Abel said.

"Heads-up? What about?"

"Admiral Delaney came looking for you earlier this afternoon."

Gus knuckled his fist against the steering wheel. "Did he say what he wanted?"

"Only that it was a matter of utmost importance. He got pretty angry when I told him you weren't in Washington and I didn't know when you'd be back. He ordered me to give him your personal cell phone number."

Dammit. Things were getting out of hand. "Here's what I want you to do," Gus said.

"Yes, sir."

"Go home right now and call in sick to work in the morning—and then don't answer your phone for anyone except me."

"Sir, that would be lying."

"Do you value your job, Johnson?"

"Sir, yes, sir."

"Then do it." Gus hung up.

He stuck his cell phone in his back pocket, got out of the car, and made his way over to the throng semicircled around Penelope's house. The fire trucks had arrived while he was on the phone with Johnson, and firemen were rushing to and fro, pumping water onto the blaze. When he got close enough to view the drama on the lawn, his heart did a double-time dance.

There was Joel, soot smeared on his cheeks, gently cradling a young dark-haired woman in his arms.

She wasn't Penelope Montague.

Where was Penelope, and what in the hell was Joel doing here? And who was the girl?

The young woman said something and pointed into the crowd. Joel raised his head.

Gus jumped behind a fireman. Shit. He had to get out of here before his son spotted him. He wasn't able to tell Joel what was going on. Not yet. There were things he had to take care of first.

Ignoring his churning heart, Gus turned and moved

away as quickly as he dared without drawing attention to himself. He went back to the Taurus, but before getting inside he stooped down and wedged his cell phone underneath the left front tire.

He slid behind the wheel, keyed the ignition, and backed over the cell phone. The crunching sound was completely satisfying.

Let Delaney try to call him now.

The bastard.

Gus might be too late to save Penelope Montague's life, but maybe he still wasn't too late to right the wrong he'd committed all those years ago.


"Hey, buddy, hey, you there in the green windbreaker," Joel shouted and jumped to his feet.

The guy turned and took off at a dead run.

Joel's pulse raced, revving with adrenaline and testosterone. His brain issued a single edict: *Stop the guy who tried to kill Marlie.*

His motivation extended past the need to see a potential killer caught. It went beyond making the man pay for his misdeed and on to preventing him from doing it again. Joel wouldn't have confessed his central reason to anyone. He barely acknowledged the impulse to himself. But the thing that drove him the strongest was his desire to look like a hero in Marlie's eyes.

When had her respect become important to him? Was it after he'd found out she'd had a crush on him twenty years ago? How pathetic was that?

"Stop that man!" Joel shouted, but no one heeded his call.

Green Windbreaker dodged around a cluster of look-loos, headed for the beach road that ran along the back side of Penelope's property.

One of the firemen called out to Joel as he zipped past the fire truck. "Mister, the arson investigator wants to speak to you."

"Yeah, yeah."

Joel waved a hand, his entire attention beaded on the man in the green windbreaker. Once he'd cleared the thick of the crowd he kicked it into high gear, sprinting around the side of the house in hot pursuit, legs churning up sand.

Firemen were back here too, dousing the bungalow from the beach side. Joel jerked his head from left to right, but Green Windbreaker had vanished.

Where had he gone?

Stunned that he'd lost him, Joel stopped. What now? He cocked his head, listening. It was hard to hear anything beyond the noise of the fire.

"Sir," a breathless and red-faced fireman said, "for your own safety I'm going to have to ask you to clear the perimeter."

Joel nodded, defeated. He turned back toward the road, but from the corner of his eye, he caught sight of something and spun around.

There, draped over a patio chair on Penelope's deck, was the green windbreaker.

The arsonist had given him the slip.

Defeated, Joel snatched up the windbreaker. At least he could have the NCIS Corpus Christi field office test it for fingerprints and trace evidence.

With the windbreaker tucked under his arm, he started for the road once more, only to notice that the fireman who'd warned him off before was walking along the beach road away from the fire and toward a black Camaro parked on the shoulder.

"Son of a bitch," Joel swore when he realized he'd been duped.

The fake fireman broke into a jog.

"Hey," Joel shouted, dropped the windbreaker, and tore after the guy. "Hey, you. NCIS. Stop right there."

They were both running at a dead sprint, and Joel was gaining on the guy. He spurred himself forward, running as hard as he could.

The Camaro engine roared to life before the guy even reached the door, and Joel realized he must have started it with one of those automatic remote starters.

"Oh, no, you don't," Joel growled.

He reached for the scruff of the guy's neck, intent on yanking him into a choke hold, but then he spotted the semiautomatic Colt 45mm with a silencer snugged onto the end of it clutched in the guy's right hand.

Immediately he changed tactics. Using moves he'd learned in Navy SEAL training, Joel came up off the ground with both feet.

Putting all his body weight behind it, he slammed the flat of his sneakers into the guy's kidneys, knocking him hard into the side of the car. At that very same moment Joel heard the soft, muffled *thwap* of the muzzled gun going off.

The bullet struck the Camaro's side-view mirror. Joel fell face-first into the sand.

Before he could scramble to his feet, the gunman had the Camaro's door open. He threw his body inside.

"Son of a bitch," Joel cursed again as he struggled to his feet and watched the black sports car speed away into the night.

# Chapter 8

While Joel had been chasing the hit man in the green windbreaker, Marlie lay on the lawn, surrounded by burly arms and legs and fire hoses, gasping for air, barely able to believe she had lived through the fire.

She squinted into the darkness beyond the light from the blaze. Her glasses were smudged with soot. She took them off and polished them with the hem of Joel's shirt and then put them back on. She stared at the spot she'd last seen Joel, before he'd disappeared around the corner of the house in hot pursuit of the killer.

Would he catch the guy? She hoped that he could, but then again she didn't want him getting hurt in the process. She nibbled her bottom lip.

Tentatively, Marlie rose to her feet and edged toward the corner of the bungalow. Chaos was erupting around her. Firemen ran to and fro. People shouted. The blaze radiated intense heat. Bystanders gaped. No one seemed to notice her.

That was one upside to being small. When you didn't want to be seen it was much easier to fly under the radar.

She avoided the firemen, staying out of the way of the

crowd, and rounded the corner of the house. She paused beside the gate between her mother's bungalow and the beach road and saw him scurrying up the path.

Marlie sank back into the shadows as the assassin passed not five feet in front of her. The green windbreaker was gone and he was now wearing a fireman's hard hat and heavy yellow slicker, but she could never forget that cold, heartless face.

Ice cubes tumbled down her spine.

He was walking fast, headed for a black Camaro parked a quarter of a mile away on the road that ran from her mother's street to the public beach.

Marlie jerked her head in the direction the man had come from, but saw no sign of Joel. She curled her fingers into fists.

He must have given Joel the slip when he switched his clothes. Joel had never seen him up close. Without the green windbreaker, there would be no way for him to identify the guy.

What if he'd killed Joel?

Marlie felt as if a giant fist punched her in the gut. The coppery taste of fear flooded her mouth. No. He could not be dead. Not big, strong, powerful, omnipresent Joel. He was the only ally she had.

But was he really her ally? She was in a position where she had to trust him, but she must not forget that she didn't know him. He could be lying to her. Trying to get on her good side.

What should she do? The hit man was getting away and there was no one to stop him. Should she run for one of the cops she'd seen questioning the crowd? Paralyzed by fear, Marlie couldn't even move, much less plot a course of action.

*Quit standing there like a wimp and do something!* Angelina bellowed.

"I can't. I'm terrified. What if the killer sees me? What if this time he doesn't miss?"

*Fine. Get out of my way and I'll take over.*

And just like that, it was all Angelina.

Marlie let go, detaching completely from the unfolding scenario. It was as if she were standing outside herself, observing everything, but feeling nothing. She was disconnected, floating.

Angelina took possession of her body.

It was lithe, strong Angelina who turned Marlie's compact little legs toward the Dodge Durango parked at the curb.

It was determined Angelina who wrenched open the Durango's back hatch, found a toolbox, wrenched it open, and unearthed a screwdriver.

It was as if Marlie were watching a movie, a quiet witness, munching popcorn in a darkened theater, along for the ride but essentially untouched by the unfolding drama.

"How did you know Joel carried a toolbox in the back?" Marlie asked.

*Guy like him? Big and strong and manly. He's bound to have all the right tools for the job.*

Expertly wielding the screwdriver, Angelina leaned across the front seat to pop out the ignition cylinder. She tossed it aside, jammed the screwdriver into the steering column that the cylinder had just vacated, twisted the screwdriver into the linkage, and then started the engine. She slammed the door shut, scooted the seat up, snapped on her seat belt, and peeled away from the curb, dodging fire trucks and gawkers' vehicles as she went.

"Wow, where'd you learn to do that?" Marlie asked in amazement.

*Comic book #12, "FBI Space Aliens." We researched it with Cosmo's cousin, Felix, who used to work for a chop shop in Baytown. Remember?*

Oh, yeah. She'd forgotten all about that.

The headlights picked up the Camaro as it shot from the beach road onto the main street right in front of her. Marlie sucked in her breath, barely able to believe how quickly Angelina had gotten the car started. Gone in sixty seconds, indeed.

Angelina was about to shove the accelerator to the floor when a man wildly waving his arms suddenly stumbled onto the road right in front of her.

It was Joel.

Joel looked up as his Dodge Durango screeched to a halt just seconds before plowing right over him.

Marlie rolled the window down, propped her arm on the sill, and said in a light, sexy tone that surprised the hell out of him, "Hop in, handsome."

*Hop in, handsome?*

Puzzled by the sudden change in her, Joel threw himself into the passenger seat and buckled up. "Hit it."

"Gotcha." She floored the Durango.

The SUV leaped forward in hot pursuit of the Camaro. Joel's head snapped back against the seat. "Easy, Ms. Andretti."

"You told me to hit it."

"You don't have to hit it *that* hard."

"I'm not letting the sucker get away. He burned down my mother's house and almost killed us."

"Apparently you're hell-bent on finishing off the job," he muttered.

"I never would have figured you for the cautious type."

"And I never would have figured you for suicidal."

"Hang on." Marlie cornered the block at Mach speed, forcing Joel to grab on to the dashboard.

He stared at her. What had happened to the shy woman who'd sat on his davenport only a few hours earlier trembling in his arms? He didn't know, but he found this new side of Marlie Montague sexy and intriguing as all get out. Now, he understood why the government might suspect her of subversive activities. She'd been hiding her light under a bushel. But which one was the real Marlie? He wanted to find out.

"You're a menace to the streets."

"Don't blame me. The guy in the Camaro started it."

"Just be careful."

"You're not even winded after all that foot chasing." She looked over at him, a tinge of awe or maybe it was jealousy in her voice. Joel didn't run ten miles a day for nothing. "What are you? Superhuman?"

"I was about to ask you if you'd qualified for the honor. You aiming for the Indy?"

"Just because I drive a Prius doesn't mean I don't occasionally feel the need for speed."

"Best to keep your eyes on the road when you're doing eighty-five," he chided.

"I'm not doing eighty-five."

"Sure as hell feels like it."

"I'm doing ninety." She grinned.

On more than one occasion, Joel himself had driven much faster than ninety. It wasn't the speed that bothered him, but rather the lack of control. He didn't like being in the passenger seat, at her mercy. He wished he could edge her aside and slip behind the wheel. "How did you get the Durango started? I've got the keys."

"I know how to hot-wire engines." She gloated. "And you really should look into a better security system."

"Where did you learn how to hot-wire cars?"

"I know people."

"You're acquainted with the kind of people who routinely steal vehicles?"

"My lips are sealed."

"Not one to kiss and tell, huh?"

Smiling coyly, she slanted him a sexy look. "You thinking about kissing me?"

"No." He snorted for emphasis, denying what he was really thinking, which was "Hell, yes." "Watch the road."

"You're dying to wrench this steering wheel right out of my hand and take over, aren'tcha?"

"Yes," he admitted.

"You're one of those."

"Those what?"

"Neanderthals who think women can't handle cars."

"You're handling it just fine." He gritted his teeth. Last thing he wanted was to get into a men-versus-women-drivers argument with her.

"But you think you could do better."

"I know I could do better."

"How so?"

"For one thing I wouldn't be weaving all over the road."

"I'm not weaving."

"Okay, fine. You're not weaving. Your left front tire just keeps repeatedly crossing the yellow line."

"It's Camaro Assassin's fault. I'm simply following him."

Joel took his attention off Marlie and put it back where it belonged, on their target. The Camaro was whipping in and out of traffic and then it turned unexpectedly.

"He's trying to shake us. Damned if I'm gonna let him." Marlie jerked the steering wheel and took a hard left.

She tossed her head and her hair fell forward, the tips of the dark brown strands grazing the tops of her breasts. She reached up and slid a lock of hair behind one ear. Joel felt her movements straight through his stomach and his groin.

Something about the way she handled the quivering thrust of his V8 engine inflamed Joel. She was like a luxury automobile herself, with her rounded curves and her bosoms protruding like high-powered headlights.

Enveloped in their cocoon of steel, she rushed him through time and space at a high speed that gushed through his brain and his body. She was fast and furious and dangerous, and he worshiped her in an orgy of pure velocity.

Joel was so busy filling up with testosterone, he'd failed to keep his eye on the Camaro. Up ahead the black sports car hit the main thoroughfare leading over the new drawbridge that connected North Padre Island to Corpus Christi. Marlie stayed right on his tailpipe and narrowly missed getting slammed into a Coca-Cola truck when she ran a Yield sign.

Sweat popped out on Joel's brow. He'd been in some hairy driving situations, but this took the prize. "Where did you learn to drive like this?"

"Now you're admiring my driving? A minute ago you were criticizing me."

"I'm jealous," he said.

"Jealous? Of what?"

"You're better than I am."

"Really?"

"Compliments don't come easy for me. Accept it and don't mention it again."

She laughed. "I learned from a video simulator. Fantastic for developing your reflexes."

"You're serious?"

"As a heart attack."

"Just when I think I have you figured out, you throw me a curve."

"Uh-oh!" She hissed in her breath. Her gaze was fixed on the road.

Joel didn't like the sound of that. He took his eyes off Marlie and jerked his attention to the action outside the windshield.

To the right of them lay the bay with a tall freighter chugging toward the bridge. Ahead of them, the bridge-crossing signal arm was coming down as the bridge was about to come up.

The Camaro sped toward the signal arm.

The Durango was four or five car lengths behind.

The freighter was getting closer. The bridge began to move upward.

Inside the Camaro, the driver gunned the engine.

The bridge jerked higher.

"He's gonna try to jump it!" Joel yelled.

The Camaro slammed into the signal arm, breaking it off clean. The piece flew back, struck the roof of the Durango, and bounced off onto the shoulder of the road.

The sports car was airborne. It leaped the gap in the bridge road and came down hard on the other side but miraculously didn't blow a tire.

The would-be killer just kept going.

That's when Joel realized Marlie wasn't slowing down either. There was fire in her eyes, and the devilish expression on her face told him that she was loving every minute of this. The woman was crazier than Treeni.

And Joel was more turned on than he'd ever been in his life.

But the bridge was much too high now. They'd never make it, but Marlie didn't seem to realize that.

Or didn't care.

Alarm shot a wad of adrenaline through his body. "Marlie, no!" he yelled. "Don't do it."

Just in the nick of time, she trod the brakes. The Durango fishtailed wildly before coming to a screeching, neck-snapping halt as the bridge reached its full height directly in front of their hood and the freighter glided majestically through the opening.

*Wham!*

Marlie was back in her body again. No longer the distant observer, she could see and feel and taste and smell and hear everything again. Angelina was gone, and she was left to deal with the adrenaline and fear pumping fast and free through her arteries.

She stared at the drawbridge, saw how close they had come to death. She gasped and splayed a hand across her heart.

What terror.

What a rush.

She gripped the steering wheel with both hands, her breath packed tight inside her lungs. Furtively, she glanced at Joel. He was staring at her.

Incredulous.

She felt a little incredulous herself. There was no

mistaking the spark of sexual attraction on his face. Desire shadowed the hollows of his cheeks, giving him a lean and dangerous look.

His eyes lowered in a heavy-lidded, totally masculine ogle. He wet his lips.

Yep, even though Angelina had almost gotten them killed, it seemed Joel had been quite turned on by her daredevil antics.

And Marlie was shocked to discover that so was she.

Oh, God. Apparently, he was one of those people who got their sexual kicks from risky situations.

Was she secretly one too?

Impossible.

*I'm just feeling insecure,* she told herself, *because of all this chaos. Don't read more into your reaction than that.*

But when Joel undid his seat belt and scooted across the seat to cup her chin in his hand, she didn't think it was so impossible.

"That," he said, "was one of the craziest, most fool-hardy things I've ever seen anyone do."

She couldn't argue. She agreed one hundred percent. But it hadn't been her. It was all Angelina's doing.

"I know." Marlie drew in a shuddering breath. "I'm sorry. I don't know what came over me."

"Probably the same thing that's come over me."

Then Joel threaded his hand through her hair and fisted it there. He was going to kiss her and she wasn't going to stop him.

Marlie held that indrawn breath, waiting, hoping, afraid to exhale. She could smell him and the linger-ing burn of smoke and danger. She wondered how many women before her had been this close to him.

Close enough to touch. To taste.

Oh, God, she was in trouble.

The threat of his lips dangled inches above hers. Angelina, that bold bitch, would have kissed him first, but Marlie was not that brave. She saw the naked truth in his face. The rawness of his need shocked her.

Time to back out. She couldn't handle what was happening. It was too much. Too soon. She didn't trust that hot gleam in his eyes. She had to stand up to him, had to draw the line in the sand before she fell into the abyss and never recovered.

"I want you to take your hands off me," she said, making sure to keep her voice calm and steady when she was feeling anything but. "Now."

"Is that what you really want?" His voice was as smooth as grade A cream.

The sweetness of his tone frightened her more than the lust in his eyes. Ah, she could be so easily lured in by him.

"Yes."

He leaned in closer until his lips were almost touching hers. "Really?"

She squirmed and felt a sudden gush of heat low in her belly. Closing her eyes, she murmured, "No."

"Yes, you want me to kiss you, or no, you don't? If you want it you have to ask for it. I don't kiss a woman against her will."

*No! No! No!*

"Kiss me."

Had she really said that? Or was it Angelina butting in again?

He didn't hesitate. His mouth came down on hers.

Part of her wanted to struggle. Part of her wanted to resist. And part of her was loving every minute of it.

A scorching heat flashed through her, hot and fast, incinerating everything in its path. Her tongue, her throat, her chest, and beyond. She burned from the glorious pressure of his lips.

Burned for him.

She hadn't been kissed a lot. Didn't possess a backlog of experience to compare it to. There'd been a couple of guys in college and a couple more after that. And there'd been Cosmo when he'd tried to convince her to take their friendship to the next level.

The only time in her life that she'd ever instigated a kiss was when she was five years old and had kissed J. J. Hunter when he'd stood up to the bullies for her. J. J. hadn't kissed her in return. In fact, he'd scrubbed his mouth hard with the back of his hand and told her that now he'd have to get a vaccination for girl cooties.

But this kiss, wow!

It was like nothing she'd ever experienced. Joel's kiss was raw and real. It was primal and fierce. And it was terrifying to a timid woman who spent most of her life simply fantasizing about such deep, damp kisses, never ever daring to hope she'd actually get to experience them.

Joel's kiss was ten times better than any dreamy reverie. Strong and rich and knowing. What woman on earth would want to be kissed any other way?

Perfectly, their mouths fit. His larger one closing securely over her smaller one. Just as it had when he'd given her mouth-to-mouth resuscitation. Except this was much better.

This, she could enjoy.

Naked need, passionate frustration, pure animal lust erupted from him into her and spun a magic that went far beyond the mere joining of their lips. This single wild union was everything.

But it was wrong. She should put a stop to this. Besides, they were in the middle of traffic.

*Yeah,* Angelina said, *but the drawbridge is still up. Go for it. Where else you gonna go?*

But what was going to happen once this was over and the drawbridge went down and they had to go back to reality?

Joel fisted his hand tighter in her hair and pulled her even closer to him, penetrating her with his tongue, exploring her fully. She stopped thinking, stopped listening to her monkey mind chattering away, stopped doing anything except allowing the moment to unfold.

He was all that she'd ever envisioned in a lover and so much more. Daring and decisive and direct. He groaned low in his throat. His body strained and pushed against hers and Marlie met him measure for measure, reaching up her hands to cup his face in her palms, marveling at the feel of his thick, warm skin.

His lips vibrated against hers and he breathed her name. "Marlie."

No name had ever sounded so sexy. Marlie, Marlie, Marlie. Hers was not a euphonic name. The hard *M* followed by the harsh *R* and ending with the girlish "lee" sound caused phonetic disharmony. But the way Joel said her name, with his slight southern drawl, it sounded like the ocean breathing. "Maaalee."

She moaned quietly and he swallowed up the resonant hum of her, like a man too long in the desert drinking his fill of ice water.

Desperately, she wished they were in private, in a bedroom, far from traffic and prying eyes. She wanted him to tumble her onto a soft mattress, rip her clothes off, and dive into her deep. She ached to feel the hard thrust of his shaft as her body closed around his.

Marlie's need was a runaway horse. Out of control. Disorderly. Unbridled.

Turmoil. She was in turmoil. Her emotions flailed giddily. Excitement warred with guilt and passion and sadness and glee. She wanted to laugh. She wanted to cry. She felt too free.

Help!

She jerked her head back, pulling away, struggling to breathe and grab hold of some shred of sanity. Joel's arms were still wrapped around her, his eyes clouded and heavy. The motion was slight, hardly noticeable, but his lips were trembling.

She wasn't the only one totally blown away. Eddies of embarrassment and sexual hunger washed over her, warring waves of boldness and timidity.

"Joel . . ." What was she going to say? That she was sorry? But she had nothing to apologize for. *He* had kissed *her.*

She reached out, not knowing what she intended to do, but got caught up in the crazy push-pull battle inside her.

But Joel raised an arm, blocking her hand, and latched his eyes on to hers.

He was breathing hard and he did not speak. He didn't have to speak. She could read the message in his eyes loud and clear.

*Come any closer, touch me again, and I will have no choice but to take you right here, right now, the rest of the world be damned.*

The resulting thrill that raced through her body was so powerful that she almost had an orgasm right there on the spot.

Behind them car horns honked.

"The drawbridge is up," he croaked in a gravelly voice and then fell back against the passenger seat.

Angelina wanted to take credit for the stunned expression on his face. Marlie's ego wanted to believe her kiss had rendered him weak and senseless.

But when she saw the dark red bloodstain blooming on the front of his garish Hawaiian shirt, her heart stopped.

# Chapter 9

The man wore a black ski mask and mirrored sunglasses. Penelope had no idea how he could see to drive in the darkness.

In his lap lay a pistol.

He hadn't spoken a word to Penelope since he'd kidnapped her. She sat huddled beside him on the front seat of his four-wheel-drive Army jeep circa 1960, afraid to ask questions, terrified of his answers. Her hands were bound in front of her with a soft fiber rope.

He drove south down the long, lonely stretch of beach of North Padre Island, away from her home, away from Marlie. Gone were the restaurants and the stores. Gone were the hotels and the condos. Gone were other cars and people. They were on government land now. On the National Seashore Preserve, in the middle of nowhere. The sky above was as vast and deep as the Gulf of Mexico stretching out to their left.

Misgiving filled her. Her heart was pounding, and she felt slightly sick to her stomach. She'd spent half her life expecting something like this, but as the years had passed she'd grown complacent. Thinking surely that if the dastardly people Daniel had been about to expose just before his death had wanted to kill her, they already would have done so.

Why was it happening now, fifteen years after the fact? She knew nothing about what had happened in Iraq during Desert Storm. Daniel had refused to tell her what was going on, refused to put her and Marlie in harm's way by giving her dangerous knowledge.

Penelope had no idea what this man wanted or where he was taking her. But even though she could not have put it into words, she knew this was the most significant event of her life. More important than her wedding day or her daughter's birth or the night she'd learned Daniel had been shot down in cold blood aboard the USS *Gilcrest* by his best friend Gus Hunter and that his body had fallen overboard and been lost at sea.

Mile after mile slipped away, the silence growing longer, louder, tenser until Penelope thought she would scream.

At last, several hours after he'd abducted her from her home, only minutes after her mysterious phone call, the man stopped the jeep. The sand dunes around them were thick and tall and eerily silent. He motioned for her to get out.

Penelope opened the door. It was dark and cold. She shivered in the chilly night air. She could see nothing but sand dune upon sand dune upon sand dune. No houses, no people, no signs of civilization.

*He's going to kill me. He's going to gun me down in cold blood, and I'll never see Marlie again.*

But she would see her beloved Daniel at long last.

Joy, hot and unexpected, jumped in her chest. Oh, to be with Daniel!

And then a sense of complete serenity settled over her. All right then. If it was her time to die, then it was her time to die. She'd waited fifteen long years to be reunited with her husband. She would not mourn the loss of this life, even though she would miss her daughter something fierce.

"Go ahead," she said, her voice clear and steady. "Shoot me. I'm prepared to die."

But he did not shoot her.

Instead, he pulled a silk scarf from his pocket.

Oh, dear God, he was going to strangle her.

He stepped closer. She forced herself not to scream or beg for mercy, but she couldn't help flinching when he draped the scarf over her head.

She would be brave. She would do Daniel proud. Penelope squared her shoulders and prepared for death.

"You're bleeding," Marlie said, stating what was now becoming quite obvious.

"Wow." Joel gave her a wan grin. "She's beautiful and amazingly astute too."

"Don't be a smart-ass."

"It's either that or pass out," he said. "Take your pick."

"What happened? How did you get hurt? How long have you been bleeding? Why didn't you tell me?"

"Please, don't nag," he said. "I'm not up for it."

"That's not nagging; that's asking questions."

He massaged his forehead with two fingers. His color was too pale, and he was beginning to ooze blood onto the seat. It must hurt like hell, no wonder he was so grumpy.

"Never mind," she said. "Don't answer. It's not important."

"I got nicked by a stray bullet," he murmured.

"The hit man shot you?"

"He didn't shoot me, he shot the side-view mirror of his Camaro, and it ricocheted off and grazed my side."

"He shot up his own Camaro? You know, for a hired assassin this guy is really a crappy shot, but I'm grateful for it."

"Where are we going?" Joel asked.

"I'm taking you to the hospital right now." Marlie sped up, whipping the SUV from lane to lane, jockeying for a better position in traffic.

"Don't panic, it's just a flesh wound. I'll be okay."

"What are you? Some stalwart knight from a Monty Python skit?"

"I'm an ex-Navy SEAL. Believe me, I've had much worse than this."

An ex-Navy SEAL?

Well, that explained the gun and the commanding way he'd thrown her over his shoulder and then busted out the window in her mother's house to save her, and his arrogant attitude, cocky tilt and all. She felt as if he'd been lying to her somehow. He could have told her before now that he was a SEAL. Before she had started liking him, before he'd saved her life and gotten himself shot up over her.

"I knew it," she muttered, her emotions a fist against her rib cage. "I told Angelina you were military, but she wouldn't listen. I mean, who could mistake it? The hair-cut, the posture, the starched white dress shirt."

"Angelina?"

Belatedly, Marlie realized she'd just referenced her alter ego to someone who didn't know how much mental energy she spent with a fictional character. Instead of answering him she said, "An ex-Navy SEAL, huh?"

"I'm retired."

"You retired from the SEALs and you're only what? Thirty?"

"Thirty-one."

"You didn't retire. Not at your age. I'm a Navy brat. I know what SEALs are like. They're tight. It's a real brotherhood. Once you're a SEAL, you don't willingly leave. You got kicked out, didn't you?"

"Yeah," he admitted. "I got kicked out."

"What did you do? Funnel whiskey down someone's throat?"

"Not exactly." He gave her a wry smile, and she admired his ability to see humor in a black situation.

"You're not going to tell me why, are you?"

"I don't like to talk about it."

Marlie nodded. She could respect that. There were a lot of things she didn't like to talk about either, and if she were the one with the gunshot wound, she'd be howling like a banshee.

By the time they reached the hospital in downtown Corpus, Joel had either fallen asleep or passed out. Marlie kept glancing at his chest to make sure he was still breathing, and every time she looked it seemed the bloodstain had spread a bit more.

She pulled up into the emergency bay. "Joel, we're here."

He didn't answer.

Marlie reached over and shook his shoulder. "Wake up, we're at the hospital."

He groaned, but didn't open his eyes.

"Come on, say something, smart-ass."

His head lolled back against the seat.

Oh, no. Oh, crap. Oh, shit.

Marlie peeled off her seat belt, jumped from the SUV,

and ran inside the emergency room entrance. Once she was through the door, she stopped, not knowing where to proceed to next.

Beyond the glass partition nurses ran to and fro, obviously working a major trauma. The front desk was empty; no receptionist or clerk greeted her. To her left lay the waiting area, crammed with people. Most sat in chairs looking miserable; a few were watching the television mounted on the wall in the corner. A bored security guard lounged against the wall, listlessly picking his teeth.

Marlie's eyes drifted to the television screen. The news was on. She turned away, trying desperately to catch the gaze of a passing staff member, when from her peripheral vision she saw her picture flashed up on the television screen.

What the heck?

Hurriedly she shoved her way over to the TV, cocked her head, and strained to listen above the hum of voices and hospital noises.

"Marlie Montague is wanted for questioning in the arson investigation surrounding the fire that burned her mother's North Padre Island cottage to the ground earlier this evening," said the News 11 anchorman. "In the garage of that home, the police have just made a grisly discovery. We go to Evita Casteda live at the scene."

Grisly discovery? What grisly discovery?

Marlie nudged aside a wino who reeked of urine, and stood on tiptoe for a better view of the television. The camera switched to an attractive Latina reporter standing in front of the burned-out remnants of her mother's home. Yellow crime-scene tape secured the perimeter. Marlie's blood curdled. To actually see the remains of the bungalow weakened her stomach and her knees.

"Mike," Evita Casteda addressed the anchorman, "here's what we've learned. The police have found a body in the ashes of the house owned by Penelope Montague."

"Mom?" Marlie whimpered and bile rose to her throat.

No. It couldn't be. Her hands shook and her skin turned as cold as a grave.

"The body is burned beyond recognition, but according to the medical examiner it does appear to be male. Cause of death is yet to be determined. We'll keep you updated as new evidence arises. Back to you, Mike."

It was a man's body. It wasn't her mother. She raised a trembling hand to her mouth.

The camera switched back to the newsroom. "Marlie Montague is the daughter of the infamous Desert Storm traitor, Daniel Montague, who was accused but never convicted of selling U.S. military missiles to the Iraqi terrorists during the first Gulf War. Montague claimed he'd been framed by someone in the upper echelon of the U.S. Navy, but Montague was shot and killed trying to escape custody before he could be tried for treason."

The anchorman paused for effect, then quickly glanced down to check his notes.

"Montague's daughter is now a comic book artist who writes about government conspiracies. Ms. Montague is no stranger to controversy. Last year she was maced by police during an arrest at a shrimp boat protest on Pier 51. The law enforcement authorities are not yet saying that Ms. Montague is a suspect, but she is considered a person of interest. Witnesses saw her fleeing the scene of the arson in the company of an unknown male companion."

Marlie's picture flashed up on the screen again.

Dear God, she *was* a suspect.

\*   \*   \*

*Tell her the truth. Tell her why you're really here.* The notion tapped illogically, an accusing intonation in Joel's brain as he sat in the Durango, drifting in and out of sleep, slowly oozing blood.

*It's me, J. J. Hunter, the guy you had a crush on when you were five. I'm on your side. I want to help you. I want to protect you.*

Aw, damn. He prayed that when she finally found out who he really was, she'd forgive him. Not only for lying to her, but for the past, for being a Hunter. For his father's part in her father's death.

His cell phone chirped and he answered it one-handed. "Yeah." He tried to wet his dry lips with an even drier tongue.

"Bring her in."

"What?"

"You deaf? Marlie Montague; bring her in."

"Dobbs?" Feeling dazed, Joel shook his head.

"No, this is Howard Stern. Bring her in, Hunter. Now."

"Why?"

"Just do it."

"I want an answer."

"Don't question my authority, just obey the order."

Joel was feeling testy. "I'm the one out here with my ass on the line, getting shot at and almost burned up in a house fire. I have a right to know what the hell is going on."

"You got shot at? Who's shooting at you?"

"Yeah. The guy who's trying to execute Marlie Montague. Got any idea why, Dobbs?"

"Don't let that mousy facade fool you, Hunter; she's dangerous."

"Sorry, Dobbs, I don't know whose bullshit you're spreading, but I don't need my yard fertilized."

"Don't be a smart-ass. They found a body in the arson fire in Penelope Montague's garage."

"Penelope Montague?" His gut wrenched hard to think Marlie's mother might have died in the fire.

"Nope. Take a wild guess."

Joel grunted. "Why don't you save me the minutes and just tell me."

"Former government-contractor-turned-weapons-lobbyist Robert Herkle."

"What was Robert Herkle doing in Penelope Montague's garage?"

"That's the sixty-four-billion-dollar question. But here's the kicker. The police found a gas can they believe was used to start the blaze, and Marlie Montague's fingerprints are all over it."

"So? She used the gas can at her mother's and the arsonist wore gloves. Dobbs, I've been watching her for two weeks. I was with her when she went to her mother's house. Someone nailed the windows shut and we were trapped inside the house together when the fire started. There's no way she ignited that blaze."

"Before you rush to the woman's defense, that's not all."

"Lay it on me." The allegations were so bogus. Joel didn't know who was behind these lies. He didn't know if Dobbs was a mere puppet or if he was one of the investigators determined to railroad Marlie, but he wasn't about to let them blame this on her.

"Just got the coroner's report. The fire was set to cover up the fact Herkle had been shot with a gun once owned by Daniel Montague. If Marlie didn't kill him, her mother certainly did, and since we have no idea where Mom is, it's time to bring your girl in. Besides, if someone is bent on killing her, it's better to have her in protective custody."

"Not if you intend to bring her up on charges for a crime she didn't commit."

"The evidence will be what brings her up on charges, Hunter, not me."

"I don't feel good about this. There's more you're not telling me."

"Yeah, and it's top secret. Just bring her in."

Joel thought about Marlie and her crazy conspiracy theories. He'd never believed that any of them could be true, but now, with his boss's adamant attitude, he was starting to wonder if perhaps she really had stumbled onto something. Some weird things had been happening. Could the Navy brass really be involved? His sense of loyalty warred with his sense of justice.

And what about Marlie? If he didn't stand by her now, what would happen to her? His protective instincts welled up inside him. She was the underdog. She needed him and he couldn't turn his back on her, even if it meant turning his back on the Navy, even knowing that if she was wrong, if someone wasn't trying to railroad her, then he would pay a high price.

He clenched his fist and made his decision to put everything on the line for her. "No."

"What?"

"You heard me. I'm not bringing her in. Not when you're already prejudiced against her."

There were so many damned unanswered questions.

Where was Marlie's mother? Why had Robert Herkle been in Penelope Montague's garage? Who had killed him? Was it the same man who'd tried to assassinate Marlie? Had he also started the bungalow fire, or had that been someone else? And how did any of this tie in to Marlie?

Joel didn't know, but he was determined to find out.

"I'm not bringing her in," he told Dobbs again and hung up the phone.

She had to get out of here. Before someone recognized her and called the police. In a futile attempt at a disguise, Marlie snatched off her glasses and stuck them in her pocket.

Turning on her heel, she fled the emergency waiting room. It was only when she got back out to the SUV that she remembered Joel.

What to do? What to do?

She stood beside the Durango, frozen, indecisive. If she went back into the hospital with Joel, she was bound to be recognized after that news broadcast. And anyway, weren't all gunshot wounds automatically reported to the police?

"Come on, Angelina, take over. I can't handle this one on my own," Marlie mumbled.

*Dump Joel out on the curb and let him fend for himself,* Angelina advised.

"I can't do that," Marlie said, shocked that her alter ego would even consider such a heartless solution. "He saved my life. I'm not leaving him."

*Suit yourself.*

"You need some help, lady?"

Marlie jerked her head around to see a man smoking a cigarette off to one side of the door. She'd been so distressed she hadn't even noticed him standing there.

"No, thank you," she muttered. "I'm fine."

"You don't look so fine. Talking to yourself is nothing to be ashamed of," the guy said. "We all hear voices now and then."

Marlie didn't answer. She jumped back into the SUV and glanced over at Joel. Actually, he looked slightly better. The bloodstain didn't appear to be much bigger, and his color had improved. Then she saw the flask of whiskey in his lap and realized he'd been dosing himself.

He eyed her. "What's up? You look like you've seen Casper the Ghost and he wasn't nearly as friendly as his PR rep would have us believe."

"We can't go in there. Or I can't go in there. You can go in if you want," she said.

"You got an aversion to hospitals?"

She shook her head. "That's not it."

"You gonna tell me what it is? Please don't make me play twenty questions. I'm not in the mood."

"They found a dead guy in my mother's garage, and the police think I killed him and started the fire to cover it up. I saw it on the TV news while I was in there."

"But that's idiotic. I was with you when the fire started."

"Tell me about it. But I have a feeling if I try to explain, they'll arrest me first and ask questions later," she said.

"Then let's get out of here."

"What?"

"Start the car. Let's motor."

"But you've got to have that gunshot wound looked at. Go on in."

"I'm not budging."

"Don't be ridiculous."

"I'm not leaving you on your own. This killer that's after you means serious business, and I'm the only thing standing between you and him," Joel said.

"Excuse me, Mr. Ego, but who appointed you my guardian?"

"You did, when you burst through my back door."

"Get over yourself." Marlie snorted.

"In case you haven't noticed, you're driving my vehicle. You have to take me with you."

Oh, yeah.

Marlie shot a look over at him. His gaze was lazy, almost sensual. How could he be feeling horny when he'd just taken a bullet?

Hell, how could he be feeling horny over her in the first place? He was major-league beefcake, and she was a farm-team rookie. Their pairing would be like mating a thoroughbred Triple Crown winner to a Shetland pony.

Who cared? It wasn't like she was looking for romance. Love was the last thing on her mind. She wasn't tough enough to handle the inevitability of heartbreak, and this guy had heartbreaker stamped all over him.

"You honestly think I'd be better off dragging your wounded butt around with me than just getting out of town on my own?"

"Running away won't solve your problems. We have to figure out who wants you dead and why. And you need a bodyguard."

"A guy with blood running out of his side doesn't make a convincing bodyguard applicant."

"I'll be fine. We'll find a place to lie low and you can patch me up."

"In case you haven't noticed, I'm not exactly Florence Nightingale."

"I have a first-aid kit in the back of the SUV, and I've had first-aid training. I'll walk you through it. Now, let's motor out of the ambulance bay before an ambulance shows up and runs over us."

"Why would you even want to help me?" She eyed him suspiciously.

"You mean besides the fact the guy made it personal when he shot me? That's not reason enough for you?"

"No, it's not. You could just go to the police."

"So could you."

"You saw the way Officer Kemp treated me."

"How's this? I'm pissed off that someone locked us in your mother's house and tried to burn us to death. Much as you might be attached to your loner status, like it or not, we're in this together."

"No, we aren't. You're shot. I'm not. Get out of the car and let the doctors take care of you."

"Okay. Try this one on for size. I've been expunged from the SEALs for eighteen months and I was bored out of my skull until you came crashing into my life. Suddenly that old adrenaline rush is back and I feel alive again. You've given me the opportunity to dust off old skills. You're doing me a favor."

He meant what he was saying. Marlie saw the truth of it in the way his eyes lit up.

"Why do you have this macho need to protect me? You don't even know me."

He got a faraway look in his eyes, peered right through her, staring hard at something from his past. "You want me to tell you my biggest regret?"

If he gave up a secret, then she would feel better about the situation. More in control. She needed something to hold over him before she could trust him. "Okay."

"I once knew another woman like you. Independent. Headstrong."

Obviously, he'd mixed her up with Angelina. She was timid and reclusive, not headstrong and independent, but never mind. "Is this the woman you were once in love with?"

"Yes. It was my duty to protect her, but she didn't want my protection."

"Why not?"

"She wanted to perform her mission alone, wanted to

prove she was as tough and resilient as any man. And she knew the only way to get rid of me was to hurt me. So she did something cruel to drive me away." He paused and she heard the pain in his voice. "I turned my back on her. I left her when I should have been watching her."

"What happened?"

"She was wounded and almost died that night, and it was my fault. If I'd ignored my ego and stayed with her, she would never have gotten injured. With you, I've been given a chance to redeem myself. So because of my past failings as a soldier and a man, you're stuck with me, Marlie Montague, and I don't care what you have to say about it. From this point on, I'm by your side twenty-four/seven until the killer is caught and your mother is found."

She shook her head. For Marlie, deception was a matter of self-defense. If she allowed herself to be totally honest with Joel, she'd be placing her life in his hands. She'd never been able to trust anyone to that degree. She had to protect herself, not only from without but from within.

"What's it gonna take to convince you?" Joel asked, his voice low and lulling.

Their gazes held. One second. Two. Three.

Marlie drew in a shaky breath. "In order for me to trust you, then you're going to have to trust me."

"Okay."

"That means believing in me."

"I can do that."

"And by answering a question."

"What's that?"

"This other woman. Who was she?"

Joel hesitated a moment and then said, "My wife."

# Chapter 10

"I'm in," Cosmo said.

Three hours' worth of hacking, and Chet Delaney's personal journal entries popped up on the screen, just waiting for Cosmo to decode them.

"You're a genius."

For his reward, Treeni leaned against his shoulder, took his earlobe between her teeth, and nibbled just a little too hard. Cosmo gulped and a groan slipped over his lips. He had to force himself to stay focused on the computer screen.

"Is there a particular date we're after?" he asked.

"Go back two, two and a half weeks. Say January third."

Cosmo scrolled down and frowned at the code. It wasn't any cryptogram that he recognized, but he wouldn't expect the head of Navy Intelligence to use something easy. The more he studied it, the clearer it became that the code was one of Chet Delaney's own creation. Cosmo couldn't believe he had the balls to do this, hacking into the private diaries of the former head of the Office of Navy Intelligence. A man who very easily could become the next President of the United States.

What a high. He felt freakin' omnipotent.

"What exactly am I looking for?" he asked Treeni.

"References to an NCIS special agent named Joel Hunter. I'm trying to find out where my father assigned him."

Cosmo knew jealousy was an ugly, trouble-causing emotion, but despite what his rational mind was telling him, he couldn't leave well enough alone. He had to open his mouth. "Who is this guy?"

Treeni shrugged. "My ex-husband."

And then jealousy did chomp into him with its sharp, unrelenting teeth. Green and dark and violent. He tasted it. Vile and bitter, instantly eradicating the sweet flavor of cream cheese and chocolate fudge and earthy pecans on his tongue. Treeni had invited him here to help her hack into her father's private records so she could locate her ex-husband.

She was nibbling on *his* ear, but thinking of another man.

Obstreperously, Cosmo pushed away from her and got to his feet.

"You want to hunt up your ex-husband, you'll have to do it on your own."

Treeni burst out laughing.

Cosmo scowled. He was beginning to understand precisely what Chief Peterson had been warning him about. "What's so damn funny?"

"You're jealous."

"No, I'm not."

"That's *so* hot."

His initial response was to deny his feelings, but then he thought, *Screw that.* His next action was totally uncharacteristic, but Treeni had goaded him into it. He grabbed her up from her chair and hauled her to her feet. She was so tall that they were almost the same height. He looked her straight in the eyes.

"Damn straight I'm jealous."

Treeni's eyes widened in surprise. "Why, Cosmo, who would have thought behind that computer geek exterior lurked the heart of a lion?"

"I won't be toyed with." He had no idea where this unexpected bravado was coming from, but he milked it for all he was worth. "I've been watching you for two weeks. Wanting you with every cell of my body. Wanting you as much as I want air. I think you knew that. I think you're using my attraction to you to your advantage. You're trying to get me to help you do something illegal. It's not going to work. I won't be treated the way you've treated other men in the past."

She gulped.

He watched the column of her throat work and saw the flutter of the pulse at the hollow of her neck.

"I've been watching you too, Cosmo. And wanting you as badly as you wanted me," Treeni whispered.

He ached to believe her, but he did not. "Are you still in love with your ex-husband?"

Treeni met his hard stare and never blinked. "I never loved Joel. At least not the way a wife should love her husband. He and I were more competitors than anything else. We had great sex and got a rush out of our one-upmanship games, sure, but it wasn't anything more than that."

"I don't understand. Why would you marry a man you didn't love?"

Treeni drew in a deep breath. Cosmo couldn't stop his gaze from being magnetized to the rise and fall of her scrumptious chest beneath the gauzy silk of lingerie.

"I spent my life trying to prove myself to my father. He wanted a son, not a daughter. I did everything I could to make him love me. Played sports. Joined the Navy. Got into the Secret Service. He always admired Joel. I thought, well, if I can't be Joel, maybe I can marry him and maybe then Father would be proud of me."

"But it didn't work that way."

"No, and I wound up married to a man as intense and cunning as I was. Not a good combo. No elastic to that kind of relationship. I wanted things my way and he wanted things his way, and neither of us knew how to compromise. It got us into a lot of trouble in Iraq."

"What happened in Iraq?"

For the briefest moment, Cosmo could have sworn he saw a mist of tears in Treeni's eyes, but then she blinked and it was gone.

"I did something unconscionable. I violated the very code I'd sworn to uphold, not to mention my marriage vows. I was a total shit to Joel," Treeni admitted. "I was trying to hurt him, trying to get him to walk away so I could run the mission my own way."

Cosmo said nothing, but a million conflicting thoughts were tumbling through his mind. What was the appeal of this woman? Why did he want her even more now that she was confessing her darkest sins to him? "Did your husband walk away from you and the mission?"

"Yes. Because I left him with no choice. I drove him away. And as a result of my stupid, stupid decision I almost died," she said. "Tunnel of white light, floating around the ER, watching the doctors and nurses do their thing on my lifeless body. The works."

"Seriously?"

"Very seriously."

"How did you almost die?"

"Fallout from a missile explosion. Head injury. I'll show you the scar later if you're still interested." Her grin was faint and tinged with a hint of melancholy.

Cosmo didn't answer.

Treeni bit down on her bottom lip before continuing her story. "The mission was a miserable disaster, but Joel— good old heroic Joel—stepped up to the plate and took the blame. He got tossed out of the Navy SEALs because of what I did. He wouldn't give me a divorce until I recovered from my injuries. But the minute I was able, I filed. It had been a long time coming, and we were both relieved."

"Why are you trying to find him again?"

Treeni's face darkened. "I just learned something very disturbing on my last trip to the Middle East. I found out that Joel had been right about our previous mission and I'd been mistaken." She swallowed hard. "I came back to the States to tell Joel what I'd learned, but when I got here, I found out he'd been sent on a secret mission through his new job with NCIS, and I'm certain my father is involved. I'm really worried it's related to what's going on in the Middle East."

"Terrorists?"

Treeni shook her head. "Worse."

"What could be worse?"

"I can't tell you that, but if I can just find Joel I'm certain he can help me shine some light on this. So, can you put your jealousy aside and help me?" She seemed nothing but sincere. "For the good of our country?"

Cosmo wanted to believe her. God, how he wanted to believe. It might turn out to be the single most stupid thing he'd ever done, but he said, "All right. I'll do it. But only under one condition."

"What's that?"

"I want to be there when you speak with your ex-husband."

Joel had to get Marlie someplace safe. He had to tend to his bleeding wound, which was hurting like hot coals were being shoved into it, and then he had to make new plans. He was cutting his ties with NCIS, going out on his own, going out on a limb, but he saw no way around it. Not if he was going to help Marlie. By insisting that he arrest her, Dobbs had left him no alternative.

Marlie sat behind the wheel of the Durango, driving them away from Spohn Hospital. She was headed back in the direction they'd come from, cruising south on North Shoreline Boulevard. The Bay of Corpus Christi stretched out to their left. Lights from the shrimp boats bobbed on the darkened water.

A fresh stab of pain shot through him. Joel winced and clenched his fists.

"Take another hit off that flask. You're starting to look sickly again."

"You trying to get me drunk? And steal my virtue?" Joel tried teasing, but his heart wasn't really in it. He did take her advice and knocked back another swallow of whiskey.

"You caught me," she said. "My life won't be complete until I get you soused and jump your bones."

"There's that wicked tongue again. Did I ever tell you that feisty women turn me on?"

"Demure it is then, all the way, from now on."

"Yeah, right."

"Please, kind sir, have you any suggestions for where we might take refuge in our time of tribulation?"

Joel groaned from another shooting pain, but he pretended it was from her awful attempt at Regency-era speech patterns.

"I fear," she said, injecting her voice with a laughable British accent, "the constables will have my abode under surveillance and your residence is too near mine to make a suitable alternative. Furthermore, it is unseemly for a young woman to be unchaperoned at the home of an unmarried gentleman."

He groaned again, and this time it *was* from her miserable rendition of nineteenth-century vernacular. "Please, I beg of you. Stop with the Jane Austen."

"Are you now appropriately turned off?" She grinned mischievously.

"Most assuredly, fair maiden." Joel looked at her, his heart feeling as if a pro wrestler had grabbed it with an iron claw. Marlie's levity in the face of adversity snipped his resistance like barber scissors, severing the connection between steely control and red-hot desire. He wanted her even more because she could make him laugh when things looked grim. He didn't know who was more deranged. He or Marlie.

"Good. Now, any idea where we go from here?"

"Motel."

"It sounds so seedy."

"No one said that it had to be a rent-by-the-minute motel."

"I'm on something of a budget," she pointed out. "No cash-ola to fund a fancy hotel stay."

Joel had a credit card, but worried about it being traced. He didn't know exactly how pissed off Dobbs was at him.

And then he suddenly thought of his father's condo on Mustang Island. He hadn't been there in years, and he had no clue what kind of shape the place was in, but it was secluded. And he did remember the alarm code that would unlock the front door. Unless his father had changed it, the numbers were the same as his birthday. Plus, the condo would be empty. Gus never went there in the winter.

"Head for Mustang Island." He gave her the address, not knowing if this was the best idea he'd ever had or the very worst. "I've got a friend who has a summer place there and he won't mind if we borrow it."

He hated lying to her but he was already walking a thin line, trying to keep his identity a secret. He didn't want to say it was his father's place and risk giving himself away somehow before he was ready to come clean.

Twenty minutes later, they were inside his father's condo. It smelled moldy from being closed up, but other than that, Joel had forgotten how swank the place was. Gus had splurged on the condo with money he'd inherited from an oil-rich uncle, and he harbored plans of retiring there someday. But Joel doubted that his stepmother Amber, who was three years younger than he, would ever leave the city.

"Wow," Marlie said after Joel flicked the light switch on. "Fancy-schmancy. Your friend must be pretty well off."

Joel shrugged. The whiskey was making his head swim, and the throbbing in his side was sapping his strength. Lying down, and the sooner the better, was his only goal. His bloodstained shirt was sticking to his skin, and whenever he moved he felt a sharp poking sensation dig deep into his flesh.

Marlie stepped farther into the room. She lifted her head and stared at the vaulted ceilings and slowly spun in a circle. "Weird."

"What is?"

"This place looks familiar to me." She walked into the living area, flicking on more lights as she went.

Watching her sashay away, Joel clasped a hand to his heart. God, she did strange and wondrous things to him.

*What's your major malfunction, Numb Nuts? Get your mind back in the game. This ain't playtime for J. J.*

Right. He was letting a little sexual chemistry and way too much whiskey cloud his judgment.

In his defense, it had been a rather action-packed day. Not since the drama of Iraq had he felt so stimulated, and that wasn't a good thing.

"Yes," she said. "I've definitely been in this condo before."

"Huh?" *Pay attention to what she's saying. This is important.*

"Yeah, when I was a kid. I don't recall much about it, but I do remember this woodwork." She ran a hand along the mahogany wainscoting. "It's pretty unique. Rich. Expensive. I remember being small and looking up at it and thinking, 'Wow, someday I want to own a place on the beach just like this one.' Who's your friend?"

Jesus. A forgotten recollection hit him like a lightning bolt. She *had* been here before.

They'd once played together on Mustang Island. Back when he'd gone by J. J. and his parents were still married. If Joel tried hard enough, he could see the two of them walking along the windswept shore, picking up sand dollars, cracking them open to find the white shell pieces inside that looked like flying birds.

She'd worn glasses even then, and the elastic of her red swimsuit had cut a groove into the top of her thigh. She hadn't interested him of course. She'd been a little kid, four or five tops, while he would have been nine or ten. Probably nine. His parents had separated just before his tenth birthday.

Their eyes met.

He remembered her hair in pigtails and how she'd been missing a couple of front teeth. He thought of the time he'd taken up for her when a couple of bullies had pestered her and tried to steal her ice-cream cone. She'd bawled for him. He'd punched the guys. They'd run off.

And then little Marlie had stood up on her tiptoes and kissed him.

He remembered being caught off guard, unnerved by her adoring admiration, but he'd been pleased too that he'd made her so happy.

Joel had the strong, damaging impulse to tell her who he really was. To come clean and confess that he was J. J., the boy she'd once had a mad crush on. The unexpected urge toward honesty was so overwhelming, he had to bite down on his tongue to keep quiet.

How innocent she seemed. He didn't think he would ever get over the paradox she presented. How could she possess such a suspicious mind and such a trusting face? He was toeing a tightrope between tipping his hand and proving to her that he was a good guy. A good guy who lied.

The essential question? Was she a good girl?

According to his bosses at NCIS, she was not. But the more he hung around her, the more certain he became that things were not what they seemed.

Just exactly why did NCIS have this woman under investigation? He'd been told it was to protect secrets of national security. But what secrets? And who was he protecting the secrets from? Marlie? Or the people who were after her?

"Who's your friend?" she repeated. "Maybe we know the same people."

*Distract her. Quick, think of something.*

He considered kissing her again. Wanted to kiss her again more than anything, but kissing her the first time had been a huge mistake. It had left him achy for something he shouldn't have. Yet he was drawn to her like a dieter to double-fudge chocolate cake.

He was caught between wanting to tell her who he was and his fear that he could be wrong about her. That she could wind him up the way no one else ever had. Joel felt as if he'd crossed some invisible line and there was no going back.

In the end, his weary body settled things. It might have been from blood loss or it might have been from the four slugs of whiskey he'd had in the car. In reality, it was probably a combination of both. His head spun dizzily and his knees buckled. He grabbed for the wall, barely able to keep himself standing.

"Joel!" Marlie exclaimed and jumped to his side.

"I'm okay." He held up his hand, resenting the sympathy in her eyes.

"Sit down, you're about to pass out."

"Navy SEALs don't pass out."

"Oh, save it," she said. "Stop trying to play the bull-headed, tough, macho male."

"Why?" He tried to give her a teasing smile, but it came off more like a grimacing wince. "So you can play the bullheaded, tender, caring nurse? Now that I think about it, you'd make one helluva sexy nurse."

Marlie snorted and leveled her small shoulder under

his armpit. "Knock off the sexual innuendo, Jolly Green, and lean on me."

He would have laughed if it wouldn't have hurt so much. The thought of this tiny woman bearing even a tenth of his weight was inconceivable. He was a good eighty pounds heavier than she.

But damn, his legs were as fluid as water, bobbing and weaving beneath him. His head wasn't much better. Had some unseen force wrapped a rubber band tightly around his skull?

Her shoulder fit just perfectly under his arm. Her earnestness was so damn endearing.

"Lean on me," she repeated.

Joel tried to shake her off, to prove he could stand on his own two feet, but his breath was ragged and he couldn't seem to draw enough air into his lungs.

"Just do it," she bullied.

Wow, she was dishing out a little tit for tat. He wanted to give her hell right back, but his body betrayed him. He leaned against her, putting as little weight on her soft shoulder as he could get away with and still satisfy her. He hated feeling this weak, this vulnerable. He was loath to admit it, even to himself, but the balance of power had shifted in her favor.

*Gotta find a way to regain the upper hand. She can't be the hero. You're the hero.*

"Where's the nearest bedroom?" she asked.

"Bedroom? Woman, are you trying to take advantage of a wounded war veteran?"

"Ha-ha. You talk a good game, big man, but if I had any worries that you could follow through with your sexual moves, I'd let you fall flat on your face."

"Sexual moves? You think that's what this is? If I were

putting my sexual moves on you, Ladybug, you'd already be on your back beggin' for more."

She peered up at him from around the side of his chest, but she didn't look the least bit intimidated by his bravado. "Go ahead, bluster away. You don't fool me one little bit."

"This isn't bluster," he growled, hating that she had seen right through him.

"Uh-huh, yeah, right."

If his frickin' knees would just stop buckling he'd show her he wasn't blustering. He would yank her into his arms, curl his fingers into the soft globe of her sweet butt, and kiss her until she lost all control. At that thought his fingers tightened securely around her upper arm and his penis stiffened.

He didn't feel the slightest pang of guilt for his inappropriate hard-on. The battlefield had taught him the preciousness of each and every moment. You had to seize the day and revel in being alive. Because your next breath might be your last.

Treeni had understood. She'd been the same way, and they'd mixed like oxygen and gasoline.

But Marlie was different. She had been hiding out from the world for so long that she had no clue how to embrace life when she was holding it in her hands. He had the strongest need to teach her, to show her everything that she'd been missing by hiding behind her comic books and her fears.

"Bedroom," she said again.

"Through there." He pointed.

Marlie guided, he hobbled. It was a relief to collapse onto the bed.

She stepped back. Joel looked at her, noticed her gaze had dropped to the very obvious bulge in his pants. She made a soft feminine sound, her eyes transfixed. Her pupils widened and she nervously nibbled her bottom lip.

Well, at least he'd gotten her mind off trying to remember who'd lived in the condo when she'd visited it as a child. He felt a certain smug, masculine satisfaction. He smiled wolfishly, his gaze on her face.

She licked her lips.

There was no denying the spark of longing in her eyes. She might be scared, but the look was undeniable. Marlie Montague wanted to jump his bones as much as he wanted to jump hers.

# Chapter 11

It was almost midnight when Gus called Abel Johnson from a pay phone outside a twenty-four-hour adult video and bookstore. The triple-X-rated establishment was the only place he'd been able to find a functioning pay phone, and conveniently enough it was located next to a bar where Gus had just downed a few shots of scotch.

The news of the arson, Penelope's disappearance, and the mention that her daughter was a person of interest in the crime was all over the news. Not only that, but the reporters kept dragging up old history, calling Daniel Montague a traitor and resurrecting every sharp edge of Gus's terrible guilt.

He knew he had to do something irrevocable, before he lost his nerve and backed out.

"Hello," his assistant answered. Abel sounded alert, wide awake, as if he'd just been waiting for Gus's call.

"I need for you to do sumptin' very important for me," Gus slurred.

"Admiral?"

"Uh-huh."

"Are you drunk?"

"Daz none of your business."

"I've never seen you drink, sir."

Gus winced. He'd given up the hooch years ago when he'd been trying to hang on to Deirdre, but now and again when he needed an antidote for his weakness, he would take up the bottle. He curled his fingers around the edge of the phone booth to keep from weaving. "Just lissen to me."

"I'm listening."

Gus forced himself to concentrate on speaking clearly. This was a matter of utmost importance. "I have documents in the safe at my house. Very important documents."

"Yes, sir."

"If you don't hear from me within the next forty-eight hours, here's what I want you to do. Get a pen."

"Hang on." Abel let out a long-suffering sigh that Gus chose to ignore.

He heard the sound of his assistant setting down the receiver. He didn't like asking the kid to do this, but it was the only insurance he had. The only thing that could save Joel and Marlie. The only thing that could redeem Daniel's name if Gus was no longer around to do it.

A few seconds later Abel was back. "Okay. I've got a pen."

"Go over to my house. Amber's out of town visiting her mother. You'll need a code to get in." Gus told Abel how to deactivate the alarm. "Then open the wall safe in my bedroom. The combination is my son's birthday."

"Got it."

"Inside there's a top secret file marked 'Iraq, 1990.' "

"Yes, sir."

"Take it to the media."

"You want me to release top secret documents to the media? Are you sure?"

"I've never been more certain of anything in my life. It should have been done years ago."

Abel sucked in his breath.

"What is it?" Gus asked.

"Nothing, sir."

"Speak your mind."

"It's just...I have a feeling this could end your career."

"If you don't hear from me in the next forty-eight hours, it'll be because I no longer have any use for a career."

"Sir, are you absolutely sure it's not the alcohol talking? Why don't you sleep it off and call me back in the morning?"

"No one appointed you my babysitter, you little snot-nose," Gus yelled, but then belatedly realized hurting Abel's feelings was probably not the best way to get his own needs met. He wasn't about to back down. He was an admiral, dammit, no matter how undeserved the title might be. "Just do what I say and that's an order."

"You take it easy. I'll go get your first-aid kit out of the Durango," Marlie said.

For once, Joel didn't argue with her and for that she was grateful. She left him lying on the bed with his jaw clenched and his eyes closed. He was hurting a lot more than he was letting on.

She went back outside, into the darkness. The cool winter night breeze soothed her heated skin. The sound of the ocean lulled her ears. The carpet of stars in the jet-black sky appeased her weary eyes.

But nothing could quiet her troubled thoughts. They crashed in on her, a house of cards. Her mother was missing. The police wanted to question her. And a man in a black Camaro wanted to kill her.

And Joel was married.

Or had been.

He'd never clarified whether he was divorced or not, and she hadn't asked because she'd been too afraid of his answer. She didn't know why it mattered. Didn't know why she cared. It wasn't like she was going to hook up with him. No matter how hot and achy he made her feel.

Marlie wondered what he thought about her and then wondered why she cared. Forget about him.

But how could she forget about him when she was going to have to go back in there and dress his wound with his naked torso exposed.

*I'll do it,* Angelina said. *You just sit back and relax.*

That's what Marlie was most afraid of. That her alter ego would take over and get her into deep trouble she couldn't get herself out of.

"I'll handle it," Marlie muttered. "Stay away."

She found the first-aid kit in the back of Joel's SUV, then hurriedly returned to the house. She wondered what had happened to the man in the black Camaro and prayed he hadn't somehow tracked them to Mustang Island. Returning to the bedroom, she found Joel lying stretched out across the mattress, with an arm flung over his eyes, blocking out the overhead light. She stood in the doorway watching him. In repose, he didn't look nearly so big and tough. In fact, he looked weary and wiped out.

She went to the dresser and flicked on a table lamp before turning off the overhead. He didn't move in response, and his chest rose and fell in a soft, regular rhythm.

He was asleep.

In such a defenseless posture, he looked far younger than the formidable Navy SEAL who no doubt knew exactly how to kill someone with a single blow from his big, dangerous hands and would do what he had to do without a moment's hesitation or regret.

She'd seen him in action today. Saving her from sure death in the fire, giving her mouth-to-mouth resuscitation, chasing after the assassin without a single thought for his own safety.

She owed him so much. Her heartstrings tugged, and Marlie felt the first stirrings of loyalty. Loyalty and honest-to-goodness trust.

She was on dangerous ground. Emotional quicksand of the most deadly kind. She had to stop thinking about this, had to concentrate on what needed doing and just do it.

The curtains were open and as the clouds moved, a blade of moonlight cast his hair in a silvery glow.

Marlie crept closer. She could see that the blood on his shirt was dried and dark except for a bright red dampness in the very center where the wound was still oozing. She had to wake him up and take care of it, even though the thought of tending to him left her weak-kneed and woozy.

*No time to be a wuss. Step up to the plate. Unless you want me to take over,* Angelina said.

"Buzz off," Marlie mumbled.

She directed the beam from the dresser lamp to shine directly on his torso and then laid the first-aid kit on the bed beside him.

"Joel."

He moved his arm from over his face, and his stormy-sea eyes met hers. For a long, stuttering moment, Marlie lost her ability to breathe. He looked so familiar, like she'd known him forever.

It's those eyes, she thought, haunting and strangely familiar.

And he didn't just look at her, he stared *into* her, and she boldly stared back, seeing something far more beyond that gruff masculine exterior he wore like a badge of honor.

His eyes told her the things that his pride and his fear of looking weak would not let him say out loud.

*Thank you*, his eyes whispered. *Thank you for helping me. Thank you for sticking by me.*

As if she had an alternative.

Without him, she had no hope of eluding the killer. He had saved her, and now she would save him.

Stop thinking like this, she scolded herself. He could be a married man.

*He doesn't wear a wedding ring,* Angelina observed.

A lot of guys didn't wear rings.

*He said he'd gotten his heart broken. That means a breakup.*

Yeah, it also means he probably still has feelings for her.

*You're here with him now, not her. Go with the flow, Montague.*

But the moment had vanished. Thank God. The gentleness evaporated from his eyes, and his macho countenance was back in place.

He dropped his hand and jokingly said, "Got a bullet for me to bite on, Doc?"

"A bullet's what got you into this fix."

"Ah, that's where you're wrong. The bullet was secondary. What got me into this was the cute dark-haired ladybug who showed up on my doorstep batting her big brown eyes and looking for a knight in shining armor."

He might have thought that he was flirting or paying her a compliment, but he actually pissed her off.

"I was trying to save my own life," Marlie snapped

peevishly. "I certainly wasn't angling for some good-looking oaf to start following me around and causing me all kinds of problems."

He laughed. "Channel that anger, Doc. You're gonna need it."

Irritated, she twisted open the buttons of his kitschy bloodstained Hawaiian shirt. The sooner they got this over with the better.

Anger steeled her nerves. When she saw the ugly way the assassin's bullet had split his perfect skin, grazing a shallow trough just under and to the right of his last rib, she was less horrified than she might have been, even though she had to bite down on her bottom lip to keep from gasping.

The bullet had passed completely through, leaving the injury raw and jagged and scary-looking, but his bare-chested, beefcake days were far from behind him.

What now? She looked to Joel.

"Sew me up."

"You want me to stitch your wound?"

"Needs closin'."

"I've never done anything like this before."

"You can hot-wire a car, you can do this."

"Yes, but I researched that. I've never researched wound suturing."

"Ever sewn a button on a shirt?"

"Yes."

"Good enough."

She hissed her breath in through clenched teeth. "It's gonna leave a scar."

He winked. "It'll get me sympathy from the ladies."

Marlie frowned. She didn't want other women giving him sympathy.

*Oooh,* Angelina said in a teasing singsong, *you're jealous. You want him as your boyfriend. Marlie and Joel sitting in a tree...*

Shut up.

She opened the first-aid kit. It was the most extensive one she'd ever seen, containing a suture kit, sterile drapes, gauze bandages, hydrogen peroxide, a scalpel, Betadine sticks, antibiotic ointment, a bottle of penicillin, and a second one of Vicodin.

"You could do surgery with these supplies. Is this some special Navy SEAL first-aid kit?"

"Yeah."

She opened both vials of pills, took out one each of the antibiotic and painkiller, and handed them to him. "I know you probably shouldn't wash the Vicodin down with whiskey, but this is going to hurt like hell so go ahead."

"I know," he said, took the proffered pills, and downed them with one long swallow from his flask. "Okay, ready. Go to it."

"Shouldn't we let the pain pill take effect first?" she asked, hoping to put off the inevitable for a little while longer.

"The whiskey has a pretty good head start. Fire away." He nodded.

Opening one of the blue drapes from the first-aid kit, she then unfolded it and tucked it between his torso and the duvet. She struggled not to notice what an exceptionally fine body he possessed. She ignored the studly ripple of his six-pack. She denied that his navel was actually the most perfect creation ever bestowed upon any man. She disregarded the dark swirl of hair that extended down from that heavenly navel to disappear beyond the waistband of his jeans.

"This is going to sting." She liberally poured hydrogen peroxide over the wound.

Joel sucked in his breath, but that was the only sound he made.

The wound effervesced as the peroxide cleaned out the dried blood. When the bubbles abated, Marlie tilted her head, trying to see better in the limited lighting from the bedside lamp. Gently, she took a gauze pad and patted the wound dry. It was ready to be stitched. Nervously, she opened the suture kit. Luckily, the thread was already attached to the needle.

For a better angle, she knelt on the floor beside the bed. "Scooch to the edge."

He complied.

"Here goes nothing. Brace yourself." Tentatively, she pushed the needle through his skin.

Joel grunted.

She stopped. "I'm hurting you."

"I can take it. Go on."

Muscles tensed, Marlie proceeded with her grim task. Joel took another slug off the flask. She felt so guilty. It was because of her that he'd been hurt.

"Got a question for you," he said a few minutes later. He sounded tipsy.

"Uh-huh?"

"What's with all the black and white?"

Marlie frowned and looked up at him.

His eyes gleamed.

"Excuse me?"

"Your clothes. Your house. Your car. Everything you own is black and white. Where's the color? Where's the zip? Where's the joie de vivre?"

She shrugged off his comment even though it bothered her. "I like black and white."

"Why?"

"I don't know. It's just my preference."

"But why?"

"You sound like a three-year-old."

"Black and white feels secure to you," he said, answering his own question. "People are less likely to notice you when you wear black and white. You use it to hide out."

"You're wrong. I like black and white because there's no ambiguity about it. It's either one or the other."

"Is this because you believe the world is made up of morally ambiguous people?"

"There's no believing to it. The world *is* made up of morally ambiguous people."

"The world is made of flawed human beings."

"Same thing."

"So what color of human being am I?"

"Red," she said immediately. "Startlingly hot fire engine red."

"I'll go along with that," he said. "Red's a power color. So what hue would you be if you couldn't pick black or white?"

It was a silly question, but it did give her pause.

"Something quiet and deep. Forest green, I suppose. Natural. Earthy."

"No." He shook his head. "That doesn't fit you at all."

"Okay, Calvin Klein. What color would you say fits me?"

"Pink," he said decisively. "Sweet, wholesome Dubble-Bubble pink."

"Gak!" Marlie exclaimed. "Is that how you see me? As a five-year-old?"

"Not at all. I see you as a ripe, lush feminine woman."

"What do you see your wife as?" She hadn't meant to say it. The words just slipped out.

*Liar,* Angelina accused.

"Ex-wife," he corrected.

Her heart fluttered hopefully. How stupid. "What's her color?"

"Most definitely scarlet."

"Two reds."

"Terrible combo," he said. "Too much color."

"What happened to ruin your marriage?"

*Don't ask this stuff. Why are you asking this stuff? It's just going to make you miserable.*

He didn't say anything for the longest time. Marlie kept sewing, kept her eyes trained on her work. If he hadn't been plied with whiskey and Vicodin, she doubted if he would have answered her at all.

"She married me to get back at her father," he said.

"Why did you marry her?"

He laughed, but it was a dry, mirthless sound. "She was the opposite of my mother."

Marlie didn't say anything. She wanted him to keep talking, and she feared that if she commented, he would shut down. Although she couldn't say for sure why she wanted to hear this.

"My mother is one of those dependent women who can't survive without a guy, but she's attracted to these hard-ass types who treat her badly."

"Those bullying stepfathers you spoke of."

"Yeah."

It was difficult to visualize anyone bullying this powerhouse of a man. But he hadn't always been a man. The thought of Joel as a kid vulnerable to oppressive adults tugged at her heartstrings.

"Treeni, that's my ex, she's tough. She didn't need any man. Her biggest dream was to be a Navy SEAL, but women aren't allowed. So she became a spy for ONI and married a SEAL instead. And spent the duration of our six-month marriage trying to show me up."

"So what ended things?" Marlie dared.

He didn't answer. Okay. She'd pushed too far. She understood. She didn't offer up her private life for just any and every one either. She kept stitching his wound, watching his chest rise and fall.

"We were sent to Iraq together," Joel said finally. "On the same detail, but we were assigned to different units. Our mission was to find weapons of mass destruction."

Marlie made encouraging "Go on" noises, but she kept her eyes down, not wanting to distract him from his story or make a mistake with her suturing.

"Treeni was determined to beat me to the punch and find those weapons. While I followed the more traditional methods of information gathering, Treeni used her training as a spy."

Marlie felt his muscles tense beneath her fingers, and she knew he'd arrived at the difficult part of his story.

"Following a hunch, I drove to the site where I believed that a cache of missiles was hidden in an underground bunker and discovered that Treeni had beaten me to the spot. There was a time bomb attached to one of the missiles, and she was in the middle of defusing it."

He swallowed. The sound was dry and raspy in the quietness of the room. "She told me to leave, but of course I refused. I didn't care who got credit for finding and defusing the damned missiles. I wasn't going to leave her alone out there in the desert. But she was determined to claim victory. She told me how she'd found out about the cache. She'd slept with one of Saddam Hussein's top-ranking officers in exchange for the information." Joel's voice broke.

Marlie's heart twisted and tears misted her eyes. She was touched beyond measure that he'd shared this with her. Even if he was a little drunk, it had taken a great deal of courage to confess this. He gave off energy as sad as her own. What made them so in tune with each other? They were strangers, but she needed this intimacy that was growing deeper with every word he spoke.

"Shhh," she said. Her rational mind wanted to stop the burgeoning connection, but her heart begged him to keep talking. "You don't have to say any more."

But it seemed, once started on his woeful tale, Joel could not be stopped.

"I walked away. I left Treeni alone in the darkness with the bomb. I let my pride and my pain override concern for her safety." He drew in a deep breath and paused.

Just when Marlie thought he wasn't going to tell her, Joel spoke.

"I was two hundred yards away, attempting to radio the bomb squad when the bunker exploded. Treeni's lover had actually placed two bombs, but she didn't realize it. She'd just walked away from the first bomb when the second one went off."

"Oh, my God, Joel."

"At the very same moment the bomb detonated, a convoy was going by on the road above the bunker. Four Navy SEALs, the men in my unit, were killed. Shrapnel from the bomb struck Treeni on the head and she almost died. And it was all because I let her hurt my feelings. I should never have left her alone. I took the blame. I said I was the one who didn't follow regulations and defused the bomb on my own rather than following protocol by calling in the bomb squad. I protected her. She filed for divorce once she'd recovered from her injuries."

"That's why you got kicked out of the SEALs?"

"Yeah," he said. "Yeah."

Marlie couldn't begin to imagine how he must have tortured himself over what had happened. He'd paid a very high price for his mistakes.

"Joel," she said. "I'm so sorry."

"I don't need your pity. I just thought if you knew the details it might make you feel better about trusting me."

"Thank you," she said. "Thank you so much for telling me."

The strange thing was she did feel better. He was a man trying to make amends, and if letting him help her would repair the crack in his soul, how could she refuse his assistance?

"I'm finished," she said and wrapped up the medical supplies before returning them to the first-aid kit.

He looked down at her handiwork and then raised his eyes to meet her gaze. "You're amazing."

"Hang on. I still need to apply a dressing."

She finished up her work, her mind filled with the story he'd just told her. When Marlie glanced up, she saw that he had fallen asleep and she was glad because she didn't want him to see her crying for him. For a man who had lost so much and still managed to pretend he didn't care.

# Chapter 12

For what seemed like hours, Penelope's captor led her across the sand. He hadn't strangled her as she'd feared, but instead used the scarf to blindfold her. She stumbled occasionally, but each and every time he was there to catch her, his hand at her elbow, gently guiding her along.

Who was this man? Where was he taking her? What did he want? She'd posed these questions to him numerous times, but he never answered and eventually she'd given up asking.

She thought once or twice about running, but something in her body language must have given her away, because each time the notion crossed her mind, her subjugator would tighten his grip on her arm and press the nose of his weapon softly against her side, a silent but deadly warning.

The surf roared unusually loud in her ears, her nose inhaling the unique smell of midnight sea, mingling with the scent of the man beside her. It was a hauntingly familiar aroma she could not quite place. It made her feel raw and vulnerable and achy for all that she'd lost.

The loneliness of her life settled over her with relentless vengeance. What more did she have to lose?

Wind buffeted, tossing handfuls of sand at them. The

hem of Penelope's dress billowed against her legs. Her mouth was dry. She was thirsty and hungry and tired.

He stopped suddenly and pulled Penelope up close against him.

Alarmed, she sucked in her breath.

He moved his face against hers, scraping her cheek gently with his whiskers, his evocative smell invading her.

How dare he?

A shiver shot down Penelope's spine when she realized he'd removed his mask.

She wanted to look him in the eyes and demand to know what she was up against. She reached up for her blindfold with her bound hands, determined to find a way to yank it off, but he was quicker and snatched hold of her wrist before she could reach the scarf.

How was it that he anticipated her every move? It was almost as if he knew her every thought.

His breathing was as rapid and raspy as her own.

"Dammit," Penelope cried. "Who are you? What do you want? Who sent you? Speak to me. I deserve an answer."

But he uttered not a word, only grunted and tugged her away from the water.

Where was he taking her?

She fought, batting at his chest with her bound fists. Unaffected, he dragged her forward. Rusty hinges creaked. She heard a heavy metal door being swung open. In her blindness, the sound escalated her fear.

As did the cool, musty-smelling air that rushed out to skim her skin.

He pulled her after him, down, down, down. They splashed through ankle-high water. Her elbow grazed the side of a wall.

Cement.

He was taking her underground. She thought wildly, crazily, *Phantom of the Opera*.

She heard skittering noises and high-pitched, irritated squeaks. Her stomach roiled. Rats. It had to be rats. Panic wrapped around her heart. What was this place? Was she to die here? Was this to be her tomb?

The last fifteen years had culminated in this moment. She'd made a grave mistake back then, giving up hope too easily, not fighting back. Balking, Penelope stopped, dug her heels into the cobblestone floor. "No, no, I won't go."

She battled him. Pushing, hitting, biting, whatever it took to survive.

He did not fight back. He let her do her worst and when she was played out, too weary and spent to struggle any longer, he tenderly but firmly pressed two fingers against the carotid artery in her neck until Penelope slipped into oblivious darkness.

Gathering up Joel's shirt from the bed, Marlie went in search of a washer and dryer. She needed clean clothes, she needed a shower, and she needed to think.

She found the laundry room at the end of the hall, shucked out of her clothes, treated the bloodstain on Joel's shirt with hydrogen peroxide, and stuffed all their laundry into the same load to wash in cold water. Stark naked, she padded back down the hallway to the bathroom adjoining the bedroom where Joel slept, stopping just long enough to snag her purse up from the floor where she'd left it.

Flicking on the bathroom's overhead light, she came face-to-face with her reflection in the mirror. Her color was pale, the lipstick she'd slapped on hours earlier was long gone, and there were traces of soot on her neck from the fire.

And was that stubble burn on her mouth?

Marlie lightly fingered her lips. She thought of how Joel had given her mouth-to-mouth resuscitation to save her life and then later, kissed her in the Durango to give meaning to the life he'd just saved.

She felt thrilled and stunned and in equal portions both powerful and overwhelmed. She was unable to make sense of her world and what was happening to her. Why was she having these kinds of feelings for Joel? And how did she stop them before things got out of hand?

*Let 'em get out of hand,* Angelina said. *It's time you took a risk or two in life.*

But it was too foolhardy. Her attraction to him couldn't lead anywhere.

*Why does it have to lead anywhere but the bedroom?* Angelina asked. *Besides, I thought you didn't believe in love.*

That comment made Marlie think of her mother. A deep sadness invaded her soul. She wanted to call Penelope on the phone and bubble enthusiastically about Joel. She wanted to giggle and share confidences. She wanted to ask her mother for advice. Ask her how to flirt. She and Penelope were close. Like sisters. Like friends. They had no family beyond each other. But she could not call her mother. Mom was missing. Her home was gone.

Was Mom dead?

No. She refused to think it. Refused to believe it.

But if she wasn't dead, where was she?

Marlie pressed her fingertips against her forehead, pushing against the thoughts. She couldn't let herself travel down this road. If she did, she'd come mentally unglued. She had to take it one step at a time. There was nothing she could do right this minute to find her mom, but she could seek comfort from the only other person she trusted.

Her best friend.

She wrapped a towel around her, fished the cell phone from her purse, and perched on the bathroom counter. Back resting against the wall, feet hanging over the sink, she crossed her legs and punched in Cosmo's number.

"Hello?"

She was surprised to hear he sounded wide awake. Cosmo's voice instantly lifted her spirits. She could kick herself for staying mad at him for so long. "Cos?"

"Marlie?" He sounded genuinely happy to hear from her. "Is that you?"

She nodded, too overcome by emotion to speak. Until this moment she hadn't realized exactly how much she missed her friend.

"Mar? You still there?"

"Uh-huh," she managed.

"Are you all right?"

"No."

"Talk to me."

And just like that the awkwardness between them vanished. As quickly and quietly as she could, Marlie told him about the assassin on her doorstep and what had happened to her mother.

"What have you gotten yourself into?"

"I don't know, Cosmo."

"One of your conspiracy theories pegged the truth and someone is trying to shut you up. We knew it was bound to happen."

"But I don't know anything," she wailed.

"Obviously you do, you just don't realize the importance of your knowledge."

"I'm really scared."

"Are you by yourself?"

Marlie hesitated. Should she tell him about Joel? But she had no secrets from Cosmo. "No, my neighbor's with me."

"Mrs. Whittaker is with you?"

"No, no. Someone new moved into the vacant house on the other side. An ex-Navy SEAL. He gave me a ride over to Mom's and he was there when the would-be killer torched her house."

"Can you trust him?"

Marlie bit down on her bottom lip. "I think so."

"Just be very careful."

"I am."

"What can I do to help?"

"It's already been a huge help talking to you again. I'm sorry we ever fought."

"Me too."

"Listen, there is something you can do for me."

"Say the word. You need me to get on a plane and come down there?"

"No. I don't want you to do anything that would jeopardize your new job." She told him then about the package she'd sent him containing the valve stems and pieces of twig. "Could you get it checked for fingerprints?"

"I'll pull some strings," he said.

"You promise you won't get in trouble?"

"It'll be fine."

"Thank you."

A fresh warmth of security washed over her. She was safe for now and she had friends. With Joel's and Cosmo's help she would find her mother and get out of this situation.

Marlie heard a woman's voice in the background saying, "Cosmo, come back to bed."

Surprised, Marlie brought her hand to her mouth. "You're not alone."

"It's okay," he said to her, and then she heard him muffle the phone as he murmured something to the other woman.

"You sly dog, you've got a girlfriend," Marlie said.

"Maybe, kinda, sorta."

She could hear the smile in his voice, and his smile made her smile. "Meaning?"

"Still too new."

"But you really like her."

"Yeah," he said, and his voice was so husky Marlie wondered if what he felt for his companion was a lot more than like.

"This is wonderful news."

"You don't mind?"

"Are you kidding? You deserve all the happiness in the world, my friend."

"Thanks," he said.

"Well, I didn't mean to interrupt. I'll let you get back to what you were doing. Have fun."

"I'll check the morning mail for your package."

"Thank you."

"Call me immediately if you need anything."

"Won't your girlfriend be jealous?"

"She'll understand."

"She sounds like a keeper to me."

Cosmo laughed. " 'Night, Mar."

" 'Night, Cos."

Still grinning, Marlie hopped off the counter and then rummaged in the cabinet until she found hotel-sized bottles of shampoo and small bars of guest soap. Desperate to scrub herself clean and erase the stench of danger from her body, she climbed into the shower and turned the faucets to as hot as she could stand it. She scoured until the water ran cold and her skin turned as tingly pink as the color Joel said she should wear.

After she got out and dried herself off, she twisted her hair up in one oversized towel and wrapped her body in another. She tiptoed out of the bathroom and padded back down the hall to the laundry room, switching their clothes from the washer to the dryer.

She edged through the bedroom on her return to the bathroom with the intention of blow-drying her hair when she saw that Joel was very much awake.

He ripped off her towel with his eyes. Lying cocked back on the bed like some nonchalant jock that had just rocketed his team to the state title, wearing his bandaged wound as a badge of honor.

His shoulders were so broad he should have been fined for looking so damned potent, and he sent up at least a half-dozen red flags on her don't-you-dare-get-close-to-this-one radar.

"Where you goin', Ladybug?"

She gestured toward the bathroom. "Dry my hair."

"Bring the dryer in here; I'll do it for you."

"You need to rest. Sleep."

"To hell with that," he said. "You helped me. Now I help you. Bring the hair dryer in here, or I'll go into the bathroom with you."

Knowing that he meant it, she retrieved the blow-dryer and a comb, brought the hair-care items to the bed, and crouched cautiously in her towel to plug it into the socket beside the lamp.

"Sit." He spread his legs and patted the duvet directly in front of his crotch.

She wasn't sure about this. Here she was in only a towel, and he was wearing nothing more than a tight pair of jeans.

"Sit."

She carefully crawled up in the bed beside him, making sure the towel was wrapped securely around her body. He removed the towel from around her head, and her hair dropped to her shoulders in thick, damp strands.

He ran the comb through her hair with a surprisingly gentle touch. "You have beautiful shoulders."

His breath was warm on the nape of her neck. She felt awkward and weird. "Really?"

"That's not the only thing that's gorgeous."

"You're serious?"

"Come on. I mean, whoa, you've got a body that won't quit."

She tentatively touched the curvy flesh of her waist. "You don't think I'm too fat?"

Joel snorted. "Good God, woman. Are you kidding me?"

"My body turns you on?"

Growling, Joel took her by the shoulder and turned her around to face him. He reached for her hand and guided it to his zipper. She'd never known a man could get so hard. "What do you think?"

Marlie jerked her hand back.

She felt a flush stain her cheeks, but she was surprised to realize it wasn't a flush of embarrassment, but one of pride. She, with her overly generous body, did this to a man like Joel.

"You've got a figure just built to cushion the weight of

a man. Stop hiding it under baggy clothes. You've got it. Flaunt it."

"Right now I'm wearing just a towel."

"Don't think I hadn't noticed."

"I've noticed you too," she said bravely.

"Like what you see?"

She lowered her lashes. "You have some nice bits."

His chuckle rumbled deep in his chest. "Nice? That's not exactly what I was shooting for."

"Well, I'm certainly not going to swell your head."

"Too late for that." His grin broadened.

Okay, things were officially getting too intense. Marlie scooted away from him, headed toward the edge of the bed.

He crooked a finger at her. "Don't run away, woman."

*Woman.*

He said that word in such a sexy way it sent goose bumps dancing over her arms. Stop it, she admonished herself.

*Oh, let loose and have some fun for once,* Angelina interrupted.

But she didn't have a chance to make a move.

Boldly, unapologetically, Joel pulled her back onto the bed, gathering her against his chest, ignoring any pain the motion might have caused him.

When she'd kissed him before it had been with Angelina's persona, not her own, but this time it was Marlie all the way.

His kisses washed over her like a hurricane sweeping the island. Nibbling, licking, tasting her. His tongue was dizzyingly accomplished. His mouth was a miracle. He was a force of nature, this one. You could either run or cling for dear life.

It went against every instinct she had, but in that moment, Marlie chose to cling.

She wrapped her arms around his neck and let her jaw relax. Storm troopers had nothing on Joel. He staked his claim. Bold and brash. Navy SEAL all the way.

But underneath all the bravado, underneath all the machismo, take-command audacity, Marlie sensed something else. Something he didn't want her to know.

He was covering up. Trying to hide that scared, emotionally dependent little child he'd once been.

Understanding came that easily for her. She did not know why, but he did not fool her one bit. No matter how demanding his kisses were, Marlie knew the truth. No matter how tough he acted, she recognized it was all a ruse. No matter what he said, she realized what he really meant.

*I'm wearin' my heart on my sleeve here, so don't slam-dunk me.*

He didn't scare her. Not in the least. Which was weird, since most everything frightened Marlie.

Had Angelina secretly taken over her body again?

But no, she was looking up at Joel with her own eyes, not detached and from a distance the way she did when Angelina was living through her. She could smell his rustic scent, could feel the burn of his body heat. She loved the novelty of him. His body was startling and new. Her brain appraised him, filed away knowledge with giddy glee.

And as he kissed the pulse at her throat, she felt new to herself as well. His fingers caressed the full swell of her breast beneath the terry-cloth material of the towel. Suddenly her extra curves weren't something to bemoan, but a plush softness to be revered. So what if she wasn't as thin as a tree branch? Joel liked her anyway.

Marlie liked his body, liked what it was doing to hers. She liked how she fit just snug in the corner of his elbow. How his unique scent teased her with recognition on a deeply primal level. She thought of something her mother once said.

*I knew your father was the One the minute I smelled him.*

At the time she'd thought that was a very odd thing to say, but now she understood. No smell on earth had ever attracted her the way that Joel's scent did.

The thought unraveled her.

Marlie hesitated. Just because he smelled good didn't mean he was her one and only. Even if he was, she didn't want a one and only. There was too much pain involved in loving someone so deeply. She didn't have the courage or stamina for that.

She was going to pull away. Right this minute.

Except Angelina wouldn't let her. *No go, sister. I'm enjoying this too much.*

Until now, Marlie hadn't realized how much she was enjoying this too. In spite of everything—the danger, the uncertainty, the fear—on another level, she thrilled to be living the adventures she'd spent years dreaming up for her cartoon alter ego.

She was no longer the pudgy little girl on the playground who talked to herself. Or later, the somber girl who had no friends because her father had been accused of being a traitor to his own country. She was strong and capable; she was seizing life by the throat and wringing out every ounce of experience she could.

Joel inched her towel down and she didn't resist. He'd shifted their bodies around, and now she was lying on her back looking up at him.

How could he be so ready to make love after having just been grazed by a bullet? His virility both excited and terrified her. She wasn't woman enough for a man like him.

*Well,* Angelina whispered, *you've always got me as a pinch hitter in case you flake.*

As kinky as it sounded, there was that.

"You're so sexy," Joel murmured and lightly traced his tongue over her lips. It was so deliciously ticklish, she wriggled into the mattress and just kept gazing up into his eyes, caught in the vortex of his electromagnetic field.

Marlie hissed in her pleasure as he deepened their blistering kiss. She entwined her arms around his neck, pulling him closer as her head buzzed dizzily.

What would it be like to make love to such a powerful marauder? To skim her palms over his naked buttocks, knead those smooth, taut muscles that rippled when he moved.

"We shouldn't be doing this," she said. "Danger, adventure, and the thrill of the chase often cause people to mistake excitement for something more than it is."

"Right," he murmured, gently flicking his thumb over the tight bud of her nipple.

"We should stop."

"Uh-huh." But he kept right on going.

It felt so good. Too good. Something this good had to be bad.

Marlie struggled to sit up, to make sense of her feelings. She felt like a wishbone, tugged in two equally powerful opposing directions at once. Her doubts jerked her from the moment. Prevented her from finding pleasure in the here and now.

But maybe, her doubts were also stopping her from making a fatal mistake.

In the end, her qualms won. She splayed her palm against Joel's chest and pushed him back.

"No," she said. "No more."

She sat up, fumbling to close her towel. She tossed her head and glanced away from Joel, unable to look him in the eyes.

A shadow passed in front of the window, breaking the shaft of moonlight that fell through the open curtain. She raised her eyes to the window, and that's when she saw a man's face pressed against the pane.

Marlie screamed.

In an instant, Joel was on his feet, scrambling for his gun, the pain making shredded wheat out of his nerve endings. But rather than slowing him down, the pain was a catalyst, propelling him into battle.

He was a warrior, and protecting Marlie was his sole purpose.

She stood transfixed, finger pointing at the curtainless window. Joel grabbed her by the shoulders, shocked to find her skin damn near hypothermic.

"What is it?"

"A face in the window. A man."

"Did you get a good look at him? Was it the same guy who tried to kill you?"

"No." She shook her head. "At least I don't think so. He looked older, unkempt."

Joel clamped down on his tongue and felt the empty deadness of complete mental control settle over him. If he was honest, he would admit that it scared the living piss out of him, this ability to go stone-cold, closing down all emotions. The talent had served him well as a SEAL; not so much as a husband or a lover. For the first time ever, he wanted to lose the ability to detach. He was suddenly jealous of all those people who could let their emotions just sweep out of them. Messy, irrational, reckless. The only emotion he felt truly comfortable expressing was anger.

How fucking sad was that?

"Come on." He grabbed her by the wrist, dragged her down the hallway to the bathroom. "Get in there and lock the door. Don't open it for anyone but me. Got it?"

She nodded.

"Know how to use a gun?"

"I fired one once when I was doing research for a comic book."

"Good enough." He leaned down, clenching his jaw against the pain, hiked up the leg of his jeans, and plucked out the small-caliber handgun he kept secreted in an ankle holster and handed it to her. "If anyone comes after you, shoot them. Can you do it?"

"Yes."

Her eyes glistened with terror, but to her credit she took the gun. Joel had to steel his heart to keep from tucking her under his arm and taking her with him. She'd be safer here than out in the darkness of the unknown.

Joel closed the bathroom door and waited until he heard the lock click into place. Now, to find the bastard who'd been spying on them.

Clutching his gun in a two-fisted stance, he ignored the pain in his battered body, shouldered his way out the back door, and then slipped around the side of the house, ready for trouble.

But he found only shadows.

Joel cocked his head, zooming in, straining to hear what was missing. The air was too quiet, too still. Where were the normal sounds? The crickets and the frogs, the whisper of wind rushing over the sand dunes. Even the steady, reliable crashing of the ocean waves rhythmically caressing the shore seemed invisible.

He waited, ready, on alert, yet relaxed in his confident ability to handle whatever might arise. He was still a SEAL in his heart, if not on the government's payroll. He was part of the darkness, at one with the silence. He waited and watched and listened. For echoes, for whispers, for quivering molecules of air.

Nothing.

Stealthily, he edged to the bedroom window. Damn, the pain was a jagged saw blade pulling back and forth against the raw flesh of his wound. He bit down on the inside of his cheek.

Fuck the pain.

He shook his head to clear it. There were footprints in the sand, but it was impossible to discern much in the darkness on such unstable ground. Already the wind had shifted the sand, blurring the edges of the footprints.

No answers here.

Who had been watching them and why?

What did Marlie know that made someone want to kill her?

He thought of her. Alone in the house. Locked in the bathroom, clutching his gun to her chest, shaken but willing to pull that trigger if she had to.

She was brave yet skittish. As if she didn't know her true measure as a person. She greatly underestimated herself. He saw the core of steel that ran underneath that plush, soft exterior. Marlie was a paradox, and damn if he wasn't compelled by both sides of her. When she was worried, frantic, or nervous, his lionhearted hero side wanted nothing more than to take care of her. Taking care of her made him feel good.

But then there was that other layer. That inner steely reserve. When *that* Marlie rose to the surface, he responded to her with pure swaggering testosterone. God, she drove him crazy and made a muddle of his brain.

Thinking about her wasn't smart, but it was a hell of an improvement over thinking about the pain.

Even now, when she wasn't even within close range, his body responded to the visions his mind conjured of her. Joel recalled how carefully her gentle fingers had cleaned his wound and sewn him up. He remembered how her dark hair had grazed her cheek, accentuating the cherubic quality of her rounded bone structure.

Something in the dead center of his chest tightened.

What was with these mushy feelings? He was a Navy SEAL. He didn't indulge in emotions. He was a realist. He was an expert at blocking out unwanted feelings. He shoved them into the back drawer of his mind and locked the key. Treeni had been the same way. Both of them had the ability to stop feeling and simply act. It was the thing that had drawn them together, and that same thing had ended their marriage.

Marlie wasn't like that at all.

She rode her feelings like an ocean wave. Joy and excitement lifted her to the crest; despair and fear plunged her to the depths. Joel was loath to admit it, but he was jealous. Of her ability to let her feelings flow freely.

Damn, he wanted her. Why was he so attracted to her? Was it her wide eyes that peeped so beguilingly from behind her glasses? Was it the tender smile that tugged at the heartstrings he'd cut so long ago? He couldn't afford to feel anything more than sexual desire. She deserved better than a used warhorse with more baggage than an airport carousel.

It had taken every ounce of control he possessed not to make love to her back in the bedroom, and if it hadn't been for the interruption of the intruder, he didn't know how long he could have held out. Not when he looked into those tempting brown eyes.

A bank of marauding clouds covered the full moon, dashing the shimmering light and bathing Joel in unrepentant blackness.

A storm was coming. The wind kicked up, sent sand skittering.

He froze. Waiting. For what, he didn't know.

He was off his game. Nowhere near as sharp as normal. His rational mind blamed the gunshot wound and the whiskey and the Vicodin, but there was a part of him that couldn't help wondering if his attraction to Marlie was really to blame.

The clouds shifted again and the moon was back. Joel followed the footprints away from the house as they led toward the beach.

A few yards ahead of him, hung on the barb of an old fence, half covered in sand at the edge of the condo's perimeter, something glimmered in the moon glow.

Joel reached the fence, went down on one knee in the sand, and plucked the item from the barb. Frowning, he raised it up to examine it more closely. Immediately he recognized the item. Had seen it sewn onto the sleeve of his father's uniform.

The emblem of Admiral.

One thing was clear. The safe house had been compromised. They had to leave.

Joel had no time to form a second thought. He heard

a sound behind him, saw a shadow fall across the small dune, but blood loss had slowed his reflexes. He wasn't quick enough.

His attacker slammed something hard into the base of his skull, and Joel fell face-first into the sand.

# Chapter 13

*Face the facts. Joel's not coming back.*

Marlie sat in the bathroom, holding the gun, waiting and waiting for what seemed like ten eternities. What if something bad had happened to him? She vigorously gnawed her bottom lip, fretting about what monsters lay out there in the darkness.

*Go after him,* Angelina said.

"But he told me to stay here."

*Where have I heard that before? He was wrong at your mother's bungalow when he told you to stay put. Just because he's arrogant enough to think he hung the moon doesn't mean you have to buy into it.*

"True."

Joel did tend to take over and tell her what to do. And part of her really liked that. How easy it would be just to let him take the lead, take care of her. But another part of her balked. Joel was the kind of guy who just assumed his way was the best way, and if you didn't challenge him on it, you never got your way.

What was her way? What did she want?

She wanted to find her mother. That's what she wanted.

*So get off your duff and go find her.*

The gun felt smooth and cool in her hand. She would do this. She'd go out there and see what had happened to Joel.

*Put on some clothes first.*

Oh, yeah.

But the clothes in the dryer were still wet. She'd mistakenly put them on low heat. She switched the setting to high and dithered a moment about what to do. To hell with it, she'd just go out in the towel. Plucking a clothespin from the shelf above the dryer, Marlie used it to fasten her towel shut.

She slipped into her shoes and cautiously tiptoed into the foyer. She eased open the front door and stepped out. The clouds were playing tag with the moon. One minute dark, the next minute the pathway was bathed in shimmering moon glow. Joel's Durango sat in the driveway, but there was no sign of him.

The towel, although fluffy and oversized, was still no match for the night air. The ocean breeze sent gooseflesh running up her arms. She shivered and inched toward the side of the house. Uneasiness settled low in her belly. She fought the urge to jump into the Durango and drive away. But Joel needed her.

She cocked her head and listened but heard nothing beyond the usual beachy sounds. In her head, Angelina hummed the theme to *Halloween*.

Shut up!

Marlie took a step.

*Dupe-dupe*, Angelina said ominously. *Dupe, dupe, dupe, dupe, dupe.*

She wanted to kick her alter ego into a dark basement and slam the door, but what if she needed Angelina again?

If something had happened to Joel, Marlie couldn't handle it on her own.

*You sewed him up just fine by yourself and made out with him too, no prob.*

"What? You want me to lock you in the basement?"

*Depends on who you lock me in there with.*

"You're incorrigible."

*Yeah, but where would you be without me?*

Marlie edged along the front of the house, gun outstretched. She was about to round the corner that would let her see the bedroom window where the man had been staring in at them.

A dizziness of dread kneaded her stomach. Who had been peeking in the window? She was almost certain it wasn't the killer. And if it had been the police, they would have just come to the door. She wanted to call out to Joel, but she was too scared to open her mouth.

She peeked around the corner and her blood ran cold.

There was Joel splayed out in the sand, a man stooping over him with what looked like a rock in his hand.

"You there!" Marlie said. "Freeze right where you are or I'll shoot."

Maybe she shouldn't have said that about the shooting part because instead of freezing, the guy tossed the rock down and took off down the beach in a lumbering gait that told her he was either old or disabled or both.

She didn't know whether to chase after the guy or go see about Joel, but in the end, loyalty won out. She ran to Joel.

His hand snaked out and, as quick as a striking cobra, his hand clamped around her ankle.

Before Marlie could even cry out, she was on her butt in the sand beside him.

Joel lifted his head, anger snapping in his eyes like electricity discharging off a Tesla coil. He looked very, very pissed off.

Marlie shrank back, terrified. She'd known better than to trust him. She'd just been waiting for him to turn on her.

With a titanium grip, he yanked her ankle downward, jerking her through the sand on her fanny until she was practically lying underneath him.

How embarrassing.

Both her legs were pinned on either side of him, his wrists pushing her heels into the sand. Her crotch was level with his pelvis, and he was leaning heavily against her body. Her breasts were flattened against his chest, and his eyes were staring straight into hers.

They were breathing in rough, tight syncopation.

She felt him grow hard, and every cell in her body sang. The tremendous power of this masculine man should have frightened her, but it didn't.

Great. They were both perverted adrenaline junkies.

For a timid person with a poor track record when it came to the opposite sex, the realization that she could turn him on even under these bizarre circumstances was a heady idea.

Marlie gasped as Joel shoved his face close and pressed his nose, dusty with sand, flush against hers. When he spoke his voice was low and diabolical as he distinctly enunciated each word while simultaneously grinding his teeth.

"Why...the...hell...did...you...hit...me?"

Normally, such a show of masculine force would have cowed her. But that was before she'd been shot at, lost her mother, been locked in a burning house, almost slammed into a drawbridge, sewn up a man's gunshot wound, and got ogled by a Peeping Tom—all in less than twenty-four hours.

"I didn't hit you," she snapped.

"Then who did?"

Marlie pointed at the lone figure loping up the beach, moving farther and farther away. "He did."

Joel caught the guy and dragged him, kicking and spitting and biting, back to the condo. For an old coot, he was pretty feisty.

"Lemme go. I didn't do nothin'."

"You whacked me on the head," Joel growled, strong-arming him into the condo.

Wide-eyed, Marlie trailed behind them, the oversized bath towel cinched just above her bosom with a clothespin, his big gun clutched in her petite little hand. The geezer had stopped kicking and was staring at her with interest.

"Put on some clothes," Joel told her gruffly. He had to stop himself from punching out the old guy's lights for ogling her.

"Oh, yeah," she said absentmindedly, as if she'd forgotten she was half naked.

But Joel hadn't forgotten. His body still hummed from being pressed against hers out there on the sand. She padded off toward the laundry room and Joel's eyes went with her, following the gentle swish of her hips until she disappeared around the corner.

"Wouldn't mind having that swing in my backyard," the old guy said.

"Shut it." Joel muscled him onto the living room davenport. "What's your name?"

He flicked on the table lamp so he could see the guy better. He wasn't as old as Joel had initially thought.

Fifty-four or -five. Around Gus's age. There was madness in his eyes, and he sprouted a scraggly gray beard, but the most arresting thing about him was the long Frankenstein scar extending across the top of his head. He'd had brain surgery and from the looks of it, he was sporting a metal plate where a portion of his skull had once been.

"Your name," Joel repeated.

"You told me to shut it."

"Well, now I'm telling you to open it and give me your name."

"Seaman Third Class Ronald McDonald, serial number…"

"Your name isn't really Ronald McDonald."

"Yes, it is."

"No, it's not."

"Wanna see my driver's license?"

"Yeah."

The old guy pulled his driver's license out of his wallet and handed it to Joel.

"I'll be damned. Your name is Ronald McDonald."

"It was my name before that stupid hamburger clown ruined it." Ronald pouted. "Spent my whole life getting into fights over it."

Marlie reappeared dressed in his white shirt and her black track pants, looking clean and fresh. She hung back in the doorway, watching him interrogate Ronald.

"What are you doing here?" he asked.

"I work here," Ronald McDonald said querulously.

"Work here?" He had a feeling old Ronald was missing more than a few marbles.

"I'm the caretaker."

Had Gus hired this retired Navy seaman to keep up the place? "Why did you hit me on the head?" Joel asked.

"I thought you were him."

"Him who?"

"The commander."

"What commander?"

Ronald got a spacey, faraway look in his eyes. "It was his fault the ship went down. He knew what we were in for."

"What are you talking about?"

The old man began to tremble. "Here it comes. The explosion. Everyone running, screaming."

"Ronald, what are you talking about?"

"He's trapped. He's beggin' me for help. But if I stay, I'm gonna die too."

Clearly the old man was flashing back to some traumatic experience. Joel backed off, realizing that pushing the guy wasn't going to get him anywhere, but Ronald kept talking.

"I left him. I deserted the ship with the rest of them. It blew. Metal fragments everywhere. Hit me on the head." Ronald fingered the scar on his skull. "I almost died. He did die." He shook his head. "The poor little boy."

"What boy?"

"Ain't never gonna see his daddy again."

Joel could hear the sorrow in Ronald's voice, and he felt like a shit for sending him back to the heat of the battle. He'd had a few war-related nightmares himself, and he understood.

"It's okay. It's over," Joel said, trying to calm him.

Ronald's eyes rolled wildly in his head. "No, no, you're wrong. It's not over. The commander's back. The boy is here. He's here, and he's gonna kill us all."

"We have to get out of here," Joel told Marlie after he'd let crazy Ronald McDonald go free. "This place has been compromised."

"Where are we going?"

"Don't know, but we'll figure it out in the car. Come on."

She gathered up her purse, the first-aid kit, and the gun he had given her and met him at the door. Joel ushered her to the Durango, making sure she was belted in tight before he went around to the driver's side. He didn't know what was going down, but his encounter with Ronald had deepened his commitment to keeping Marlie safe. As soon as he got a chance, he was calling Dobbs and demanding some answers. Top secret or not, somebody better start talking.

He bumped along the beach road leading from Gus's condo to the main highway back to Corpus Christi. Languid rumbles of thunder rolled in off the Gulf, resonant and cavernous, echoing from one tip of the island to the other. Joel turned right onto the highway. Behind him, another car also turned onto the road, the swath of headlights cutting across his rearview mirror.

He narrowed his eyes suspiciously.

It was three o'clock in the morning, and Gus's condo was off the beaten path. Was it coincidence that another car had come up the isolated beach road behind them? Probably just young lovers, returning from a midnight rendezvous, but he wasn't taking any chances.

Reaching up, he adjusted his mirror. The headlights were positioned low, like those of a sports car.

He sped up.

So did the vehicle behind them.

"Hang on," he said.

"What is it?" Marlie asked in alarm.

"Just brace yourself."

He trod the brakes, whipping the Durango around in an insane U-turn, and flew past the other car.

It was a black Camaro.

The chase was on.

Fat raindrops splattered the windshield. Lightning flared a vivid forked-tongue pattern across the night sky. Thunder rolled.

Joel stomped the foot pedal. Marlie clung to the armrest. The black Camaro had made the same life-threatening U-turn that Joel had just made and was now coming at them like a demon from hell.

The Durango's tires thrummed. The windshield wipers squeaked against the glass. Marlie turned her head and saw that the Camaro was gaining on them.

"He's going to ram us," she cried.

"I can't go any faster."

The Camaro crossed over into the next lane, pulled even with the back of the Durango, but then he began a deadly drift back into their lane.

"If I can't outrun him, I'll outmaneuver him." Joel twisted the wheel to the right. Gravel from the shoulder flew up, pelting the car with *ping-ping-ping* noises.

*Bam!*

The Camaro hit the Durango's rear fender well, trying to force them off the road. Marlie's teeth smacked together at the force of the impact.

Joel turned the wheel back to the left. The Camaro and the Durango were jammed together, metal screeching, crying out like a demented patient on a psychiatric ward as they raced down the dark, rain-slicked road.

A deadly version of bumper cars.

The Camaro reduced its speed just enough for the vehicles to separate. His sudden deceleration caused Joel to rocket into the left lane.

The sports car rammed them from behind, jarring the SUV. Marlie moaned. Joel tried to get back into the right-hand lane, but the Camaro swerved to block him.

Marlie closed her eyes and prayed.

"Oh, shit," Joel said.

Her eyes flew open and she gasped. Up ahead was a suspension bridge with black water shimmering below.

"We're dead," she cried.

"Quick." Joel's gaze was hooked on the road. "Unbuckle your seat belt, slide over here, and take the wheel."

"I can't do that."

"Sure you can, I've seen you drive. You're amazing."

"That wasn't me! That was Angelina."

"Angelina?"

"My cartoon character."

"Huh?"

"I sort of channel her in difficult situations."

"Then channel her now and take the wheel."

"It's not that easy."

"Make it happen, Marlie." Joel was already out of his seat belt.

"What are you doing?"

"Have faith, Ladybug."

"Have faith? Hello, have you even met me?"

"Just get behind the wheel. You can do this."

*Angelina, you hear that? Come on. Take over.* But Angelina didn't answer her call. Where was the bitch?

The Camaro rammed them from behind again. Marlie shrieked.

"Listen to me. This is the only chance we've got," Joel said. "Get behind the wheel."

She had no choice. Joel was already climbing over

the seat into the back of the Durango. The SUV slowed immediately and the Camaro hit them again.

Marlie jumped into the seat Joel had just vacated, grasping the wheel in her sweaty palms.

Angelina, Angelina, come on, come on.

The bridge loomed.

Marlie perched on the very edge of the seat so her feet could reach the accelerator; she hadn't had the chance to move the seat forward so her short legs would fit. She stomped down on the accelerator with all her weight.

The Durango shot forward.

She heard a thump as Joel fell backward. "Are you okay?"

"Forget me; keep going."

The tires made a *rat-tat-tatting* sound as she hit the metal slats of the bridge.

Joel was rummaging around in the back, making all kinds of noises. His motions caused the Durango to rock. Because she was so much shorter than Joel, she couldn't see in the rearview mirror, but she was afraid to take her hands off the wheel to adjust it.

The Camaro's engine revved, and she knew that the driver was going to strike the SUV again. The killer was going to force them off the bridge and into a watery grave.

She felt a cold blast of air, heard loud road noises, and realized Joel must have opened the back-door hatch. She heard a loud boom but felt no impact.

Fearfully, she sneaked a peek in the side-view mirror just in time to see the Camaro shoot off the bridge and go flying into the water like a movie-studio stunt car.

She slowed the Durango and turned to look over her shoulder. She couldn't see Joel. Where was he?

Panic shot through her.

She pulled to a stop, hopped out, and saw Joel's mangled toolbox in the middle of the road. She realized at once what had happened. Joel had tossed the toolbox out the back, and the Camaro struck it at a high rate of speed. That's what had propelled the sports car into the water.

"Joel," she screamed, running around to the back of the truck.

Marlie found him lying on the floorboards, clutching his side and panting hard. Blood soaked the dressing she'd applied to his wound.

"You're hurt!"

"I'm fine." He sat up, trying to hide his grimace from her.

"You saved us," she cried, rain streaming down her face.

"We saved each other."

It was only then that Marlie realized she'd done it all without a drop of help from Angelina.

Together, she and Joel peered over the edge of the bridge and watched the Camaro's taillights disappear beneath the churning waters of the Gulf of Mexico.

# Chapter 14

Joel was fading fast. He needed fuel to keep running at this pace. Food and a long sleep.

Marlie used her cell phone to put in an anonymous call to the police, telling them that she'd seen a Camaro go over the bridge. She made Joel stretch out in the backseat while she changed his dressing. He got a kick out of her fussy mother-hen bossiness, and they were both relieved to see her stitching job had held up well under the exertion of heaving the toolbox into the path of the diabolical Camaro. She applied a new bandage to his wound, taped it securely, and then they took off again.

As tired as Joel was, he was in much better shape than the Durango. It rattled ominously as they drove back to Corpus Christi.

"Is it stupid that I feel badly for not pulling the guy out of the water?" Marlie fussed.

"He was trying to kill us."

"But he was still a human being."

Her innocence twisted him in knots. "Look, we did what we had to do to save our own lives."

"I know."

Joel didn't know how to comfort her. Reality sucked. "At least you can stop running," he said.

"Yeah, now only the cops are after me." She turned to look at him. "Maybe I should just turn myself in."

"Then who's going to find your mother?"

"I'm so tired and hungry I can't even think." Marlie massaged her forehead with a thumb and finger.

"Never fear," Joel said, turning into the parking lot of an all-night diner. "Denny's is here."

Ten minutes later they were sipping orange juice at a booth in the back corner, waiting for their Grand Slam breakfasts. Joel insisted on sitting against the wall. He didn't want anyone sneaking up on him.

Marlie was nervously shredding a paper napkin and avoiding his gaze. He wondered if she was thinking about what had happened between them before she'd seen Ronald McDonald's face in the window. His mind kept being drawn back to how they'd almost made love, even though he didn't want to think about it. He needed all his concentration for figuring out this puzzle.

"I've gotta ask you something," he said.

"Uh-huh."

"Look at me."

Shyly, she tilted her head. "What is it?"

"Do you think there's any chance that the stories about your father could be true? Do you think it's at all possible that he might have been a traitor?"

"Lies." Marlie smacked her tongue down hard on the word. "My father found out that someone high up in the Navy was involved in a cover-up and he was going to blow the whistle when he was murdered by his supposed best friend, Augustus Hunter."

Joel wasn't prone to guilt, especially for something that

he hadn't done. But when he looked into Marlie's eyes, the pinch he felt in his gut had nothing to do with his injury or hunger and everything to do with the pain that his father had caused her family.

Gus hadn't talked much about the shooting. Joel had heard more from the local gossipmongers than from his old man. According to the official story, Daniel Montague had been arrested for treason when he'd reboarded his ship after a stop in Basra, Iraq, in 1990.

They'd transferred Montague to the USS *Gilcrest*, the ship his father had commanded. Because they were old friends, Gus had personally seen to the exchange. As Gus had escorted Daniel to the brig, Montague had made a break for the railing. Gus had meant to fire only a warning shot, but in the rush of excitement one of the young MPs had jostled Gus's arm and his bullet had struck Montague in the back. Daniel's body had fallen overboard and was lost at sea.

Now, in retrospect, the story sounded pretty damned fishy. If they weren't above framing Marlie for Robert Herkle's murder, who said they weren't above inventing an entire cover story around Daniel Montague's death?

The question was, who were "*they*"?

If Marlie was correct and her father had been used as a scapegoat and then killed to keep him quiet, where did Gus fit into the scheme? Was his father part of the conspiracy?

It was an agonizing question.

And what crimes was it that the Navy was really covering up? Only concerns of national security warranted such extreme secrecy.

A sense of menace lifted the hairs on the back of his neck. Sweat warmed his scalp at the thought that his beloved Navy was corrupt. That everything he'd ever believed in and cherished was a lie. Someone in the upper echelons of the organization had committed an egregious act, and apparently they would stop at nothing to cover it up.

The realization was a punch in the gut so swift and hard, Joel exhaled a groan.

It was unfathomable that the one true place where he'd ever felt he belonged was no longer something he could trust. The Navy had provided him with discipline and the guidance he'd lacked at home. It had brought him closer to Gus after years of estrangement. But it was all a house of cards. Falling down around his ears. Shaking his faith, shattering his confidence in a system he'd pledged to defend, honor, and uphold.

Had he been a fool? An utter dupe?

He studied his hands. Hands that had killed in defense of his country. He curled his fingers into his palms, tightly squeezing them into fists.

Emotion washed over him in waves. Anger, betrayal, sadness, guilt. He closed his eyes, breathed deeply, pushing away the torrent, forcing his shoulders to relax and his fingers to loosen. Focusing the electric tide tingling over his skin into a narrow laser he could draw into his gut.

Joel opened his eyes, glanced over and caught Marlie studying him intently. "What is it?"

"You've got some soot on your cheek."

She licked her thumb with that devastatingly pink tongue, leaned across the table, and slowly rubbed the flat of her moist, soft thumb across the ridge of his cheekbone.

For some reason, this gentle contact unnerved Joel more completely than if she'd reached down and touched his crotch. What was this feeling muscling in on his psyche? He'd tried shutting it down, but the damn thing kept popping up like a jack-in-the-box, springing out at the most unexpected moments.

He was smiling, yes, frickin' smiling, because she was rubbing the dirt from his cheek with her wet thumb. He felt the smile crinkle his eyes, and a sudden warmness burned his chest just left of dead center.

She was looking into his eyes and he was looking back, unhinged as a teenager having his first sexual experience.

Oh, shit, he was in deep trouble.

They stared into each other's eyes, Marlie's hand still frozen on his cheek, still leaning across the table, hearts smoldering in the heat of their white-hot gaze. He found, in her face, a view of paradise.

He melted like chocolate in a damp palm. Her face triggered his slavish devotion. He made no sense of it. Absolutely no understanding of why it was happening. He simply knew the feeling was absolute in its tyranny.

Her eyebrows lifted in that wide-eyed eager look of hers, and then she shyly lowered her eyelashes and lifted her cheeks in an almost imperceptible smile. Then she glanced back at him once more, caressing him with her eyes. Breathlessly, she sat back down. Her thumb was gone from his face, but he'd been imprinted for life.

Joel too had forgotten to breathe.

On the surface, Marlie was cute, yes, with her round cheeks and that crooked little nose and her compact, curvy body. But as he looked at her now, in the unflattering yellow light of a Denny's fluorescent bulb, wearing his white shirt, he saw the most beautiful woman on earth.

A startlingly honest face, intelligent brown eyes, and a spirit so brave it caressed his soul. She was burning bright, nervous like someone with a high fever. Her inner beauty washed over him in a tidal wave, drowning him.

He was a convert to love. One of the faithful now. A skeptic no more.

Their waitress shuffled over and plunked down two plates in front of them, jarring him out of the aching sweetness of the moment. "Two Grand Slams."

"I'm starving." Marlie reached for the maple syrup, poured it over her pancakes, and attacked them with a soft moan of exquisite pleasure that just about made Joel come unglued.

He tackled his eggs, trying to focus on the food, but his mind was caught up with this new revelation that he had been wrong and she had been right.

Joel was not accustomed to being wrong, nor was he one for overthinking things. The way he'd always looked at the world was changing, and good or bad, it was all Marlie's doing.

After she'd polished off her breakfast, she excused herself and went to the ladies' room. He watched her go with a sigh in his heart.

The waitress led two Corpus Christi police officers to the table next to where Joel was sitting. One of the men unclipped a two-way radio from his belt and set the device on the table in front of him.

Instantly Joel went on alert.

His eggs went to sawdust in his mouth. Every muscle fiber in his body tensed. He watched the cops, but when he realized his scrutiny might draw their attention, he forced his eyes to his plate.

The two-way radio squawked. "Unit 45, come in."

The cop depressed the talk button. "Yeah, Maisy, what is it?"

Joel leaned forward, straining to hear what the dispatcher was saying. His fingers gripped his fork until his knuckles ached.

"Got an APB out on that suspect in the Herkle murder case. Name's Marlie Montague."

"Go ahead," the cop said.

The dispatcher went on to give a description of Marlie, but it was difficult to make out everything she was saying over the radio static until the end. "And her male accomplice has been identified. He's a rogue NCIS agent. An ex-Navy SEAL named Joel Hunter. Be careful out there. He's considered armed and extremely dangerous."

"Where are we going?" Marlie asked after Joel rushed her out of the Denny's. The sun had risen and the streets were starting to clog with drive-to-work traffic.

"I don't know. We need somewhere to hide until we can figure out exactly who is framing you and why, and who really killed Robert Herkle."

"And what happened to my mother." Her voice clotted with sadness. "Please don't forget my mother."

"I haven't forgotten her," Joel said. "But her disappearance is obviously part of what's going on, and I have a feeling it's all related to one of your conspiracy theories. Question is, which one? How many conspiracy theories do you have, by the way?"

Marlie tilted her head, counted on her fingers, did a little mental math. "Two hundred, give or take."

Joel whistled. "I had no idea there were that many conspiracy theories floating around."

"Hey, it's a complex world."

"Any way we can narrow them down? Throw out some of the more outlandish ones?"

"Since all this is coming to a head now, I'm thinking it's got to be a theory in one of my most recent comic books. Are you sure you want to get roped into this with me?"

Joel's eyes met hers. "I have never been more certain of anything else in my life. What they're doing to you is a gross injustice, and if I have to single-handedly overthrow the United States government to clear your name, then that's what I'll do."

Marlie felt as if the Marines had landed. Joel was throwing in his lot with her, and she was pitching a tent in his back pocket. They were a team. He'd earned her loyalty. They might have had a rocky start, but now they were sharing a foxhole in the war zone. She'd gladly take a bullet for him and die with a smile on her face. There were only two other people in the whole world to whom she was equally committed.

Her mother and Cosmo.

"First step, find a place to hole up. With the cops looking for you, we can't just check into a motel and we'll have to ditch the Durango as well." Joel idled to a stop at a traffic signal, pulling up behind a clamoring diesel truck that bore a bumper sticker advertising Corpus Christi Buccaneer Days.

Buccaneer Days was an annual spring event honoring the town's colorful past. The weekend celebration featured a flotilla parade, arts and craft fairs, food vendors, a ceremonial kidnapping of the mayor by the chamber-of-commerce-turned-buccaneers, and a huge fireworks display, among many other events. Marlie wasn't a folk festival/street fair kind of gal, but Cosmo's family organized the flotilla parade. Cosmo had been forced to pitch in every year, and he'd often tapped Marlie to keep him company.

The three or four weeks before Buccaneer Days were crazed. Hundreds of volunteers worked around the clock getting the floats ready. Off season, the floats were housed in an old dockside warehouse owned by Cosmo's parents.

Attached to the warehouse was a small apartment and during the prefestival rush, the Villereals hired a fry cook to keep the volunteers fed.

Many a night Cosmo and Marlie labored into the wee hours, discussing computer hacking and conspiracy theories, while painting or welding or nail-gunning the displays. It had been heady fun, eating greasy food, not getting enough sleep, being part of the behind-the-scenes action. The rest of the year the warehouse and adjoining apartment lay empty, waiting silently for the annual Buccaneer Days madness.

And Marlie knew where the Villereals kept the spare key.

"Make a U-turn at the next intersection," she told Joel.

"Why?"

Marlie grinned. "I've got the perfect place for us to hide out."

The warehouse was silent and musty. The floats loomed like quiet dinosaurs, waiting to be brought back to life. They squeezed past a pirate ship flying the Jolly Roger, and Joel almost hit his head on a diving board turned gangplank. They had to traverse King Neptune's water palace rising up from a fiberglass clam and slip around the bumper of the Mermaids' Cotillion. Two years ago Marlie and Cosmo had been the ones to paint the Mermaid Queen's scales with shimmering aqua paint.

Marlie sneezed against the dust and dampness seeping in from the docks.

"Don't get sick," Joel said, as if it were a choice. He was so used to taking command he thought he could tell a virus what to do. Who knew? Maybe he could. He'd certainly shaken off that grazing gunshot wound as if it were nothing more than a shaving nick.

"I'll try to keep your advice in mind."

"We need to sleep," he said. "Where's the bed?"

"Through here."

She led him into the tiny, three-hundred-square-foot apartment that consisted basically of a sink, a bed, a stove, and a bathroom. The bed bore a full-sized mattress covered with a well-worn but clean handmade quilt.

An hour later Joel sat propped up in the bed staring down at Marlie, who lay curled beside him making adorable little snoring noises that churned his insides. Her face was nestled into a pillow, her wrist curled under her chin, her warm breath feathering across his knuckles.

Here he was, in bed with the cutest woman who'd ever turned his heart topsy-turvy, and he couldn't do anything about it.

Aw, hell, it was for the best. He was just settling into his bachelorhood again after Treeni. He didn't need any new entanglements. It was too soon, and he wasn't ready to go under again.

Falling in love was so damned tricky. While he might miss the magnetic power, the celestial tug in his gut, the endorphin rush to his brain, love was always, always a complication. When you were caught in that first headlong dash of it you forgot that a shattered relationship could rip the lining right off your heart. Love, as Pat Benatar so accurately pointed out, was a battlefield, and Joel was a warrior who never ran from a skirmish.

He wasn't given to romantic conjecture. Endless mental debating was for college professors and scientists. But Marlie stirred something in him, something primal and pure that Joel had a hard time denying.

*You're supposed to be watching over her, not trying to get into her panties, Hunter.*

The feminine smell of her was on the pillow near his head. He sniffed the air, stunned by how she could cause such a hollow ache inside him, as if someone were rapping steadily, patiently against the vault of his heart.

He felt as if all action had stopped. He was waiting, frustrated, frozen, the world slack and unmoving. Silent. Disturbingly silent. And yet his pulse was thrashing, a buck in rut crashing through the forest.

Things hadn't been like this with Treeni. He'd wanted her. Oh, yeah. He had been on fire for Treeni from the moment he laid eyes on her and she for him. They'd burned and flamed and scorched and then fizzled out like two Roman candles with their fuses tied together. One giant explosion and then utter destruction.

It was different with Marlie. The chemistry was there. No doubt. But it was unique. His desire for her didn't have that same doomed incendiary quality. It was better. Deeper. Truer. More solid.

Right now, Joel wanted nothing more than to wake her up and make love to her until they both walked funny. And that was a very scary thing. Out-of-control passion he could handle, but this... this was something else entirely.

He'd had hot sex before. Lots of it. He'd been with tall women and short ones, plump ones and thin ones, blondes and brunettes and redheads. But he'd never been with one that charmed him on so many levels the way Marlie did. Her timid side fed his masculine ego.

Around her he felt like a strong protector. But just when he feared that she might be too much of a pushover for a guy like him, he would do or say something that ignited that spark in her eyes and she'd be off, giving him a hard time, standing up for herself, telling him off, engaging in the verbal sparring Joel thrived on.

He'd had her under surveillance for more than two weeks, and he'd drawn all the wrong conclusions. He'd mistaken her quietness for weakness, her lack of vanity as mousiness, her predictability as boring. But she was neither weak nor mousy nor boring.

Marlie was nothing like any other woman he'd ever known. She pushed him beyond his comfort zone in a way no one else ever had. He was the one who forced people to push their personal envelopes, not the other way around. Sure, brazen Treeni had stood up to him, but Marlie did more than that. She had him questioning his values and beliefs. Had him wondering why he'd made some of the life choices that he'd made.

Through Marlie's eyes Joel was beginning to see that his need to be strong was nothing more than an illusion. Because how could he really know when he was truly strong enough? He'd pursued courage all his life, while deep down inside he didn't feel any braver now than he had at twelve when one of his stepfathers had beaten him with a leather strap.

He found her endearing and interesting and totally adorable. He admired her compassion and her intellect and her off-the-wall wit. He respected the way she stood up for what she believed in, even if it wasn't a popular stance. Marlie possessed a noble nature and a kind heart. Her caring quality was evident in the way she advocated underdog causes. But she was more comfortable expressing her anxieties than her braver feelings.

It was almost as if she were alternating between two characters, the timid, caring hermit and the bold, calculating adventuress.

And he loved both sides of her equally.

Most of all, he loved the fact that when he was with her

they were an exciting team, balancing each other out. She kept him on his toes, and around her, he felt that he had a true sense of purpose. And his sweet Ladybug deserved far better than having his mangy-ass world dumped on her doorstep.

He brought to her the very things she'd feared. Secrets and lies and betrayal. She'd already been through so much. All her illusions about the world shattered at such a tender age. Her innocence destroyed when his father had killed hers.

And innately, Joel understood that Marlie possessed the power to hurt him far deeper than Treeni ever could.

He fought against the raging need inside him. It was vicious and demanding and made him throb for things he could not have.

Things that could cut him to the bone.

And he'd been wounded enough in this lifetime.

He had to force loving thoughts of her from his mind. He could not afford this softness. For her sake as much as his own. But as he lay beside her, his nostrils consumed with the scent of her, the doom of eternal loneliness ate at his soul.

*Feelings are for females and fools. Your softhearted tendencies are your only failing as a soldier,* Gus had told him after Iraq.

Joel winced at the truth of it. The only way to combat his weakness was to keep his concentration on what truly mattered.

Keeping her safe.

The assassin might be dead, but Joel knew with certainty the man hadn't acted alone. Someone with a lot of power wanted her dead. And he was the only thing standing between Marlie and absolute destruction.

# Chapter 15

Marlie woke confused and disoriented. Her body ached and throbbed as if she'd run a marathon in lead boots. She hurt in places she hadn't even known existed. Blinding sunlight fell through the window. She wasn't in her bed, wasn't in her room with the foiled windows.

Where was she?

Squinting, she rolled on her side and found herself eye-to-pecs with a hard-muscled masculine chest.

A shivery thrill ran through her body. She was in bed with a near-naked incredibly handsome man. She. Mousy Marlie.

*Somebody pinch me; I must be dreaming.*

She stacked her hands under her cheek and lay there watching him breathe, savoring the moment. Joel. Joel Jerome. Savior and he-man deluxe. Joel, Joel, Joel, Joel, Joel.

How had she gotten here? She meant metaphorically of course. She knew how she'd gotten here physically. Hiding out in the Villereals' warehouse had been her idea.

Her gaze trailed from his chest up to the strong column of his throat to the underside of his jaw to his face.

Rugged. Tough. Scarily good-looking. Chiseled chin. Proud nose. Sculpted cheekbones. His eyes were closed.

Marlie looked and looked and looked. Happiness bubbled inside her.

"Stop staring at me," Joel said, his eyes closed.

"I'm not staring at you."

Joel opened one eye and peered at her. "Liar."

She smiled at him.

He scowled. Apparently he was one of those people who woke up crabby.

She kept smiling.

"Are you always this happy in the morning?"

"It's not morning." She showed him her watch. "It's one o'clock in the afternoon."

He jerked to a sitting position, groaned, and immediately fell back against the pillow, one hand going to his wounded flank, the other to the back of his head where he'd been hit by Ronald McDonald the night before. "Ow. That didn't feel so hot."

"I've discovered that no sudden moves seems to be the best policy."

He smiled. "We're quite a pair, huh?"

"Hey, we survived the night. There were several times I was beginning to have my doubts that we'd make it to this point."

"Me too," he said.

Their eyes met and in that moment Marlie felt the bond between them solidify.

"I'm used to getting up at six A.M.," he grumbled.

"We didn't go to bed until long after that."

"Still, one o'clock." He shook his head and then winced. "I gotta stop doing that."

"Sometimes I don't wake up until three or four."

"In the afternoon?" He looked at her as if she were a degenerate layabout.

"Depends on my schedule. When I'm working on a tight deadline I slip into this creative fugue. I might not eat or sleep for twenty-four hours or longer. Then I crash. I slept for eighteen hours once after a long grueling session."

"Doesn't sound like a particularly healthy way to live."

"When you've got the muse by the tail, you gotta hang on."

"Weird. I've never known an intensely creative type before."

"It's a crazy life, but totally exhilarating. Probably the same kind of high you Navy SEALs get from pushing your bodies to the limits of endurance."

"Ah," he said. "A reference I can understand."

Marlie studied him. Physically, they were so different. He was one hundred percent mesomorph. Lots of lean muscle tissue, hard, sculpted. She was little Miss Endomorph. Round and soft and small-boned. But mentally they were more alike than she'd first assumed.

They believed in truth and justice and standing up for the underdog. They were both loyal and protective. And they both liked being in control, although whereas Marlie took evasive action to ensure her safety, Joel ruled the space around him with his physicality.

Maybe this relationship could work, if they lived to tell the tale.

"Stop worrying." He reached over and pressed the pad of his thumb between her eyebrows, smoothing out her frown line.

"I can't. It's my nature."

"You need a distraction."

"What kind of distraction?" she asked hopefully, eyeing his lips.

"The best kind," he answered, draping one leg over hers and pulling her closer. His deep, rumbling voice, combined with the pressure of the back of his knee against her thigh, sent an electrical charge tumbling down her spine.

"Oh?" she murmured. "And what's that?"

His eyes narrowed seductively. He looked more handsome than any man had a right to look.

He drew his thumb down the end of her nose. Their gazes met. She dared him with her eyes. Dared him to kiss her.

He leaned closer.

Marlie pursed her lips. She was burning, wanted him as she'd never, ever wanted another. The longing inside her was so strong she felt faint with it.

She turned her face up to his, waiting for the mystery, the magic to begin.

Joel pressed his mouth to hers. It was the smallest movement of his lips, yet it captured her emotions quick as kindling.

He gazed into her eyes and she peered back at him, giggly as a teenager whose boyfriend had just sneaked in through her bedroom window for the most forbidden of kisses.

The membranes of her lips throbbed, deliciously receptive and incredibly sensitive to the slightest brush of his.

Their breaths merged, a mystical embodiment of their essence, fusing the bond.

Then Joel pulled away and threw back the covers. "Daylight's burning," he said and swung his legs off the bed. "Let's roll."

What? Just like that he was going to kiss her and then break it off?

Her face burned with embarrassment. Inside, she was

as fragile as spun glass in the hands of an amateur juggler. Why had he so quickly distanced himself? Was it her? Had she done something wrong? Marlie fretted.

She searched his face, trying to find meaning there. He jerked his head away, ostensibly searching for his shoes, but deep inside she knew he was purposefully avoiding looking at her.

Why? Was he wishing that he hadn't kissed her? Was she that lousy of a kisser?

Marlie pressed two fingertips against her lips. She felt like someone left stranded on a deserted island, watching the supply ship sail away without her.

Alone. She'd never felt more alone in her life.

Her skin felt hot. She wanted to run away, but she could not. She was trapped. Trapped in a dangerous situation. Trapped with a man she barely knew and did not understand.

But she'd be damned if she was going to let him see how much his abruptness had bruised her ego. She might be scared, she might be shy, but at heart, she was a fighter.

"Where are we going?" she asked.

"To get our hands on your comic books," he said. "We have to find out who sent an assassin after you and why."

"We can't go home. I'm certain the police have my house under surveillance."

"Yeah," he said. "So where's the nearest comic book store?"

"Mel's New and Used Comics at Padre Staples Mall."

Quickly they showered and redressed each other's wounds. Marlie applied a new bandage to Joel's injury and gave him another penicillin pill from the first-aid kit. Joel took the pressure dressing off her wrist, secured the laceration with a butterfly closure, and they were off.

"Soon as we can," Joel said, "we've got to ditch the Durango. She's in bad shape. Don't want to get pulled over for having a brake light out."

"After we see Mel we can rent one."

They pulled into the mall parking lot. Marlie noticed several police cars parked in the fire lane near the main entrance. She figured they must have busted a shoplifting ring or something. It never dawned on her that the police could be there for her until they drew near Mel's.

Marlie stopped short right by the Dippin' Dots kiosk across from the comic book store. When she saw a man in a trench coat had cornered Mel at the cash register and several uniformed officers were searching the inventory, her heart thumped.

She and Joel watched as one of the officers left the store, carrying a stack of comic books. Marlie caught a glimpse of the cover, and that's when she realized they were confiscating all Mel's copies of *Angelina Avenger*.

The man in the trench coat putting the squeeze on Mel's store was Special Agent William Dobbs. Joel grabbed Marlie's elbow and dragged her to the General Nutrition Center.

"In here," he said brusquely and maneuvered her behind a shelf of herbal remedies.

If Dobbs had flown out here from Camp Pendleton, things were worse than he'd imagined. He was in deep shit without a shovel.

Just what the hell *was* in those comics?

"What are we going to do now?" Marlie whispered.

"Wait them out."

"May I help you, folks?" asked a voice from behind them.

Simultaneously, they pivoted to see a Jack LaLanne look-alike beaming at them as if they'd been delivered to the promised land and he was the Messiah. The dude was seventy if he was a day, but possessed muscles Arnold Schwarzenegger would envy.

He reached between Joel and Marlie to pluck a bottle of pills from the shelf. "This is the product you're looking for; trust me on this."

Marlie pushed her glasses up on her nose and narrowed her eyes at the bottle. "What's it do?"

The salesman winked. "Increases potency, strength, and endurance."

"So it's a high-performance drug?"

He nudged Joel with his elbow. "Oh, it's much more than that, know what I mean?"

Joel got his drift loud and clear.

Marlie took the bottle and studied the label. "Is it for men or women?"

"In a manner of speaking"—the Jack LaLanne wannabe chuckled—"it's for both."

"Well, I could certainly do with more endurance," she said and jerked a thumb at Joel. "He wore me out yesterday."

Joel lowered his head and hissed, "Marlie, shhh."

"What?" She blinked up at him.

"It's herbal Viagra."

"Oh, no." She thrust the bottle of pills back at the randy version of Jack LaLanne. "Take a good look at him. He don't need no stinkin' herbal Viagra."

Joel grinned. Okay, he'd admit it. Marlie's confidence in his virility without proof of the fact stroked his ego.

They lurked among the vitamins and dietary supplements waiting for Dobbs and company to exit Mel's comic book store. Randy Jack trailed after them trying to convince Joel and Marlie that they were one step away from nirvana and all it would take for them to achieve perfection was to slap down a lot of dead presidents for his pricey potions and powders.

Joel saw Dobbs leave the comic book store. "Call your buddy Mel," he told Marlie. "And tell him to meet us at Chili's in the food court."

She dug her cell phone from her purse, called Mel, and made the assignation. After bidding the disappointed herbal salesman good-bye, they headed for Chili's.

While they waited for Mel to appear, they ordered hamburgers. Ten minutes later, the comic book store owner appeared looking harried and harassed. He spied Marlie and ambled over.

Mel was a tall, gangly guy in his early forties with a half-assed goatee, long gray hair pulled back in a ponytail, and an Adam's apple the size of a pomegranate. He shot a suspicious look at Joel. "Who's he?"

"We can trust him."

"Well, if you're vouching for him, that's good enough for me." Mel sat down beside Marlie. "Nobody gets past your radar unless they're completely trustworthy."

Joel felt a twinge of guilt at Mel's statement. He had fooled Marlie and slipped past her radar. He'd been trained to be proud of such an accomplishment, but he was not. He felt like a traitor.

"What happened in your store?" Marlie asked.

"NCIS came in and confiscated my copies of *Angelina Avenger*," Mel said.

"NCIS? But why?"

"Dude wouldn't tell me, but he did ask all kinds of questions about you. Don't worry, I didn't tell him anything.

You know my zero cooperation policy when it comes to government agencies."

"Thank you," Marlie murmured and touched Mel's forearms in a gesture of appreciation that made Joel stone-cold jealous.

"Hey, their appearance at the store just underscores the things you write about in your comic books. Big Brother is watching."

"Did they get all my comic books?"

Mel nodded. "Didn't pay me for them either and didn't say when I'd get them back."

"I'm sorry."

"It's not your fault," Mel said. "I called a lawyer."

"Do you know who might have more copies of my comic books?"

Mel shook his head. "I already got calls from other comic book dealers in the town. They got tapped too."

Why were her comic books being pulled from store shelves by NCIS? Joel wondered. It made no sense.

"Damn. I need them."

"Don't you have copies of your own?"

Marlie shook her head. "I can't go home to get them. Cops are watching my house."

"One of your conspiracy theories was right." Mel nodded. "You've pissed off the wrong people."

"But I don't know which ones. Joel's here to help me figure it out. He's an ex-Navy SEAL."

Mel narrowed his eyes at Joel. "You're trusting a SEAL?"

"Navy did him wrong too," Marlie said.

"Ah, okay. So he's cool." Mel extended his hand across the table. "Sorry, dude, I'm just naturally suspicious of the military, after what happened to Marlie's dad and all. No hard feelings?"

"No hard feelings." Joel shook the other man's hand. Apparently by getting thrown out of the SEALs he'd passed Mel's criteria for trustworthiness. That was a sad state of affairs.

"But don't you know what's in your own comic books?" Mel asked. "Why do you need copies?"

"Of course I know, but I've been racking my brain to figure out which one could actually be true. I thought if Joel helped me look through them, he might see something I don't. I'm too close to the material."

"You know what you need," Mel said, snapping his fingers.

"I'm open for suggestions." Marlie canted her head in that cute little way of hers that grabbed Joel's gut. "What's on your mind?"

"Something to distract the cops so Mr. Special Forces here can slip into your house and get those comic books for you."

Actually, Joel thought, it wasn't a bad suggestion, but he could have done without the Mr. Special Forces crack.

"But what kind of distraction," Marlie said, "that wouldn't put me in jeopardy of getting arrested?"

"I'm thinking what Angelina did in 'Spy Queen of the Yukon,' " Mel said.

Mel and Marlie looked at each other and in unison said, "Flash mob!"

"Huh?" Joel asked.

"Never mind, dude," Mel said. "You just get inside her house. We'll handle the distraction."

"We're also going to need a different vehicle, Mel," Marlie said. "You willing to exchange your car for a Dodge Durango?"

"Hell, yeah." Mel pulled his keys from his pocket. "This is exciting."

"The Durango's a little worse for wear," Marlie said.

Mel grinned. "You've seen my car."

"Touché."

*That's just great,* Joel thought. *What was she getting him into?*

"You need a place to stay?" Mel offered. "My mom's always looking for company."

"Thanks," Marlie said. "But we're okay at the Villere-als' warehouse. We don't want to get anyone else involved in this mess unless it's absolutely necessary."

Mel nodded.

"Can I speak to you in private?" Joel inclined his head.

"Sure."

He took her elbow and led her to a secluded corner of the restaurant. "Do you think it was smart telling Mel where we're staying?"

"I've known him a long time," she said. "And Mel hates the government. He'd never rat us out."

"What if he was threatened or tortured?"

Marlie's eyes rounded. "Oh, gosh. I hadn't thought about that."

"I'm sure no one will torture Mel, but do remember to watch what you say."

"Hey, who knew? You're more paranoid than I am."

"While you and Mel set up this flash-mob thing, I've got a few recon details to handle. Meet you at the Internet café at 1500."

"Gotcha."

"Be careful, Marlie."

"You too." She went up on tiptoe and gave him a quick kiss on the lips that sent Joel's heart reeling against his rib cage as he realized it was far too late to play it safe.

\*    \*    \*

The Corpus Christi police had sent Kemp to stake out
Marlie's house. Of all the frickin' luck. He would recognize Joel on sight, which was probably why Kemp had
been selected for the detail.

Joel also knew that there had to be an NCIS agent
secreted somewhere nearby, probably inside his house,
watching Marlie's place on the surveillance camera they
had no doubt repaired. It might even be a whole team.
Dobbs wouldn't leave this mission strictly in the hands of
the locals. Hell, Dobbs might be in his house right now,
cocked back in his chair just waiting for him to show up.

Joel grinned. NCIS might be good, but the SEALs
were better.

He'd left Marlie parked inside Mel's 1979 Chevy
Impala, which looked like it hadn't been cleaned out
since 1979, on the next street over from Oleander Circle
and slipped silently through the yards of the surrounding houses. He was dressed all in black to blend in with
the gathering dusk and he'd synchronized his watch with
Marlie's and Mel's.

Five minutes until six P.M.

He blended into the shadow of a palm tree by the house
on the other side of Marlie's. His body tensed, his senses
on full alert. He waited.

At precisely six P.M. they descended.

Appearing seemingly out of nowhere, car after car
started turning onto Oleander Circle. People materialized
on the sidewalks, in the street, gathering quickly until
there were four hundred or more.

The flash mob.

Called up by mass e-mailings Mel and Marlie had sent
out from the Internet café to college students and activists
and conspiracy theorists and comic book aficionados.

And they were all carrying bowling balls and singing "Anchors Away."

Joel had exactly five minutes to get in, get the comic books, get out again, and blend in with the flash mob before they dispersed, or Dobbs would fry his ass for breakfast and Marlie would be on her own.

Down the block, Marlie hid in a hedge of red-tipped photinias. She clutched a pair of Bushnell binoculars that she'd borrowed from Mel. His flash-mob idea had been brilliant, particularly since his brother Kelvin ran a bowling ball manufacturing plant and he'd just been piling up the imperfects in storage for years. The e-mail had instructed the mob participants to stop by Kelvin's, pick up a ball, and head on over to Oleander Circle by six P.M.

Marlie pushed her glasses up onto her forehead, raised the binoculars to her eyes, and watched gleefully as more than four hundred people stood at the head of the street. They were singing at the top of their lungs. In rhythmic waves they began rolling their bowling balls down the cul-de-sac. The people at the front of the line would roll their balls and then they would peel off to the sidewalks on either side of the street and let the next group take their place.

Kemp jumped from the patrol car parked in front of her house. He looked taken aback.

Would Joel make it? Marlie's palms sweated against the metal of the Bushnell.

Neighbors popped from their houses, staring agog at what was happening to their quiet little street.

With four hundred bowling balls bearing down on him, Kemp must have realized what a bad idea getting out of the vehicle had been. But it was too late to get back into the car, and he ended up jumping onto the trunk as the balls whizzed toward him.

The door to Joel's house opened and two men came running out. Marlie recognized the lead guy as the NCIS agent from Mel's store. They quickly assessed the chaos, then the lead man motioned his partner back inside Joel's house while he drew a weapon and headed for Marlie's place.

Oh, dear! Were they going to catch Joel inside?

Marlie glanced at her watch. Three minutes after six. In two minutes the crowd would be gone, and Joel would be exposed with no human shield to cover him.

The winter twilight was deepening, making it harder to see. She propped her elbows on her knees to keep her arms steady while she scanned the remaining crowd. The cul-de-sac was a sea of bowling balls.

Where was Joel?

Everyone had finished throwing their bowling balls and were hurrying away. Gingerly, Kemp climbed down from his patrol car.

Where was Joel?

Kemp slid behind the wheel of the car and hit the lights and siren but there wasn't anywhere for him to go. He was hemmed in by four hundred bowling balls.

Where was Joel?

"Looking for me?" When he tapped her on the shoulder, Marlie startled and would have let out a shriek if she hadn't been gnawing her thumbnail.

"Come on." Joel grabbed her hand. "Keep your head low."

Marlie slung the binoculars around her neck and dropped her glasses back down on her nose. Ducking their heads, they scurried along the hedge row to the next street. Laughing and panting, they tumbled into Mel's Impala.

"Didja get the comic books?" Marlie asked as Joel put the jalopy in gear.

He lifted up the waistband of his shirt and pulled out the last six issues of *Angelina Avenger.* "That answer your question?"

"I guess you didn't have time to get me a change of clothes like I asked, huh?" Unless he had something more stuffed down his pants, an affirmative answer did not seem in the offing.

"Look in the backseat."

She turned her head and spied a sack from The Gap, where he'd bought his black outfit at the mall while she and Mel had been sending out the flash-mob notifications.

Several police cars sped by them on the opposite side of the road, headed in the direction of her house.

"You bought me something at the mall?"

Joel grinned.

"That's so sweet."

Marlie dragged the sack into the front seat with her and dug past the clothes Joel had changed out of in the mall men's room. At the bottom, she found a gauzy, romantic feminine dress. It was a floral print of forest green and pink.

Her heart punched strangely against her chest as she removed it from the sack. Last night, he'd asked her what color she would wear if she couldn't wear black or white and she'd said forest green and then he'd told her she looked like a "pink" to him. Not only had he remembered the silly conversation, but he'd used the knowledge to buy this incredible dress that was a combination of them both.

She didn't know what to say. No man had ever bought her a dress before.

"Do you like it?" He sounded anxious, eager for her

approval. His nervousness was as touching as the gift. "If you don't like it, I'll take it back, get you another."

"Joel." She breathed.

Dazzled, she raised her head. She couldn't have been more moved if he'd given her diamonds or rubies.

"You needed something clean to wear. Is it too fancy? It's too fancy." He answered his own question. "I knew I should have gotten you jeans and a T-shirt."

"No, no." She blinked against the mist of happy tears pushing against her eyelids. "It's perfect."

He was at his most alluring: dark eyes filled with anticipation, his mouth quirked up at one corner, warm, inviting, sexy.

And she was at her most suggestible. In a flash of sudden knowledge that almost knocked the breath from her body, she recognized she was in love with him.

Deeply and irrevocably in love.

She loved his masculinity, his cleverness, his intricacy. She loved his bravery and his code of honor and his loyalty. She considered what he was revealing about his feelings by giving her this dress. She touched the mother-of-pearl buttons on the dress. They glimmered in the dome light he'd switched on when she'd reached for the sack. The buttons were so delicate. The dress so utterly feminine. Was he saying that he saw something special in her? Something no one else had ever seen?

Wings of panic fluttered against her rib cage. The new understanding that she'd fallen in love with him altered her reality. She wanted to make love to him.

Now and for always.

But how had this come about? She didn't believe in love. No, that wasn't true. She believed in it all right, had seen the evidence of it resonate throughout her parents' marriage. And she had seen the loss of that love almost destroy her mother.

She was scared, terrified, that this glimmer of happiness would evaporate if she studied it too hard. How could she trust in this tenuous feeling? She barely knew him. She felt as if she barely knew herself.

Confusion wrapped her in its grasp and the most she could manage was a simple "Thank you."

Joel said nothing, just sat there watching her with the engine running.

She didn't expect him to love her back. It was too much to hope for. But the dark expression in his eyes told her that he wanted her. Badly. That was easy to read. His eyes roved over her body and his jaw tightened.

Could sex be enough?

She swallowed hard, enveloped by unexpected melancholia. Marlie shook her head, mentally warding off the sadness. She wanted him. She would take whatever she could get. If sex was all he had to offer, she'd convince herself that it was enough.

# Chapter 16

Twenty minutes later Joel and Marlie were back at the float warehouse on the opposite side of town.

"Time to get down to business." Joel extended three of the comic books out to Marlie and kept three for himself.

"Do you think I could change first?" Marlie held the dress to her chest. "I'm sick of wearing these clothes."

"Sure."

"I'll be right back," she said and hurried into the apartment to change while Joel climbed up on the Jean Laffite float and walked out to sit on the gangplank.

Marlie took a quick shower in the apartment's tiny cubicle of a bathroom, toweled herself dry, and slipped on the dress Joel had bought for her. There was no mirror so she couldn't see how she looked. Which was just as well. She had no makeup with her anyway.

Lightly, she fingered the floaty material of the dress. She hadn't worn such a frilly garment in a long time and she would never have chosen it for herself. But she loved it and not simply because Joel had picked it out. The pairing of colors, although unusual, worked. In the dress she felt like a tulip in springtime, like a ripe, desirable woman.

It was fitted to her curves but not too snugly, and the V-neckline showed off just the right amount of cleavage.

Sexy but not blatant.

She wondered how Joel had known her size. Had he been with so many women that he just had an instinct for knowing what a size 12 felt like?

Oh, dear, he was so much more experienced than she. How could she hope to compete with all the other women that had come before her? How could she hope to measure up to someone as wild as his ex-wife?

*Maybe he's had enough of wild,* Angelina said. *Maybe he just wants you.*

And that's when Marlie knew she was going to seduce him.

The problem was, she wasn't exactly sure how to go about it.

*One step at a time.*

She brushed her hair and removed her glasses and set them on the shelf above the sink. She looked down at her sneakers and realized she had no shoes to wear with this gorgeous dress. Better to go barefooted than clomp around in unglamorous sneakers.

Resolutely, she kicked off her shoes, took a deep breath, and almost ran into the bathroom door as she turned to go back into the warehouse.

Slow down, she warned herself; maneuvering without either her glasses or her shoes on was going to take some extra effort.

Joel didn't hear her approach. He was deeply engrossed in the comic book, sitting on the gangplank with one leg bent at the knee and the other dangling off the board. She paused a moment to admire him in the dim glow of the overhead lighting.

Even in studious repose, the man exuded a raw animal sexuality that took hold of Marlie and wouldn't let go. He scared her a bit.

Maybe that was the very reason she wanted him so much. He brought life and color and excitement into her drab, colorless world.

She ran her hands along the dress, touching the soft, cheery material. How much she wanted him!

And how afraid she was to go for what she wanted.

Tentatively, she licked her lips and then climbed up onto the float.

She heard the sound of something slithering to the floor, looked up, and saw the comic books falling from Joel's hand and hitting the ground one by one as she toed the gangplank toward him.

"Jesus, Marlie."

Startled, her hand flew to her throat. What? What had she done wrong?

"You look so damned *hot*."

The gleam in his eyes sent a flush of pride pumping through her body. He thought she was hot. The atmosphere couldn't have been any tenser if she'd been a palsy victim juggling nitroglycerin.

Okay, she was just going to do it.

Marlie took a deep breath, looked Joel straight in the eyes and gave him the sultriest look she could muster, even though her heart was hammering so loudly she feared he could hear it.

He was so damned handsome, the embodiment of the fantasy heroes she'd read about and dreamed of but never believed she'd find in real life. Making this first move was both terrifying and empowering. What if he rejected her? But what if he didn't?

She raised her chin. She might not have much experience at seducing men, but she was going to do her best to try to turn him on. She winked and slowly ran her tongue over her lips and made soft enjoyment noises as if she were licking a dollop of Häagen-Dazs triple-chocolate fudge from her mouth.

He grinned.

She raised her hem, coyly giving him a shot of her upper thigh.

He whistled and applauded like she was a showgirl at a topless Vegas review.

How embarrassing.

How nerve-racking.

How absolutely *exhilarating.*

An eyebrow arched up on his forehead and Joel regarded her with a wicked stare.

Her stomach plummeted and she nearly lost her nerve. But the need to feel him inside her body stiffened her spine. She had to have him. If only for one night.

He made a come-to-me motion with his fingers.

Bumping her hips the way she did when she danced alone at home, she inched closer.

The springboard rebounded against her weight, scaring her. "Uh-oh," she whispered.

"I'm here." He reached out his hand.

She took it and carefully eased herself down beside him.

They looked at each other.

Marlie smiled and tentatively leaned in to kiss him. The gangplank wobbled more.

"Um, I thought it might be fun to seduce you out here, but I've changed my mind."

"About seducing me?"

"No, no." She shook her head. "About doing it on the gangplank."

"Nervous?"

"Yeah."

"Excited?"

"Yeah."

"That's a good combo. Don't tell me you've never done the gangplank boogie with anyone before."

She knew he was just teasing, but the answer was, hell, no. She'd never done it much of anywhere. Technically, she didn't qualify as a virgin. She'd had a couple of partners. Neither long-term romances, and she'd never had an orgasm with either one of them.

And that's how she feared it was going to be with Joel.

It turned out she worried for nothing.

Gently, he laid her across the gangplank, kissing her with the magical embodiment of him. Strong, confident, decisive. He boldly explored her mouth with his tongue and she felt a primal comfort that bound her to him, strengthening her tentative trust and cementing their pair bonding.

Their radiant energy fused. She wrapped her left arm around his neck, pulling him down closer to her lips vibrating with receptiveness.

He pulled back, chuckling.

"What?" She blinked.

"You're humming."

"Was I?"

"Yeah."

She wrinkled her forehead. "Was I really?"

"Uh-huh."

"What was I humming?"

His grin covered half his face. "I think it was 'Holding Out for a Hero.'"

Marlie felt a blush burn from her scalp all the way to

her toenails. "Oh, gosh, I'm so embarrassed. I had no idea I was humming that song."

"It's okay," he said. "I feel like I've been holding out for a hero too."

Gently he unbuttoned her dress. Marlie propped herself up on her elbows to watch him. Uncertainty swept over her again and she scooted to the edge of the gangplank, ready to drop off.

But Joel rested his open hand against her right knee and ran his palm up her thigh, fingers drumming as if playing her leg like a musical instrument. With his other hand, he tilted her chin up and brought his mouth down on hers for another searching kiss.

She melted into him.

Enveloped in each other, pasted together by contact at the shoulder, hand, leg, hip, and chest, Joel and Marlie sealed their destiny and closed their fate with the stoppers of their mouths. She wrapped her legs around his waist, her heels bumping into his muscular hamstrings. It felt as if their very cells were entwined. They were oblivious to everything on earth beyond themselves and this moment.

They had fallen down the well of each other, absorbed in each other's very beings. Joel's deep inner vitality and rich, amazing restlessness for life filled Marlie with rapture. It rolled off every inch of her in glorious waves. He evoked in her an immeasurable desire, a thirst so vast all the oceans of the world evaporated in a single drop of it.

How was this possible? How could she have become so deliriously intoxicated with him so quickly?

Her thrill terrified her.

The gangplank vibrated between them; one wrong move and they could fall off. Their entire time together had been like this. A daring adventure, and now they were embarking on a dangerous affair.

At last Marlie understood why she'd hidden behind Angelina's cartoon facade all these years. Through Angelina, she could gamble without risks. Feel without feeling.

But now all that had been stripped away. She was naked. Exposed.

It felt glorious.

She was being bold and sassy all on her own. She was feeling, touching, tasting, hearing, and seeing everything with her own five senses. Nothing was blunted, nothing distant or muted, nothing viewed through the filter of her alter ego's eyes.

Alive.

She was finally totally and completely alive.

"You've been deprived," Joel said, smoothly caressing the delicate skin under her arm with a tickle touch so light she couldn't believe it was his big masculine fingers doing the stroking, sensing somehow what she was thinking. "I can see it in your eyes."

She was barely aware of what he was doing, because she was so busy staring into his face, but he was unhooking her buttons one by one. She finally noticed what he was up to when the cool air kissed her heated skin.

It was too much for her to handle. She shrank back, retreated, called Angelina in to take over and finish the deed.

"Stop it," Joel growled.

"Stop what?"

"Stop holding back. Let yourself go."

"I...I can't."

"Yes, you can."

"I don't know how."

"Just relax, sweetheart." Joel dipped his head, lowered

his lips to her chin, and nibbled. She shivered at the delicious sensation radiating through her nerve endings.

"I've always had bad luck with men," she said, dragging out the words.

"Don't mean to brag, Ladybug," he nestled his mouth next to her ear and whispered, "but your luck's just turned."

"It's not bragging if you can live up to it," Marlie said smartly. "Can you deliver on the hype?"

That had been a stupid, cocky thing to say. Joel had thought he was being charming. He realized now he had probably sounded like a jerk. His arrogance fled, and he was left thinking what a bad idea it had been to get this whole thing started on top of a board hanging off a pirate ship float. What had they been thinking?

*You weren't thinking.*

"You're supposed to say, 'Ladybug, "Deliver" is my middle name.'" She winked at him.

He wanted to tease back, but suddenly his tongue was stuck to the roof of his mouth. He wasn't sure how to proceed. He had to be careful. Should he call it off? Back down? Turn away from the sweetest thing that had ever happened to him?

But he wanted her so badly. More than he'd ever wanted any woman.

He reached out to stroke her, his fingers dangling just above her exquisite bosom. Her body heat radiated up through the air and into him, invading his bloodstream, filling his heart.

He couldn't resist her. Even when he knew it was a bad idea. He was helpless. He stroked her hair. God, she had such beautiful hair, long and dark and wavy. Her cheek. Her chin. Her lips.

Lightly, he trailed his fingertips over her skin.

He brushed the delicate bones of her jaw, traced a powdery blue vein down her throat to her breast.

What a woman!

But she had no idea what she was getting into. She'd finally placed her trust in him when he'd been lying to her. He couldn't make love to her. Not until he came clean about who he really was.

"Marlie," he said, "we have to talk."

"Not now," she murmured. She took his hand and kissed his fingers and then slowly took his thumb into her mouth.

Joel groaned. "You don't know what you're getting into."

"I don't care."

"Listen...," he said, but he could not talk, could not think with her wicked little tongue licking around and around his thumb. She might look angelic, but the woman was deceptively devilish. "I'm not who you think I am."

"Shhh, Joel. I know you."

*What?* he thought fuzzily, his brain bathed in testosterone. Did she really know who he was? Had she known all along he was J. J. Hunter?

"Marlie."

She was staring up at him with such an expression of awe on her face—as if he'd created the galaxy just for her. How had he gotten so lucky? What had he done that was so right?

"Joel," she said, "you have no idea how hard this is for me to say."

"I'm listening. It's okay."

"I'm used to hiding out. For me to step forward and ask you to make love to me is a big deal. I have no idea when

I'll have a normal life again. Or if I'll ever see my mother again. We have no idea where to look for her. Please, I need this respite. I need to escape. Just for a little while. Please, make love to me."

How could he refuse that heartfelt request? Especially when there was nothing else on the face of the earth that he wanted more than to love her?

"Let's get away from this damn gangplank," he said.

He took her hand and led her off the board. When they reached the main part of the float, he scooped her into his arms and carried her to the apartment.

She was so feminine. Her buttocks, waist, and breasts all nicely fleshed and curvy.

He laid her on the bed, stripped off both their clothes, hurriedly palmed a condom from his wallet, and then got in beside her. They'd been dancing around this moment from the first time their eyes had met across the broken glass in his kitchen.

Marlie was underneath him. Joel had all his weight on his elbows and was peering down at her as if staring at the Grand Canyon for the first time.

Flesh against flesh. Skin on skin. Their hearts pounded so loudly in the same rhythm they both could hear it.

The sensation was so vast, so indescribable, that Joel felt awkward all over again. He'd never experienced anything like it, wasn't sure how to deal with his feelings or what they meant in the long run.

He tried to pull back, to reevaluate what was happening, but Marlie pushed her pelvis against him and made pleading noises.

"Easy, Ladybug." He was so hard, so turned on, and it had been so long since he'd had sex that Joel feared he would come way too soon and ruin it for her.

She pressed her lips into his throat, nibbled, and moaned softly. She ran her hands up the back of his neck, combing her fingers through his hair.

It felt so frickin' good.

He tucked the condom under her pillow and then ran his hands over her breasts, cupping them in his palms.

"I want to please you," he said, feeling desperate and hating his desperation, but there he was. He'd lost all control of the situation, and she was in full charge whether she knew it or not.

"Just being with you pleases me."

"Tell me, what do you like? How can I make it good for you?"

Her eyes widened. "I don't know."

"You don't know?"

"I've never...no one's ever pleased me."

"You're a virgin?"

"No," she said and a lone tear pearled in the corner of her eye. "But I wish I were. I wish I'd saved myself for you. I just never thought you existed. I never thought I would ever feel this way. My mother told me—" She broke off.

He cuddled her close, threaded his fingers through her hair. "It's okay. We'll figure it out together."

"Just don't stop kissing me," she said and pulled his head down to her lips.

She tasted so good. Hot and spicy and salty. Joel kissed her long and deep and hard. The kiss was fat and rich and full of promises. He was caught in an expense of time, in an expanse of spirit, and they melded. One into the other.

He didn't want to feel it. It had sneaked up on him swift and sure, and in that instant when their lips joined and their eyes connected and their bodies made head-to-toe contact, Joel Jerome Hunter gave Marlie Montague his heart.

Fully. One hundred percent. Forever.


A magic carpet ride. That's what this was. A magic carpet ride to the stars.

"Fly Me to the Moon."

This was the dream she'd never dared to dream. It happened just as her mother had said it would.

*Mom? Where are you? I wish I knew where you were so I could tell you about Joel.*

"Marlie?" Joel had been kissing her neck, but he stopped.

"Uh-huh?" She kept her eyes closed, trying to will her thoughts off her mother and back into the moment, but it wasn't working.

"What's wrong?"

She shook her head.

"Open your eyes and look at me."

Slowly, she did as he asked and found his gray-green-blue eyes brimming with compassion.

"Talk to me."

"I don't want to talk. I want you to make love to me."

"What were you thinking about?"

She swallowed, paused. "My mother."

He pressed his lips together and caressed her cheek with the crook of his finger. "I'm sorry. I knew this wasn't a good idea."

Joel moved to slide off her, but she grabbed him around the waist with her legs and held him in place.

"Please, don't go. I need this. I need you."

He nodded, understanding in his eyes. "We'll find your mother, Marlie. I promise you. I can't wait to meet her."

"She'll be so excited to meet you too." The tender

expression on his face made her feel better immediately. He smiled at her and she smiled back.

She wanted to get things back on track with Joel, wanted to recapture the mood. She latched her legs tightly around him, careful to avoid the area where he'd been grazed by the bullet, and boldly reached down to touch his inner thigh.

Her hand moved beyond, cupping him. He was so hot and heavy, smooth and hard and excitingly male. Her breathing quickened, but his did not.

It should have.

She opened her eyes and found him staring down at her with a look on his face that unraveled her completely. He was still concerned about her.

Darn it. She didn't want him to worry, didn't want to take away from this moment, from their first time together. She wrapped her fingers around his shaft and whispered, "Wow, wow."

"Oh, babe, you have no idea how you're undoing me."

And then she realized the concern on his face hadn't been just for her, but for him too.

He kissed her again, gently, sweetly.

He was opening up to her. Not with just his body, but with his mind and soul as well. She could feel it in the way his fingers trembled as he caressed her face. Opening up to her in a way he'd never opened up to anyone.

He was risking his heart.

She felt honored beyond words. She let go of her last remaining shreds of doubt, let go and gave him every part of her. Including her trust.

Especially her trust.

He'd proved he was worthy of her loyalty. She would stick with him through thick and thin. No matter what.

Finally she understood what her mother had been trying to tell her all these years.

In his arms, she had found what she thought would never be hers.

A soul mate.

Joel's lips absorbed her essence.

With her legs wrapped around his waist and her hands threaded through his hair, with her body cradled against his, he was having difficulty even recalling where they were, never mind remembering why he'd hesitated.

"I want you, Joel," she whispered, took his hand, and guided it between her legs. "Now. Inside me."

Her directive couldn't have been clearer if she'd printed up frilly pink cards that said "You are invited to a party." Joel wasn't about to refuse the call. She was so hungry. Her appetite fueled his own. He touched her down there, lightly at first, then more deeply, increasing their intimacy. She was supple and silky and unreservedly female. Not to mention that she was hot and dripping wet.

For him.

She was giving herself over, surrendering her concerns, letting down her guard.

There was a reason this wasn't completely right. There was something he'd forgotten to do. It was lurking back there in his brain, fuzzily beyond the reach of his intense fog of pleasure. But his mind wouldn't work, wouldn't focus. He couldn't concentrate on anything except Marlie and the mind-blowingly erotic sounds of ecstasy she was making. He was working her to a fever pitch, pushing her beyond all boundaries of both their endurance.

"Inside me!" she commanded. "Now!"

He couldn't stand it any longer. He was just about

to plunge himself into her ripe, willing body when he remembered the condom he'd tucked under her pillow.

"Wait, wait," he said, rolling off her.

"No," she cried, "you can't stop now."

He shoved his hand under the pillow, came up with the condom, and held it up for her to see.

"Oh," she breathed. "Oh, God, I didn't even think about protection."

"It's okay," he said. "I gotcha covered."

"I could have... we could have..."

"But we didn't," he said, putting an end to her speculation.

She had a tendency to spiral into conjecture, and now was not the time to let her wander loosely down that path. He fumbled with the package but she was too impatient. She surprised him by snatching the condom from his hand, pushing him back against the mattress, and straddling his torso.

Would the woman ever cease to amaze him? Just when he thought he had her figured out, she'd dumbfound him again.

She ripped open the package with her teeth and with a sigh of pure glee she rolled the condom into place. Then she shifted her body forward and slid down on him, as wet as a seal.

He hissed in his breath. Nothing had ever felt so damned good as her hotness sheathed around his penis. She dangled her breasts in his face and he took one nipple in his mouth, suckled her hard.

"Joel," she moaned, wriggling and writhing on top of him. "Joel."

Everything stopped for him as he watched her moving above him. The sight of her long dark hair tumbling loosely about her shoulders, her skin eggshell-luster like palest bone china, full grapefruit breasts stretched taut, her lips pursed, rapture glowing in her eyes. The sweet perfume of her body made him dizzy, and he felt something far beyond awe.

"Oh, oh, oh," she cried.

She was about to come; he could see it in her face as her features pinched.

And he wasn't far behind her.

"Marlie," he gasped.

They moved in unison. She in a circular motion, he a pump, bucking underneath her.

Together, they cried out. His essence spilled out of him. Marlie fell forward, clinging to him as she broke apart. He flew with her. In pieces. As his world exploded in a rain of light and sensation and sound.

He lay there trembling, his body slick with sweat.

She raised her head and looked down at him, her eyes shimmering with trust.

With *trust*.

Aw, hell.

An infusion of shame replaced his earlier joy. Now he remembered what he'd forgotten to do. He'd thought it was just the condom, but he was wrong.

He'd forgotten to tell her who he really was and that he'd been sent to spy on her for the U.S. Navy.

Essentially, he was her enemy. There's no way this could last, Joel thought. No way at all.

# Chapter 17

Cosmo wasn't having any luck decoding Admiral Delaney's personal journal. Granted, he hadn't had much time to spend on it. The job had been slammin' hard today, and he was just getting around to his snail mail that the mailroom runner had dropped off several hours earlier. The last two nights with Treeni had been incredible. He'd had the most stupendous sex of his life, and he couldn't stop thinking about her.

He'd promised himself he'd stay up all night working on the project for Treeni. He had to be careful using the office computer system. He knew his every keystroke was being monitored. It was the ONI after all. But he also knew how to obstruct their spyware without his block being detected. Still, it was risky. You never knew who could be watching or how.

Trying to multitask, Cosmo opened his mail with one hand, ate a tuna-fish sandwich on rye with the other, and kept his eyes occupied with the code on his computer screen. Chet Delaney might be damn good at creating his codes, but Cosmo Villereal was even better at breaking them.

He picked up an express mail envelope from the stack

and didn't even look at the address as he set his sandwich down and peeled the envelope open.

A baggy with tire valve stem caps and pieces of broken twigs fell out.

It was the package Marlie had called him about. And he'd totally forgotten about it until now. Feeling like the worst friend on earth, he pushed aside Delaney's code and turned his attention to Marlie's evidence.

He'd need help from the guys in the evidence lab, but Cosmo hadn't worked at ONI long enough to build up favors owed so he could pull strings. But he knew who could. Cosmo picked up the phone and called Treeni.

"Cos," she purred.

It wasn't his imagination. She was glad to hear from him. His spirits soared again.

"You get something?"

"Not yet, but I'm hard at work on it," he said. "Treeni, I need a serious favor."

"All you have to do is ask."

Was she buttering him up because she was desperate for him to unearth the information on her old man, or did she really mean it? Cosmo supposed it didn't matter. Right now what mattered was getting help for Marlie.

He told Treeni what he needed. She told him that she would contact the evidence lab and tell them the prints on the valve stem caps were for her. He thanked her, hung up, and carted the baggy to the evidence lab.

"I should have something for Treeni soon," the lab tech said.

Cosmo nodded.

"So you're her latest conquest." The guy grinned.

"I don't know what you mean by that," Cosmo said stiffly.

The tech shrugged and gave him a look that said, *You'll figure it out soon enough, buddy.*

He didn't care for the man's innuendo and would have told him so if he didn't need his help. Cosmo went back to his desk; propping his feet up on the top, he maximized the screen with Delaney's code on it.

Suddenly the pattern leaped out at him. Of course! Why hadn't he seen it before? It was a convoluted substitution for a classic code.

Hurriedly, Cosmo began to decode Admiral Delaney's entries. With any luck, tonight he would have valuable information to share with both of the important women in his life.

At two o'clock in the morning, Joel and Marlie sat up in bed eating canned peaches they'd found in the cupboard, her comic books strewn across the quilt in front of them. They'd both read the last six issues of Angelina Avenger's adventures all the way through five times each, and they'd come up with nothing.

"There's nothing in any of these comic books that is even remotely related to the Navy," Joel grumbled. He thumbed through them again. "This one's about Atlantis, and in this one Angelina uncovers a conspiracy by a pharmaceutical company putting additives that cause cancer into their vitamins so they could sell more chemotherapy drugs."

Marlie nodded and wiped a drop of peach juice from her chin with the back of her hand. "I thought it was just me. I kept racking my brain trying to figure out which one of these comic book theories could be true, but honestly, they're all pretty far-fetched. I was hoping your fresh, objective eyes would see something that I missed."

Not so objective, he thought, and wondered how in the world he was going to break the news to her about his identity. He should have done it before they'd ever made love, but he hadn't, and now he couldn't think of a way to begin.

*Don't be a coward, Hunter, just do it.*

Not yet. She looked so happy.

"If the clues are there, I'm not seeing it," he said, instead of saying what was really on his mind. "What about your next comic book that's due to hit the stands? What's it about?"

"Zombies."

Joel contemplated her. He knew she hated the word "cute" in reference to herself, but she was so darned well impossibly cute, with her knees drawn up to her chest and her hair mussed, sucking on the back of a plastic spoon. She was cute like the black-and-red ladybugs he'd collected off his mother's rosebushes as a kid and kept in a jar with holes poked in the lid so they could breathe. That is, until Gus made fun of him for collecting "sissy" bugs. Joel had let them go, watching them fly away from him in the summer heat.

"Zombies?"

She shrugged, took the plastic spoon out of her mouth, and stuck it in the empty peach can on the windowsill above the bed. "After twenty-eight comic books, the ideas start running a little thin."

"Do you ever think about doing anything else? Something a little less paranoid and isolating?"

"No." She blinked behind her black-framed glasses, going all studious at his question.

"How did you get into the comic book business in the first place?"

"I always loved to draw. Created Angelina when I was eleven or twelve. This may sound weird, but I channeled her. She came through me, but she wasn't part of me. Whenever I have a problem, she sort of takes over and solves everything for me."

"Interesting."

"Weird, you mean."

"No, it's interesting how you've split your personality into two distinct sections. You claim the timid you, but not the bold you. Why's that?"

"I'm not bold. That's Angelina."

Joel shook his head. She actually saw her cartoon character as separate from herself.

"Did Angelina appear to you before or after your father died?"

"After."

"Do you think you created Angelina as a wish fulfillment, as a way to avenge your father's death? You were a kid, powerless to do anything, so you invented this fearless persona who would dare anything for justice."

"Possibly."

"Ever considered that you might outgrow her?"

Marlie looked horrified. "No."

"Just a thought. What's going to happen to Angelina when you don't need her anymore?"

"I'll always need her."

Joel arched an eyebrow.

"What?" Marlie demanded.

"You've changed a lot over the last couple of days."

"That still doesn't mean I have to give up Angelina."

"It's hard letting go of a security blanket."

"She's not a security blanket." Marlie glared at him, clearly agitated.

Time to back off. Joel raised his palms. "You're right. Let's get back to the conspiracy theories and government cover-ups. Let's assume for a minute that we've gone down the wrong track and none of this has anything to do with your comic books."

"Okay."

"Who else might want you dead?"

"Shrimp boat operators?"

Joel chuckled. "I doubt the brotherhood of shrimpers put a contract out on you for your involvement in a protest rally."

"Maybe the assassin wasn't a hired hit man at all, just some wacko who didn't like my politics," Marlie suggested.

"Then why are they trying to frame you for Robert Herkle's murder?"

"Maybe they're not trying to frame me. Maybe that's just where the evidence is pointing and they're simply doing their jobs."

"What about your mother? How does she fit into all this?"

Marlie chewed her bottom lip. "I don't know."

"Maybe it's got something to do with your mother."

"But what?"

He shook his head.

"This is getting us nowhere." Marlie shoved the comic books to the floor.

"Maybe it's related to what happened to your father fifteen years ago."

"There were a lot of threats against Mom and me back then. That's why we moved to Corpus from Maryland. To escape the fallout from the Navy's propaganda. People used to come up to my mother in the grocery store and tell her my father got what he deserved." Marlie's voice cracked. "They believed the lies the Navy put out about him."

"And you have no idea what it was that your father had uncovered? What corruption or scandal he was about to blow the whistle on?"

"I don't know. He wouldn't tell Mom for her own safety, and I was a kid."

"Thing is, why has this resurfaced now? Who was around fifteen years ago that's still around today?"

Marlie's face darkened. "That bastard Gus Hunter, for one."

Joel didn't know what to say to that, so he just drew her into his arms. "We'll keep working on it."

"Do you have any old contacts in the SEALs? Someone you can trust to help us?" She looked into his face. "See what they can find out?"

*This is the time to come clean, buddy. Tell her the truth.* But he didn't know how to begin.

Instead, he said, "I could make some calls. We'll find your mom, I promise."

"Thank you." She kissed him.

Her lips, still sweet with peach juice, were the most delicious things he'd ever tasted.

Marlie whispered his name, again and again. His scent filled her head, became her world. His mouth was soft and warm, his tongue teasing her slowly, sensuously.

He held her gaze as his body filled hers. He moved slowly, deliberately taking his time, torturing her with his leisurely strokes.

"Joel," she whimpered. "More."

But he refused to let her call the shots this time. Each time she tried to move with him, to spur him onward, to push him more deeply inside her, he resisted. Pulling away, a teasing smile on his face.

"You're wicked," she gasped. "So wicked."

"Ladybug, you have no idea."

"You're driving me crazy."

"I know. I want you crazy out of control for me the way I am for you."

Fine then. If he wanted to be in the driver's seat, she would let him. She lay back and opened herself up to him fully, letting her legs splay open.

"That's it," he murmured. The entire time he kept moving slowly. Exasperatingly, heart-stoppingly, scrumptiously slow.

If she tried to do anything to speed him up, he stopped moving. It was only when she let go that he gave her what she was aching for.

And she allowed him full control. Trusting him.

It felt glorious to let herself go. To release her fears. To trust this man.

She watched his face as she surrendered herself to him completely. And as her climax swelled, as it grew and rolled through her in surge after infinite superb surge, unadulterated delight and extreme gratification flashed in his eyes.

"Take me with you," he said. "Let's go together."

His heartfelt request was enough to shove her over the lip of another orgasm. She hung on to him, plunged with him, strapped her legs around him, and drove him into her. She clung to Joel, her lifeline, her support.

She trusted him as she'd never ever trusted another. She trusted him with her secrets. She trusted him with her life. But most of all, she trusted him within the very depths of her soul.

He'd stamped himself into her heart. She belonged to him now and there was no turning back.

Near dawn, Cosmo had translated all the admiral's journal entries. He reread what was written there and his blood ran cold. All these years of listening to Marlie and her wild conspiracy theories and she'd been right.

But what did this new knowledge mean for him and Treeni?

As Cosmo stared at the screen, not knowing what to do next, the phone on his desk rang. Mind whirling with the startling information, he answered it.

"Villereal, this is Willis from the evidence lab."

"Yeah?"

"Got the ID back on your prints."

"Who do they belong to?"

"NCIS agent by the name of Joel Hunter. Used to be a Navy SEAL."

"Thanks," Cosmo said and hung up the phone. Treeni's ex-husband and Marlie's new neighbor were one and the same. And he'd flattened Marlie's tires. No coincidence there.

He looked at the screen again. Thought of Marlie and Treeni. He was torn in two opposing directions. Not sure what he should do next. Did he choose love? Or loyalty?

Marlie was his best friend.

But Treeni was his new lover.

Cosmo closed his eyes, took a deep breath, and in the end did the only thing his conscience would let him do. He picked up the phone and made the call that would irrevocably alter his life forever.

The ringing of her cell phone tugged Marlie from a deep, dreamless sleep. She tried to ignore it. She was too happy with Joel spooned up against her. She didn't want to move, did not want to disturb her bliss.

The phone rang again.

Joel didn't move. He must be exhausted, poor man. Marlie grinned to herself. She'd worn him out.

The phone kept on.

What if it was her mother?

The thought spurred her. Careful not to wake Joel, she inched out from under his arm, which was thrown across her waist, and eased her feet to the floor. She slipped on a comic book and almost fell, but managed to brace herself against the counter.

Her purse was on the floor by the refrigerator. She snatched it up, dug out her phone, praying that if it was her mother she wouldn't hang up before she answered. Without bothering to waste time looking at the caller ID display, she flipped the phone open and murmured, "Mom?"

"Marlie?"

At the sound of Cosmo's voice disappointment shot through her, but interest quickly replaced the disappointment.

"Cosmo, hi."

"Mar, I'm so glad you answered."

"Did you get my package?"

"Yes."

"Were you able to get fingerprints off it?"

"I was." There was something more he wasn't telling her; she could hear it in his voice.

"Do you know who flattened my tires?"

"I do."

"Cosmo, what's the matter? You sound strange."

"I have bad news."

She raised a hand to her throat. Oh, no. "Yes?"

"The prints belong to an NCIS agent."

"An NCIS agent is trying to kill me?"

"No, he was assigned to spy on you."

Well, that explained the wiretap on her phone. "Who is this guy?"

"He's a former Navy SEAL."

The hairs on her arms lifted. She didn't want to ask, but she had to know. "What's his name?"

Cosmo heaved in a deep breath. "Joel Jerome Hunter. He's Gus Hunter's son."

Marlie couldn't have been more stunned if someone had told her she was sitting on a ticking time bomb. She swung her eyes to Joel's sleeping form.

Numbness and confusion, thick and significant, enveloped her. She felt at once nothing and everything. A million tiny teeth of shame, regret, and sorrow bit her, sharp and relentless. Her heart scalded, her stomach turned inside out.

*J. J. Hunter?*

So it was him. The boy she had once loved. Marlie hiccuped in a shaky breath.

"Mar? You okay?"

"Why did they send him to spy on me?" she asked, a strange coldness settling deep in her bones.

But Cosmo didn't answer because the line had gone dead.

Treeni stood in front of Cosmo's desk, her duty weapon clutched in her hand. She pointed it straight at his heart. "Hang up the phone."

Stunned, Cosmo broke his connection with Marlie.

"Who were you talking to?" Treeni demanded as Cosmo raised his hands in the air and kept his eyes trained on the gun. He knew Treeni was an expert markswoman. If she wanted to shoot him, then he was dead.

"My friend, Marlie Montague."

"Dammit, Cosmo," she said through gritted teeth, "I thought I could trust you." She racked the Glock.

Sweat popped out on his forehead and a hard bullet of fear lodged in his throat. "Wait, wait, it's not what you think."

She narrowed her eyes. God, she was both gorgeous and deadly. In fact, her willingness to do whatever needed to be done, no matter what the consequences, was an incredible turn-on.

"I translated your father's journal. You're not going to believe what I found out."

"I already know," Treeni said. "I just needed proof. What I wanted from you was to find out where he'd sent Joel."

She'd claimed she didn't have any lingering feelings for her ex-husband, but the look on her face told Cosmo that wasn't entirely true. His gut roiled. She'd been using him, just as he'd feared. How stupid of him to believe a woman like Treeni could ever be interested in a guy like him without an ulterior motive.

*What a fool you are, Villereal.*

"Where did my father send him?" Treeni repeated.

"That's just it. Your father didn't send Joel anywhere."

"Then who did?"

"I don't know, but your father is being investigated by NCIS, and your ex-husband is involved."

"So where is Joel?"

"In Corpus Christi. Spying on my friend Marlie Montague for NCIS. I don't know what's going on down there, but it's got something to do with your father." He shook his head. "And here I always thought Marlie was off her beam with her conspiracy theories. It's looking like I owe her a huge apology."

"It's about the Mohawk missiles," Treeni said and slowly lowered her weapon.

Cosmo trod across the room, wrenched the gun from Treeni's hand, and roughly squeezed her upper arm. "Tell me everything you know. And I swear to God, if you lie to me..."

He let his words trail off. He couldn't threaten Treeni's life; he cared about her too much, and it didn't matter if she didn't care about him, but he had to let her know he meant business. "What's the real reason you wanted me to find your ex-husband?"

He didn't intimidate her. He figured nothing much intimidated Treeni Delaney.

"I'll tell you," she said, attempting to wrench away from him. "But not because you're going all macho on me."

"Dammit, if anything happens to Marlie, there will be retribution." He pressed his fingers harder into her flesh. "Someone's going to have to pay."

"You're in love with her, aren't you," Treeni said coolly, as if she didn't care, but Cosmo could have sworn he saw a flicker of jealousy in her eyes.

"I love Marlie, yes. But not in the way you think. She's like a sister to me."

"She's not your lover?" Treeni sounded hopeful.

He was going to lay his cards on the table. He had nothing to lose. "Once upon a time I thought I was in love with her, but that was before I met you and realized the difference between affection and real passion."

"Yeah?" Treeni grinned.

"Yeah."

"For me it was the opposite. I was well acquainted with lust, but with you, Cosmo…" She paused and trailed her fingers over his face. "I'm envious of your loyalty to your friend. No one's ever shown me that kind of loyalty."

"Not even your ex-husband?"

She shook her head. "I never gave him the chance. Poor Joel was just a pawn in my pathetic attempt to get my father's attention. How stupid I was."

"Don't envy Marlie." Cosmo pulled Treeni close to his chest. "I'll always love her, but my feelings for her will never rival my feelings for you."

"Honest?"

He kissed her then, rough and demanding.

Treeni liked it. She threw back her head, exposed her throat to him. He nibbled her skin for a moment, burning kisses along her pale, swanlike neck, but then he forced himself to stop. "As much as I'd love to make love to you again, Treeni, there's no time. If the things in your father's log are true, we're all in serious trouble."

# Chapter 18

Marlie couldn't believe it. She refused to believe it. Cosmo had to be wrong. Joel couldn't have betrayed her. She'd let herself love him. How could she have let herself love a liar and a spy?

Proof. She had to have proof before she could swallow the whole horrible story.

*Check his pockets,* Angelina said.

Joel's pants lay on the floor. If he was an NCIS agent, he would have some kind of identification, a badge, handcuffs.

She tried not to notice how good he looked in the pre-dawn light shining through the window, but it was like ignoring a Rembrandt. The beard stubble at his jaw was heavier now, darker, making him look doubly sexy. In spite of the dark circles ringing his eyes, he looked strong and resilient and breathtakingly handsome. She couldn't keep her eyes off him. He was that compelling. That masculine. That alive. He was everything she had ever wanted but had been too afraid to wish for.

And then she had finally dared to let go, to trust him, and he'd ruined her.

Marlie shuffled across the room, slow and tentative, as if she'd been drugged, afraid to look, afraid to have the truth confirmed, afraid to have her worst fears about Joel verified.

Sweat trickled down her neck even though the room was cold, unheated. She moved across the floor, praying her knees would not give way. She reached his pants and bent to pick them up. Fingers slick with perspiration, she felt in his back pockets.

She found the handcuffs first.

They slipped from her hands, jangling as they hit the floor. Marlie whipped her head around to see if Joel had awakened but he slept on, oblivious to her discovery, still peaceful in the knowledge that he'd successfully deceived her.

The pain of his betrayal was intolerable.

She'd known better than to trust, but bit by bit he'd chipped away at her defenses and she'd stupidly allowed herself to be tricked.

Leaving the handcuffs on the floor for now, she pulled out his wallet and then his badge. She flipped it open. NCIS Special Agent Joel Jerome Hunter.

Joel Jerome.

J. J.

The boy she'd loved as a child all grown up into a manipulative, dishonest Navy cop.

She wondered if anything he'd told her had been true. Had everything been a lie? Did he even have an ex-wife? Had he ever been to Iraq? Or was it all made up simply to gain her confidence?

Anger popped like expanding bubbles to the surface of her mind. She wanted to hurt him as much as he'd hurt her. She wanted revenge. A distant rage made a sound like white noise in her head.

Marlie did not stop to think. She simply acted. She reached down, picked up the handcuffs, and stalked over to the bed.

Joel opened his eyes then and looked up at her, smiling a goofy, carefree smile that broke her heart. "'Mornin', Ladybug."

Fury consumed her. She clamped one cuff around his wrist and the other to the bed.

"Marlie?" He sat up, hair mussed, face bearing the imprint of a creased sheet. "What's wrong?"

"What do you think?" she said, her tone pure glacier.

He looked at the handcuff and she could see from the expression on his face that he was trying to figure out what to say next.

"You went through my pants?"

"Oh, no." Rage shook her like a sapling in a storm. "Don't you dare take that tactic. You're not turning this around on me. Be a man. Own what you've done, Special Agent Hunter." Marlie spat out his name as if it were a foul taste in her mouth.

"Marlie, wait. Unhandcuff me. Let's talk about this."

She shook her head, unable to speak to him. Without another word, she turned and strode out of the room.

This was not exactly how Joel had imagined things would play out the morning after their first night of lovemaking.

*What did you think, Numb Nuts? That she would plant a big ol' smooch on you for deceiving her?*

Frustrated, Joel jerked on the handcuff. It clattered noisily against the metal bed frame. Did she have to put the thing on so damn tight?

Hell hath no fury like a woman whose trust has been betrayed.

He understood her feelings of violation. He'd misled her. From the very beginning of this assignment, he'd hated lying to her. He just hadn't expected his actions to have such repercussions. He'd never expected to start liking her so much.

Never expected to love her.

But if she thought he was just going to lie here and take this, then she was sadly misguided. He tried to chuff himself up on anger, reaching for the only strong emotion he ever really allowed himself to feel with any regularity, but he couldn't seem to dredge up the energy.

He'd tried so hard to shore up the weak places in his soul. Fought to block the tenderness. That was probably why he'd hooked up with Treeni. She was the first woman he'd ever met who was more emotionally shut down than he was.

And Marlie was the opposite.

She was full of feeling. Emotions oozed from her in a messy tangle. She scared him because she made him feel things too. Things he didn't know he could feel.

Deep, intense, moving things.

Those feelings indicated weakness. Right? That's what Gus had always told him. That's what his stepfathers had shown him. What the SEALs had taught him. Men weren't supposed to admit when they were lonely or scared or vulnerable. They were supposed to have heart attacks and leave their families with lots of insurance. Heroic men didn't get all touchy-feely about what was going on in their heads and their hearts. They sucked up their disappointments and swallowed them down like poison.

But he didn't want to do that anymore. He was weary of shutting off his emotions, pretending they didn't matter, sublimating toughness for self-expression.

When he'd been trained that way, how did a guy learn to change? Was it impossible? Was it too late?

Could he ever hope to win Marlie back?

Joel realized then that the fact he was even asking himself these hard questions was a step in the right direction. If he was willing to examine issues he'd previously ignored, that was progress.

Joel thought of how she'd looked straddling his body, such a fierce expression on her cherubic little face as she'd locked the handcuffs in place, catching him completely by surprise. He grinned in spite of himself.

She'd been wearing the dress he'd given her, looking all green and pink and dewy like spring. Yet at the same time, with her small mouth pressed in a determined line and her eyes narrowed, she'd looked more pugilistic than a championship boxer fighting to hang on to his title.

God help him, he was in love.

Stone-cold. Deaf, dumb, and blind in love.

Joel wasn't exactly sure when the lightbulb had switched on in his brain, but she'd gone to his head.

And his heart.

He had to get out of these handcuffs. Had to get out of here. Had to find Marlie before the wrong people got to her.

And he had to apologize for all he was worth.

The key to the handcuff was in his wallet, and his wallet was on the floor over by the refrigerator. And the refrigerator was eight feet from the bed. He should be able to drag the bed that far.

She'd locked him down in an awkward position. His right arm was over his head, and she'd clamped the other end of the cuff in the middle of the rod metal of the headboard. But there was wrought-iron grillwork that prevented him from sliding the cuff all the way to the end of the headboard. If he tried to stand up, his body was bent over the bed, and he had trouble getting enough leverage to scoot the bed sideways toward his crumpled black denim jeans lying on the floor. Not to mention the uncomfortable position put added pressure on the gunshot wound at his right flank.

His body was in a weakened condition. He hadn't eaten enough protein in the last few days to help him heal properly, and the iron bedstead was heavier than it looked. He managed to drag the bed a couple of feet but then he had to stop, sit on the edge of the mattress, and rest a minute.

If the SEALs could see him now, they'd be laughing their asses off.

He glared down at the floor, spied one of the *Angelina Avenger* comic books lying open. He started to scoop it up and toss it out of his way when something caught his eye.

Picking up the comic, he began to read, flipping the pages faster and faster. He'd read it last night, but the significance of the secondary story line hadn't registered. He'd missed it because he'd been looking for conspiracy theories, not paying attention to the subplot involving Angelina's personal life.

When he'd finished reading the comic book from cover to cover twice, Joel knew not only why he'd been assigned to watch Marlie, but who held the key to a big chunk of the puzzle.

His father.

Marlie felt utterly broken.

Darkness and confusion haunted her soul. The blood rushed to her head and her sight dimmed. She pulled over to the side of the road and cut the engine of Mel's decrepit

Impala. Resting her hands on the steering wheel, she dropped her head and allowed herself to mourn the loss of her short-lived bliss.

"Dear God, how can it be?" she cried. "How could I have fallen in love with a man who has so deceived me? A liar, a cheat, a traitor. I made love with him. I took his body into mine, tasted his lips, felt his heartbeat; I *loved* him—and he was only using me."

Her body trembled and her stomach rose up to crowd her throat, the taste of bile bitter in her mouth.

"I should have known better. I did know better. And yet I foolishly let myself fall for him. Why? Why? Why?"

Her anguish was vast. Deeper, wider, sharper than any physical pain she'd ever experienced. It tore at her with vicious claws. Ripped and shredded and gnawed.

She felt nameless, faceless, stripped of everything she held dear. No home, no mother, no father, no love.

Nothing.

*Not quite,* Angelina said. *You've got yourself. You've already proved it. Inside you there's a core of something more.*

"Yeah," Marlie muttered. "And it's you."

*I am you.*

"No you're not. You're this courageous, fearless, independent Amazon-warrior woman I created in my head. I'm nothing like you. I'm scared and small and..."

*Braver than you give yourself credit for.*

"I'm not."

*Stop being so cautious and nearsighted. Take your glasses off and really see.*

"If I take my glasses off, I won't be able to drive."

*I'm speaking metaphorically and you know it,* Angelina said saucily. *Look around you, Marlie, and get a*

*good look at the big picture. See where you fit in and how*
*you can trust others.*

"Uh, excuse me. Have you not been listening? I just
trusted Joel and look what happened."

*You didn't really trust him.*

"Yes, I did. I gave him my heart and he stomped on it.
Rather savagely I might add."

*If you really trusted him you wouldn't have stormed out*
*of there. You would have given him a chance to explain.*
*But you don't want to know that he could be trusted. You*
*wanted him to screw up to prove yourself right.*

"That's ridiculous."

*Is it?*

Was there some truth to what Angelina was saying?
Had she given up on Joel too soon? Was she laying blame
on him that really might lie with her? Was she so unprac-
ticed at faith that she had no real idea what it was?

Even if he had betrayed her, shouldn't she give him a
chance to redeem himself?

And give him the opportunity to hurt her all over
again? Did she look like an idiot or what?

*You gave up on Cosmo when he took a job at ONI, and*
*you perceived his leaving as a betrayal. But then he came*
*through for you. Your trust in him wasn't misguided.*

But there was so much more at stake with Joel. She was
in love with him.

*All the more reason to trust that he'll come through*
*for you.*

But it was so hard changing the patterns of a lifetime,
and what if she gave him a second chance, only to discover in the end that she'd been right all along and he
wasn't trustworthy? She couldn't take that risk. It hurt too
damned much.

In her mind's eye she saw Joel as a ten-year-old, help-ing her build sand castles on Mustang Island. She knew now why the condo on the beach had looked so familiar. Her family had spent a week there with Joel's family that dreamy summer. How ironic that the only boy she'd ever had a crush on was the same man who'd just broken her heart.

Forget him.

She had to stop thinking about Joel. Focusing on what had gone wrong with their relationship was bringing her down when she needed all her mental energy for finding out what had happened to her mother. She couldn't rely on anyone to save her.

She was in this alone.

She had to be her own hero.

Joel finally pulled the bed close enough to reach his pants and was working on dragging them to him with his foot when a sound from inside the warehouse arrested his attention.

Was it Marlie? Had she gotten over her pique and come back to unlock him?

He sure as hell hoped so, because he was damn worried about her running around out there alone unprotected, but he didn't want her to catch him like this, handcuffed naked to the bed and fishing for his pants with his toe.

Another inch closer and he was able to bend down and snatch the pants up off the ground. One-handed he took his wallet from the back pocket and rummaged around inside looking for the key to the handcuffs.

More noise from inside the warehouse.

Hurry, get yourself undone before she gets here. In his haste, he fumbled his wallet. The key dropped out, hit the floor, bounced twice, and disappeared under the refrigerator.

*Dammit!*

The doorknob jiggled.

He was stuck. No way out of it. He was going to have to admit to Marlie that she had bested him. He raised his head, strapped his most charismatic grin on his face, and prepared a glib line.

But when the door opened, it wasn't Marlie he saw standing there.

Rather, it was his ex-wife.

# Chapter 19

Penelope dreamed of Daniel.

They were both young again and in the heated throes of lovemaking. His kisses were hot on her face, his thick strong arms tight around her waist. The delicious Daniel smell of him was all over her.

In her nose, in her hair, on her hands.

What sweetness. What heaven.

And then the dream was gone, and she opened her eyes to darkness.

A deep, abject loneliness filled her soul and her head ached from an awful throbbing in her temples. How many times had she dreamed wonderful dreams, only to have reality thrust rudely upon her when she awoke?

Closing her eyes, she willed herself back to sleep, back to the lovely, impossible dream.

But the sound of a lamp clicking on snagged her attention, causing her to remember where she was and how she'd gotten here. Her eyelids flew open and she sat bolt upright on the narrow metal cot. Penelope's gaze swung to the broad-shouldered man in the ski mask looming in the doorway of the cramped, damp underground room.

He carried a tray of food in his hands.

Her stomach rumbled, betraying her stoic desire to refuse any and all physical comfort from her captor. "Take it away. I don't want your food."

He set the tray on a small dressing table across the room from her cot and moved toward her, his boots clomping loudly against the cement floor.

Penelope gulped but did not shrink back, even though she was terrified. "What do you want from me?"

Slowly, he raised his hand and she braced herself, expecting to be struck, but to her surprise, he reached up and tugged off the ski mask.

She blinked in the dimness, so shocked she could not believe what she was seeing. On the man's right cheek was a disfiguring scar. It was the first thing that captured her attention. Her gaze fixed on the scar silvered with age even as a tremendous, gripping dread twisted her stomach.

No, no, it simply could not be.

Over the years, her psyche had been numbed by the presence of emotional pain too strong to bear. Her ability to believe in miracles had been shattered long ago. If she was really seeing what she thought she was seeing, then she must be either dead or mad.

"Daniel," she whispered, staggering to her feet. Alive after all these years. "Is it really you?"

The air flew from her lungs. There was no breath left inside her. She gasped, hung on the impossibility that her husband was not dead.

"It's me, Pen." His voice was a gravelly rasp, his jaw clenched as tight as her fists.

He needed a shave, she noticed inanely. He'd always had a heavy beard.

She wobbled as if he'd cut her off at the knees. Part of

her wanted to fling herself into his arms and press wild kisses all over his beautiful, scarred face, but another, less noble part of her wanted to pummel his chest with her fists and demand to know why he'd let her believe that he was dead. Why had he let her grieve so fiercely for so long?

Delicate tremors shook her body and she could see Daniel was shaking too, his hands trembling, his eyes glued to her face.

"I know I have so much to explain, and I will," her husband said. "But the important thing for you to know is that I did what I had to do in order to protect you and Marlie. I never meant to cause you pain. It was like ripping my heart out, being away from you."

Penelope could not speak. The words weren't there. The emotions, the tension, the dark sorrow in them both charged the stale air like lightning on a hot day in tornado season. She turned away, unable to look at him any longer.

He took her by the shoulders and turned her back around to face him.

She shrank away. She hadn't meant to react so panicky, but she'd just been touched by a ghost.

Immediately he released her and stepped back, anguish in his eyes.

Shivering, she hugged herself, running her palms up and down the outer side of her upper arms.

"Pen," Daniel beseeched, "speak to me, say something. Yell. Slap me, curse my soul to eternal damnation for leaving you to raise our daughter alone."

"Why would I do that?" she said, feeling strangely calm now. "You've suffered enough."

"You forgive me?"

"There's nothing to forgive."

She met his eyes, and every bit of love they'd ever

shared drew them into each other's arms. One minute they were like strangers, awkward and hesitant, and the next they were kissing with the hungry, gleeful passion only true soul mates can know.

They kissed until their lips were raw and their arms achy.

They pressed their bodies together, their hearts pounding in tandem beats. They couldn't get enough of each other, trying desperately to cram fifteen lost years into one prolonged embrace.

Finally, panting for air, they broke their kiss, but they did not stop touching. Daniel trailed his fingers through Penelope's hair. Penelope traced the ragged outline of Daniel's scar.

"When you abducted me, why didn't you tell me who you were?" she whispered. "Why did you hide from me?"

He ducked his head. "I was afraid you wouldn't want me anymore. I'm not much to look at."

"Oh, Daniel." Her heart caught in her throat.

"Why didn't you realize who I was?" he asked. "Who else would call and whisper our secret code? Who else would say 'rendezvous'?"

"I suppose I did know," she confessed. "But I was too afraid to believe. Too afraid of getting my hopes up and having them dashed. Too afraid of losing you all over again."

"Pen, Pen." He took her hand, drew her closer.

The air between them crackled, high voltage, but the look Daniel sent her was tender and soft.

"You still wear the wedding ring I gave you," he said, gently taking her left hand in his right.

"Daniel, in fifteen years there hasn't been a moment when I haven't felt married to you. Why would I take off your ring?"

"There hasn't been anyone else?"

His insecurity was touching. "There's never been anyone else for me from the moment I first laid eyes on you at the spring cotillion, Daniel Montague, and there never will be."

He kissed her again, and the second contact was even sweeter than the first and sent them down onto the cot, arms entwined.

Their reunion was everything Penelope could have hoped for and more. At first, she was worried; what would Daniel think of her body as he undressed her? The passage of time and gravity had done things to her figure.

But she needn't have fretted. The joy on his face when he unbuttoned her shirt and touched her bare skin with reverence convinced her that he still saw her as the young woman she'd once been.

Gently, he finished undressing her before taking off his own clothes and then lowered his head and deferentially kissed her breasts. Penelope gasped with wonder and angled her legs around his hips as her husband pressed her back into the thin mattress. He levered himself over her, the hard tip of his shaft lying hard against her belly.

Nothing had ever felt so miraculous.

They tore into each other, stunned, amazed, awed to be merging their bodies together once more. They held on for dear life.

"Pen," he whispered.

"Daniel," she murmured right back.

Magic lifted them up, carried them over the wall of exaltation. They rose together as one once more. Up, up, up, they flew until they were consumed by the exquisiteness of it all.

After fifteen long years, the impossible dream had come true.

*      *      *

"Joel?"

"Treeni? What are you doing here?"

"I could ask you the same thing," she said, raking her eyes over him and then waggling a finger at him. "Looks like you've been learning a few new tricks."

Joel rattled the handcuff against the bedstead and did his best to act as if the situation were nothing out of the ordinary. "What? Don't try to tell me you've never seen a guy chained to a bed before, because I'm not buying it."

"But not you. I never would have thought you'd let down your machismo enough to allow someone to chain you to a bed. Although since it appears you're partnerless at the moment, perhaps your trust was a bit misplaced. Darn it, where's my camera phone when I need it most?" Treeni was enjoying the moment way too much.

There was a noise behind Treeni and then a studious-looking dark-haired man appeared behind her. He was carrying a laptop and looking down at the computer print-out in his hand.

"Treeni...I—" He stopped short when he spied Joel.

"Hi," Joel said, going for debonair, with a little devil-may-care thrown in for good measure.

"Who the hell are you?" The guy scowled darkly. "And what are you doing handcuffed naked to the bed in my parents' warehouse? Did you break in to do kinky things on the floats? This ain't a bordello, buddy."

"Cosmo"—Treeni rested her hand on the guy's shoulder, and Joel was happy to report he didn't feel even a twinge of possessiveness—"meet my ex-husband, Joel Hunter. Joel, this is Cosmo Villereal. He's a cryptographer with ONI."

Cosmo glared. Joel might not be jealous, but the guy clearly was.

"You're Marlie's friend. She's said a lot of nice things about you," Joel said, this time shooting for charming and disarming.

"You know Marlie?"

Joel's smile was starting to get a little forced, but he was determined to keep it up. "She's the one who hand-cuffed me to the bed."

Cosmo straightened and glared, offended. "I don't believe you."

"Hey, it's true. She's a lot feistier than she looks." He couldn't help throwing in the last comment.

"Where is Marlie?" Cosmo demanded.

"Do I look like I have a clue?"

"Boys, boys. Let's ignore the petty jealousy for a moment. While this situation is a lot embarrassing—mostly for you, Joel—and a little humorous, we have more important things on the agenda."

"Yeah, like letting me loose so I can get dressed."

Treeni took pity on him and at his direction retrieved the key out from underneath the refrigerator. She unlocked the handcuffs without an excessive amount of snickering, but as she did so she muttered under her breath, "I think you've finally met your match, Hunter."

Ignoring Treeni's comment, he zipped up his jeans, thankful to be covered again, and tugged his black T-shirt down over his head. But she was right. He had met his match.

Joel thought of Marlie, how fierce she'd looked when she'd snapped the cuff around his wrist and then mana-cled him to the bedstead. Eyes blazing, her chin hardened with determination, she hadn't in the least resembled an angel on old ladies' Christmas dishes. She'd looked like three kinds of dangerous.

"So what brings you to Corpus?" Joel plunked down on the edge of the bed, shoved his feet into his black boots, and laced them up.

"I'll let Cosmo do the honors. He's the one who broke my father's coded diaries."

"Code? What code?"

Cosmo set his laptop on the table, turned it on, and while it booted up, he leveled a serious look at Joel. "There's something I have to get off my chest before we get started."

"Shoot." Joel snapped the hem of his pants down over his ankle holster and met the other man's gaze.

Cosmo held Joel's stare and never blinked. "I'd like to date your ex-wife."

"Uh, okay." Joel didn't know what he was expected to do with that information.

"I just thought you should know." Cosmo nodded curtly. "In case you still have feelings for her, you've got me to contend with."

As if that would have been a contest. From the looks of his wimpy arms, the guy was lucky to bench-press a hundred. But Cosmo needn't have worried. Things between Joel and Treeni had been over a long time ago. While Joel felt a certain sadness that they'd really put each other through the wringer, he was actually quite happy for Treeni.

The incident in Iraq seemed to have changed her for the better. She seemed softer, less pushy, more willing to consider someone else's opinion. Or maybe this Cosmo character was the one responsible for the changes in her.

"Thanks for telling me, Cosmo," Joel said. "I appreciate the man-to-man, but Treeni is a free agent. You should probably be discussing this with her, not me."

Cosmo turned to Treeni, but before he could get the words out of his mouth, she was in his arms and branding him with a red-hot kiss.

"Um. Do you two need a moment?" He jerked a thumb over his shoulder. "I could just go wait out in the float warehouse with the fiberglass mermaids."

Treeni broke off the kiss and sat down at the table beside Cosmo, crossed her legs at the knee, and put her hand on his arm.

"Do you remember the Mohawks that you and I found in Iraq?" Treeni asked Joel.

"Ended my career as a SEAL, not something I'm likely to forget soon."

"In the midst of the ensuing chaos, no one bothered to ask how U.S.-made Mohawks from Desert Storm got into an underground bunker in Basra."

"I heard they were stolen and part of Saddam's weapons of mass destruction package."

"Who'd you hear it from?"

Joel frowned. "Your father."

"Ever think he could be lying?"

"Lying?"

Treeni looked to Cosmo and he answered for her, "According to Chet Delaney's private journal entries, he had Robert Herkle hide Mohawks all over Iraq in 1990. And, he also stored a half-dozen of those missiles in an abandoned World War II naval bunker on North Padre Island."

"But why?"

"They were defective. My father planned all along to use those defective missiles to his advantage. He knew that one day he was going to run for president, and he was determined to win. During the first Gulf War he actually gave a shipment of the defective Mohawks to Iraqis, but made it look as if they'd been stolen. And he kept six of those missiles in reserve for his own use."

Treeni paused to let it sink in and then continued. "His scheme was to detonate the missiles just before the election, knowing that Iraqi terrorists would be blamed for setting them off. Since he has a reputation for being tough on terrorism, he figured he'd be a shoe-in for president. But he was careful to choose that stretch of Padre Island in the national preserve where no one lives. He didn't want to kill anyone. Just cause enough of a commotion to get the desired results. The missiles aren't particularly powerful as far as missiles go. Even when all six are detonated together with the warhead that my father attached to cause them to explode simultaneously. There would be plenty of damage to the island itself and anyone that was in the immediate vicinity. But no one in Corpus or in Port Aransas or on Mustang Island or any of the surrounding populated areas would be affected," Treeni said, looking as cool as if announcing she'd chipped a nail and was off for a manicure.

"Holy crap." Joel exhaled.

"But here's the kicker. Your father just found out about the missiles on North Padre. Gus stole the remote-detonation code from my father, and now he's gone missing."

Penelope lay beside Daniel on the cot, inhaling his breath, drawing in the essence of this stalwart man who'd sacrificed his very existence for her. Even in slumber, he held her in his arms, the fingers of his right hand entwined with the fingers of her left. One of her ankles was crossed over his. They couldn't stop touching each other. They had so much touching to catch up on.

For the first time since the blindfold had come off, she really noticed the small room. The accommodations consisted of the Navy-issue rusty cot and saggy mattress they were sleeping on, the dressing table near the door where Daniel had set her tray of food the night before, the floor-to-ceiling bookcases lining the wall at the end of the cot.

Penelope squinted to see the titles, noticed they were mostly law tomes or books on ocean biology. There was a ham radio on a spindly legged nightstand beside the bed and framed pictures of her and Marlie. Her heart wrenched.

She shifted in his arms, turning to study Daniel's face in the muted lamplight, tracing her eyes over the weathered skin, the cruel ravages of the scar, the thick swath of salt-and-pepper hair falling over his forehead.

Over the course of the past few hours she'd seen him in vulnerable moments, glimpses of sadness, devotion, hunger, grief. Watching him made her bite back a moan of unbelievable happiness. He was hers again. She was a widow no more.

He made her feel warm and tender and cherished. The lingering effects of their lovemaking burned inside her, a hot, sweet candle, melting over fear, temporarily sealing her in this bliss.

His eyelids opened and she smiled at him, timid and tentative.

"We have to talk," he said.

She knew he was right, but she yearned to stopper her ears so she could bask in the glow of reunion and not hear the ugliness of what he had to tell her. She curled against his chest, kissed one of his nipples while gently plucking at a thatch of chest hair.

He caressed her hair with a palm. "Are you listening?"

Penelope sighed and snuggled deeper against the pillow. "I'm listening."

"Let's go back to the beginning of the first Gulf War," he said. "When I was second in command of the USS *Gilcrest* and Gus was my superior officer."

Penelope wished she didn't have to follow him there, but she owed it to Daniel to hear every last horrible detail. He deserved to speak his peace. She thought of how lonely he must have been, living in this cold, damp bunker for fifteen years, forced by circumstances to hide. Away from his wife and the daughter he loved. She'd thought she'd been lonely without him, but her loneliness was incomparable to what Daniel had endured. She'd had Marlie. He'd had nothing.

"Let me set the political stage as well. At the time, Chet Delaney was in charge of the entire Desert Storm fleet."

"I remember."

"His position allowed him to campaign for the Navy's acquisition of the Mohawk missiles manufactured by Herkle Industries. What I didn't know at the time, but discovered long after the fact, was that through his Jordanian-born wife's relatives, Delaney had purchased stocks in Herkle and had hidden his underhanded dealings in a Swiss bank account."

"Chet Delaney didn't buy the Mohawks because they were the best missiles to use in Desert Storm," Penelope said, repeating it back to him so she could get the facts straight in her mind. "But because he would end up making a fortune off a government contract with Herkle."

"That's right. But what Delaney didn't know was that there was a glitch in the computer software and about ten percent of the Mohawks were defective." Daniel grimaced. "The USS *Gilcrest* found out the hard way."

"I remember when you called me, distressed over something that had happened in the Gulf, but you couldn't talk about it."

"I couldn't afford to tell you, Pen. The less you knew, the better. The *Gilcrest* was the first ship to be outfitted with the Mohawks. One night we were fired upon by Iraqi patrol boats and Gus ordered me to launch two of the Mohawks. One hit its target, but the other missile misfired and exploded inside the launcher rather than being propelled outward like the other missile. One of my sailors was killed and another was badly injured."

Daniel detailed what had happened on board the *Gilcrest* in a way that sickened Penelope's stomach and tugged her anguish through the minute filter of his isolation. The empty timbre of his voice spoke louder than his words. He had to distance himself from what he was saying or he'd be unable to utter a single syllable.

She looked at him, tears on her face. He reached over and gently flicked the tears away with his thumbs. "Don't cry for me, Pen, or for yourself. We both did what we had to do to survive."

"So much time wasted. So much of our life together gone."

"We're here together now," he said softly. "That's all that matters."

She swallowed back her tears. She had to hear the rest of this, had to understand. "What happened after the missile misfired? There was never any public mention of damage to the *Gilcrest*. No word that we'd destroyed Iraqi patrol boats."

"Gus received orders from Chet Delaney to keep the incident hush-hush, citing matters of national security. We were to report the dead seaman AWOL and the injured man had suffered a brain injury and couldn't remember what happened. He was given a medical discharge and put on seizure medications that suppressed his recall." Daniel paused. A faraway expression came over his face. "The other members of the crew were given a cover story."

After a moment, he continued. "Gus obeyed Delaney's orders without questioning, but I couldn't live with that. I was determined to find out what had happened, why the missile had malfunctioned, why my man had died, and why Chet Delaney was so damn eager to cover up an accident. I started researching the Mohawks and Herkle Industries but kept coming up against brick walls. The paper trails had been destroyed. People had been bought off or hushed up with threats. The less I found, the more determined I became."

"You always were stubborn." Penelope couldn't hide her admiration. No matter what the personal consequences had been for their family, she could not fault her husband for doing the right thing.

"One night during shore leave, I was attacked on a side street. A man beat me within an inch of my life with a metal pipe." Daniel touched the scar on the side of his face. "He told me to stop investigating the misfiring missiles or next time I'd lose more than my looks."

Penelope hissed in air through clenched teeth, her mind conjuring up the horrible circumstances in which her husband had found himself. He was an honorable man and she respected his decision, even if it had torn their lives asunder. She loved him for who he was. No matter the cost. She felt badly that she couldn't have been there, that he'd had no comfort so far from home.

"But still you couldn't let it go."

"No. I went to Gus. I tried to convince him to stick

with me, that together the two of us could make a difference. We could blow the whistle on the Delaney-Herkle connection. Delaney was getting rich off the purchase of the Mohawks. He wasn't about to pull the plug on the contract."

"You wouldn't let it go," Penelope interjected. "And Delaney wouldn't give up."

"And Gus wouldn't step up to the plate."

"He's always been a coward," Penelope muttered. "He couldn't even stand up to Deirdre for joint custody of J. J.; how could you expect him to stand up for you?"

"Gus helped me the best he could. I can't blame him for taking the easy way out. I've paid a very high price for my integrity." Daniel lightly grazed her cheek with a knuckle. "And unfortunately, so did you and Marlie. Forgive me. I can never make up for my flaws."

"Gus is the one I can't forgive. He condemned you to a half-life in this hole." She waved her hand at his underground home.

"Don't be bitter, Pen. You're above that. I was stupid. I started telling everyone who would listen what Delaney was up to. I had no concrete proof to back up my allegations, but I was going public anyway. I called a press conference, but never got a chance to tell my side of the story. I was young and hotheaded and so certain that I would be vindicated simply because I was right and Delaney was wrong. Lord, how dumb I was. When Delaney realized he wasn't going to shut me up with beatings and threats, he upped the ante."

"Accusing you of treason."

"Yes. Delaney and Herkle devised a way to detect the defective missiles. They found them, separated them from the rest of the lot, and then shipped them to Iraq. They put my name on the requisition sheet and then staged a robbery of the supply ship. They manufactured more false evidence against me, even found an Iraqi soldier to swear that he'd seen me meeting with one of Saddam Hussein's top-ranking military leaders. Because they were so good at framing me and buying people off, their case against me was airtight; and if that wasn't enough, Herkle visited me in the brig."

"Why?"

"To threaten me into silence. He said someone was watching you, and if I ever breathed a word about what happened on board the *Gilcrest,* he'd have you and Marlie killed."

"What a horrible position they put you in." Penelope pressed a hand to her mouth.

"I was trapped. No way out. Not only was I going to be hung for high treason, but if I dared to mount a defense, the two people I loved most in the world would die. I was doomed."

Penelope pulled him close, cradling his head against her shoulder. "Shh, you don't have to say any more. Stop reliving it. It's in the past. Gone forever."

"No." He pulled back. "I have to tell you everything. At least once. It's important to me that you hear the entire story."

"Okay, whatever you need."

Penelope swallowed, bracing herself.

"Gus was both my salvation and my damnation. He came to see me in the hold on the night before they were to transfer me to the ship that would deliver me to the U.S. He came up with the plan to fake my death and he knew the perfect place where I could hide for a lifetime. In this old Navy bunker."

"What have you been doing down here for fifteen years?"

"Missing you," he said, and Penelope spied a misting of tears behind his eyes.

She kissed him gently. "What about the law books?"

"I've been studying. Trying to find a way to bring Delaney to justice through the court system without letting him know I'm still alive and putting you and Marlie at risk."

"Where do you get your supplies?"

"Gus makes sure I'm taken care of. He's got Ronald, the man who was injured on the *Gilcrest,* keeping up his condo on Mustang Island and looking in on me from time to time."

"Ronald is the man who lost his memory?"

Daniel nodded.

"But Gus has never been here to see you himself?"

"No. But we pass messages back and forth through Ronald, and Gus pays for everything I need."

Penelope sniffed. She had an exceptionally low opinion of Gus Hunter. "What made you call me? Why did you come out of hiding? Why now, Daniel, and not eight or ten or twelve years ago?"

Her husband leaned across her, his bare chest grazing her upper arm, opened the drawer on the nightstand beside the bed, and pulled out a copy of Angelina Avenger's latest adventure.

"This," he said and handed her the comic book. "Our daughter outted me."

Before Penelope could comment, they heard something in the distance, something or someone moving through the tunnel outside their sanctuary.

Immediately Daniel sprang from the bed, scrambling

for their clothes. He thrust Penelope's slacks and blouse at her and then tugged on his pants.

Hands trembling, she got dressed as the noises grew louder.

Footsteps. The sound was definitely footsteps. Someone was coming.

Daniel placed a finger to his lips, urging her to stay silent. She followed him, determined never to leave his side again. As he crept to the nightstand and retrieved his gun from where he'd left it, Penelope went with him, staying right behind his tall, broad back.

Closer and closer the footsteps came. They could hear someone's raspy, labored breathing. The intruder was almost upon them.

Daniel cocked his gun, jerked the door open, and shoved the weapon into the face of the panting man standing there clutching his chest.

"Daniel, don't shoot; it's me. We've got big trouble," Gus Hunter gasped, just before he collapsed on the floor at their feet.

# Chapter 20

Are you trying to say you think my father is going to detonate your father's missiles?"

"Pretty much."

"Crap." Joel shoved a hand through his hair. "But why?"

Treeni shook her head. "We don't know, but Cosmo thinks he can create a command override that will block the detonation code. The code is on the warhead that's been attached to all the missiles so they can be detonated at once. The problem is that it's going to take time."

"And," Cosmo said, "we have no idea how much time we have."

"I'll call Gus and get the scoop from the horse's mouth," Joel said to Treeni and Cosmo.

"Good luck with that," Treeni said. "We've already been to his office at the Pentagon and his house. No Gus, and no one is admitting to knowing where he is."

"What about his executive assistant, Abel Johnson?"

"He'd called in sick and when we went to Johnson's apartment, he wasn't home either."

"Did you try calling Gus's private cell?"

"We didn't have the number."

Joel whipped his cell phone from his pocket and punched in Gus's number. After three rings, his father's voice mail picked up. The automated voice asked him to either leave a message at the tone or to contact Abel Johnson if he needed further assistance and then provided the alternate phone number.

Joel called Abel.

"Chief Petty Officer Johnson," Abel answered.

"Abel? This is Joel Hunter, Gus's son."

"Yes, sir."

"Do you know where my father is?"

Johnson didn't answer immediately. Joel heard the hesitancy in his silence, knew something was afoot, and pushed. "Tell me the truth; is he missing?"

"Not exactly, sir."

"What exactly?"

"I don't know where he is, but I have been in contact with him."

"And?"

Abel hesitated again.

"He's in big trouble, Johnson."

"I know."

"Tell me about it so I can help." Joel wanted to jump through the phone and wring the words from the kid's throat. He flicked a glance over at Treeni and Cosmo, who were hanging, wide-eyed, on his every word.

"Your father called me two nights ago and told me to go over to his house and retrieve top secret documents from his safe."

"What kind of documents?"

"They're sealed. I haven't opened them, but they've got something to do with Desert Storm."

"Yeah?"

"Gus told me that if I hadn't heard from him in forty-eight hours, I should release the documents to the news media. That's eight hours from now. I wasn't sure he really meant it, so I called in sick to work and caught the first flight to Corpus this morning."

"You're here now?"

"Yes."

"Why did you come to Corpus?"

"When he was talking to me, I heard the sound of the ocean in the background. I know he has a condo on the beach at Mustang Island, so I did some checking and found out he bought a ticket to Corpus on Continental Airlines on Wednesday afternoon."

"I have to see those documents." Briefly, Joel thought about asking Abel to come to the warehouse but dismissed the idea. This was the closest thing they had to a safe house. He couldn't risk compromising it or putting Treeni and Cosmo in jeopardy. "Where can I meet you?"

"The documents are top secret."

"I know that, but this is my father we're talking about, and a lot of lives are at stake, Johnson. You want that hanging over your head?"

"No, sir, but..."

"I'll take full responsibility for the consequences. Meet me on Padre Island at the pier just south of the new drawbridge in half an hour," Joel commanded. "And make sure to have the documents with you."

"Yes, sir."

Joel hung up.

"Well?" Treeni arched an eyebrow.

Joel relayed the conversation. "I'm going to find Gus. You two stay here and get cracking on blocking that code."

Cosmo was already at work, squinting seriously at the computer screen, typing furiously.

"Be careful," Treeni said. "This could get very ugly."

"Yeah."

"I didn't see a car outside. I'm assuming your bondage babe absconded with it after she left you tied up. Here, take my rental." Treeni tossed him the keys to her car.

"Thanks." Joel caught them with one hand.

He left the warehouse, grateful Marlie wasn't involved in any of this. He regretted that she hadn't let him explain himself, but he was glad she was out of harm's way. He drove to the rendezvous spot and parked on the shoulder of the road behind a tan Toyota minivan.

A man stood at the far end of the pier. Had Johnson beaten him here? Or was this merely a tourist taking in the view of the Gulf? Joel had never met Abel in person. He had no idea what the guy looked like.

It took Joel several minutes to walk the length of the pier. The man remained gazing out at the ocean, never once turning around to see who was approaching.

"Abel Johnson?" Joel asked as soon as he was close enough so that the wind didn't snatch away his words.

The man turned.

And Joel found himself staring into the glacial blue-eyed glare of the man from the black Camaro.

Marlie had spent the morning driving aimlessly around the city, not sure where to go or what to do. Without Joel, she felt rudderless, adrift. Plus, she kept getting teary-eyed thinking about Mom. She was afraid to go home, certain that NCIS still had her house under surveillance.

*My heart is shattered,* she thought, *like a block of salt hit by an anvil, and there's nothing to do but sweep it up.*

Resolutely, she pushed away her melancholy thoughts. She found herself drawn to Padre Island and the burned-out remains of the bungalow. Perhaps she could find some clue the investigators had missed. Something to take her mind off Joel and help her find her mother.

She drove over the drawbridge, remembering the car chase with the black Camaro and how she'd almost driven off into the ocean in hot pursuit. Recalling how Joel had kissed her, hotly, passionately, ignoring his injury because he'd wanted her so much.

Her lips tingled at the memory. She ached for Joel and what they might have had. Mourned for what they'd lost before it ever really started.

Blinking, she turned her head and stared out the passenger-side window at the pier near the drawbridge. She spotted a tall man dressed all in black striding down the length of the pier. Her heart leaped into her throat.

Joel?

*Come on,* Angelina scoffed. *It can't be Joel. You left him handcuffed to the bed in the warehouse.*

"He's pretty wily. He could have gotten loose."

*What are the odds you'd drive right by and see him?*

"Corpus isn't that big of a town, and if he was looking for me, Mom's cottage would be a logical place to start."

*He's not at your mother's cottage. He's on a pier. Meeting someone.*

"I'd recognize that walk anywhere," she said resolutely. "It's him."

Angelina sighed. *Whatever.*

"I'm going back. I have to find out who he's meeting and why." Marlie trod the brakes. The Impala fishtailed. She guided it off the road, bumping over the sand, looking for a place to hide it in the dunes in case it really was Joel and he recognized Mel's car. She found a lovers-lane spot off the beach road, stopped, and got out.

As quickly as she could, she navigated the dunes, heading in the direction of the pier and praying Joel and his cohort wouldn't have already left by the time she arrived. She crested a large sand dune. The pier was on her right.

Except Joel and the other man had turned and were walking swiftly toward two vehicles parked on the shoulder of the road near the drawbridge. No doubt about it. The controlled way he held himself, the military square to his shoulders, the walk that yanked at her heart; it was Joel.

Marlie squinted, trying to identify the other man but she couldn't. Dammit, why did she have to be so nearsighted?

Who was he with, and what were they up to?

She scurried down the dune, hit the hard-packed damp sand, and then ran along underneath the pier, splashing through shallow pools of salty ocean water, praying the men didn't turn around.

They climbed into a tan minivan, Joel in the driver's seat, the other man riding shotgun. Joel backed up in an aggressive display of acceleration, spraying sand across the pier.

Then just as he pulled the minivan toward the highway, the man in the passenger seat turned his head, and for the first time Marlie got a clear look at his face and her blood ran cold.

Why was Joel driving away with the man who'd tried to kill her?

"Drive south," Abel commanded.

Joel obeyed because Chief Petty Officer Abel Johnson

had his duty weapon shoved up under Joel's rib cage. But what scared him more than the gun was the crazy, out-of-control look in the man's eyes.

"What's this all about, Johnson?"

"Revenge."

"Against who?"

"Your father, Chet Delaney, Daniel Montague, Robert Herkle."

"You killed Herkle."

"Yes."

"Why?"

"He knew the software was defective when he sold the Mohawks to the government. And Chet Delaney knew it too, but he had stock in Herkle Industries. All they cared about was making money."

"I'm not following you."

"My father was killed aboard the USS *Gilcrest* because of those defective missiles. They just wanted to cover it up to save their own asses."

"I'm sorry. I didn't know."

Abel shoved his weapon deeper into Joel's side, stirring up the gunshot wound. Joel grimaced and clenched the steering wheel tighter. "Liar."

"I didn't know, I swear."

"You talked to Ronald McDonald. I was in the condo, hiding in the coat closet, listening when you interrogated him."

"You're the boy Ronald was talking about."

"Yes."

"But Ronald is not in his right mind. How was I to know he was speaking the truth?"

"Your father took care of Ronald. Gave him a job, paid for his medication. But what did my family get?" Abel was breathing hard, and his glacier blue eyes had turned as darkly turbulent as the North Sea. "Squat. Zero. Nothing. Your father reported my father as AWOL. Said he'd abandoned his post. My father would never do that. My family never got a penny from the Navy. No life insurance. No military funeral for my father. No acknowledgment for giving up his life for his country. He was cheated. My mother and I were cheated."

"Oookay." Clearly Johnson had some serious issues.

"My mother was distraught. My father never came home. The Navy was accusing him of desertion. We had no money. My mother started using heroin. They turned my mother into a drug addict."

Joel's mind raced as he tried to piece it all together.

"My mother died of an overdose when I was ten. I had no mother, no father, no relatives who would take me in. I got bounced from foster home to foster home. You know what foster homes are like?"

"I had a few shitty stepfathers," Joel said, trying to form something of a bond with him.

"Not the same," Abel howled. Joel heard the deadly metallic sliding sound of a round being chambered. "You had a mother. You had a father. You had a place where you belonged. Don't you get it? I had nothing."

"You had nothing," Joel repeated in a quiet voice, hoping to calm Abel before he accidentally put a bullet into his gut. One belly wound per week was enough.

"I knew my father hadn't abandoned us, and I lived for the day I was old enough to vindicate my father's name. I joined the Navy the day I turned eighteen. I studied computer programming, worked hard, got promoted swiftly. I plotted to go to work for your father, gain access to any and all files pertaining to the USS *Gilcrest* and Desert

Storm. And it worked. In my determination to find out what happened the night my father supposedly went AWOL, I made myself indispensable to Admiral Hunter."

"Wow, that's a lot of work for a vendetta."

"'Revenge,'" Abel quoted, smiling, "'is a dish best served cold.'"

"So why strike now?"

"Because the final pieces of the puzzle just came together when I read *Angelina Avenger* and learned that your father helped Daniel Montague fake his own death."

In the comic book story Angelina had learned her father was still alive. That he'd faked his own death to protect the family he loved from an evil government mastermind bent on framing him for treason when he was trying to blow the whistle on a cover-up. Joel recognized it as fantasy wish-fulfillment on Marlie's part, but now it seemed it was true. Her father was still alive.

"All this time I thought Montague was a hero, and then I find he took the easy way out. Rather than going to trial, standing up for what happened to my father and Ronald McDonald, Montague slinked off into hiding like a coward."

"Why did you try to kill his daughter? She didn't do anything to anyone." Would he ever see Marlie again? The thought of never wrapping his arms around her again, never holding her lush body against his, never smelling her scent or hearing her voice, tore a hole right through the fabric of his soul.

"I went after her to force Montague out of hiding."

"Did you force him out?"

"I couldn't flush Montague out, but I did push your father into leading me to his hideout." Abel patted the briefcase in his lap. "It's all right here in Gus's top secret files. There's a full confession detailing his part in the cover-up.

"And that's not all." Abel smiled maliciously.

"What the hell else is there?" Panic set in, and Joel had to clench his fists around the steering wheel to stop his body from shivering.

"I know something your father doesn't know."

"What's that?" Joel growled. More than anything he wanted to wrap his hands around Johnson's neck and squeeze the life right out of the little shit.

"Delaney had Herkle hide six missiles in a bunker on North Padre Island in the very same place where Gus later took Montague to hide out. Is that ironic or what?". Abel chortled, low and ugly. "And the fun doesn't end there. Gus recently stole the remote-detonation code for the war-head from Delaney and hid it in his safe. I suppose he intended to use it as leverage against Delaney. But guess who's got the code now?"

His wheedling tone and sharklike grin told Joel everything he needed to know.

Abel Johnson had the remote-detonation code, and he was going to use it.

Marlie followed the minivan, making sure to stay as far behind the vehicle as she could and still keep it in sight. Every muscle in her body tensed as brittle as bones.

How could it be? The man who'd gone over the bridge in the black Camaro was still alive.

Alive and with Joel.

Were they partners? Had Joel been lying to her all along?

No. She could not accept that. Her heart refused to believe it.

There had to be another explanation.

Had the killer taken Joel hostage?

But why?

She followed them for over an hour, traveling down the long, lonely stretch of beach highway. The road played out completely, giving way to miles and miles of tightly packed sand, with the ocean to the left and acres of rolling sand dunes to the right as they entered the National Seashore Preserve. Marlie dropped even farther behind until the minivan was nothing more than a moving dot against the flat, broad horizon.

Where were they headed?

She drove and drove and drove. After another half hour, when she was almost certain that she'd lost them, she came across the minivan parked on the beach.

Tentatively, she got out of the Impala and skulked toward the minivan. Terrified of what she might find, she held her breath and peeked in the window.

The minivan was empty.

No sign of Joel or Mr. Assassin Man.

Perplexed, she turned, hands on her hips, and spied a silver Ford Taurus bogged down in the sand beside a dune several yards away and next to the Taurus sat an old military jeep.

What in the hell? This secluded patch of beach was starting to look like a used car lot.

Stomach in her throat, she edged over to inspect first the Taurus and then the jeep. The Taurus was a rental, and the jeep was standard government issue from the late sixties or early seventies. The floorboards had rusted out and the camouflage green paint was peeling.

Where was everyone?

She leaned against the jeep, not knowing what to do next, and then she saw it.

There, buried in the side of the sand dune, was a heavy metal door leading to an underground concrete bunker.

Penelope and Daniel dragged an unconscious Gus up onto the cot. "His color is ghastly," Penelope whispered. "Do you think he's had a heart attack?"

Daniel placed two fingers on the inside of Gus's wrist. "His pulse is weak and erratic. We've got to get him to a hospital."

They exchanged looks.

"Can we risk it?" Penelope whispered.

"We have to, Pen. He saved my life. I'll do my best to save his."

"No need to worry," said a scarily cheerful voice at the door that they'd neglected to shut while carrying Gus to the cot. "You're all going to die today."

Simultaneously Penelope and Daniel spun around to see two men standing in the doorway. The one who'd spoken stared at them with cold, soulless eyes. He had a gun lodged in the rib cage of the other man.

"Abel?" Gus said from the bed. Penelope swung her eyes back to him. He was sweating profusely and blinking at the men in the doorway as if he couldn't see them well. "Is that you? Thank God you're here. Do you have those files? Or have you already given them to the media?"

"I've got the files."

"Good man."

"Dad?" the other man said. "Do you have any idea what's going on here?"

This was Gus's son, Joel, all grown up? Feeling as if she were at a Ping-Pong match, Penelope shifted her eyes back to the doorway.

"Joel? You here too?"

"You don't look so good, Gus," Abel said. "Guess you didn't notice your Inderal prescription looked a little different this time."

Gus furrowed his brow in confusion. He wasn't catching on. "You tampered with my medicine? But why?"

"I'll let your son explain," Abel said and shoved Joel into the room ahead of him.

Daniel was staring at the soulless-eyed man as if he were seeing a ghost. "Johnson? But you're dead."

"Not me, Montague," Abel Johnson said. "My father, Aaron. The one who paid the price for your little cover-up. The one who didn't make it back from Iraq. The one who didn't get a hero's funeral."

"I don't understand," Gus said, struggling to sit up.

"Lie down, Dad," Joel said. "I'll explain it to you later."

"Here's the deal," Abel said. "All you bastards are going to pay for ruining my life. I'm going to lock you up in here together. You may talk among yourselves for whatever time it is you have left and hash this all out. In the meantime, there's a collection of Mohawk missiles hidden somewhere in this bunker, and thanks to stupid, trusting Gus, I now have the detonation code he kept in his top secret file. Just remember as you're sweating it, you're all dying because of what you did to my father."

"What about Delaney?" Joel asked. "He's not paying for your father's death, and other than Herkle, he's the main one responsible."

Abel grinned. "Don't you see, that's the sheer beauty of my plan. The detonation of the missiles is going to lead NCIS straight to Delaney. He's the only one who is supposed to have the detonation code. Gotta thank you, Gus, for having the foresight to steal the detonation code from Delaney. This way, I don't have to kill him. He'll be accused of murdering you all and he'll get the death penalty. Won't even cost me a bullet. In the meantime, I get to watch him squirm like a worm on a hook."

"But if you detonate the missiles, won't you die too?" Penelope asked.

"It's a remote-detonation code," Abel said, sneering. "I'll be in Corpus when it goes off."

Penelope clenched her fist. The kid was totally insane. Consumed with rage and revenge.

"You have every right to be angry," Daniel said. "You and your family were treated shabbily. But please, let my wife go. She had nothing to do with this. She's an innocent bystander."

"I was an innocent bystander. So was my mother. Collateral damage, Lieutenant Commander. Your wife stays."

"No." Daniel lunged for Johnson.

"Daniel!" Penelope screamed.

Johnson swung the gun around and leveled it right between her husband's eyes. "I could just shoot you right now. You want a few minutes to say good-bye to your friends, I suggest you sit down and shut up."

Penelope suddenly felt an odd calmness come over her. Everything would be okay. At least this time, if Daniel was going to die again, she'd be right there with him.

# Chapter 21

Back at the warehouse, Treeni paced the length of the apartment while Cosmo frantically keyed various configurations into his computer keyboard.

"When this gets out," she said, "my father is going to be destroyed."

"What he did was wrong, Treeni," Cosmo said.

"I know. I also know that I'm responsible for putting this all in motion. If I hadn't gotten you to hack into his private journal entries...," she trailed off.

"It was bound to come out. Gus Hunter had already stolen the detonation code. This was your father's doing, not yours. He's brought this upon himself," Cosmo said as kindly as he could.

"He's wrong, I know that, but he's still my dad, and I feel horrible being the one to send him to prison."

Cosmo heard the pain in her voice. He stopped typing and turned in his chair to look at her. She sank down onto the mattress, dropping her head into her hands. "Would you have it any other way?"

She shook her head. "I've learned that eventually justice must be served."

He got up, went over to her, slid his arms around her. "You've made the right decision."

Her shoulders shook. It freaked him out a little to see her crying. Treeni was so tough, so strong. He'd thought her invincible.

Cosmo wasn't sure how to comfort her. He cupped her chin in his palm and tilted her face up, forcing her to look him in the eyes. "Our friends are in trouble. The future of America could hinge on what happens here. We can't let anyone detonate those missiles. You know firsthand how dangerous the Mohawks are."

She nodded, wiped her eyes with the back of her hand. "Get back to the computer, Cosmo. Block that detonation code. Do your job. Save our country."

Like Alice down the rabbit hole, Marlie went into the bunker. It was pitch-black beyond the outer door and she literally could not see her hand in front of her face. The darkness smelled of the sea.

She stood in ankle-deep water, one hand splayed on the concrete wall, head cocked, listening and letting her eyes adjust to the loss of light.

And then she heard it.

Voices.

Following the sound she edged forward, running her fingers along the wall as a guide. She heard the scurrying of tiny feet, realized it was probably rats. Taking a deep breath, she forced herself to continue.

She reached a bifurcation in the bunker. She stopped again, listening, trying to determine which tunnel the voices were coming from. The sounds were too muffled to hear what was being discussed. After a couple of seconds, she felt certain they were coming from the tunnel on the right side.

What to do? She had no idea what was waiting for her at the end of the tunnel or who was even down there. Had the assassin already killed Joel? Or was Joel the one he was speaking to? Had confederates joined him? It seemed likely, considering the Taurus and the jeep parked outside.

She shifted her weight and her purse brushed against her hip. She heard something inside clank and recognized the sound. It was the noise a smoke bomb makes rubbing up against a can of Mace.

A smile came over her face. What a brilliant idea. She'd throw a smoke bomb down the tunnel, hurry outside, secrete herself on top of the bunker, and then mace the assassin when he came stumbling out. Certain that her plan would work, Marlie fumbled in her purse and found the smoke bomb.

She pulled the triggering mechanism and hurled the bomb as far down the tunnel as she could throw, then before she could be consumed by smoke, turned and ran for the door.

Thick black smoke began to fill the bunker.

Abel's face immediately paled. He darted his eyes around the room as he wildly swung his gun from Daniel to Joel to Penelope to Gus. "What is it? What's going on? Is there a fire? Where's the fire?"

"You're afraid of fires, aren't you, Johnson? Your father died in a fire on board the *Gilcrest* when the Mohawk misfired. You found that out, didn't you, and you've been terrified of fires ever since," Daniel said coolly.

Joel was amazed at Daniel's ability to think on his feet. But where was the smoke coming from? This was a damp underground cement bunker. Not much to burn.

What if it wasn't a fire, just smoke? Like, say, from a smoke bomb?

There was only one person he knew who carried smoke bombs around with her. His paranoid Marlie.

"Gotta get out," Abel said, pulling on his collar. "Can't breathe." He turned and disappeared down the tunnel.

The choking smoke swirled thicker, blacker. Joel couldn't let Abel get away. Daniel must have had the same thought because they slammed shoulders as they bolted for the door, unable to see each other in the heavy smoke.

"Let me," Joel said. "Stay with your wife and my father. There's no fire. It's Marlie with a smoke bomb."

"Marlie?" Daniel's voice was reedy with emotion. "Go after him, son; don't let that bastard get hold of my girl."

Marlie waited on top of the bunker, Mace can cocked in her hand, finger on the button ready to fire off a round the minute the assassin came running from the bunker.

A minute passed. Then two.

Just when she was beginning to think her plan had failed, that the water in the bunker had doused her smoke bomb, the assassin came tumbling out along with a trail of thick smoke.

Geronimo!

She dropped down onto his shoulders. He fell to his knees in the sand. She shoved the Mace nozzle in his face and fired.

He screamed, whacking at her with his free hand, struggling to keep hold of his gun in the other.

But Marlie was determined. "Try to kill me, willya," she hollered and unloaded another squirt of Mace on him.

The assassin staggered to his feet, still trying to dislodge her from his shoulders. He tried to point his gun at her, but she squeezed his neck tight with her thighs, attempting to cut off his blood supply. He wobbled, wavering.

"Marlie, I've got him. Jump off," Joel yelled.

She turned her head, saw the most splendid sight in the world. Joel, coming to help her.

He took the guy down at the knees at the same time Marlie leaped from his shoulders. The assassin's gun flew out of his hand and spun across the sand. He and Joel grappled in hand-to-hand combat.

Marlie started for the gunman's weapon, but at that moment, another person came out of the bunker.

She froze in her tracks. Unable to believe her eyes.

It could not be.

And yet it was.

"Daddy?" Marlie whispered, wondering if he was a mirage, if she was dreaming or hallucinating or all three.

Nodding, her father spread both arms open wide.

All those years of wishing and hoping and praying that he wasn't really dead fell away, and she lived a miracle. Through her comic book, she'd taken a leap of faith, declared her deepest wish—*that her father was still alive*—and it had come to pass. Secretly, deep inside, she had never stopped believing that the impossible was possible.

She flung herself into his embrace.

"Baby girl, baby girl, baby girl," he murmured over and over, crushing her against his chest, smelling her hair, raining joyful kisses over her face, hugging her with all the love he had to give.

She clung to him as wave after wave of emotion washed over her. Sadness, awe, confusion, breathtaking joy. She quivered against him. She burrowed her face in the curve of his neck the way she had as a child.

Behind her, Joel and the gunman struggled on, but in Marlie's world everything was perfect. "You're alive. Daddy, you're alive."

Joel let out a cry of pain, but before Marlie and her father could look to see what was happening, the assassin screamed in outrage. "No! You cannot have a happy ending. I don't get a happy ending; you don't get a happy ending."

There was a loud popping sound, and a blinding white pain shattered through Marlie's back. The impact took her breath away. Blood trickled down her shoulder, hot and sticky.

Her head whirled. God, it hurt so bad. Nobody ever told her getting shot could hurt so badly. She gritted her teeth, fighting off the pain, fighting to hold on.

"Marlie," her father gasped. "Don't die. You can't die."

He cradled her in his arms, tears streaming down his face as he patted her hair. Her heart thumped. Her back burned. Her vision blurred.

"Daddy," she whispered, "I love you, always."

And then she spoke no more.

The sound of an intercom paging Dr. Jones to the cardiac cath lab tugged at Marlie's consciousness. She smelled the odd combination of antiseptic and powdered eggs. She heard the clank of metal dishes, the squeak of rubber-soled shoes against linoleum. The mattress underneath her was stiff and unyielding. When she moved, the plastic cover crinkled noisily. And oh, yeah, there was definitely an undesirable draft in the back of her nightgown.

She was in the hospital, and she had no idea how she'd gotten here. The last thing she remembered was looking up into her father's eyes as he begged her not to die.

Daddy? Had she dreamed it all?

By degrees, she pried her eyes open and looked up into the concerned faces of her mother and father. They sat in side-by-side chairs, perched just inches from her bed, tightly holding hands.

Marlie smiled and smiled and smiled in spite of the dull pain just under her right shoulder blade where she'd taken a bullet. It felt so good to see her parents together again. Her heart lub-dubbed, rich in iambic pentameter. Early morning sunlight streamed through the east window. Bright yellow sunlight. New and fresh and dazzling.

Everything had changed. Her world had color again. It had hope.

And love?

She lifted her head off the pillow, glancing around the hospital room, looking for Joel. She didn't see him. The movement exacerbated the pain in her back and she slumped back against the pillow.

"Joel?" His name was the first thing she said, and it came out in a croak. Her throat was as dry and scratchy as if it had been scrubbed by sandpaper.

Where was he? Her euphoria slipped. Had he been shot as well? Was he...?

"He's all right," her mother said. "He's been by your side ever since the shooting. Hasn't left to eat or sleep, but Gus was going in for a cardiac catheterization, and Joel felt he should be there after the doctors moved you out of ICU and assured him you were stable. He'll be back."

"How *is* Joel's father doing?" It was hard thinking kindly of Gus Hunter after years of believing he was her father's murderer, but she would try. For Joel's sake.

"Gus did have a heart attack. They're doing the heart procedure to find out how much damage and to learn if he's got clogged arteries that might require surgery."

"I'm sorry to hear about that."

"Gus has been worried about you too," her father said. "He feels responsible for what happened."

"What did happen after I got shot?"

Her father told her everything that had transpired, ending with, "Joel tackled Abel, and let's just say that it was very lucky for poor Johnson that Special Agent Dobbs and his NCIS team showed up when they did. Otherwise, Joel would have killed him," Daniel said. Admiration tinged his voice.

Marlie's head felt stuffy, her brain slowed by medication, but goose bumps crept over her skin at the impact of her father's words. Joel was her hero. Ready to kill for her if need be. "NCIS was at the scene?"

Her father nodded. "They've been on the investigation since I called and told them I would turn myself in if they opened a full-fledged investigation of the Mohawk missiles and assigned Joel to watch you twenty-four/seven."

"You're the one who requested me for the assignment," Joel spoke from the doorway.

Joel!

Marlie sat upright in bed, ignoring her dizzy-headedness. She had to see him. Had to get a good look in those amazing gray-blue-green eyes.

"Yes," her father said to Joel. "Once Marlie's comic book came out, I knew I had to do something to protect my family. NCIS had their stipulations too. In exchange for my testimony, they wanted to keep Marlie out in the open and let things play out with Herkle and Delaney. Nobody knew about Abel Johnson of course. The only way I would agree to it was if they assigned you to the case. You took damned good care of her when you were ten. I knew you wouldn't let anything happen to her. You're a real hero."

Tough, macho Joel looked downright embarrassed. "Thank you for your vote of confidence, sir, but I was only doing my job."

Only doing his job?

"Oh, so I'm just a duty to you, J. J.?" Marlie challenged.

"That's not what I meant...I..."

"Sewed yourself up tight in that one, son." Her father winked at him and got to his feet. He held a hand out to her mother. "Come on, darlin', let me take you to breakfast."

After her parents left, Joel perched on the edge of the bed. "I really didn't mean that the way it sounded. Your dad just embarrassed me, calling me a hero. I'm no hero; I just wanted to protect you and I failed."

"You didn't fail."

"You got shot."

"I'm still alive."

"I was terrified you were going to die."

She saw the truth of his fear in his eyes. "I didn't."

"Thank you for not dying."

"You're welcome."

They looked at each other a little warily. Not sure what to do next.

"We haven't talked since you found out I betrayed you," he said at last. He shifted awkwardly and cleared his throat.

"No, we haven't."

"I should have told you before we made love." Joel looked miserable, confused and afraid. "It wasn't fair of me."

"Yes, you should have." She didn't make it any easier on him. A tiny part of her was still a little angry. She deserved an explanation and an apology.

"I knew you had a hard time trusting people, and I

also knew you were forced into a situation where you had to trust me. It was my job to take advantage of that and I did."

She said nothing, just watched his face, saw how much he was struggling with his conscience, with the choices he'd been forced to make.

"You have no idea how hard it was for me. I'm a good soldier, or at least I was." His laugh was harsh, not amused. "I did what I was told. Everything was black and white. You either followed orders or you didn't. There was no in between, no middle ground, no gray areas."

Marlie brought her hand to her mouth, rubbed her fingers over her lips. She felt a great settling inside her. Her life too had been about black and white. Outside world bad, family good. She'd left no room in her heart for other people and places and things beyond the familiar. But her world had changed. People were people. Some good, some bad. Sometimes they let you down, but sometimes they far exceeded your expectations.

"My assignment to spy on you struck me wrong on a personal level, but it was my assignment. Professionally, I did what I had to do and yes, I lied to you and I'm sorry. I did what I was told. That is, until your mother's bungalow burned down and they found Herkle's body inside. Dobbs ordered me to bring you in at that point, but I refused. You have no idea how much I struggled with the decision. But in the end, Marlie, I turned my back on my job and I followed my instincts. I did what I thought was best for you."

Marlie's bottom lip quivered. He was torturing himself over her. She could no longer keep a stone face. She forgave him for violating her trust. She understood fierce loyalty. She didn't give it lightly, but once she'd given someone her loyalty, they had it for life. Joel had given his loyalty to his country in the same way she'd given her loyalty to him. How could she punish him for that?

"Please, Marlie, forgive me for deceiving you. It's been eating at my soul." He got down on one knee beside the bed and peered deeply into her face. He looked so woeful, she almost laughed. "I don't want to lose you over this, Ladybug. I'll spend the rest of my days proving that you can trust me."

"You already have." She held out her arms to him and wrapped him in her embrace.

His shoulders sagged and a sigh of relief left his lips.

"There's no blame," she whispered. "Only forgiveness."

He held her lightly, not wanting to hurt her, she knew, and sweetly kissed her lips. Then he eased her back down on the pillow and took a step back.

"I've got something for you," he said.

"You brought me a present?" She perked up. "Is it another dress?"

"I'm afraid it's not a dress, but I'm hoping you like it as much." He pulled something from his shirt pocket and dropped it into her upraised palm.

"What's this?" It was a baseball card, yellowed with age. "You're giving me an old baseball card?"

"Not just any old baseball card."

"Where'd you get it?"

"Gus gave it to me. He'd stuck some of my childhood keepsakes in the same envelope with the Desert Storm file."

"So this is top-security stuff," she teased.

"Of the highest level." He grinned back.

Marlie studied the ballplayer on the front. A catcher for the Texas Rangers, Joel's favorite team, circa 1985. "What's so special about Jim Sundberg?"

"It's not Jim Sundberg that's so special, but the reason I saved his card."

"Why's that?"

"Flip it over and find out."

She turned the card over and there, written in a childish scrawl with a felt-tip marker below Jim Sundberg's faded stats, were the words: *Maybe I can give Marlie a shot so she won't have girl cooties.*

"I knew it," she whispered. "I knew you were lying when I kissed you when you were ten and you said you'd have to get a vaccination for girl cooties. Admit it. You loved me even then."

He took Jim Sundberg out of her fingers and dropped him onto the nightstand. Then Joel gently stretched out on the hospital bed beside her and gathered her carefully into his arms. He softly kissed her.

"You loved me then and you love me now," she taunted. "Admit it."

"Well, you know what they say."

"What do they say?"

"You only love twice. So this is it, Ladybug. I'm all you get."

"Lucky for you, J. J. Hunter"—she cupped his cheek in her palm—"I've never wanted anyone else."

# Epilogue

Marlie was right smack-dab in the middle of getting ready for a bowling tournament when her front doorbell chimed, playing a computerized rendition of "Holding Out for a Hero," courtesy of Cosmo.

She'd traded her glasses for contact lenses, her black track pants for crisply ironed green slacks, and her white cotton T-shirt for a fashionable pink silk top. She'd forgone the ponytail and instead had used a flat iron to tame her unruly locks.

*You look elegant, trendy, and sophisticated,* Angelina said. *About time you started living up to your potential. Now if we could just get you to quit bowling.*

"Keep your opinions to yourself," she said as she capped her lipstick and hurried for the door.

She threw the door open without looking through the peephole. She no longer feared what was beyond the insular cocoon of her imagination. She'd learned the world was a larger, more magical, more complex place than she'd ever understood, and only through taking a leap of faith had she found her true self.

And her true love.

Who just happened to be lounging nonchalantly against the door frame, gazing at her with adoring eyes.

"Your escort has arrived," Joel said and held out his arm. He was dressed in jeans, a red bowling shirt, and his very own bowling shoes.

Their team didn't win the bowling trophy, but that didn't stop the celebration. Everyone she and Joel cared about had shown up for their impromptu engagement party at the Starlight Lanes.

Penelope and Daniel cheered them on from the sidelines. Cosmo and Treeni sat sharing kisses in between bites of messy bowling-alley nachos. Gus bounced Joel's half sister, Amy, on his knee, dutifully drinking apple juice instead of beer. Mel was bowling on their team, as was his brother Kelvin, who'd provided the bowling balls for Marlie's flash mob. Even NCIS Special Agent Dobbs had shown up, as had several of Joel's Navy buddies.

"Your friends are a sexy lot," Marlie whispered to Joel. "No wonder women go gaga over SEALs. Talk about hot."

"Hey, hey," he said. "No ogling my buddies in front of me."

"Oh, come on, babe." She wrapped an arm around his waist and leaned into him. "You know you're the hottest of them all."

"Hear that, guys?" Joel hollered to his friends. "My lady thinks I'm hotter than all of you combined."

"Darn you, J. J." Marlie blushed, embarrassed. "You didn't have to tell them that."

"The wee thing has to say such nonsense to ya, Hunter; it's your ring that's on her finger," teased Donovan Stewart, a burly SEAL of Scottish descent.

"If she thinks you're the hottest, then obviously she's never seen you naked," joked Rob Jacoby, another SEAL.

"You've got to remember," Dobbs pointed out, joining in the fray. "It's not been that long since she got shot. Still on the pain medication, Marlie?"

"I can't get any respect around here," Joel grumbled, pretending to be miffed.

"Certainly not with that bowling score," Treeni piped up.

"Okay," Joel said. "Who wants to bowl for it? First one to get a strike is the hottest guy in the place."

In an instant all the competitive Navy SEALs were picking up bowling balls and selecting a lane, with Cosmo joining in.

"You're going down, Hunter," Cosmo said. "I've been bowling since I was five."

"Twenty says J. J.'s gonna take it," Gus called out, and then the bets started flying.

"I'll take that action," Dobbs said. "My money's on the Scot."

"Anyone who bets against Cosmo is crazy," Treeni said confidently.

Blanketed in a warm, comfortable glow of happiness, Marlie watched her husband-to-be tease with their family and friends. In that glorious moment, she felt as if she'd finally come home after a long, arduous journey, finally integrating into the person she was always meant to be.

Six weeks had passed since Marlie had been reunited with her father. Six weeks since she'd accepted that she and Angelina were one and the same. Six weeks since she'd fallen hopelessly in love with the grown-up version of J. J. Hunter, finishing the process they'd started all those many years ago.

A lot had happened in those six weeks. Her parents had renewed their wedding vows and gone on a second honeymoon. After recovering from his heart attack, Gus had come forward and told the entire story of Robert Herkle and Chet Delaney's conspiracy to hide the truth about the Mohawk missiles. Citing his culpability in the cover-up, Gus relinquished his position at the Pentagon. No charges were brought against him and he officially retired from the Navy. The Mohawks in Iraq had been located and safely destroyed along with the missiles on Padre Island. Abel Johnson was in jail, pending his murder trial for killing Robert Herkle.

Chet Delaney was awaiting court-martial and he'd been indicted on several conspiracy charges. Treeni was dealing with the exposure of her father's criminal behavior as well as could be expected. Marlie empathized with what she was going through. She remembered all too well what it had been like when Daniel had been accused of treason. She reached out to the love of Cosmo's life and Treeni had reciprocated, opening up to her in unexpected ways. It was the first time either of them had had a close female friend and they were enjoying getting to know each other.

In the aftermath of media exposure, Marlie's career shot off the charts. Sales of her last *Angelina Avenger* comic quadrupled. She'd been approached by several publishers to write a book about her experiences, and she'd received a lucrative offer from a video game design company who wanted to turn Angelina into a video game. She was still mulling over the opportunities. Much of her choice depended on whether Joel was going to return to the SEALs (Treeni had come forward to set the record straight about what had really happened in Iraq, and he'd been offered his position back) or if he was going to stay with NCIS. Marlie wanted him to do whatever would make him happiest.

"Ready, set," Treeni called out. "Bowl."

Eight men bowled in unison.

But not Joel. He left his ball sitting in the lane, took Marlie's elbow, and hustled her away.

"Eight strikes!" Treeni's voice carried over to them as Joel escorted her out into the parking lot.

"Darn, now we'll never know for sure who's the hottest of them all," Marlie said as the door closed behind them.

"Like there was ever any doubt in your mind, Ladybug."

"So why did you run off?"

"And show up those other guys? Please, I'm not heartless." He grinned. "I couldn't stand not having you all to myself for one minute longer."

"Oh, no?"

"No. You're in my blood, Marlie. I can't ever get enough of you." He pulled her to him, kissed the top of her head.

She laughed and entwined her arms around his neck. "Yeah, keep talking to me like that, babe."

He kissed her long and hard until the door opened and his SEAL buddies came out to rib him for not bowling. He nuzzled Marlie's neck and whispered, "Let's go find someplace a little more private."

"What do you have in mind?"

"I was thinking the Villereals' float warehouse. We never did get to try out Neptune's clamshell."

"Deviate."

"I knew you'd like it." He grinned.

As his buddies sent up catcalls, Marlie pulled Joel's head down and kissed him again, happy in the knowledge that this was indeed one hero worth holding out for.

FBI agent David Marshall has a big
headache and all because of two women.
He'd enlisted Cassie Cooper in a sting
operation, but she's disappeared. Now,
determined to find her sister, Maddie
Cooper charges into the picture, sticking
to his side and making him tingle in all
the right places...

Please turn this page for a preview of

# *Charmed and Dangerous*

from the upcoming Lori Wilde
collection,

## *Double Trouble.*

Maddie Cooper was twenty-two minutes into her Monday afternoon kickboxing class, her students' collective heart rates zeroed perfectly into their target zone, when she heard the incessant gallop of the *William Tell Overture* humming from inside her gym bag. She could just make out the digitalized noise above the thumping beat of Salt-N-Pepa's *Let's Talk About Sex* blasting through the state-of-the-art surround sound system and she surmised her cell phone must have been ringing for quite some time.

Bad news.

Only two people ever called during her classes and both of them always wanted the same thing. It was either her mom asking her to go salvage her sister from her latest exploit or it was her identical twin Cassie begging Maddie to come haul her butt out of some pickle or the other.

The upshot was always the same. Good ol' Maddie to the rescue.

Like in college when she had to bail Cassie out of jail for streaking through the Alamo during rush week on a dare from her sorority sisters. Or the unforgettable incident when her rambunctious twin called her for a ride at three A.M. after getting tossed out of a Hells Angels Christmas party—which she'd audaciously crashed—for unruly conduct.

"Jab. Jab. Upper cut," she commanded into her headset and tried to pretend she was having an auditory hallucination.

A courageous shaft of February sunshine battled the gloomy clouds and slanted through the open blinds, momentarily illuminating the room with the hope of spring. Maddie studied her disciples in the floor-to-ceiling mirrors, monitoring them for correct form. She kept her own posture in rigid control. Shoulders straight and knees slightly bent, setting a good example.

"Nice work ladies," she called out. "Squeeze those abs. Keep your glutes clenched tight."

Phone? What phone? She didn't hear no stinking telephone.

"Bob. Weave. Roundhouse kick."

But no matter how hard she tried to deny it, beneath the sexy grind of hip-hop, there was no mistaking the bastardized version of classic Rossini. As much as she longed to ignore the summons for help, she simply could not. Her sister needed her.

Dammit.

"Water break," she instructed the class. "But keep moving."

Her more serious students frowned. They had been flying Zen and didn't want to stop, but her newer apprentices ran for their water bottles, gratitude for the unexpected reprieve shining on their sweaty faces.

Only slightly breathless, Maddie trotted across the room, wiping her slick palms against the thighs of her black cotton Lycra workout pants. She bent to scoop her gym bag off the floor.

William Tell was still giving it hell as she dug to the bottom of the bag and retrieved her "track and field" themed Nokia. She jabbed the 'talk' button with a short, unpainted fingernail.

" 'Lo."

"Maddie, it's Mom."

The connection came across faint, staticky, but then she didn't expect anything else. Costa Rica was a long way from Fort Worth, Texas. Her stepfather built bridges all over the world and Maddie was never sure where her mother would be living next, but she could be certain it was always some place interesting.

"I'm in the middle of class."

"I know sweetheart, I'm sorry to interrupt, but this is urgent."

Wasn't it always? Maddie suppressed a sigh and shook her head. A flop of streaky blond hair broke free from it's Scrunchie and fell across her nose. Irritated, she tucked the phone under her chin, stabbed back the errant lock with her fingers and rewrapped her ponytail.

"What's Cassie done now?"

"How do you know I'm calling about Cassie?"

"Because she is always our main topic of conversation."

"That's not true."

"So why *did* you call?"

Her mother paused. "Because I've been trying to reach your sister all weekend and she's not answering her phone and you know she calls me every Sunday."

Bingo! Maddie could have gloated, "See, see, see, you did call about Cassie." Instead a stab of worry winnowed through her.

She hadn't heard from her twin either. Usually, Cassie phoned her two or three times a day. She should have been suspicious over the unexpected silence. Instead, she'd self-ishly enjoyed the peace and quiet. She should have known better than to relax her guard.

"When did you last see her?" Mom asked.

"I don't remember," Maddie hedged, not wanting to unduly upset her mother. "I'm certain it was sometime this weekend."

"You haven't seen her since Friday afternoon, have you?"

"All right. We had lunch on Friday and I haven't heard from her since."

"Hmm," her mother mused.

Maddie pinched the bridge of her nose between her thumb and forefinger. "Hmm what?"

"This is like that semester you and Cassie were living in Madrid and she was working at the Museo del Prado. Remember?"

How could she forget? That was the autumn after she had faltered at the Olympics in Atlanta and blown her chances for winning the gold. She had gone to Madrid both to lick her wounds and to keep an eye on Cassie who was on a work/study program for her degree in art history.

"And," her mother continued, "Cassie took off for a long weekend in Monaco with that Greek guy." She snapped her fingers. "What was his name?"

"Dominic Koumalakis."

"Oh yes. I'm hoping this is the same sort of thing. That she's just off for a lark with this new boyfriend of hers."

"New boyfriend?"

Another long pause. "She didn't tell you about Peyton?"

"Uh, no."

"Oh dear." Her mother sighed. "I guess I wasn't sup-posed to say anything."

Pulling Cassie's impetuous fanny from various and sundry fires, had honed Maddie's protective instincts to a fine point and she was getting bad vibes. Her gut clutched and the hairs on her arms stiffened. Something was amiss.

The idea of her twin not bragging about a new boyfriend was like getting a box of Cracker Jack's without finding a prize inside. It rarely happened. If Cassie wasn't talking, that meant she *knew* Maddie wouldn't approve of the guy.

"Now, now," her mother said, uncannily reading her mind. "Don't go making snap judgments."

"So what's wrong with this guy?"

"Nothing's wrong with him. He's British and a few years older than she is, which I believe is a good thing. He does something in the art world, but I'm not sure what. Import, export maybe."

"Oh, that's just ducky. Mother, the guy sounds like a drug dealer."

"You're jumping to conclusions, drawing assumptions. He's not a drug dealer."

"How do you know?"

"Cassie uploaded his picture in my e-mail. He's quite the snappy dresser."

"And drug dealers don't wear nice threads?"

"Stop being so suspicious. I swear he looks just like Tony Curtis in *Sex and the Single Girl*."

"That's what you said about Dad and Trevor and Vinny and look how those relationships turned out."

"Can I help it if I used to be attracted to dashing irresponsible dark haired men? Besides, I'm with Stanley now and all's well that ends well, even if the poor darling is as bald as a cue ball and about as dashing as a pumpkin."

"But he loves you and he treats you right."

"Yes he does. I learned the hard way a sharply dressed man with a thick head of hair isn't everything. Give your sister time. Eventually, Cassie will come to the same conclusion I did."

"So how long has she been seeing this Peyton character?"

"About three weeks and she says he's a phat kisser."

"Mother!"

"What? Phat means pretty hot and tempting."

"I know what it means." Maddie didn't realize that she'd raised her voice until she spotted her students gaping at her. She turned her back to them, hunched her shoulders and whispered fiercely into the receiver. "Why does Cassie tell you these personal things?"

"I'm proud she lets me in on what's happening in her life. You, on the other hand, didn't even tell me when you first started your period. I wish you could be as open and honest with me as Cassie is."

"About my love life?"

"Do you have a love life, Maddie?"

"Jeez! That's kinda private don't you think?"

Her mother sighed. "Just as I suspected. No man in sight."

"Why is that so important?"

"I worry about you being alone. You're always sequestered in that gym. How are you going to meet anyone if you never get out, mix and mingle?"

"I'm not looking to meet anyone."

"Nonsense. You're pushing thirty, dear."

"And?"

"Tick-tock."

Maddie bit her tongue to keep from saying something she would regret. Apparently, Mom would prefer her to be like Cassie, with a new guy every few months, none of whom stuck around.

"You and your sister are night and day," her mother said. "If you two didn't look exactly alike I would have sworn someone switched one of you at birth."

"I feel like someone switched me at birth," Maddie muttered under her breath.

Hell, she frequently felt as if she was the only one in the family who had a firm grip on reality. Although in her mother and Cassie's book her steadfast practicality meant that she was dull as paste.

Okay, so maybe she wasn't a glam gal with a string of boyfriends lining up outside her door. Have curling iron, will travel was not her motto. But she paid her bills on time and she rarely forgot to take her vitamins and she never missed the opportunity to vote.

Omigod, she *was* boring.

Well, somebody had to be the responsible one, especially after Dad had bailed on them. She shuddered to think where they would all be if it weren't for her level-headedness. She'd taught herself to cook when she was ten, learned to drive when she was thirteen. And when she was fourteen, in order to keep Mom from bouncing checks willy-nilly all over town, she'd taken over paying the household bills. She loved her mother with all her heart but if common sense were cupcakes her mother would starve to death. Thank heavens she'd finally found Stan.

"You overindulge Cassie," Maddie said. "You always have. She gets away with murder."

"We almost lost her."

"I know. I was there."

Maddie closed her eyes and a rubber band of memory snapped her back to the past.

Eighteen years disappeared and for one brief moment she was nine years old again and her sister lay in a coma in that stark antiseptic hospital room filled with ominous sounding machines. Their mother and father hovered over Cassie's bed, fear and worry lining their faces, the nurses moving silently on their rubber soled shoes.

Nobody noticed Maddie standing statue still in the corner feeling utterly responsible for the accident. Nobody understood the guilt and shame racing through her because she was supposed to have been looking after her sister. Nobody recognized the sheer terror weighting her stomach at the thought of losing her twin.

From that moment on, Maddie had sworn to God that if he let her sister come out of the coma she would never again give Cassie the opportunity to inadvertently do herself in.

"You weren't responsible," her mother said. She'd never blamed her for what happened, but Maddie had never forgiven herself. "One of these days you're going to have to let yourself off the hook."

Tension churned her stomach. She forced herself to take a long, slow cleansing breath and realized her students were milling around, clearing their throats, checking their watches. Salt-N-Pepa had given way to Pink who was in the process of enthusiastically getting a party started.

"Listen, I've gotta go."

"So you'll track Cassie down?" her mother asked.

"You know I will."

"Call me when you find her."

"Yes, yes. Good-bye."

Maddie switched off the cell phone and turned to face the class. No way could she go back to work now. Not when she kept picturing her twin battered and bleeding and lying in a ditch somewhere.

Besides, she owned the gym. She could cancel the session with impunity, even if it did grate against her work ethic. She shooed the students toward the door with a wave of her hands.

"Class dismissed."

Thirty minutes before closing time, Cassie Cooper met her contact at the Ridgmar Mall food court, right across from *Spank Me,* her favorite edgy clothing boutique. In fact, at this very moment, she was wearing a *Spank Me* ensemble.

She had on a tight black sweater with a large diamond shaped cut out right at the level of her cleavage, revealing a nice display of tanned skin. The iridescent material of her short tangerine skirt caught the light as she stalked across the tile in her knee-high, tiger-striped leather stiletto boots. She wore a matching orange leather coat and carried a small silver handbag.

Many masculine heads turned in appreciation as she strutted by, but she pretended not to notice, even though she couldn't resist putting a breezy little wiggle into her walk. Cassie was a woman on a mission. Flirtation would have to wait.

For the first time in her life she was doing something important, something meaningful, something that would finally earn her Maddie's respect and by gosh she was proud of herself.

He was seated at a bistro table across from *Steak-on-a-Stick,* the man who two weeks earlier had offered her the opportunity of a lifetime and in the process turned her world topsy-turvy.

Cassie scooted her fanny onto the black wrought iron

café chair across from him, folded her hands in her lap and offered her most seductive smile.

"Hello, handsome. We've got to stop meeting like this," she teased in a low sultry voice.

FBI special agent Reis Marshall *was* righteously handsome, in a rather rugged, unkempt sort of way. He was tall and muscular with a granite jaw and chiseled cheekbones that oddly enough, lent him a sensitive air. His nose was neither too big nor too small for his face, but it crooked slightly to the left at the bridge, as if he'd once used it to stop an irate fist.

He wore bland, nondescript clothing; often sported a five-o'clock shadow and he had this habit of jamming his hand through his short sandy-blond hair and mussing it up. Cassie had to resist the urge to smooth it down again. It seemed he didn't give a hoot about what he looked like. She got the distinct impression there was no Mrs. Marshall around to *GQ* him up.

And while he did possess a brooding magnetic quality that appealed to her, the guy simply wasn't her type. He was too intense, with his determined dark eyes that pinned you to the spot until you squirmed. Too By-the-Book-Straight-and-Narrow for her taste. Cassie liked her men sharply dressed with debonair smiles, easygoing personalities and a touch of wildness around the edges.

This uncompromising guy was much better suited for someone like her sister Maddie. A woman who enjoyed a good argument. Except Maddie was likely to fry this decisive man's last nerve with her incessant analyzing, deliberating and fretting. When would her twin learn that sometimes you had to fling caution to the wind, take a chance and live a little? Like she had by agreeing to spy on her new boyfriend for the FBI.

"Yes," Reis said grimly. Did the guy ever smile, she wondered. "We will stop meeting like this."

Cassie sobered. "What's up? You sound mad. Did I do something wrong?"

"I'm not mad and no, you didn't do anything wrong."

"What is it then?" She smelled fried corn dogs and chili cheese dip, popcorn and fajitas. The wide-open food court seemed to close around them like a kitchen pantry. Cassie held her breath and waited.

Reis steepled his fingertips. His bland expression was meant to calm, but if she looked closely she could see tension tightening the corner of his dark eyes. He wasn't fooling her a bit.

"I'm afraid we've got trouble," he said.

"Trouble?"

Her curiosity was piqued. Trouble usually spelled excitement and Cassie loved excitement. As long as it was good excitement, like driving a Corvette too fast on the freeway. And not the bad kind of excitement, like peering into the barrel of a gun. Not that she had ever been in trouble *that* bad.

"I'm pulling you off the case," Reis continued. "I was never for involving a private citizen in the first place, but we didn't have much of a choice. However, now that Peyton Shriver is consorting with the likes of Jocko Blanco, I refuse to allow your continued participation in this investigation. Blanco is a ruthless character and I won't endanger your life."

"No!" Cassie fisted her hands. This wasn't what she'd expected to hear. She'd expected praise for a job well done. She'd expected encouragement to keep up the good work. She'd expected a pat on the back not a boot to the butt.

"Yes," he said.

Reis couldn't be taking her off the case. Not now. Not yet. Not when she was so close to convincing Peyton she was madly in love with him and would do anything he asked. Like embracing his illegal lifestyle. Plus, she had a feeling he was falling for her just a little bit. Cassie had unerring instincts about that sort of thing. If she played her cards right, she would soon have Peyton surrendering his ace of hearts.

She envisioned herself on the cover of *Art World Today* magazine with the grabby headlines, *Museum Employee Nabs International Art Thief, Proving to Her Naysaying Sister She's Not Such an Airhead After All.*

A thrill ran through her at the thought. Try that on for size Maddie. Me, on the front page of a magazine, for capturing a renowned art thief.

Of course there was the teeny issue that Peyton *had* snookered her into believing he was an overseas art dealer completely smitten with her beauty. She would have been just another hapless victim, if Reis hadn't shown up and recruited her to help take down Shriver. He'd told her Peyton's M.O. was to cozy up to female museum employees, gain their confidence, use their security clearance to make off with priceless works of art and then leave the women to take the rap.

"Haven't I been doing a good job?" Cassie asked. His words had punched squarely in the solar plexus and she was finding breathing evenly a chore.

"You've done an excellent job. It's not you."

"What is it then?"

"The situation has changed. You're no longer safe."

"But Shriver is about to make his move." Cassie struggled hard not to sound desperate. *Please, please, please let me help you nail him.* "I can feel it."

"Cassie." Reis reached across the table and laid his big hand over her small one. "Don't worry. We will get him. I promise you that."

She shuddered at the resolute set of his jaw, the determined lust for justice in his eyes. She'd hate to be in Peyton's shoes right now. Reis Marshall was as indomitable as a badger in urgent need of an attitude adjustment.

"Yeah," she murmured. "But I wanted to be there when you arrested him. I wanted to see the look on his face when he realized that scatterbrained Cassie Cooper was the one responsible for bringing him down."

Reis shook his head brusquely. "I'm afraid that's no longer an option."

"Listen, I'm tougher than you think. I can take care of myself. And I do know how to make use of my feminine wiles." She winked and toed his shin under the table with the tip of her boot.

He gave her the once over, assessing her outfit, her make-up and her soft, curvy physique with an amused quirk of an eyebrow.

"Sweetheart," he said, and she grinned. Cassie liked being sweet-talked. "Forgive me for saying so, but while you're as appealing as all get out, you're no match for Jocko Blanco."

Anger ripped through her. Oh hell. He was no better than Maddie. Treating her like a kid. Acting as if she were some helpless southern belle who needed his big bad male protection in order to survive. She'd spent her life being babied and coddled by her mother and her sister and she was sick of it. She could stand on her own two feet, dammit. And working with the FBI was supposed to be her chance to finally prove how strong she was.

Drats. Everything was slipping through her fingers.

She was about to try again to persuade Reis to give her another chance, when he raised a palm and cut her off in exactly the same high-handed manner Maddie might have used. Cassie grit her teeth.

"We want you to take a vacation. Get out of town on the taxpayers' dime. How about Padre Island? We'll arrange with the museum for you to take time off from work and we'll send an agent with you. What do you say?" he coaxed. "Sun, surf, a little R&R. You've earned it."

"You're telling me that I might be in real danger?" Cassie gulped and splayed her fingers over the base of her neck. Momentary panic squeezed her heart.

Okay, she wanted to prove she was as tough as Maddie; she just didn't want to have to die for it. She was an adrenaline junkie, no doubt, but she was not a fool.

"It's simply a precaution. In case Shiver figures out you've been helping us and he decides to send Blanco after you."

"Oh."

At the thought of being hunted down by Peyton's creepy scar-faced, tattooed pal, Cassie began having second thoughts. Maybe being a wussy wasn't such a bad thing after all. Maybe being smothered in the cocoon of your overly protective sister's love wasn't such a horrible way to go.

"We want you to know that we appreciate all the information you've passed along to us. You've been a valuable asset to this team." Reis was still giving her his "so-long-sucker" speech. It was the most she'd ever heard him speak. Normally he was rather taciturn.

Cassie nodded, but she wasn't hearing him any longer.

Something across the length of the food court caught her gaze. Something tall and blond and furious. Something that could strike terror even into the heart of someone as cold-blooded as Jocko Blanco.

Her bossy twin sister Maddie on a rampage.